"TAUT AND ENGROSSING . . . an unusually thoughtful, exciting thriller." —*Publishers Weekly*

"HEART-STOPPING. . . . Within the main plot is also a murder mystery and stories within stories that will keep readers' fingers flicking the pages." —*Library Journal*

When an angry white mob poured out of the bar on San Francisco's Geary Street and surrounded an innocent black man, Kevin Shea was the only one who tried to fight through the crowd and stop the violence. His heroic attempt failed, leaving him bruised and battered. And now, thanks to a deceptive news photo taken during the melee, he is wanted for the murder himself—and the real culprits have threatened his life if he says a word.

As riots rage and politicians posture, Lieutenant Abe Glitsky finds himself under pressure to bring Shea in at all costs. And as respect for the law crumbles—even among those sworn to uphold it—true justice is the only thing that can prevent the death of another innocent man. . . .

"A West Coast take on *The Bonfire of the Vanities* . . . richly satisfying." —*Kirkus Reviews*

"Hits the ground running. . . . Lescroart blends keen social comment with sizzling suspense and comes up with a winner." —*Blade-Citizen Preview* (Oceanside, CA)

"A gifted writer. . . . I read him with great pleasure." —Richard North Patterson

continued . . .

ALSO BY JOHN LESCROART

A
CERTAIN
JUSTICE

. JOHN LESCROART

SIGNET BOOK

SIGNET
Published by New American Library, a division of
Penguin Group (USA) Inc., 375 Hudson Street,
New York, New York 10014, USA
Penguin Group (Canada), 90 Eglinton Avenue East, Suite 700, Toronto,
Ontario M4P 2Y3, Canada (a division of Pearson Penguin Canada Inc.)
Penguin Books Ltd., 80 Strand, London WC2R 0RL, England
Penguin Ireland, 25 St. Stephen's Green, Dublin 2,
Ireland (a division of Penguin Books Ltd.)
Penguin Group (Australia), 250 Camberwell Road, Camberwell, Victoria 3124,
Australia (a division of Pearson Australia Group Pty. Ltd.)
Penguin Books India Pvt. Ltd., 11 Community Centre, Panchsheel Park,
New Delhi - 110 017, India
Penguin Group (NZ), cnr Airborne and Rosedale Roads, Albany,
Auckland 1310, New Zealand (a division of Pearson New Zealand Ltd.)
Penguin Books (South Africa) (Pty.) Ltd., 24 Sturdee Avenue,
Rosebank, Johannesburg 2196, South Africa

Penguin Books Ltd., Registered Offices:
80 Strand, London WC2R 0RL, England

Published by Signet, an imprint of New American Library, a division of Penguin
Group (USA) Inc. Published by arrangement with the author. Previously published in Donald I. Fine and Island editions.

First Signet Printing, February 2006
10 9 8 7 6 5 4 3 2 1

 REGISTERED TRADEMARK—MARCA REGISTRADA

Printed in the United States of America

PUBLISHER'S NOTE
This is a work of fiction. Names, characters, places, and incidents either are the
product of the author's imagination or are used fictitiously, and any resemblance
to actual persons, living or dead, business establishments, events, or locales is
entirely coincidental.
   The publisher does not have any control over and does not assume any responsibility for author or third-party Web sites or their content.

*To Alan Heit
and
to Lisa Marie Sawyer—
the reason God made California*

ACKNOWLEDGMENTS

Several generous and talented colleagues bear witness to the reality that it's not such a cutthroat world out there after all. I have to single out Karen Kijewski as a constant source of inspiration, support and ideas when the well runs dry or the creek don't seem it's ever going to rise again. She is a great writer and an even better friend.

Also thanks to Dale Brown and Bill Wood for the "attitude check" when it was sorely needed; Dick and Sheila Herman; Dennis Lynds and Gayle Stone; Brian Garfield for not cutting his hair too soon; and Rick Patterson and Jon Kellerman, both of whom found something to like and were kind enough to say it.

In San Francisco I'm indebted to those people who lent their time and expertise to try and keep this story within the realm of "reality-based" fiction—Assistant District Attorneys Bill Fazio and Jim Costello; Supervisor Kevin Shelley (and from his office, Mindy Linetsky and Eric Merten); and John L. Taylor, Clerk of the Board of Supervisors.

To the others whose contribution is ongoing—sisters and brothers and in-laws, Al Giannini, Don Matheson, Mike Hamilburg and Joanie Socola, and especially Justine Rose and Jack Sawyer—your support is invaluable. Thank you.

Finally, I must gratefully acknowledge the tireless efforts of Don Fine, Carole Baron, Leslie Schnur, Dave Nelson, Mike Geoghegan, Bernie Kurman, Bob Gales, Jason Poston, Fred Huber, and my dear friend Jackie Cantor. What a great team!

Our progress in degeneracy appears to me to be pretty rapid.

—ABRAHAM LINCOLN

To those white people who have whatever hang-ups they have, get over it.

—MARION BARRY

Pain reaches the heart with electrical speed, but truth *moves to the heart as slowly as a glacier.*

—BARBARA KINGSOLVER

June 19–28

1

At about eight-ten on an unusually hot and sultry evening a couple of weeks before the Fourth of July, Michael Mullen, a thirty-nine-year-old white accountant with a wife and three children all under eight, stopped his new black Honda Prelude at the corner of 19th and Dolores in the outer Noe Valley District of San Francisco. Dolores is a divided street with a wide grassy area occasionally pocked with trees between the north- and southbound lanes.

According to witnesses, a young black male was walking in this divider strip when Mullen pulled up to the stop sign at 19th. The driver immediately behind Mullen, a kid named Josh Cane, noticed that, with the heat, Mullen had his driver's window open, his elbow sticking out resting on it.

The young man in the divider strip, who'd been walking north, the same direction both Mullen and Cane had been driving, closed the remaining feet between himself and Mullen in a couple of athletic bounds, "like he was jumping over some mud or something." (Rayanne Jonas, fifty-six, an African-American day-care provider, walking home from the center on Army, where she worked.)

"I saw he was already holding something, which then, I mean at that time, I thought was a pipe, and then I realized . . ."

It turned out it was a gun, which the man stuck into Mullen's temple. He pulled the trigger. The report was loud enough that Cane—in his car with *his* windows up and his air conditioner blasting—heard it "like a crack of thunder."

The only witness with the wherewithal to move in the following seconds, to try to do anything at all, was a fifteen-year-old Hispanic youth named Luis Santillo, who was on *his* way home from his after-school job at the fast food place down the street on 16th and Guerrero. He, too, saw the athletic man take the leaps, aim the gun, and fire.

"Hey!" he yelled. "What the hell . . ." He started running toward Mullen's car.

Meanwhile, ignoring Luis and everything else, the assailant pulled the door of the car, reached in, unbuckled the seat belt, and with one hand pulled Mullen out, lifted his wallet, and dumped his body on the street.

Luis, twenty feet in front of the car and still coming, still yelling, froze as the vehicle accelerated, the driver's door swinging half-open. The car fishtailed slightly on the pavement, corrected, then jumped forward through the intersection, its left bumper hitting Luis, bouncing him first off the hood and windshield, and then throwing him seventy-six feet into a juniper bush in the divider strip, which saved his life, although the pins in his hip would probably prevent him from ever jumping athletically like the shooter.

The car, gaining speed, "went off like a rocket, just going and going 'til it was out of sight" (Riley Willson, a car mechanic at his own shop, Riley's Garage, on the northeast corner of 19th and Dolores).

On June 20, the car—or what was left of it—was recovered. Its doors were gone, as were the tires. The body had been tagged by what must have been every kid with a can of spray paint in the neighborhood. The car had been abandoned on Moscow Street hard by the Crocker-Amazon Playground, a common dump spot south of the 280 Freeway, almost to the city limits.

Besides the traces of cocaine, marijuana seeds and roaches, beer cans and other debris, the car yielded such a beautiful fingerprint—in blood—on the back side of the steering wheel, that Shawanda Mboto, the San Francisco Police Department specialist in these matters, let out a war whoop from her perch by her microscope.

It took less than a day to verify that the blood was in fact Michael Mullen's. The fingerprint belonged to an African-American career criminal named Jerohm Reese.

*   *   *

Jerohm Reese was twenty years old. He had first visited the Youth Guidance Center at the age of fourteen when, without a regular domicile, he was convicted in juvenile court of stealing a pair of Air Jordan tennis shoes from Ronda Predeaux after he had beaten him up.

His "accomplice" in that crime—the boy who had held Ronda down by kneeling on his upper arms and pounding away at his face while his shoes were stripped off—was another youth, Wesley Ames, better known as Tooth because he had only one left on the top, right up-front.

Over the next four years Jerohm Reese acquired a juvenile rap sheet, mostly stealing and, when he needed to, doing some minor violence, often with his fists although once he used a metal pipe and once a rock.

He spent his eighteenth birthday in a courtroom. Though Jerohm had not yet turned eighteen when he robbed the Portola Liquor Store on Ocean, this time he had had a gun in his possession, which on his arrest he said had been a toy. (Jerohm's toy—never located—had given a concussion to Meyer Goldsmith, the owner.)

Jerohm's public defender, Gina Roake, had prevailed with her argument for leniency, on the grounds that technically this was Jerohm's first offense (*as an adult*). Whether persuaded by this argument or exhausted at the end of another long day at the bench, Municipal Court Judge Thomas Langan had sent Jerohm upstairs to the county jail for a year, of which, due to the overpopulation of the jail, he served five months and twenty-one days.

Between the ages of eighteen-and-a-half, when he got out of jail on the Portola robbery, and twenty, when his bloody fingerprint was identified on Michael Mullen's steering wheel, Jerohm kept a low profile, and though he was brought to the Hall and questioned several times, he was charged with no new crimes.

Although Jerohm lived and hung mostly in the Bay View district between Hunter's Point and Candlestick Park—one of the coldest and most inhospitable environments in the state—at about midnight on June 21–22, he was arrested by an African-American inspector sergeant of homicide named Ridley Banks as he exited the Kit Kat Klub just north of Laguna, a long walk from Candlestick, after his presence had been reported by that establishment's owner,

Mo-Mo House, who had some sort of arrangement with Sergeant Banks. Accustomed to the drill, Jerohm offered no resistance.

A search of Jerohm's given address, an apartment he shared with an eighteen-year-old unemployed hairdresser named Carryl Joyner and her two-year-old Damien, turned up one of Michael Mullen's credit cards.

Jerohm professed ignorance as to how the credit card had come to rest between the cushions of his couch, saying that maybe it had fallen out of the pocket of his friend, Tooth, when he'd been visiting. Tooth, sadly, had died only a few days ago when he had gotten hold of some extra-pure Mexican brown heroin and mixed up a speedball with it. That's how Jerohm's fingerprint must have gotten onto the steering wheel, said Jerohm. Thinking it had been Tooth's car, Jerohm had had to drive Tooth home in it that night—the man was really messed up and his woman would kill him if he spent the night out again. Jerohm hadn't noticed the blood—it must have been on the seat or something, got transferred to his finger.

Two days after Jerohm's arrest, a Friday, he took part in four separate police lineups. On the good side of the glass, on these four occasions, respectively, sat Josh Cane, who had been the driver behind Michael Mullen; Rayanne Jonas, the day-care provider; Luis Santillo, still in a cast with a bandage wrapped around his head; and Riley Willson of Riley's Garage.

All of the witnesses picked out Jerohm Reese as the one who looked the most like the shooter. None, however, could be one hundred percent certain it was him. The man who had hijacked Michael Mullen's car had been tall, like Jerohm, and had appeared to be well-muscled and athletic, like Jerohm. But he had also been bearded, and Jerohm today was clean-shaven (had been, he said, for months). Further, the man had been wearing a sleeveless down jacket, which may have made him look more buffed-up than he had actually been. Finally, after eight on a muggy June night, the waning light wasn't any too good. None of the witnesses could be sure.

Even without the eyewitnesses, however, the incident report and record of arrest went down one flight to the office of the district attorney. Inspector Banks was interviewing other potential witnesses, people who might remember, for example, whether Jerohm had worn a beard recently, people who could perhaps place Tooth in an alternate locale at the time of the crime—normal, dogged police procedural work.

On the following Tuesday, June 28, District Attorney Christopher Locke announced that his office was declining to charge Jerohm Reese with the hijacking of Michael Mullen's car and the murder of Michael Mullen. There was no way, he said, that the charge could be proved absent compelling eyewitness testimony. The credit card and the fingerprint were explainable, especially given that Tooth's residence was within three blocks of the Crocker-Amazon Playground and his prints, too, were all over the car's front seat, along with ten others.

Jerohm was ordered released from jail, and signed out on Tuesday afternoon at two twenty-eight. He waited until after they had served lunch.

Tuesday, June 28

2

A large drinking crowd was gathering at the Cavern Tavern, a workingman's bar in the Richmond District of San Francisco. Jerohm Reese's victim, the CPA Michael Mullen, had been a regular at the Cavern—he'd been that establishment's accountant—and June 28th would have been his fortieth birthday. The management of the pub decided they were going to say good-by to Mike their own way—they'd have a party for their boy.

Mike's younger brother Brandon, a thirty-five-year-old telephone repairman who had taken the day off, and his cousin and best friend, Peter McKay, currently between jobs, hadn't had any luck getting Mullen's widow, Paula, down to the Cavern. She'd had her fill of Irish wakes, the rites of burial, drinking. Mostly she was already sick of her grief, and what she wanted was to get back to her normal life with her children, which, she was beginning to suspect, was never going to happen.

Brandon Mullen and Peter McKay were depressed enough about Mike's senseless death, but Paula's refusal to accompany them to the Cavern's special memorial had put them into even blacker moods. Mike's own wife!

There was a huge head shot of Mike blown-up against the dart wall and this reinforced their loss—their brother and friend was gone. Goddamn, pour some whiskey.

The Cavern's oval-shaped bar ran the center of the room, and Jamie O'Toole wasn't letting any of the regulars buy a drink. This was the Cavern's wake, for its patrons, and the place was plannin' on losin' its ass tonight, thanks. It was the least they could do for Mikey.

By quarter to nine, close to sixty men had poured into the Cavern—ready to get half-tanked coming in after their

wives and kids and supper, or hot and sweaty and thirsty
from their daytime jobs on construction sites, body shops,
road crews. Jamie O'Toole poured and they raised their
glasses to the poster-sized photograph of Mike Mullen's
smiling mug.

Neil Young's "War of Man" was playing on the jukebox,
loud, throbbing and insistent. Somebody kept playing it
over and over, and Jamie O'Toole kept the volume up.
Guys were starting to sway, shoulder to shoulder, packed
in, sweating, spilling their beers.

Kevin Shea, a twenty-eight-year-old graduate student in
history at San Francisco State University, was clean-cut and
red-cheeked and he was lucky if he looked twenty. He had
thick, nearly black hair, a sardonic grin he liked to trot out
from time to time, and a recently acquired predilection to
drink that he thought he was shepherding along nicely.

He leaned into the wall by the jukebox, on his third free
pint of Harp. He hadn't known Mike Mullen, hadn't come
down here specifically for the send-off, although he guessed
that subliminally he must have heard about it—he was at
the Cavern most every day anyway.

Neil Young was getting on his nerves. When the opening
riff for "War of Man" started up for the fifteenth straight
time, he jammed his hip into the side of the box, sending
a jarring screech through the room.

"Watch your arse!"

The place was quiet. The Irish call such a moment
"angel's passing," but if that was it, no angels stayed
around long. At the bar, in the hole of silence, Peter
McKay happened to glance at the television, which suddenly seemed to be blaring. He grabbed heavily at Brandon
Mullen's shoulder, spilling more beer over his glass, down
the sides, over his hand.

"Hey, look at that!" he yelled. "Up there. That's the
nigger that killed Mikey, isn't it?"

All eyes were glued on the newscaster, who stood holding
her microphone on the steps of San Francisco's Hall of

Justice, empty food wrappers and other debris swirling around her in the late afternoon wind.

"In local news," she was saying (Jamie O'Toole had turned the sound up as loud as Neil Young had been), "Jerohm Reese, who last week was arrested in connection with the daylight carjacking of a man in the Mission District, was ordered released today with no charges being brought against him. According to the district attorney's office, there wasn't enough evidence—"

Brandon Mullen, the victim's brother, slammed his beer glass on the bar and screamed at the newscaster at the top of his lungs, as though she were standing there with him. "What are you talking about? There were four eye-witnesses!"

Somebody back by Kevin Shea took it up. "He had Mikey's credit card, didn't he?"

"He had the damn gun!"

"What do they need anymore to put somebody away?"

"Damn niggers gettin' away with murder . . . !"

"More than that, with anything . . . !"

Peter McKay had finished his beer. He backed it up by throwing down another shot of Bushmills, his fourth. Standing on the rungs of his barstool, he rapped his empty jigger at the top of the pitted bar four times—*crack, crack, crack, crack*—"I'll tell you what they need. I'll tell you what *we* need. We need some justice!"

McKay had a grand speaking voice, deep and resonant, and now it had the added authority of an impassioned hoarseness. But he had no need to argue. Everybody was already with him. He was their voice. He was standing on the bar. "They need a message. We got to give 'em a message."

"Fuckin' A!"

"Right on!"

Over and over now, guys poking each other in the shoulders, in the guts, pumping up.

3

Just at that moment, Arthur Wade could not believe his good luck. Here, on Geary Street, he had found a parking place directly in front of the Cavern, not two doors down from the French laundry where he was supposed to pick up the cleaning. The door in between was a hardware store that had locked up for the night. You just didn't find good parking places in San Francisco, not when you wanted them. And he had only ten minutes before the laundry closed at nine. He was going to make it. It was a good omen.

Karin just hadn't had the time to get his shirts. Both of the twins were down with one of what seemed like the never-ending cycle of children's ailments and his wife hadn't been able to get out all day. She was cooped up, going crazy. So he'd told her, no sweat, on the way home he'd pick up the cleaning.

He really did try to do his share with the household stuff, but when you're a black man in a professional job, your first priority had better be to give your bosses no reason on the planet to think you weren't giving a hundred and fifty percent at all times. Which was what Arthur Wade, a four-year associate attorney at Rand & Jackman, did. It didn't matter that Jess Rand and Clarence Jackman were both African-Americans themselves. They had set themselves up to compete with the best of the all-white firms, pulling in major corporate accounts from all over the country, and their associates could get to partner if they gave every minute of their time for eight years and were also brilliant, tireless and blessed with an entrepreneurial spirit.

Which, fortunately, Arthur Wade was.

He got out of his BMW and slammed the door, in a

hurry, his mind still on his work. Shivering at the sudden blast of heat, he realized he'd been isolated from the weather all day—ten hours of grueling depositions. Luckily the depos had finally burned everyone out, which was why he had time to help Karin. Getting off work anytime before eight was more or less a holiday.

He had closed the car door, but he wasn't even walking fifty feet in this heat with his coat on. He took it off, and holding it, reached inside his pants pockets to take his keys out and put his coat back over the seat. The keys weren't there. They were still in the ignition.

Locked out.

He slammed his hand in frustration on the roof of the car, which set off his two-toned, shrieking, ear-piercing alarm. *EEEE-eeee! EEEE-eeee! EEEE-eeee!*

Peter McKay was still standing on the bar, in the middle of his rant against the release of Jerohm Reese, the rotten unfairness of the way black people could get away with absolute murder, all of that, when he heard the racket of the car alarm and could see Arthur Wade outside the Cavern's front window, doing something around a nice, new-looking BMW. Stealing it, he thought, the black bastard.

"Hey, look-a here!" he called out. "I don't *believe* this."

Kevin Shea liked to tell himself that pretty soon he was going to get his act together and even finish his damn dissertation and get his Ph.D. and maybe after that get a job teaching, or something else, just as long as it included time for drinking and didn't want too much of his soul. He wasn't giving up any more of his soul. That was settled.

But for the moment it was all just too much to sort out. Changes. The relationship thing. Where he was going, what he was doing. All the hassles. Forget it. It was easier to drink. Not take anything too seriously.

But he didn't like this.

Okay, he'd gotten rid of Neil Young, but these guys were really getting obnoxious now. Nigger this and nigger that. He hated the word—God knew he'd heard it often enough growing up. But it was frightening here. Guys yelling stuff he couldn't believe in modern-day San Francisco. And some jerk standing on the bar going insane.

He'd had enough of this. Kevin Shea was leaving, out of here.

EEEE-eeee! EEEE-eeee! EEEE-eeee!

The car alarm was blaring.

McKay jumped down off the bar and was through the crowd, men—his cousin Mullen, all the others—falling in behind him. Even the bartender Jamie O'Toole coming over the bar, into it.

Then McKay was at the front door, yanking it open, out into the twilit street.

Arthur Wade, embarrassed, turned, his hands spread in a what-can-you-do gesture, trying to be heard above the sound of the screeching alarm.

McKay was at him before he could be heard, shoving at him, pushing him away from the car. "What the hell you think you're doing?"

"Hey!" Wade didn't push back. He didn't like getting pushed but this obviously was just a misunderstanding. He'd explain to this hothead, get it cleared up. "This is my car. I got locked out—"

McKay pushed him again, up against the truck parked next to him, both hands in the chest. "Your car, my *ass.*" Then, turning—screaming over the noise—"Nigger says he owns a BMW! I say my *ass.*"

The alarm continued to shriek.

"I say he's *stealing* the car!"

Wade straightened up, set himself. A dozen men had come out of the bar, and more kept coming. So did this drunken guy, right at him. These were bad odds. Arthur Wade didn't like it but the better part of valor was to walk away and come back when things cooled here.

"Hey! Where you going? Where do you think you're going?"

One step backward. Two. Hands up, moving away. "Look, I'm just walking away, I don't want any trouble—"

The drunk kept at him. "Hey, you don't want any trouble, you don't try to steal cars." A rush at him, then another push. And then somebody behind him, blocking him.

"Hey now, look, guys—"

EEEE-eeee!

A shove from behind now, from the other direction. The drunk in his face, screaming. "You guys get away with murder. Anything you fucking want to do—"

And then another sound—even over the screech of the alarm—the picture window of the hardware store exploding in a shower of glass. Jamie O'Toole had thrown one of the Cavern's heavy beer mugs into the window of the hardware store. Now he was in the front display area, amid the lawn mowers and power tools, the coiled clotheslines and the sledgehammers, yelling something.

The violence of the noise, the shrill cacophony, the huge display window smashed, alcohol and testosterone, ratcheting it all up notch by notch.

EEEE-eeee! EEEE-eeee! EEEE-eeee! ·

O'Toole was in the hardware store window, grabbing something from where it hung on the wall. What the hell was that, a rope?

A rope. A heavy yellow nylon rope.

Kevin Shea heard the yelling, the screech of the alarm outside. What was happening out there? Whatever it was, the mass of men from the bar continued to stream outside, as though a plug had been pulled.

Shea, moving toward the door to leave, got caught in it. Men behind him pushing to be part of it, forcing him along, screaming. "Keep moving, move it along, everybody, now, *move it.*"

Then, from the street, out of Shea's vision, chilling him. "Hold him down! Don't let him go!"

Arthur Wade was strong and agile. He worked out whenever he could, at least three times a week, at the Nautilus place they had installed upstairs at Rand & Jackman. His percentage of body fat was a lean fourteen, and he still weighed the same one-ninety-one he had maintained at Northwestern, where he had played varsity third base his last two years.

But this thing had developed too quickly, taking him

completely by surprise. Something hit him—hard—in the head behind his ear, knocking him sideways, against the pickup he'd parked next to, slamming the other side of his head.

"Hey . . . !"

A body slammed into him. Another. Fists into his sides. What was going on? But there wasn't any time for figuring. He elbowed one man, then another, with his arms free swung at a third.

But they just kept coming, ten of them, twenty. More.

One of the men he'd elbowed came back, hitting low, jamming his genitals and he half-crumpled. There was no winning this one. He turned, kneeing up, connecting with a jaw. He kicked at the man, broke for the street.

But they'd come around parking spaces, spilling over from the sidewalk. Cars honking now in the street, but pulling around the crowd, no one stopping. He straight-armed the first guy he ran into, but the guy was big and didn't go down. Somebody caught the back of his collar and pulled back at him, choking him.

"Get him! Hold him."

His legs got hit. They had him from both sides now, between his car and the truck. He turned back, chopped at the arm that held his neck and heard a crack. The surge abated for an instant. He raised a leg onto the truck's running board and hurled himself over the roof of his car, rolling and coming down kicking by the street, twisting his ankle. Shit.

But there was a hole. He could get through. He punched another man, straight-armed again and had a clear break. A couple of steps, the ankle giving under him, but he could force it. He had to. But then a car, turning onto 2nd Avenue, out of nowhere, was blocking his way.

He slammed up against it—more honks now, and the squealing of brakes—was somebody finally going to help him? Panting, he broke left, up 2nd, but the crowd had overflowed onto the street, screaming "Get him, get him!"

There was a crushing hit from the side of his knees—somebody who had been trained to tackle—and he went down, skidding five feet on the pavement, ripping the leg of his suit and the skin off his leg. A bunch of the beer-smelling men were pinning his hands and feet. He couldn't get any movement.

With disbelieving horror, he realized that somebody was forcing a rope over his head.

At the periphery of the mob, Kevin Shea decided he couldn't let this happen.

The jerk, the lunatic—he guessed it was still him—had thrown one end of the yellow rope—almost glowing in its brightness—over the arm of the first streetlight up 2nd Avenue. Now some of the men were jumping underneath the free end, trying to grab it, while the rest of them were chanting, "Pull him up, string him up!" He had to move.

He put a shoulder down and pushed. He got pushed back but everybody's attention was on the scuffle on the street and he kept pressing into the tight mob.

But it kept getting tighter the closer in he got. Pulsing, almost. Pushing toward the center.

He raised his head. Someone had gotten on some shoulders and as Shea watched, he gained the rope and pulled it. Both sides, which had been dangling, came straight. Taut.

"Yeah! Do it! Do it *now*!"

The unbelievable bedlam rose around Shea and he used his elbows and knees, pushing, now within ten feet. He got his first glimpse of the man—bleeding from the head now, still struggling, in what looked like a white shirt and tie.

He dug in again with his elbows, and somebody jabbed him back. With all his strength he threw the back of his arm into the man's face, pushing forward.

"Hey! Come on!" *Was that him,* yelling? Screaming at the top of his lungs. "Wait a minute. Don't do this!" But whatever he was saying was getting lost in the rest of the din.

He was hit again. And again. On the mouth. His sides.

He kept pushing. The Swiss Army knife he always carried—it was out, opened. He slashed at the legs of the man in front of him, and he went down, yelling. Shea stepped on him, pushing forward.

But he wasn't any closer. The mob holding the black man had moved closer to the light, everyone else parting before them.

The noise, the noise. Unlike anything Shea had ever heard or imagined—a kind of sustained moan, tension wound to the nth, like the last minute of a close basketball game, except with this inhuman, animal quality. There was a guy next to him in the streetlight's glow, spittle coming from his mouth, yelling non-words. Others had started mooing, the way they used to do in the halls in high school. And always the teeth-on-edge screech of the car alarm, underscoring it all.

He kept fighting, using the flow now to help him, getting closer, his knife still out. He jabbed again, randomly, in front of him, striking out with his other hand, getting people out of the way.

But not enough of them.

Suddenly, the tension released itself with what almost sounded like a cheer. The black man, only four feet in front of him, was off the ground, above the crowd, the rope tight. At the rope's other end half a dozen of the men kept pulling, raising him up, higher—now his waist at the height of Shea's head.

The hanging man reached above his own head, grabbing at the rope. A second's reprieve. Maybe a minute's. How long could he hold out? Somebody yelled that Shea should grab the feet, pull down on his feet.

God. Animals.

Suddenly, pushing all the time, Shea got himself there—to the man's feet. He was still holding the rope above his head with his hands. Shea hugged the legs and lifted up, trying to relieve the pressure.

He pushed his right hand up. "The knife," he screamed above him. *"Take the knife."*

Maybe he could cut himself down. He seemed to hear him. There was a shift in the weight and the knife was grabbed from Shea's hand. There were flashes of light—somebody taking photographs? Drops of something wet splattered against his jacket.

Someone in the crowd yelled. "That's it, pull down! Pull!" The rest of the crowd took up the word in a chant. "Pull, pull, pull, pull . . ."

The hanging man was struggling above him trying to slash the rope with the knife, but with only one arm, even partially held by Shea, it took an immense and sustained effort. He was not getting it done.

4

Paul Westberg was the photographer.

He was a twenty-three-year-old freelancer trying to break into the small time, the free presses, some ad sheets, boudoir shots of housewives a couple of times a week. He'd been walking, taking the occasional "art shot," heading east on the north side of Geary near 2nd a couple of blocks from his home as the dusk snuck up behind him. The light was terrific, casting a burnished glow over the city.

And then he heard the crowd over the hum of six lanes of traffic on Geary. News! And—astoundingly—he was here. Prepared. Hooey!

But the light—the fantastic light—had changed. With the sun now just under the rim of the horizon he'd need his flash on the north-south street, where the action was. He had to get it attached, change his stops. All almost automatic, but taking time.

He did it all before crossing to the south side. But something was really happening over there, like a rally or something. He made his way, jay-running, through the eastbound lanes, waited on the center strip, darted forward.

Cars were stopped in the right lane, swerving around, causing a slowdown. He squeezed off one shot, figured it was a waste, got to the other side. There was no chance of seeing above the crowd so he stood on the hood of the nearest car. You had to take some chances if you wanted to get ahead.

Finally he saw what was happening.

The mob around him pulsed back and forth, rocking the car he stood on, then moving away from it. He didn't know how long he'd get. If anybody saw him . . .

But there was some guy, his arms around a *hanging* man,

holding a knife to his throat. God, what a shot! The shot of a lifetime.

His hands were shaking but he had to get the focus, he had to take the time.

There! One.

Snap. Another.

Someone below was grabbing at him, yelling. "Hey! Get this guy!"

He kicked out, jumped off the back of the car and ran like hell. He was home in three minutes.

5

The crowd closed in. Someone hit Shea at the knees. The knife fell, clattering to the street. Above him, he heard a creak and a guttural sound—a deep *hnnh* as the rope took the man's full weight again.

The men who held the other end of the rope were coming toward Shea now. There was a fire hydrant he saw for the first time. They were looping the rope around it.

Shea grabbed up the knife from the street, lunged at the first man, cutting at the arm that held the rope. The man cried out and, for an instant, let it go.

Somebody hit Shea again. Fists. He struck out with his knife, then someone kicked it. He heard it clatter away. A kick in the head. Then another one. Then darkness.

Helter-skelter before the distant wail of the first sirens, and still the closer, unending alarm klaxon that had been shrieking for half of eternity, the mob was disappearing around the corner onto Geary, down 2nd Avenue into alleys and doorways, over Dumpsters and back fences. Coming to, Shea heard panicky voices, the scrambling of feet, men running.

On his knees, he struggled to clear his vision. Whoever had beaten him had done some damage—his face was crusted and it felt like some ribs had been broken and perhaps his left arm, too. He tried to lift it but it hung dangling from his side.

The rope was still there, tied to the hydrant.

Looking up, seeing the man hanging, looking now very much dead, he forced himself to the hydrant. Maybe there was still a chance to save his life if he could get him down.

He tried to pull at the mass of knots that had been tied at the hydrant, but with the weight from the man pulling on the rope from the other end, tightening it all down, there was no way, with only one hand, that he could even get a start. The knots wouldn't give.

His left arm was a throbbing, useless burden. Still, he tried to use it, tried to take some of the pressure off the rope with his good hand and use the bad one to untie one of the knots. Or something.

He had to do something.

He pulled. Something new gave in his arm and without intending to, he screamed, nearly blacking out for a second, going down to one knee. He hung his head, gritting through the pain, hearing something else.

A pair of lights came around the corner up at Geary, tires screeching, heading right for him. It pulled in front of him, a door opened and two men jumped out of the open bed of the truck, another from the front seat.

"Thank God, guys. You gotta—" But they weren't listening. One of them had a hand on his bad arm, pulling. Another grabbed his leg, lifting. "Hey! What . . . ?" They had him by both legs now and lifted him over the sides of the truck into its bed, the three men holding him down.

"He in?" the driver yelled, but without waiting for any answer, the tires squealed again.

One of the men who had grabbed him snapped Shea's head against the metal floor. "You don't know nothing," he said. "You tell anybody anything, you're dead meat. We'll find you."

They were gaining speed, taking one corner, then another. He was all turned around, held down, trying to get some bearings, anything. The three men were panting, holding him down.

Then, he didn't know if there was some signal or what, but the truck screeched, pulled over, stopped. With one last warning that they would kill him if he said a word, they threw him out, then were off in a spray of gravel and the stink of burning rubber.

Wednesday, June 29

6

"What is this about, Chris?"

"It's about civil war, Elaine. Is your television on?"

"Almost never."

"Well, check it out. Now. I'll wait."

"What channel?"

"Any channel."

Elaine Wager had been asleep. The call was from her boss and self-appointed mentor, San Francisco District Attorney Christopher Locke, who took a special interest in Elaine Wager.

She, like Locke, was black. She was also intelligent and already, though just barely twenty-five, a good lawyer, a tenacious prosecutor. Added to this were her considerable physical charms—mocha-colored skin as finely pored as Italian marble, a leggy, thin-waisted body, an Assyrian face. Of more importance to Chris Locke than any of these attributes, though, was Elaine's mother, Loretta Wager, a United States senator and the first African-American of either sex to be elected to that office from California.

Elaine Wager swung her bare legs to the floor. On top she wore a man's Warriors T-shirt. Waking up as she walked, she found herself becoming dimly aware of a concert of sirens down below, out in the city. The digital clock on her dresser read twelve-fourteen. Her apartment was a one-bedroom, twelve stories up, a few blocks north of Geary Street on Franklin near Lafayette Park. She glanced out the window—there seemed to be several fires a few blocks away in the Western Addition. To the south, too, the sky glowed orange.

Still carrying the phone, she moved quickly now through her sparsely furnished living room.

"What's going on, Chris?"

The tiny portable television was on the counter in the kitchen area. She flicked it on.

"We're in riot mode, Elaine. The projects are on fire. They lynched one of the brothers tonight." Elaine sat down hard on one of the stools by the counter. "Arthur Wade."

"What about Arthur?" she asked stupidly.

"You know him?"

"Of course, I know him. He went to Boalt with me. What about him?"

There was a pause. "Elaine, Arthur Wade is dead. A mob lynched him."

"What do you mean, *lynched*?" She was babbling, trying to find a context for it, an explanation for the inexplicable.

On the television, more of the now-familiar visions— already the crowds were out in the streets, already the shop windows were being smashed, buildings were burning. Her eyes left the screen, went out to the real city again.

"Chris?"

"I'm here. I was wondering if you'd heard from your mother."

"No, not yet. I'm sure I will. Meanwhile, what are we going to do?"

"Are you still in front of your TV?"

"Yes."

"Look at it now."

On the screen was a still photograph that would in the coming days become as famous as the Rodney King videotapes. Arthur Wade was hanging from a streetlight, and under him a white male was hugging him, apparently pulling down on his legs, trying to break his neck. Wade, in his last futile seconds, was holding the rope above his head with one hand, and with his other appeared to be trying to strike the man pulling his legs, to drive him away and purchase himself another few seconds of life.

Elaine stared transfixed at the horror of the scene. She had never expected to see it played out in her lifetime again, especially here, in supposedly liberal San Francisco.

She forced herself to look again—the black man hanging by the neck, surrounded by the white mob. All the faces were blurred except the two in the center, and they were in perfect focus. Arthur Wade and the man who'd hung him, whoever it was.

Chris Locke sounded raspy, drained. "We're going to get proactive here, Elaine. That man's got to be found. And then we've got to crucify him. Can you come down to the Hall . . . ?"

"You mean now?"

"I mean yesterday, Elaine."

7

Shea made it home, walking.

It took him over two hours to make it on the smaller streets from where he had been dropped in the grassy center divider of Park Presidio Boulevard to his apartment on Green Street near Webster.

The details kept coming back. The black man struggling. Reaching for him. The man's weight on his shoulders while he was still alive.

Maybe, Shea kept thinking, reliving it, he shouldn't have gone for the guys near the fire hydrant, should have just stayed holding the man up, maybe then it would have turned out . . .

It still wasn't real.

He limped, stopped, leaned on things, vaguely aware of sirens, of the sky glowing now off to his right. At the moment, he couldn't put it together.

There were six apartments in his three-story building, three up front and three in the back. He had the one all the way back and all the way up. He wasn't sure he could make it.

He'd better see a doctor soon. Maybe he should call the police, although they'd already be all over the scene back at the Cavern. Still . . .

Finally he made it, took out his key and got inside, locking the door back behind him. God, his arm was killing him. His ribs. Everything.

From his cupboard, he took down a bottle of vodka, poured about six ounces into a glass, added two ice cubes and a spoonful of orange juice concentrate and, drinking, went into the bathroom. He finished the drink before the shower had gotten hot, before he'd been able to strip off his shirt.

He looked at himself in the mirror. He shouldn't be drinking now, he told himself. He should call the police, a doctor, somebody. But first he needed the one drink tonight, now. Who'd blame him for that, after what he'd been through? And the shower, wash off the blood, check the damage. Then he'd have one more before bed, dull things a little, the pain. There was nothing they could do tonight anyway.

That poor bastard . . .

8

By three in the morning units of the police force, fire department and emergency crews had been mobilized within the city and county of San Francisco. The mayor, Conrad Aiken (no relation to the poet), had also put in a call to the governor's office in Sacramento requesting that the National Guard be called out, that martial law be declared. There were already nineteen fires and property damage was going up faster than the national debt.

Here in the middle of the night Aiken had forsaken his ornate digs at City Hall in favor of the Hall of Justice at Seventh and Bryant streets, the home of the police department, the district attorney's office and the county jail. He had commandeered District Attorney Chris Locke's outer office and sat behind what was usually a secretary's desk.

The mayor was an imposing figure in spite of considerable physical drawbacks for a politician—he stood only five-foot-seven and was so thin that the joke was when he stood sideways, unless he stuck out his tongue you couldn't see him. He was also nearly bald, with a half-dollar-sized portwine stain that ran under his left eye and halfway across the bridge of an aquiline nose with a bump in the middle of it.

Most people put him a decade younger than his stated age of sixty-two. He had that spring in his step, contained energy and piercing gray-blue eyes. He had all his teeth, and they were pearly white, though he wasn't flashing any of them now.

With him in the office were Locke, Assistant DA Elaine Wager, Police Chief Dan Rigby, Assistant Chief Frank Batiste, County Sheriff Dale Boles, who was in charge of the jail and its prisoners, Aiken's administrative assistant, a young man named Donald, and Lieutenant Abraham Glitsky, a forty-four-year-old Jewish mulatto who headed San Francisco's homicide detail.

Aiken had started off by wanting to get a report on the status of the riots from Chief Rigby—the affected areas, what measures were being taken, how many men were on the street and so on. Rigby was in the middle of running it down for him.

". . . mostly containment at this stage. We don't have a hope of any real control until we get more people on the streets, and of course we've got the usual looting—"

"We're not gonna have that," the mayor said. "I want you to put out the word. We're not tolerating looting. This isn't Los Angeles." He looked around the room for effect, his port-wine stain glowing. "This isn't Los Angeles," he repeated.

"No, sir," the chief replied, "but how are we planning to stop it, the looting?"

"I'm in favor of shooting to kill."

Rigby looked shocked. Pleased, but shocked. "Well, we can't do that."

"Why not? Don't they do it in the Midwest after tornadoes. We'll do it here. Why not? I'm not going to allow looting in San Francisco."

Chris Locke took a step forward. He was a big man, half again the mayor's weight, the only person present in a business suit. "Sir, the only people you'll shoot will be black. It's racist."

Aiken didn't like that. "I'm no racist, Chris. The only people I'd have shot would be looters. Black, white or magenta, I don't give a damn."

Elaine Wager spoke up. "But the only people rioting so far are African-Americans, sir, the same as you had in Los Angeles—"

"There's a lot of rage," Locke added.

"I don't want to hear that shit. I don't want to hear about rage. Rage isn't an issue here, and it sure as hell isn't any excuse. Keeping the law is what this is all about."

Rigby said, "It's moot. Black officers won't shoot black looters."

Lieutenant Glitsky almost spoke up for the first time to say that he would—half-black and half-white himself, he had little patience with the posturing and excuses from either side. But he kept his mouth shut, for now.

"What the hell?" Aiken said. "Don't black officers arrest black lawbreakers every day?"

Rigby shook his head. "It's not the same thing."

The mayor wasn't buying. "Look. I'm talking about preserving the city, protecting all its citizens. Let's not turn this thing into a race war."

Elaine Wager spoke up again. "But that's what it is. That's the issue. A black man's been lynched . . . sir."

"Goddamnit, I know *that.* But what we're talking about now, this minute, is not a racial question. It's about *people who're breaking the law.* Riot control."

Rigby repeated that he couldn't shoot looters.

Aiken held up a hand. "Look, I don't want to talk about shooting looters. I don't even know if we've got looters at this stage, but I don't want them tolerated. I think we've got to make a stand somewhere. We're not going to just sit and watch 'em. I want them prosecuted—"

"Where do we put 'em?"

This was Dale Boles. His jail upstairs was already filled to capacity. If Aiken wanted the police to start arresting looters he was going to have to take responsibility for housing them.

Aiken glared at him, chose not to respond and turned to Glitsky. "What have you found out about the lynching itself? Was it random or what? Maybe we can get some handle on how to stop this thing faster if we know what started it."

Glitsky, in corduroys and a leather flight jacket, was sitting on a low filing cabinet at the back of the room. He had a hawkish nose and an old gash of a scar running through his lips, top to bottom, almost as though he'd had an operation for a cleft palate. He was a light chocolate color, wore his hair in a buzz cut, and had startling blue eyes. Answering Aiken, he nevertheless fixed a flat gaze on Chris Locke. "Jerohm Reese," he said, "not that that's any excuse."

The mayor cocked his head. "Who's Jerohm Reese?"

"What's Reese got to do with this, Abe?" Locke said.

"I said 'Who's Reese?' " Aiken repeated.

Glitsky stood up and quickly told the story. The carjacking. Mike Mullen. The release. Glitsky looked at his watch, glanced at Locke—disdainful. "Reese was released less than thirteen hours ago. We have a couple of witnesses, not to the lynching itself but they seem to think the mob came from the Cavern, a pub on 2nd and Geary."

"Okay," Aiken said. "And?"

"And I was down there. I went into the Cavern myself. Place was empty except for a bartender named Jamie O'Toole who told me it had been dead all night. Slowest night they'd ever had. He'd heard the mob outside, of course, but got scared and didn't want to go out and check—"

Locke interrupted. "Jerohm Reese, Abe."

The scar between Glitsky's lips went almost white—perhaps he was smiling. "On the back wall of the Cavern was a huge blown-up picture of a guy. I asked O'Toole who it was and he said it was Mike Mullen. He'd been the accountant for the place. Seeing as I was a homicide cop and all, maybe I'd heard of him."

Silence in the room, finally broken by Elaine Wager. "You mean because Jerohm Reese was released . . . ?"

Chris Locke answered everybody. "I released Jerohm Reese because there wasn't going to be a conviction on him."

Glitsky looked at him. "Well, some of these people seemed to take it wrong, sir."

Aiken rubbed a hand over his face. "You're telling me that this mob happened because of the release of this Jerohm Reese?"

"That's how I read it, yes, sir. Just the way some people took it wrong when they let off the cops who beat up Rodney King." He paused and added, "Again, in Los Angeles."

Locke wanted to get back to the nuts and bolts. "Have we identified any of the mob?"

"No, sir, not yet. We're working on it, but it's a stonewall out at the Cavern."

"We've got one." Elaine Wager felt free to talk whenever she wanted. Glitsky thought it must be great having a U.S. senator for a mother. "Have any of you seen the news tonight?"

Glitsky nodded at her. "Yep," he said, "we're working on him, too. Real hard."

9

Rolling over on his arm woke Shea up. It was still dark out, about the time the somnolent effects of the alcohol usually wore off. His mouth was dry. Unlike most mornings when the throbbing was an insistent dull pounding inside his head, today he lay in his bed immobilized by the pain.

The pulse of the jackhammer in his skull made him fear to lift his head from the pillow—his ribs, his arms, his hips. He wondered for a moment if he was seriously hurt. This, he told himself, was not a hangover. Hangovers didn't feel like this. (Many mornings he would tell himself that he wasn't hungover, he was sure he hadn't drunk enough to make him hungover, he just hadn't had enough sleep.)

He rolled to his side and bile came up on him. Staggering in the dark, he bumped five steps to the bathroom and barely made it, crumpling to the floor and hugging the commode.

Finally he stood and urinated. The jackhammer was not going to let up. He had to try to get back to bed, to sleep some of this off. He should call a doctor.

The bathroom light was an explosion that nearly knocked him down again but he had to wash his face, brush his teeth. There were two of him in the mirror, he couldn't focus down to one.

Cold water on his face. Washing off crust from the beating. Still two faces, both swollen, cut.

Back on his bed, the room spun some more.

The jangle of the telephone ringing next to his ear almost tossed him out of the bed. He jolted up, arm and ribs feeling ripped from their sockets, joints, whatever it was that attached them.

He got it halfway through the second ring.

"Kevin?"

A girl. Melanie. No, it couldn't be. They'd broken up—face it, he'd dropped her—three weeks before. He flopped back on the bed, the phone pressed to his ear. "Timezit?" he moaned.

A pause while she processed the slur in his voice. He was sure that was it. Now, if tradition held, would come two minutes of rebuke.

Okay, he was drunk. Did she want to fight about it? Again? Well, not tonight, honey, I've got a headache. He almost hung up, then heard her say, "It's five-fifteen." The time didn't surprise him. During the school year, when they'd still been going out, she'd always set her alarm for five so she could get up and study and get a jump on the day. It was another reason they'd broken up.

"Melanie . . ."

"God, Kevin, how could you *do* it?"

"Do what?"

She told him.

10

The streetlights glared off the wet-looking street. The whole short block—it was a cul-de-sac that backed up to the Presidio—was empty, dark, forbidding. The windows facing the street caught a glint here and there, ghosts flitting across the fronts of the buildings.

Abe Glitsky, noticing all this, told himself he didn't used to think this way. It was only since Flo had died. *Only*. Sure, *only*. *Only* nine months of her struggle against the ovarian cancer that killed her in its own quick time, in spite of the chemotherapy and other atrocities they had colluded to commit to ward off the inevitable. Nine months with Glitsky at her side every step of the way, both of them struggling against the urge to despair and—perhaps more difficult—the random appearances of their irrational yearning to hope. And then, after she was gone, trying to maintain the facade these last fifteen months—not to show the pain, not even (and it tortured him on the days he managed it) to feel it as fresh as it had been.

Fifteen months. *Only* fifteen months. God.

It was—unusually—still shirtsleeve weather in this the darkest hour before the dawn. Since his duplex didn't come with a garage, he'd wound up parking in the nearest spot—four blocks away—and by the time he hit his block, he was almost shaking from fatigue. But still, in no hurry to get home. He never was anymore.

There was a sliver of moon through the trees in the Presidio—the morning was dead still and his footfalls echoed. He realized he hadn't heard a siren since he'd started walking. That knowledge didn't fill him with any hope. He knew what it was—he knew what false hope was and he wasn't going to indulge anymore. Today would be hotter than yesterday, and today it would all break loose.

Behind him as he turned up the sidewalk a bus rumbled by on Lake Street. Turning, he saw that it was empty except for the driver and a passenger sitting alone way in the back.

His wife Flo had always wanted a real house. Their plan was to have Flo stay with the kids until the youngest, Orel, got into junior high, which would have been, would be, the next September. At that time Flo would have gone back to teaching and they would have saved for a couple of years, maybe moved out of the city, got their house.

Would have, should have . . .

Putting it off a minute longer, he stood in front of the cement stairs leading up to the second floor. The light over the door had blown out or Rita, his live-in housekeeper, had forgotten to leave it on. It was a long twelve steps to the landing—his own self-improvement, one-day-at-a-time program.

Inside, there was the old sense memory—the familiar smells, the shadows. A tiny bulb burned over the stove in the kitchen and he quietly made his way back. When they had first moved in eleven years ago he and Flo hadn't been able to get over the spaciousness of the place—two bedrooms, study, living room, dining room, kitchen. They had only had the first two boys then—Isaac and Jacob—and they had put them in one bedroom, used the other themselves, and still had an adult's room where they kept files, wrote checks, locked the door when they needed to get away. After Orel came around (they called him O.J. back then—they'd since dropped the nickname), the older boys shared a bunk bed until they finally had to acknowledge there was no room for three of them—their beds and all their stuff—in the one ten-by-twelve room. They had given their eldest, Isaac, the old study as his own bedroom.

Now, with Rita living on the premises, space was an issue. Half the living room, the area around the couch set off by a changing screen, was Rita's. The only place to sit was at the kitchen table. Glitsky's Barco-Lounger was still where it had always been in the living room, but it was awkward sitting there while Rita was trying to go to sleep across the room.

So he went and sat at the kitchen table, made tea and was drinking it, feeling the ghosts.

Glitsky usually wore his gun, even at home, but tonight for the call-up he had left his holster hanging in the closet in his bedroom, so when he heard the "chunk" he grabbed a butcher's knife from the block on the drain and switched on the light in the hallway leading back to Isaac's room.

Where all was quiet.

He stood in the open doorway, pumped up, breathing hard. After all that had gone down already tonight he was ready to explode. If anybody touched his home . . .

The only light came from the hall, but Isaac's room wasn't much bigger than a bread box, and all of it was visible. His son was completely covered by his blankets—Glitsky could see them rising and falling.

The back door was locked. He told himself it could have been a raccoon getting into the garbage, dropping the lid on the cement. It surprised people to hear it, but there were lots of raccoons in the city, big and fearless as mastiffs, breeding like rabbits in the brush of the Presidio.

As he passed Isaac's door again Glitsky decided to take another look. Still covered. In the past, whatever time he got in, he'd always check the boys before he went to sleep. Not that they ever needed it. It was just a habit he'd acquired—walk to their beds, look at their faces, check their breathing, make sure the blankets were over them. Dad stuff.

In three steps he was by the bed. Leaning over, planning to gently pull the covers off his head, he saw the shoes sticking out from under the blanket. Ike didn't normally sleep in his shoes.

"Hey," he whispered, sitting on the edge of the bed, laying a hand on his son's shoulder. "Nice try." For another few seconds the form was still. Sighing, Glitsky lay the knife on the desk, crossed his hands, elbows on his knees.

The blanket moved. Glitsky pulled it down. His oldest son—seventeen next month—had been crying. He was also fully dressed.

Glitsky tried to pull the boy toward him, to get an arm

around his neck and hold him there against him. "Come here."

But he jerked away. "Leave me alone!"

The first time Glitsky had heard that from him, it took what he'd thought was the last unbroken piece that was left of his heart and stomped on it. Now, he wasn't used to it, exactly, but he'd heard it enough that it had lost a little of its hurt. "All right." He got to where he knew his voice would sound controlled, nonchalant. "You been out?"

No answer.

"Do me a favor. Don't go out. It's bad out there."

Still no answer.

"You heard all the sirens? They lynched a black man tonight, not ten blocks from here. It's not safe out there."

Isaac was one-fourth black, with light skin and his father's kinky hair. But everyone with an ounce of visible black knew the reality—you were white or you were non-white. Black.

Glitsky was looking straight into his son's eyes, which were doing their best to avoid his. He saw enough of that at the Hall every day. He wasn't going to lose this boy, or his brothers. But he believed that the way to keep people's respect was demand that they keep some for themselves. He moved ahead. "The rules committee has a meeting and didn't invite me?"

"The rules committee is a joke."

The rules committee was something Glitsky had implemented in the first months that he and the boys were all trying to survive after Flo. It was made up of all of them, including Rita, the housekeeper. The adults had two votes, the boys one each, and so if there was unanimity between them they could outvote either Glitsky or Rita alone.

The rules committee had navigated them through some rough seas—when the boys had felt that there was no order, that life itself was precarious. Glitsky believed it gave them some sense of control. It also caused a lot of fights—but fighting was all right. Glitsky could take fighting. Just don't give him silence.

Which was what he was getting now.

He stood up. "Look up here, Ike, look at me." The son

moved out of the light so he wouldn't get the glare from the hall light. He raised his eyes—red.

"You weren't home. When I heard you go out—"

"They've got an emergency downtown, Ike. All over the city. They called me. I had to go."

"You always have to go."

Glitsky ran a hand through his hair. "I know," he said. He was too tired to go into it. It was true, but so what? "I don't want you going out there, Isaac. Not for a couple of days."

"You're grounding me? The middle of summer you're grounding me?"

"I'm saying I don't want you boys to go out."

"For how long?"

"I don't know. Maybe a day, maybe two. I don't know. It's not safe out there."

"Oh, but it is safe for you, huh?"

Glitsky hated the tone but it was his house and his sons were going to obey his rules and that was that. "Don't give me any grief, Ike. We can talk about it in the morning."

He felt the need to reach and touch his boy, soften it somewhat, explain, but didn't dare try. It would just escalate, like everything else. He stood up. "Sleep tight."

Closing the door behind him, he walked out.

Rita was asleep. Glitsky heard the regular sibilance of her breathing on the other side of the screen as he lowered himself into the old lounger on "his" side of the living room.

Closing his eyes, the events of the night came racing up at him—from Isaac to the Cavern Tavern to the meeting with the mayor and the brass downtown. Then, suddenly, to Elaine Wager—why had *she* been there?

Oh yes, of course. Her mother.

Loretta Wager.

Startled by the unexpected clarity of the memory, he opened his eyes. The quiet room. The deep shadows. That was all. Suddenly, his brain exhausted and his emotions frayed—perhaps he was starting to doze in dawn's first light—there was the vision of Loretta Wager again, as she'd been back in college, the first time, in her apartment with

the Huey Newton chair and the two dominating wall posters: for Eldridge Cleaver's *Soul on Ice,* and the other, of
Martin Luther King's face with his dream and the crowd
in front superimposed.

She'd invited Glitsky up to go over some of the San Jose
team rosters and choose likely candidates they could recruit
for the Black Student Union, the BSU. Glitsky had pretended that it was innocent—hoping it wouldn't turn out
to be, but not even daring to admit that. They were in her
bedroom, actually looking over the lists, when she excused
herself for a minute and went out to get a Coke or something. Then she called out his name.

At twenty-two, she was near-perfect in form, a goddess
reclining naked with her legs parted on the couch in her
living room, the slanting rays of the afternoon sun streaking
her, her fingers stroking herself, asking him if she scared
him, if he wanted her and had the balls to take her—

He sat up, opening his eyes. This, he thought, was pa-
thetic indulgence, stupid, recalling an adolescent encounter,
getting half-tumescent on his Barco-Lounger across the
room from his children's nanny as she slept and the city
burned.

Disgusted with himself, he pushed himself up and went
into his bedroom. There was Flo's picture on the dresser,
smiling at him. He turned off the overhead, got undressed
in the half-light and fell into bed.

He didn't want to see Flo smiling. Or fantasize about
some romanticized past with Loretta Wager. Especially, he
did not want to think about what was going to happen in
a few hours, when the sun came up again, as it always did.

He tried to force himself to sleep, to forget, to ignore.

He was still hard.

11

After finally forcing himself to get out of bed an hour after the sun had come up, Kevin Shea had stood at his widest back window taking in his view. Nothing in his vision resembled an area struggling with poverty. His apartment on Green Street backed onto Cow Hollow, whose artery in turn was Union, San Francisco's yuppiest mile. Beyond Union were the upscale Fort Mason and Marina neighborhoods. To Shea's right, looking east, he could catch a glimpse of Russian Hill and the glittering bay beyond. To his left, the green expanse of the Presidio provided a lush foreground to the red spires of the Golden Gate Bridge.

This morning seven distinct columns of smoke rose in an arc through the panorama. Opening the window a crack to look further around, he heard a constant wail from sirens, dopplering nearer, then farther in the streets below. He closed the window and lowered the blinds, darkening his living room.

In the kitchen he fumbled for coffee beans, half of which he spilled before he got them into the electric grinder. He got some water over one of the burners, then turned on the television.

He was beginning to hope he had only dislocated his arm. It had regained some mobility and in certain positions didn't hurt so much, and he thought if it was broken that wouldn't be the case. His ribs, on the other hand, hurt like hell in every position.

A mug normally intended for beer was full of coffee. Slumping nearly horizontal in a stuffed chair of worn, cracking yellow faux-leather, he was too low to see over the ledge of any of his windows, and anyway the shades were drawn.

Melanie on the phone had started out being convinced by what the television was saying about his role last night, and that really worried him. Did she *really* think that he had somehow been a ringleader in the lynching? She should have known he was incapable of anything like that. But if even *she* thought he'd been involved, he had bigger problems than a few broken ribs.

In his hungover daze he had managed to ask her how she could think what she was saying was possible?

"You've got to see the picture," she had told him, and then had hung up.

The television cast its muted glow back into the half-lit room. Shea, hunkered down in his chair as though against an onslaught, sipped his coffee. The screen filled with a close-up of an anchorman as the morning news came on the air:

"The lead story here and across the country today is the lynching of a black attorney by an all-white mob here in San Francisco last night and the devastating escalation of violence and rioting that has swept the Bay Area and is already being reflected in other major cities—New York, Chicago, Atlanta, Detroit, Washington, DC, and Los Angeles.

"Here in San Francisco Mayor Conrad Aiken has called for a dusk-to-dawn curfew and has asked the governor to declare a state of emergency for the city and county. Property damage is already estimated at some two hundred fifty million dollars and that figure is certain to go up, perhaps into the billions. The Red Cross and other relief organizations are setting up tent cities and emergency medical centers in Golden Gate Park, Dolores Park, Marina Green and several other locations around the city for those who need shelter or assistance, and even at this early hour, people are flooding to these areas. Our News Center crews report nineteen fires are still burning in several areas of the city, including the site of the lynching itself. We're going to take you there now, live . . ."

Shea had forgotten his coffee. The fire he was seeing on the tube was in the process of consuming nearly the entire square block bounded by Geary (and the Cavern Tavern) and Clement streets between 2nd and 3rd—businesses and family duplexes.

The anchorman was talking to his stringer over the images of the flames: "We understand, Terri, that authorities are especially concerned about the location of this blaze . . . ?"

"That's right, Mark. This appears to be a very different reaction from the frustration and rage we saw in Los Angeles after the Rodney King verdict. As you know, this is not a ghetto area and police were here earlier this morning when these fires began with a kind of drive-by firebombing attack centering on what used to be the Cavern Tavern, which is where the mob reportedly first developed."

"An attack?"

"That's right. Witnesses tell us that several cars converged here at one time, crashed the police barricade and started throwing Molotov cocktails. Fortunately there weren't many people on the street or it might have been much worse. The police on the street were shot at from the cars and two were wounded. So it was more a planned raid than a spontaneous explosion of rage."

"A call to arms? The start of a civil war?"

Terri shook her head. "Let's hope not, Mark, but it could be, it certainly could be."

And then, suddenly, Shea was looking at the picture—*his own picture*—hearing the anchor's voice-over. "And here is how it all began. Police Chief Dan Rigby speculates that there was an informal memorial service for a man named Michael Mullen who was shot to death during a carjacking a couple of weeks ago. The man arrested for that crime was an African-American named Jerohm Reese and he . . ."

They kept the picture on the screen, and his face was the clearest thing in it. But to him it still looked like it captured what he had actually done—held up the guy, tried to get him the knife to cut himself down. His attention came back to the screen: ". . . and the mayor is asking this man, who is still unidentified, to come forward . . ."

The mayor was on a street somewhere in the predawn, in shirtsleeves, looking haggard. A fire burned behind him. "We must not let this divide us," he was saying. "This does not have to be black versus white. This was a small group of individuals, of misguided white men who broke the law and who will be punished. Every decent person in San

Francisco, and that's the overwhelming majority of us, wants this group, and especially its leader, brought to justice."

In disbelief, Shea watched and listened to more of it. Senator Loretta Wager had flown in overnight and they had caught her coming off the plane at the airport. "Certainly the first step before we can ever talk about starting to heal these wounds," she said, "has to be a good-faith effort on the part of San Francisco's authorities to apprehend these murderers, to demonstrate to the minority communities, to all of us, that hate-based lawlessness will not be tolerated. And this can't be done with talk—only with results. We've had enough of talk. If the mayor and the police chief want us to believe they are truly concerned about the black community and all our decent citizens, then this man in the picture, and the others, have got to be found and put on trial. And quickly. Give them the benefit of a justice that they denied Arthur Wade. And, if they are found guilty, give them the penalty that fits the crime."

The coffee was cold and so was his sweat. Shea did not feel his ribs or his arm anymore as the news broke for a commercial and he heard yet another siren outside.

12

Lieutenant Abe Glitsky sat at his desk in the homicide detail on the fourth floor of San Francisco's Hall of Justice. After an hour of no sleeping he had given up and gone back downtown. He had been in since seven-fifteen, trying to get a handle on the madness, to coordinate the efforts of his department, which had already, previous to yesterday's incident, been up to its eyeballs in domestic-violence homicides, drive-by homicides, drug-related homicides, senseless, stupid homicides—the usual harvest of the urban streets.

Now, the workday not even officially begun, and not including Arthur Wade and of course the still "unsolved" murder of Mike Mullen, he already had two new verified homicides—victims of the street violence. These were a three-year-old white child who'd been burned to death in one of the duplexes that had gone up in the aftermath of the firebombing of the Cavern and a Korean store owner who had caught a brick in the head while he had been trying to defend his fresh-fruit and vegetable store in the lower Fillmore.

To say Glitsky had an open-door policy at work would have been a misnomer—in fact, his office had no door. There used to be a door. Then, one day, it was removed to be varnished or painted or something and had never made it back. So anyone who desired an audience with the lieutenant could simply walk into the large room that held the twelve desks of the homicide detail inspectors, turn left and pass into his inner domain—a fourteen-by-sixteen-foot area set off by drywall.

There were two windows. From his desk, looking right, was the double-door entrance to the detail, a not-so-early warning system that told him—if he was looking—who might or might not be coming through his doorway in the next moment or two. In front, his view was not the touristy one seen on postcards of Baghdad by the Bay. Instead it featured a foreground of the old, pitted and cluttered desks of homicide detectives, an unpainted concrete column stuck with official department announcements, wanted posters, joke faxes that made the office rounds, pictures of male and female prostitutes, the occasional morgue shot, yellowing newspaper articles . . . the column was the detail's unofficial bulletin board.

Beyond the desks and the column was a six-foot window of crisscrossed panes, thick with grime, through which—when the fog allowed—one used to be able to spy the artery of the 101 Freeway, pulsing with life, and beyond that, the rooftops south of Market. At last, on clear days, in the distance rose the glitter-dome of Nob Hill, with its fabled hotels, architecture, history.

Now, and for the past two years, the view through the soot-stained panes consisted of parts of the second, third and fourth floors of the new jail, a truly hideous committee-designed incarceration unit whose rounded glass and chrome exterior was somehow expected to meld aesthetically with the hulking gray box that was the Hall of Justice.

Just outside the detail was a small reception area that due to budget cuts had not been manned—or womanned—in four years, so that anyone who took a notion to could waltz directly in—both to the open area and to Glitsky's own office.

Glitsky loved it on television where the buzzer sounded and the lieutenant said, "Yes?" and the receptionist—usually a twenty-something knockout in full makeup and no uniform—informed him that the mayor or the district attorney or Mr. Flocksmith was there for an appointment, at which the lieutenant, sighing, said, "Keep him on ice for a mo, Marcia, then send him in." He really loved it.

Chris Locke was in the doorway, through it and standing in front of Glitsky's desk, knuckles down on it, hovering, before the lieutenant had a chance to look up.

"I'd like a few words with you, Abe, you got a minute."

"Come on in, Chris. Make yourself at home."

Locke was alone, which was unusual. Glitsky wondered if he had gone home and gotten any sleep. He was dressed in his coat and tie as he had been in the middle of the night.

Glitsky started to lean back in his chair, to look up at the district attorney. It occurred to him, though, that Locke enjoyed putting people in this position, so instead he stood—Locke was a big man but Glitsky had an inch on him. "Coffee, Chris? Tea?"

Locke wasn't buying the hospitality. "Abe, I'm confused."

"So am I, Chris. All the time. But I've stopped worrying about it."

Locke took his knuckles off the desk. He was, Glitsky thought, one of those people who didn't like to stand unpropped, and no sooner had he straightened up than he half-turned and rested his hind quarters on the front of the desk.

Glitsky went into his best at-ease, hands clasped behind his back.

"I always thought we got along"—Locke began—"and then this crap you drop last night about Jerohm Reese. I take it you didn't agree with my decision to let him go, even though he had no chance in hell of turning into a conviction."

"Perhaps."

"What does that mean?"

"It's a seven-letter word that means 'maybe,' Chris. I thought letting Jerohm go, after we went to the trouble of finding him, then arresting and booking him and all, seemed a little, well, precipitous."

Locke picked a piece of Scotch tape off the roll on the desk, working it between his fingers. "This is really about the lieutenant thing, isn't it?"

He was referring to the test the city gave, and which Glitsky had taken a year ago, to determine eligibility for promotion to lieutenant. While the candidates had waited for the results Locke had invited Glitsky up to his office and said he was going to use his pull to get him bumped to lieutenant even if he failed the test. He had gone on to explain that "people of color" were discriminated against by the testing process, that Glitsky was a good cop and deserved the promotion even if his grades didn't measure up.

Glitsky had felt insulted by the assumption that he wouldn't pass (he got a ninety-seven, second highest among the candidates). Also, he didn't like the obvious politics of it—a mixture of backass affirmative action and loading up the police department with lieutenants for whom the DA had done "favors."

"A little of that, Chris," Glitsky was saying. "But mostly just plain old Jerohm Reese. And now, of course, the rest of it." Glitsky raised his head, indicating the world outside.

Rolling the tape between his fingers, Locke sighed. "Anything about Reese going to help us now?"

"You mean like arrest him again? I doubt it. But I thought it would help last night if hizzoner got some understanding of what might have started this whole thing."

"What started this whole thing, Abe, was lynching Arthur Wade. And what's going to end it is finding the guy that led that mob."

"You really think so?"

"Yeah, I do, Abe. Other people do, too."

Glitsky took a breath, letting it out slowly. New to his so-called leadership role, he was still mostly a street cop in his heart—a protector of victims, a collector of evidence, the man who made the arrests. All of his training and experience was in enforcing laws and policies, not in making or interpreting them. But now, as head of a department, he caught a whiff of a change and it didn't smell too good. "Well, as I mentioned last night, Chris, we're investigating it."

Locke stepped closer and leaned over the desk. "I don't know if that's going to do it, Abe. If that's going to be enough."

13

Shea's hand was on the telephone.

He had pulled up a couple of the blinds so he could have a sense of what was happening outside. The television stayed on.

He had decided that there was really only one thing to do—call the police and turn himself in, tell them what had really happened. The longer he let this thing grow of its own accord, the more this crazy interpretation was going to be accepted as reality. He had to stop it *now*. He picked up the receiver.

The face of Philip Mohandas suddenly filled the television screen. Mohandas was the leader of the African Nation movement and the embodiment of the voice of African-American separatism. Shea had written an entire chapter of his thesis— *Segregation to Integration and Back Again*—on Mohandas, and now the face on the screen caught all his attention. Like the mayor had earlier, Mohandas was speaking outdoors, live, in what looked like one of San Francisco's projects. They punched up his voice in mid-sound-bite.

". . . we don't *believe* that the white man's government don't know who led the mob that murdered Arthur Wade. We don't *accept* their lies. We don't *believe* that there's any commitment to punish the guilty, because the truth is that the white man's law don't punish the white man. If we want justice, we're going to have to make it. If we want our streets back we're going to have to take them!"

The gleaming face turned. Mohandas seemed to have an understanding of where the camera was. "You're out there," he said, pointing at Shea through the television, "we know you are. And we are going to find you. And you are going to pay."

As the picture cut away from Mohandas, Shea again saw the photograph of himself on the screen in a blurry close-up. Then the camera pulled back and the anchors chattered away, explaining what Shea needed no explanation for. His face was the centerpiece of a wanted poster, offering a reward of one hundred thousand dollars.

Suddenly the voices of the anchors came back into Shea's consciousness. ". . . denial that this is, in effect, a contract on the man's life, isn't that right, Karen?"

"That's true, Mark, but the talk here in the streets is that the money is being offered for the man's death. Even if somebody gets to him after he's been arrested, even if he's already in jail . . ."

Shea put the telephone back down in its cradle. Calling the police and giving himself up had just turned into a bad idea.

Melanie Sinclair had never done anything wrong until she'd met Kevin Shea, and now it seemed that *everything* she did turned out badly. The last thing she had wanted to do was get him mad at her again, accuse him of anything, put him on the defensive. That, she had come to believe, was how she had lost him.

But then on television she had seen what he'd done last night, or what it looked like. She couldn't believe it, that wasn't Kevin. But what was she supposed to think?

Before she had met Kevin Shea, Melanie had always done the right thing. She had gotten A's all the way through school. She kept her shoes neatly arranged in her closet underneath her color-coded hangers, on which hung, in order, dresses, skirts, slacks, blouses, coats, sweaters, vests. She combed her hair a hundred strokes every night, smiled easily without putting it on, was a genuine asset to any organization she decided to join. She loved both her parents and her younger brother and sister, and they felt the same about her.

Up until now, at age twenty-one, she had experienced only one serious wrinkle in the otherwise smooth fabric of her life, and that had been Kevin Shea, who was not all, but quite a lot, of what she tried not to be.

It should have worked out. Kevin was the right age for

her, unattached, with an aura of sophistication that implied experience. Whatever his flaws—none of them *too* serious—she could help him with them and thereby ensure his appreciation and love. *Plus,* to tell the truth, she had been very much physically attracted to him. She knew that that was important.

Just how important, she couldn't be sure since she was still a virgin. She had decided that Kevin Shea was going to be the man to deflower her and then marry her. Melanie Sinclair truly believed in the old-time values and virtues.

And for a few months it had worked. Melanie had good genes, shining auburn hair, nice breasts, shapely legs. She was considered a catch and she was honest enough to know it. She had picked Kevin Shea to be caught by. And then, five months after their first date, two months after they had been making love, three weeks ago, he had said good-bye.

Just like that.

He was sorry, he didn't love her and didn't want to change. He didn't want to stop drinking, for example. Or laughing out loud. In fact, he had said maybe *she* should consider changing—lightening up a bit. People should try for excellence, he said, not perfection, because perfection, after all, was impossible, whereas excellence was occasionally attainable. Something to shoot for.

Well, to hell with him! That had been her original reaction. If he didn't believe in even *trying* for perfection, then certainly he'd never get there, or even all the way to excellent. It was a phony distinction anyway.

But she hurt. God, how she still hurt!

And now she'd gone and made it worse. Calling him that way . . . she'd just thought there might have been something she could do.

She hadn't been able to keep that judgmental tone out of her voice. Why did she *do* that? She loved him. She *knew* he hadn't done what they were saying, but she was only trying to play a little devil's advocate, get him to understand the *seriousness* of it. Except, of course, he would know, she didn't have to tell him. He could figure things out on his own. But Melanie—dumb, dumb Melanie—she just couldn't leave well enough alone. And now she'd gone and lost him . . .

*   *   *

Kevin hadn't liked Cindy either. Cindy Taylor, her best friend. That had been another big problem.

"She's tooling you," he had told her. "She's using you, Mel, and you're carrying her. You watch, she's jealous, she's using you."

(That was another thing—he called her Mel. No one had ever called her Mel and she kept correcting him about that too, until he broke up with her.)

"How is she using me?"

"She's holding *you* back so that she can be the wild one, the exciting one. Not that she's exactly Madonna herself." He'd even told her that Cindy had come on to him, which couldn't be true, because Cindy had told her that she didn't even think much of Kevin. Although, come to think of it, Cindy *had* been the one to notice him at school, to get her interested.

Well . . . no matter now, that was over. And Cindy, for better or worse, was still her best friend, and she had to talk to somebody . . . The tears wouldn't stop. She was going crazy.

"My God, that *is* Kevin." The call had awakened Cindy too, but Cindy was used to it. "What are you going to do?"

"I don't know. I called him. He was . . ." She was going to say hungover but held it back.

"What did he say?"

"I didn't let him say much. I just asked him why."

"And what did he say?"

"He didn't say anything."

"He didn't even deny it?"

Melanie had put that down to shock, but the fact was that he hadn't. "No . . ."

"I *knew* he was capable of something like this." The way she said it made Melanie feel uncomfortable, the effect Kevin seemed to have on her. It was too strong a reaction somehow. But she couldn't think about that now.

Dead air. Melanie could hear Cindy's television. "They're saying anyone who can identify him should notify the police," Cindy finally said.

"Well, I'm not going to do that."

"I don't know, Melanie."

"Cindy, come *on.* This is Kevin we're talking about. Whatever it looks like, he didn't—"

"It sure does look like it, though, doesn't it? If he did, the police should—"

"He didn't! I know he didn't."

"I don't know that."

"Cindy!" Calling her had been a mistake, too. Everything she did nowadays was turning out wrong. "Cindy, come on, don't *you* do anything either, okay?"

Silence.

Then, calling on every reserve of calm she had: "Just promise me you won't do anything, would you. *Promise*?"

A long pause. Then: "I'll try."

14

"Kevin Shea. And he was home as of about an hour ago. The snitch supplied the address, too."

Glitsky didn't much like this emphasis on one man. After all, it had been a mob, and even if this one guy had been the leader—and it did look that way—he wasn't the only guilty party. There were somewhere between twenty and sixty people somewhere in the city who'd had a hand in this. Glitsky had sent out a team to go and persuade Jamie O'Toole, for example, the bartender of the Cavern, to drop down to the Hall before noon for a few questions. He also craved an audience with Paul Westberg, the photographer, whose identity he had only just learned.

But now there was nothing to do but move on this Kevin Shea. Glitsky gave the order to dispatch a black-and-white to the address they had been given. Then, thinking about it, he made two more decisions: to send second and third cars as backups to Shea's place, and to stroll over to his chief's office and get the latest version of how things stood, bureaucracy-wise.

"To tell you the truth, Lieutenant, I don't know how to react to it. It's the least of my worries at the moment."

Chief Dan Rigby sat in his leather chair behind his desk. Glitsky had been a department head for less than a year and the two men had never met socially. Nevertheless, when the lieutenant had come calling the chief had admitted him right away. Now Glitsky stood on the Iranian rugs and looked across the shining expanse of mahogany desk that separated him from his boss. He wondered, briefly, if

Rigby's desk would fit into his whole office, and decided it might but it would make walking around a bit of a chore.

"I'm just saying that, technically, sir, we don't have much in the way of evidence if we're going to charge—"

"What about that picture?" Rigby gave Glitsky a hopeful look, knowing as well as his lieutenant that normally a photograph such as Westberg's would have to pass a battery of tests for authenticity before it could go before a grand jury or any finder of fact as admissible evidence.

Glitsky stood impassively, as though considering the chief's words. "Yes, sir," he said at last, finessing the question. "But to charge someone with murder before the grand jury has had a chance—"

"I'm hearing, Lieutenant, that we need something, almost anything, and right away if we're going to have any hope of containing this thing."

"Mr. Locke came by my office this morning and that was pretty much the message he delivered, so I've heard it, too, but frankly, it makes me nervous. That's why I came here to talk to you. I don't exactly know how to handle it—"

"What's to handle? We arrest the guy, book him, give him to Locke. Everybody takes a deep breath, maybe the streets settle down. Do you have any doubts about this man, what's his name, Shea?"

"No, sir, but that's not my point. I'm saying we don't have a usual case to make an arrest on. We could take a lot of flak on it. In normal times we wouldn't go near this yet."

"These aren't normal times."

"No, sir, they're not. But I'd like an eyewitness all the same. Something to make the arrest more . . . defensible."

"Well, you've got that."

Glitsky waited.

"The photographer, he's downstairs on three getting questioned right now."

"By the DA? How'd that happen?" They both knew this was way outside the realm of procedure, that normally the police interrogated everyone associated with a crime and the district attorney pretty much stayed out of it at least until there was enough to present a case to the grand jury.

"Locke told me, as a courtesy, that they were talking to

him. As a courtesy," Rigby repeated. "They're building their case on Shea."

"Before they knew who he was?"

"They *decided* who he was, Abe."

"Who did? Locke?"

Rigby nodded. "Locke. The mayor. The senator."

"The senator?"

"Loretta Wager, in the flesh. She flew in here this morning, last night. I gather she's sold this idea to the mayor—offer up Shea, although you didn't hear it here. Focus it on him, then deliver him, restore the faith of the black community and even the score. Let justice take its course. And now you say we've got him, right? Shea?"

"I sent some cars to go pick him up. We'll worry about a warrant later."

"Okay, then, we've done our job."

Glitsky bit his lip, surprised at the length of time the chief had given him, and the confidence he'd shared. "What if it doesn't work?" he said.

"What, our job?"

"No. What if we get Shea and the place still keeps erupting?"

"Loretta Wager says it won't. The mayor's betting it won't. And Chris Locke's betting his job on it."

If wasn't exactly an answer, but perhaps there wasn't one. Glitsky nodded. "I'd like to go talk to the photographer."

"He's downstairs. Help yourself."

After he got the picture developed in his darkroom and ran it down to the KPIX studios, Paul Westberg had not been able to talk himself into going back home. There was no way he would get back to sleep.

They had offered him five hundred dollars for his picture and all rights, but he had studied the scenario that had developed around the Rodney King videotape—every photographer's dream—and had fantasized about some similar piece of good fortune happening to him, planning how he would handle it. And now it had happened. He had held out for twenty-five hundred dollars, retaining world rights to the shot.

Fielding the calls in the middle of the night in the studio basement, he'd then sold licenses to air the picture on CNN, Fox and the major networks for their news shows only. In the past sixteen hours he had grossed some twenty-four thousand dollars. He had three agents and a couple of lawyers sniffing around and he hadn't even been home yet. They'd found him.

What he hadn't counted on was the police. He was, after all, not only a photographer, but a witness. He was the only one who couldn't deny that he'd seen it all. He'd *been* there—the downside to fame and glory.

The two officers had been polite but firm. He was going to go downtown with them for questioning. Sure, he could take his own car. They'd follow him.

They hadn't taken him to the police station upstairs but through the district attorney's corridors on the third floor of the Hall of Justice and for twenty minutes left him sitting alone, sweating, in a small room, unguarded and abandoned. He had stopped feeling on the cusp of untold good fortune. In fact, he had become vaguely fearful—his mouth sour and his eyes bagged and he wanted to go home and crawl into his bed.

Finally the heavy wooden door creaked open and a beautiful young black woman wearing a business suit had been standing in front of him, smiling, identifying herself as Assistant District Attorney Wager. After assuring him that he wasn't a suspect in the lynching, she asked if he wanted a lawyer present anyway. He had sipped at the excellent coffee (she had brought him a fresh cup), and said no, what did he need a lawyer for? He hadn't done anything illegal or wrong.

She proceeded to walk him through the events of the previous night, and she had helped him reconstruct the truth as he remembered it, how he had been walking down the other side of Geary Street, heard the commotion, looked over and thought it might be news. Finally, getting to the moment of the picture, how the crowd had been yelling, "Pull on him, pull, pull!" and the guy had been doing just that. No, there was no doubt about it. Sure, he'd testify to it. He *saw* it. That was what had happened.

And then the hawk-faced black man with the flight jacket and scar through his lips, breaking into the room and scaring the shit out of him, taking over from the lovely assistant district attorney. Ms. Wager had been cool about it, composed, but still struck him as somebody caught doing something wrong.

The man, Lieutenant Glitsky, he said, the head honcho of the homicide detail, suggested they go upstairs to continue the interview. Convinced that he hadn't much of a choice in the matter, Westberg had gone along with him.

"This is Lieutenant Inspector Abraham Glitsky, star number 1144. I am currently at an interview room in the Hall of Justice, 880 Bryant Street, in San Francisco. With me is a gentleman identifying himself as Paul Westberg, a freelance photojournalist, Caucasian male, born March 4, 1971. This interview is pursuant to an investigation of case number 950867731. Today's date is June 29, Wednesday, at 0825 hours in the A.M."

Glitsky was going to do it by the book, as a regular interview conducted in the course of a murder investigation. He sat across from Westberg at a small pitted wooden table, a tape recorder switched on between them. After walking through the standard battery of questions, again going over the basics of what Westberg claimed he had seen the night before, they got down to the crux of it:

Q: So the crowd was yelling, "Pull, pull!" Something like that. And what happened then?
A: Well, this man was pulling on him, hanging on him, like in the picture.
Q: He was pulling on the hanging man, pulling him down?
A: Yes.
Q: How do you know that?
A: [Pause.] Well, it was obvious.
Q: That's my question, Mr. Westberg. How was it obvious? Look at this picture. [Glitsky had the late edition of the morning *Chronicle* in the room.] The man has one arm around the victim, another holding up what appears to be a knife.
A: It *was* a knife. He had it at the guy's throat.
Q: Okay. Then what?
A: Then what *what*?
Q: Then what happened?
A: I took the picture. Two of them.

Q: In quick succession?

A: Yes.

Q: Have you seen the other one?

A: Yeah, sure. I developed them both at home. It didn't come out as good.

Q: Do you mean it wasn't as dramatic, or there was some technical problem—focus, lighting, like that?

A: No, there wasn't a technical problem. It was only, like, two seconds away from this one. Basically the same picture, just not as good.

Q: All right, let's go on. After you took these pictures, what did you do?

A: I ran. The crowd reacted a little to the flash. A couple of guys started coming for me. I thought they were going to smash the camera, maybe me, too, so I ran.

Q: You used a flash?

A: Yeah. It was in shadow, the street, near sunset, maybe right after.

Q: So how long in total were you there, witnessing all this?

A: I don't know. A minute, ninety seconds, something like that. It was pretty scary, crazy.

Q: And before you snapped your pictures, did you happen to notice this man who you say was pulling on the victim?

A: He *was* pulling on the victim. Look, that's what the lady downstairs told me, too. She said stick by my story. I thought you guys were on the same side.

Q: The lady downstairs, Ms. Wager?

A: Yeah, that was her.

Q: She told you to stick by your story? Which story?

A: That he was pulling down on the guy . . .

Q: Well, is that a story or is it what happened?

A: [Pause.] It's what happened. It's what I saw. The picture shows it plain as day—look!

Q: [Pause.] If he was holding on with two hands and his feet were off the ground . . . but you're saying you *saw* him pull down. That's your testimony?

A: Well, what else could it have been? He was in the mob . . . [Pause.] Yes, that's my testimony.

15

Melanie was crying. "Cindy told them."

"Cindy told them *what*, Melanie?"

"Who you were."

"*What*? Why? Why did she do that?" But he knew. "How did . . . ?"

"I called her, Kevin. Oh, God. I needed somebody. I just felt so bad, Kevin. I needed to talk to *somebody* . . ."

"I've told you a hundred times, Cindy is not your friend." But this was a stupid discussion, he decided. "Anyway, thanks for the tip—"

"Kevin, don't—"

"Don't! You tell *me* don't . . ."

She was crying. It tore at him, and he realized he still cared about her, didn't want to hurt her, but now she'd gone and done this . . .

"Kevin, I'm so sorry. I love you, I still love you and I can help you. You can come stay here—"

"Why would I need to come stay there, Melanie?"

"Cindy . . . Cindy told them where you live."

He took the receiver away from his ear and stared at it. This was too bizarre.

Goddamn Cindy, Kevin thought. This is where the dick leads you. That one night with her—before he'd hooked up with Melanie—was turning into the worst mistake of his life. And it had been nothing but a casual one-nighter, nothing like what he had had with Melanie.

Letting go of the phone, leaving it off the cradle, he went to the window and looked down over the rooftops. He stepped out onto the fire escape, climbed the iron ladder holding on with his one good arm, up to the roof. God, it was hot. It was *never* this hot in San Francisco.

His head throbbed and this time he was willing to concede that it might be part hangover. He was dressed in a pair of old 501 Levi's jeans, running shoes, a UCLA sweatshirt, and he moved in a crouch to the front of his building, looking over the ledge down onto Green Street. Two black-and-white police cars were pulled up at the curb, and he saw four men talking.

Again, a sense of disbelief. This could not be happening. Damn that Cindy. Hell hath no fury indeed . . .

Now the policemen split up, two of them going toward the front door, the other two separating, going around the two sides of the building.

Surrounded.

16

Glitsky knew that he was on edge—a bad sign. He was chomping on ice cubes, sitting at his desk, warning off all would-be intruders with the evil eye as they appeared in his doorway.

Not very professional, he knew. It was the kind of body language he would use on occasion when he'd been a sergeant and wanted solitude, but now that he was the boss it had a different feel, a kind of self-aggrandizing . . .

Well, screw it, he thought. Things were starting to pile up—he'd known they would—but as was usually the case in emergencies, you knew it was going to whack you but you could never predict where or how hard. The answer was starting to turn out to be—really hard and almost everywhere.

Maybe it was the lack of sleep last night, maybe his biorhythms were low; Isaac, Flo, the whole Wager family; but events were hitting him the wrong way and he was struggling to contain himself.

The patrolmen had not been able to arrest Kevin Shea. The suspect was gone when they'd gotten there—he had left suddenly. The apartment manager had been cooperative and let them in and the back window had been open. There was a half-consumed cup of still-warm coffee on an end table. The television set was still on. The phone was off the hook, the receiver lying on the bed. Someone had obviously tipped Shea and he had gotten out with minutes to spare.

Contributing to Glitsky's ill humor was the impression he had taken away from the interview with Paul Westberg, which was that Elaine Wager's chat with the witness had affected the man's testimony. And there was a bigger issue—the reason he had felt compelled to visit Chief Rigby earlier in the morning: the district attorney's office, perhaps at the urging of Senator Loretta Wager, seemed to be opting for a political solution to the problems, and this was asking for more trouble than Glitsky cared to consider. They were building a case on Kevin Shea which would not allow for the fact that he might, in fact, be innocent.

Actually, on the basis of what he knew, Glitsky didn't think Shea was innocent. But he was uncomfortable with something that smacked of a witchhunt, and that's what Elaine Wager's interrogation (and Westberg's responses) had reeked of.

Evidently the powers had decided that Kevin Shea was the quintessential white racist, and that feeding him to the maw of the mob was the best answer to the complicated questions they were facing. That this was a fairly typical response didn't make Glitsky hate it any less.

He knew—Christ, he should, he embodied it—he knew that while all the bureaucracies in the land were meeting de facto quotas, providing hard, statistical support for the notion that the country was making progress toward integration and racial harmony, in reality the polarization was increasing every day. Glitsky was on the street enough—he saw it.

The truth was that racism was all around him—the enlightened white workers here in the Hall always referring to black people as "Canadians," the black parents at his boys' schools who wouldn't let their kids play with white children.

On the surface everything was working. People were generally polite, proper, friendly. Now the thing that had become unfashionable—and in San Francisco the worst crime was to be unhip—was acknowledging the depth of the problem. Race? Please, didn't we do all that in the sixties? Better to pretend it wasn't really there. Certainly it wasn't an issue in San Francisco. Everybody accepted everybody else nowadays. This was the nineties. We solved all that stuff years ago. Get real.

And then, one sunny summer evening, a black man named Arthur Wade gets lynched.

And that brought him to the last cause of his ice crunching—the one person who was calling the infection systemic, Philip Mohandas, was abandoning any hope for understanding because he was taking it too damn far. There were so many other things, constructive things, he could do. He could be responsible. He could call for some restraint. Dialogue.

Instead, because Mohandas knew that nobody was going to arrest an African-American leader in the coming days for what amounted to sticks and stones, he would be *excused* for not doing the right thing. He had cause, he was a victim of his own rage. Old-fashioned laws didn't matter if you had a good enough reason. Ask the Menendez boys.

What most got to Glitsky was when the leaders who claimed to represent all the black people caved in to that temptation and then those failures were cited by white people as a justification—hell, the white side of Glitsky even felt it himself—for distrusting legitimate black motives and aspirations.

And now Mohandas was clearly breaking the law, openly calling for vigilantism, being allowed—even encouraged—to rant and vent to his heart's content. And his presence and rhetoric were raising the odds.

Glitsky felt it made no sense to let him inflame the situation but no one seemed to be inclined to try and stop it. Glitsky thought he wouldn't mind a shot at it—he had a few ideas that might get Mohandas's attention—but it wasn't his job. His job was homicide. All this other political crap was just that—crap.

But such sensible thoughts weren't doing his mood any good. He continued to crunch his ice, his eyes fixed ahead of him.

The telephone rang in his office. His receptionist being the same person who guarded his door—nobody—he picked the phone up with a more than usually unpleasant "Glitsky. Homicide."

A pause, an almost inaudible sigh. "Abe Glitsky." He might have imagined it, but there was a sense of relief in the words, as though at great personal expense she'd broken through some psychic barrier. He recognized the voice instantly.

"Loretta . . . ?"

"One word and you sound exactly the same."

Glitsky, adrenaline still running, answered her words. "No," he said, "I'm pretty different. You'd be surprised." It sounded more hostile than he felt but the words were out, unchecked, and maybe some truth . . .

"Well, of course." That deep throaty laugh. "We're all different, Abe, we've all changed. But we're all still the same, too, deep down."

This was as strange an opening as he could have imagined, bantering with his ex-lover who was now a United States senator as though they'd seen each other, perhaps intimately, a couple of days before.

Grabbing the cup, a quarter inch of ice water, he drank it for time to get his bearings, then asked what he could do for her. This, he figured, had to be about Elaine.

"I was just in the mayor's office," she said. "When he mentioned . . . I mean, there aren't many Abe Glitskys . . ."

"I'm in the phone book, Loretta, always have been."

She seemed to hesitate, then went on as though he hadn't responded. "But when Conrad brought you up . . . he said you were a lieutenant . . ."

Suddenly Glitsky's edge sharpened—a red anger flared. Loretta was looking for a toehold to satisfy her curiosity and he wasn't going to help her out. "You thought you'd just call and catch up?"

This time the hesitation was more pronounced. "You're still mad at me? After all these years?"

"I'm not mad at you at all, Loretta . . ."

"At what I did, I mean?"

"I'm still not sure I know what you did, or why you did it. But I can't say it's been a big deal the last, oh, couple of decades or so. I have a family . . ." His voice was winding down.

"I was sorry to hear about your wife . . ."

Glitsky's knuckles had stiffened around the telephone and he opened and closed his fingers. One of his inspectors, Carl Griffin, knocked on his doorjamb and got waved away. "I just suddenly wanted to hear your voice, Abe. See if you were all right, how you were doing. Is that so odd?"

No answer.

He heard her let out a breath. "All right, Abe. I'm sorry to have bothered you."

She was hanging up. He hadn't meant to cut her off. He should have . . .

"Loretta!"

But the connection was gone.

17

Kevin Shea did not want to think about the jump he had taken to the roof next door. It looked maybe eight feet across but it felt like twenty—he would have to go back and measure it someday if his life ever became normal again. He *really* didn't want to think about how far *down* it was. Far enough.

Fortunately the roof was flat and, like his own, had a low ledge. After he had landed, rolling over on his bruised arm and aching ribs, he made his way back to the ledge and lay down against it in the wide shady lane made by the early-morning sun. He heard the police come up to his roof next door, the one he had just abandoned. He heard them go down again.

After an endless ten minutes he had risked a glance over there. Okay, they were really gone. It seemed safe. Relatively.

The door that poked up through the roof was unlocked, and Shea limped his way down the four flights of stairs, seeing no one. On Green Street the police cars had pulled out. The curb was empty. He turned right and started walking, as normally as he could, away from his building.

Shea had grown up in suburban Houston, attended Rice University, majoring in economics, intending to get into some kind of management role in his father's company.

His mother's maiden name was Janine Robitaille, of the New Orleans Robitailles. She was a statuesque Southern belle who favored beehive hairdos long after they were out of style. But on her, somehow, the hairstyle never looked dated—those piles of her dark hair lifted away from the creamy cameo of her face, framing its near-flawless lines, making her always appear taller than her husband Daniel.

His father—Daniel Shea—was half-owner, along with Fred Bronin, of Flexitech, a company that manufactured athletic accessories and supplies—batting and golf gloves, wristbands, orthopedic tensors, hard little rubber balls ("Flexits") that you held in your hand and squeezed to strengthen your grip.

When Kevin was twenty-two and just out of college, Daniel had come home early one afternoon after an extended sales trip to find his beautiful wife Janine in bed with his best friend and partner Fred Bronin.

Being a good ol' boy, Daniel's reaction perhaps should have been to take up the nearest gun and shoot them both, but he fooled them. Kevin's father had always had a streak of insecurity, a tendency to melancholy, and though he had raised a good family (two boys and a girl) and become, after a fashion, successful, he never quite believed in the worth of anything he accomplished, that it had any real meaning. And the double betrayal of a wife and best friend rocked him—and he turned the gun on himself instead.

In the aftermath, the Sheas' world and everything in it fell apart. Janine and Fred Bonin did not get married and live happily ever after. They had a bitter legal and personal battle over Flexitech, which Fred eventually lost because he had a stroke in the middle of it, leaving Janine with de facto ownership of the company. She, having never spent a moment of her life on business, subsequently orchestrated the company into bankruptcy in just under two years.

Meanwhile, Kevin Shea and his younger brother Joey had both appalled their Vietnam-era mother, as they had intended, by enlisting in the army. During their three-year hitch the boys had been trained in survival, weapons, strategy, then sent separately to Desert Storm. Kevin had done a lot of marching and sweating but saw no action. His brother Joey was inside the one bunker that had been destroyed by an Iraqi Scud missile—and had been killed. Kevin's mother and little sister Patsy blamed Kevin for talking Joey into enlisting in the army in the first place, and they had made it clear he was unwelcome in Texas forever, not that it had been his intention to go back there anyway.

Kevin Shea was completely alone. Sometimes he even felt he deserved to be.

Kevin had really made only one connection since he had gotten out of the army and decided to settle in San Francisco and go to graduate school on his GI Bill. There was an older guy—maybe late forties—named Wes Farrell, who was in his program at SFSU. Farrell and Kevin had done some drinking together, had a few semi-serious talks about life. Farrell had been a lawyer, raised his own family, then something had happened—Kevin didn't know what exactly—and he had quit. He didn't believe in the law anymore. Or justice. Or in most people much either.

They had both gravitated to studying history. Somehow it was more acceptable that all they were studying was in the past and so, presumably, couldn't affect anybody ever again.

They were, in their fashion, a good team. They also both liked to drink, which tended to help.

Shea was at a public phone in the Julius Hahn Playground at the southern edge of the Presidio. The smell of smoke was everywhere now in the heated air, even here in the shade of the cypresses, and he could hear sirens and see spires of smoke rising to his left in what he presumed was the Fillmore District and to his right, over the big hill, around what must be Clement.

"Wes? Kevin." He didn't know what he was expecting—that Wes would hang up, yell at him, be astounded at the call? Something.

"Hey, Kev. What's happening?"

Kevin waited a long moment. Surely Wes knew all about his problem, about the Arthur Wade tragedy, what was going on in the city—he must be pulling Kevin's leg. "So what's up?" he asked. "Can you believe this heat?"

Then again, maybe not.

18

The mayor saw to it that Loretta Wager got a temporary office—after all, she was a U.S. senator—downtown at City Hall. It was on the second floor, up from the rotunda, down an echoing corridor, behind an anonymous door. And that suited her fine.

Her feet were sore. For some reason, her feet always hurt after plane flights. After she became president, she'd modify something on Air Force One that would . . .

Smiling, she settled for rubbing her bare feet. Her shoes were off under the desk. She leaned back in her chair, checked her watch. Twelve-fifteen. Elaine should here anytime.

She wasn't sure how she felt about the level of Elaine's involvement. On the one hand, it was good to be in the middle of things, in the loop, with a hand in the outcome. Elaine, thanks to Chris Locke, had already drawn the short straw—she was, single-handedly it seemed, handling the prosecution of Kevin Shea. And seemed to her mother to be doing a good job of it. The downside was that Elaine would shoulder the lion's share of the blame if anything went wrong. And this early in her career, that could hurt her. But, Loretta thought, that was the price of playing with the big boys.

Loretta had left a message at Elaine's as she was leaving Washington last night, and her daughter had called back within two hours, reaching her on the Airfone, filling her in on the status of events so that by the time Loretta had landed, she'd not only grasped those events but had had time to put the right spin on them in front of the media who had gathered to meet her at the airport.

Kevin Shea, she said, was the symbol of what was wrong,

not only here in San Francisco but across America. The fact that he had not yet been apprehended, arrested, even located, was proof that the white man's system wasn't working, didn't work for the black man.

Her plan was simple: the crisis had come at a moment when she could use it to her political advantage. If she could now just keep the focus on apprehending Shea, Loretta might in fact have a forum that would take her a large step toward the Oval Office. And no smiles this time.

It really wasn't out of the question. She was the right age—only forty-seven and a young-looking one at that. There wasn't much doubt in her mind that within sixteen years there would be a woman candidate. There would also, she felt, be a black candidate. And if they were one and the same person . . .

Now, nearing the end of her first term as senator, she had an interesting and, she thought, ironic problem to solve, and her instinct had told her, as soon as it had arisen, that this crisis, if properly handled, could be the solution. For Loretta Wager had spent the better part of the past six years learning the historic lesson of survival in American politics—compromise. If you wanted to get ahead, especially in the white men's club that was the Senate, you had to move within an extremely narrow band of exposure.

Loretta had been good at that, had always been skilled with people. Unfortunately, the pre-campaign polls she'd conducted were beginning to confirm what she had already begun to suspect—while she'd retained and even added to her fund-raising rolls, her voting record, her perceived moderation had gone a long way toward alienating her so-called "natural" constituency of African-Americans, and this turnaround had to be corrected or it could, and quite probably would, cost her everything she'd worked for up to now.

In her last campaign she had won eighty-seven percent of the African-American vote. Now the polls were giving her thirty-five to forty-five percent. Even if she picked up another one or two percent of the white vote she wouldn't win with those black numbers. She needed the perception that she'd reconnected with her community.

And Kevin Shea was the way to do it.

*   *   *

"Where's the staff?"

Her daughter smiled tentatively, closing the door behind her, putting down a brown paper bag. Elaine looked exhausted, her sculpted, angular face now blotched with worry, lack of sleep, and something else that Loretta didn't recognize.

But Loretta put her questions on hold and got up and came around the desk barefoot, her arms outstretched, letting herself be enfolded in her daughter's embrace. Elaine was several inches taller than her mother and held her tightly for a long moment.

They separated, stared at each other. Both of them sighed. Elaine said, "Hi," broke half a self-conscious smile, though again, Loretta couldn't read all of it.

"Hi, honey. How you handlin' this?"

"Scared, I guess. Other things." A pause. "I knew Arthur Wade, you know. He was at Boalt with me."

"Just makes it worse, don't it? You get any sleep?"

"Not yet. I brought us some lunch."

"I could eat. It's near four in DC. What'd you get us?"

When they were alone together, in private, there was a faint echo of Loretta's roots in their rhythms. Elaine took out and opened the white cartons on the desk: cornbread, roast beef, mashed potatoes, greens, diet Cokes.

Finally Loretta asked, "What other things?"

"Oh, office stuff." She took a quick drink of her Coke. "Chris . . ."

"Everybody had gone home. I was leaving, too. I'd just called you, you know? On the plane?"

Loretta, her face a mask, nodded. Her hands were folded on the desk before her. She'd forgotten her sore feet.

Her daughter was continuing. ". . . but Chris wanted me to stay. He said he needed me to help him sort this out, how we were going to handle it. I told him it was too late, I was . . ." She shook her head. "I was too tired, I supposed, to be of much help, 'specially knowing what today was going to be like. And he said that wasn't it exactly."

Knowing what was coming, Loretta closed her eyes. A long breath escaped. "He needed you personally."

"I'd never seen him like that, Mom. Really. I mean, this was my boss. We're both lawyers. We know all the rules about sexual harassment so we tiptoe around each other. And he's older, and married, I know all that. But this wasn't sex, or just sex. Mom?"

Loretta opened her eyes. "I'm here, child. How far did he take it?"

Elaine looked at the floor. "All the way," she whispered, "as far as it could go." She exhaled, the tension of letting it out.

"You sayin' you and Chris Locke made love in his office last night?"

"Don't be mad at me. I—"

Loretta held up a restraining palm, cold fury in her face. "It's not *you,* child, not you. I ain't likely gonna be mad at you." It was her turn to sigh. "But you are *my* baby. How could he . . . ?"

"It wasn't just him . . . I guess I—"

"I know, I know," Loretta said. "I know how it goes." She stared over the desk at her beautiful daughter. "The man got the heat, don't he?"

"He's always been so distant, I mean, good and kind and my true mentor, but distant. And I know you and he . . . I know he helped you, politically. But it was like, I don't know, this whole thing—this lynching, all of it—it just suddenly seemed to break him down." Elaine looked across the desk, asking for understanding. "He needed me, Mom, he really did."

"I believe you, honey. So where are you now?"

Her head down. "I don't *know.* I haven't slept. I feel guilty. Confused. I don't know what it meant, means . . ."

"How's he . . ."

Elaine sighed. "Back to business today, but what can you expect with all this going on?"

"And you think you might love him?"

"I don't know." Their eyes met and held for an instant, and Loretta knew that here, self-protectively, her daughter wasn't telling the truth. God help her, she was in love with her boss.

Loretta took a bite of her now-tasteless food, a sip of her Coke. "I just want you to think on one thing, hon. I'm not sayin' word one against you now. But you consider that it might be your boss hit on you when *you,* not him, when *you* weren't able to stand up—"

"He didn't force anything, Mom."

"I'm not sayin' he did. I'm sayin' you are emotionally drained—your old schoolmate is the victim, for God's sake. You haven't slept all night. The city's burning and you're suddenly elevated to the man's right hand. You're the one who's vulnerable here, you're the easy mark, child. Your boss, *Mister* Locke, he ain't got a damn thing to lose."

"It wasn't like that . . ."

"That's all I'm asking, that you be sure it wasn't, that's all. Because it could have been."

"It wasn't."

Loretta reached out her hand, a peace offering. Elaine looked at it for a moment, then put her own hand over her mother's halfway across the desk.

"I believe you," Loretta said. "I just don't want you hurt. You still ain't too big to get hurt." She softened it with a smile. "Now tell me about Kevin Shea, what you all got?"

19

Bowing to pressure brought to bear by the District Attorney, the mayor and a visit by the United States senator from California, the grand jury met in special session, adjusted its agenda and took only three hours deliberating before it issued an indictment on Kevin Shea for the murder of Arthur Wade.

Which had a double-edged effect on Glitsky's team—they were no longer responsible for making the decision about whether Shea himself had to be brought in; on the other hand, their work trying to identify the other members of the mob who might have been equally involved fell back under the mantle of normal procedure, with nominally still a high—but in practice a far lower—priority.

"I am . . . I *was* Mike Mullen's brother."

Brandon Mullen had tried to make himself presentable—decent clothes and neatly combed hair—but he had failed. Glitsky thought he looked like hell, lips cracked and swollen, eyes bloodshot. Blood, too, had seeped through the sling he wore on his right arm.

Glitsky had farmed out the interrogations—he had Jamie O'Toole down the hallway with Marcel Lanier, Brandon Mullen here in Homicide A with his African-American rookie inspector Ridley Banks, Peter McKay in the B-room with Carl Griffin.

Later the inspectors would get together and see if they could make something out of the stories, see where they connected and where they fell apart, and later still Glitsky planned, if he got the time, to read all the transcriptions, and maybe even view the videotapes, but for now he was getting a feel, looking in on one, then the other.

It still wasn't one o'clock. Around the Bay Area, Oakland, Richmond and East Palo Alto were on fire. In the city itself, there were ongoing civic disturbances—Conrad Aiken, sensitive to terminology even in crisis, had decreed that riots should be called civic disturbances and thus, somehow, lessen their severity—in the Tenderloin, Hunter's Point, the Western Addition, and down by City College. The homicide count in San Francisco for the day had risen from two to four, going on five—a sniper had killed a black man getting into his car on Fulton, and two white teenagers had been pulled from a convertible while they'd been stuck at a stoplight at 3rd and Palou. One of them was still alive, though his condition was critical.

Glitsky had called his home four times, ordering Rita not to let the boys out, he didn't care what. He'd deal with getting them somewhere safe as soon as he could.

Now he stood in the witness room by the door behind Ridley Banks and looked across at Brandon Mullen with his hurt arm and cracked lips. He'd assigned Banks to Mullen because a week before, when *Mike* Mullen—the brother— had been a righteous innocent victim, Ridley had been the inspector on the case, going out and seeing the bereaved family. He'd be a sympathetic interrogator, on Brandon's side.

Glitsky would go in and play bad cop. He was in the right mood for it.

"It started there, yeah," Brandon Mullen was saying.

"The Cavern?" Glitsky, of course, knew this. He'd gotten the men's names from Jamie O'Toole the night before. It was why they were down here getting questioned.

"The Cavern, yeah. I mean, Petey and I . . ."

"Petey?"

"My cousin, Pete McKay, we were together, so . . ."

"And you had some drinks there. And cut your arm on a wineglass?"

This wasn't bad cop, it was pure belligerence, and Glitsky knew better. Mullen drew himself back on his seat, his head to one side, hostility now all over him.

"Look, man, I'm here voluntarily. I thought I could help.

I don't even have a lawyer 'cause there's nothing I'm afraid of. Now you want to listen or hassle me or charge me with something? It's your choice."

Ridley, the good cop, said they weren't planning to charge him with anything. "We're just trying to get a sense of what happened." He glanced at Glitsky, a hand extended. Back off.

"That's what I'm trying to tell you."

"Okay, go ahead."

"I thought I should go, y'know. They were havin' this, like, memorial, so Petey and I thought we'd go down an' have a drink. For Mikey. How would it look if we didn't?"

"And what time was this?"

"Must have been seven, seven-thirty."

"Okay."

"So we drank a few pints . . ."

"Was the place filling up by then?" Glitsky, in a calmer tone, leaned casually against the door with his arms crossed.

"I don't know. Half the bar, maybe. Fifteen or twenty heads spread around."

Banks leaned over the table. "Was Kevin Shea there?"

"I didn't notice."

Glitsky again: "You know Shea?"

Mullen's eyes went from Glitsky to Banks. "To nod at, I guess."

Banks picked it up. "And then . . . ?"

"And then we thanked Jamie and packed it up."

"You went home?"

"To Petey's. Do a wake of our own." He spread his hands, sincere. "We knew we were gonna get good an' pissed and we didn't want to drive." At Glitsky's expression Mullen said, "Believe me or don't."

Glitsky shrugged it off. "So what happened to your arm?"

"Petey and I got to swinging at each other . . ."

"About what?"

Mullen's hands were still out on the pitted table. Now he turned them up, guileless, with maybe a touch of embarrassment. "Who knows anymore? We were pretty drunk, Petey and me, mourning for Mikey. We sort of crashed through the sliding door."

Glitsky came up to the table and put his mouth near Banks, whispering just loud enough. "The famous Irish break-the-sliding-door ritual to lay the dead to rest."

"It's what happened, like it or not."

The lieutenant laid a hand on his inspector's shoulder, then turned and walked out the door without a glance back at the witness.

20

The idea was that Wes Farrell and Kevin Shea would meet at Saint Ignatius Church on the campus of the University of San Francisco and from there Farrell would drive them to his apartment on Junipero Serra down by Stonestown, where they would try to figure out a strategy.

The problem was that to get to USF, Kevin—on foot—first had to climb the second steepest hill in a city justly renowned for them, then had to find his way across the Western Addition, which was burning down. He had overlooked those details when he'd suggested USF as the meeting place and they were proving to be significant.

The temperature was an unbelievable, for San Francisco, ninety-four degrees. The air smelled of fire. The sky was a white-edged pewter plate pressing down on him. Kevin limped his way up the Divisadero escarpment, panting through his ribs, trying to ignore the throbbing in his useless arm, the remains of yesterday's alcohol still pounding behind his eyes, doubling his vision, forcing him to sit every three or four houses, resolve to continue, move another twenty feet up the hill.

He had to get something nonalcoholic to drink, put something in his belly or he wasn't going to get anywhere. But when he finally reached the top of the hill there was nothing resembling a fast-food place. As he would have known if he'd been thinking, if he'd been able to think. This area—with the view and, normally, the freshening breeze—was prime real estate, full of embassies and private mansions. Shea knew that the mayor lived up here, one of the senators.

It was the wrong place to be if you craved a Slurpee.

He stood a minute at the crest, breathing hard, looking

north—the million-dollar view from the Pacific to Berkeley. The Golden Gate. The Presidio. Alcatraz. Today none of it gleamed—the air was too bad. The water was the color of lead—poisoned and flat.

A siren wailed nearby and Kevin turned too quickly, bringing on another rush of dizziness. He collapsed into a planter box filled with rosemary, leaning back into the hedge. The patrol car passed, slowly over the hill, gunning it down into . . .

Were the cops staring at him? He'd forgotten how exposed he was. He forced himself up, walked a block west, then turned south again onto a tree-lined street, blessedly shaded. Under the boughs, and then farther on over the low, dun apartment buildings of the Western Addition, he could see the spires of Saint Ignatius not a half mile away as the crow flew.

But between it and where he stood, several plumes of smoke roiled upward. And directly in front of him, on California, he saw an overturned car and what looked like army troops in some loose formation along the sidewalks.

Then another black-and-white patrol car—or was it the same one?—turned into the street and was coming up toward him. For an instant he thought he'd step out, turn himself in and beg for an isolated cell. They could at least protect him, couldn't they?

Except that even here, already, stuck on one of the trees, was the wanted poster with his own face staring out at him, grimacing with the effort of holding up Arthur Wade. Or—for the first time now he saw it objectively—contorted in what could have been taken for hatred.

The numbers were printed on the bottom. One hundred thousand dollars. But, more chillingly, hand-lettered, the addendum—"Dead or Alive."

Hoping that the shadows had camouflaged him, he turned into the nearest walkway, a brick path between a manicured lawn leading to a shingled Victorian with a covered entryway, a front door with a large pane of inset cut glass. Kevin curled himself back inside the recess.

The patrol car passed again, slowly. He didn't dare look.

A light came on overhead and the door to the house opened. A well-dressed woman in her mid-fifties, the television news droning in the background. "Can I help . . . Oh . . ."

Recognition. She must have been glued to the tube all morning. Backing up a step, she got herself behind the door, putting something between them. She whispered through the crack. *"You're Kevin Shea."* Suddenly she was begging him, terrified. "Please go away, I don't want any trouble."

The door closed. The bolt slammed to.

21

When he wasn't working the streets Philip Mohandas had arranged to base his operations out of a converted two-room storefront in the Bayview District, a mile or so north of Hunter's Point, only blocks from the apartment building Jerohm Reese called home.

Having been out on the barricades from the middle of the night until nearly noon, he was now taking a moment of rest on a low couch in the darkened room in the rear of the storefront. The coat to his business suit hung on the back of a folding chair, and he lay there breathing easily, his tie loosened the half-inch that allowed his prominent Adam's apple to pass unobstructed under his collar when he swallowed. His eyes were closed and a folded damp towel rested on his forehead. On his chest, his hands were together in an attitude suggesting prayer.

Philip Mohandas was not going to sleep very long. He never did, getting by, often for days at a time, on catnaps. He had two personal assistants—Allicey Tobain and Jonas, with the unfortunately phonetic last name of N'doum—who travelled with him at all times, scheduling his time and protecting his privacy. Now they were stationed outside his door on their own folding chairs.

In the outer room, copies of the Kevin Shea poster vied for wall space with several different color posters of Mohandas in mid-speech, invariably with one fisted hand held in the air—his trademark.

The afternoon sun was beginning to stream through the plate-glass windows. Newspapers littered the floor and the wide windowsills. A long, folding table had been set up along one wall, sagging under the weight of African Nation literature and cases of bottled water. Reporters, the occasional minicam crew, professional activists, and concerned citizens all ebbed and

A CERTAIN JUSTICE   85

flowed through the outer doors, speaking—mostly—in low
tones.

Out in the street, a late-model green Plymouth pulled to
the curb and stopped. An attractive, diminutive black
woman, from the looks of her maybe forty years old,
opened the driver's door, squinted at the bright facade of
the storefront and started to come around her car.

One of the reporters recognized her. "My God, that's
Senator Wager." In the back, Allicey Tobain knocked once
and pushed open the door she'd been guarding.

"What is that woman doing here?" Mohandas swung his
feet to the floor, wiped his face quickly with the damp
towel, then stood and let Allicey arrange his coat. "I have
got nothing to say to her. She is in the wrong camp."

His assistant touched his hairline briefly with a comb,
correcting it, then without a word handed him two Tic-Tac
mouth fresheners.

Mohandas was frowning, apparently trying to find an advantage in this. "Did she call?"

"No calls." Allicey pulled an imaginary strand of lint
from his coat. "No word at all. She's making a play."

"But what for?"

Allicey crossed to the door and flipped the light switch.
A tall, big-boned, ebony-skinned woman with an enormous
bust, her hair done in corn rows, she was wearing black
pants, sandals, and a black, red and yellow dashiki cinched
at the waist by a gold thong.

She straightened his coat again and ran a finger over
the side of his face. "Votes," she said. "Don't forget that,
Philip. Votes."

"Senator, how are you? What a wonderful surprise! Welcome." Mohandas wasn't big but his voice boomed, cutting
through all the chatter. Flanked by Allicey and Jonas, he
came forward, his arms outstretched. The front office crowd
parted, television cameras rolled and the two leaders embraced, only to be interrupted by a reporter.

"Senator, what brings you down here? Isn't this an unexpected call?"

"An unexpected *pleasure.*" Mohandas held on to Loretta's hand, both of them now turned to face the camera.

"I'm here to help," Loretta said. "If I can. Any way that I can."

Mohandas intoned a deep "Amen."

"This community has suffered not only the tragic loss of one of our brightest stars, not only the insult of the horrible crime itself, but the far deeper and meaningful abandonment by the very power structure that we are struggling, against great odds, to work within."

Loretta took a moment to include the crowd in her vision, then raised Mohandas's hand halfway in a conscious imitation of his own trademark gesture.

"This is a time, and I think Philip would agree, that we African-Americans, as well as all people of color, must unite—not only in justifiable anger but to create out of this chaos some spirit of hope and renewal, some sense that now, finally, we are going to make changes that will make a difference in the way we live, how we're treated, the voice we have in how things are done!"

A chorus of "amen" and "right on" followed, through which the senator picked her way, with Mohandas, to the back door, flanked again as though by magic by Allicey and Jonas.

Which closed on their passage inside.

"You want to just make noise, Philip, or you want to get somethin' done here?"

All alone with her in the tiny, hot room, Mohandas didn't feel like he needed to listen to a lecture from an Oreo. "*I* get things done, Senator. I haven't sold anyone out." He jerked his head sideways. "Those are *my* people out there. They have heard enough lies, they know who is not lying to them, and that's me, Senator, that's me."

"I'm not lying to anybody, Philip. I haven't sold anybody out."

Mohandas showed his teeth briefly, then pulled at his collar. His stock in trade was certainty. He was right and that was the way it was. "That doesn't seem to be how many of us are reading it."

"Then you're reading it wrong." This was the problem

she had flown out here to solve. And she wasn't going to succeed facing off against Mohandas, getting into a shouting match. He didn't play on her field, so he couldn't understand. She had more knowledge, and she had to use it. "Wait. Let's stop." She stepped closer to him. "Out there, just now, that was no lie. I came down here to help if I can. And I think I can, Philip. I can help you."

"I'm listening."

"Why don't you talk instead. Tell me what you want."

This, she knew, was the crux. If she could get him away from the generalities that marked his agenda. From the rhetoric. "You know what we want, Senator . . ."

She smiled at him. "How about Loretta, Philip? Loretta, not Senator. And I don't know what you want. I don't know the specifics. If you could have anything you want, what would it be? Because listen to me—now's the time you can get it."

Mohandas stopped pacing the small room, pulled at his collar again, then sat in the folding chair, motioning Loretta to the couch he'd napped on. "The African Nation platform is clear."

"Philip, when you say you want a voice, you want representation, the end of oppression, you want the laws applied fairly—who doesn't? But then you go on to say you want your own separate system, and that just don't fly. Can't you see that? The numbers aren't there, and the numbers drive the dollars. You want to take over a state? Move the people back to Africa? You want a black Israel on some sand in Africa? That what you want?"

Mohandas was sweating as the heat built in the room, leaning forward, his elbows on his knees. "We want it here. We can get it here."

"You tell me how, Philip."

"I'm talking about equality under the law, I'm talking about our entitlements, our *rights* . . ."

Loretta shook her head in frustration, found herself raising her voice. "*I'm* talking money, Philip. I'm talking federal funds. Today, here and now. For this good cause. This situation can get it for us, for you . . ."

Mohandas walked to the closet door, listened through it, then came back in front of where Loretta sat. "All right, Senator," he said, "talk to me about money."

22

Kevin knew he wasn't going to make his meeting with Wes Farrell at USF.

The realization came to him after he had crossed California Street and came out of the trees. Now there was no cover at all, just apartment houses on both sides of the one street in the Addition that didn't appear to have community problems just at this minute. He was halfway down the block when a police car turned the corner up ahead, coming toward him.

Ducking into another apartment building's paper-strewn entryway, he looked back where he'd come from. Another police car. Two on the one street, closing in.

The door was locked but there were six mailboxes and he pushed all the buttons beneath them. The front door buzzed and he pushed it open as the cars passed behind him.

"Yes? Who's there?" A raspy male voice from up the stairs.

"Sorry. Wrong place."

Kevin opened the door again, closed it loudly for effect. But he stayed inside the building in the hallway, thinking, Now what?

Apartment 3, on the ground floor in the back, had its mailbox stuffed with envelopes. The residents were either very popular or on vacation. Kevin had to hope it was the latter. He tried the old credit-card-in-the-doorjamb and, to his amazement, it worked. For the first time that day, he almost laughed. Maybe his luck was turning, but he thought it still had a hell of a long way to go before it got to good.

He tried Wes's number first. Ten rings, no answering machine. Wes was probably waiting for him less than a mile away. Maybe he should just call the cab and make a run for it. What were the odds that some random cabbie would know who he was? Still, credit card or no, he couldn't bring himself to risk it. This seemed like a time for caution—one hundred thousand dollars was a lot of money for a cab-driver or anyone else. He was pacing the apartment, limping a little, trying to decide—footfalls on hardwood.

He froze as he heard a knock on the door, then a voice. "Dave? Dave, you home? Anybody in there?"

He supposed there had to be places in his body that weren't cramping, but he didn't know where they were. He barely dared breathe.

The shadow of feet under the crack in the door remained. Kevin fought back the adrenaline, the pain, lack of oxygen, fear—he couldn't let himself pass out. He felt on the brink of it.

The neighbor was stubborn. He'd heard something—Kevin pacing?—and wanted to be sure. So he stayed and listened.

Please, Kevin thought, please God, don't let him have a key.

The neighbor was gone. Kevin gave it another five minutes, stretching, trying to get some relief to his burning muscles, then tiptoeing across the room and lowering himself into the thick upholstered chair—the couch was closer to where he'd frozen but it looked like it might creak. Besides, the phone was on an end table next to the chair. With infinite care he raised the receiver and punched some numbers. Maybe Wes had given up on him and gone home.

Nope.

He put his head back and closed his eyes.

23

It was midafternoon.

"So what do we have?"

Glitsky was in a booth with three of his inspectors—Carl Griffin, Ridley Banks and Marcel Lanier. They were having an informal meeting convened by the lieutenant at Lou the Greek's, the cop and DA watering hole across the street from the Hall of Justice. You got to Lou's either through an alley and an unmarked side door or down a stained, carpeted stairway dark enough not to show what was making it smell that way.

Lou's was what it was—they poured a good shot cheaply. The food was usually tasty, hearty, possibly nutritious. Lou's wife was Chinese and Lou, of course, was Greek, and you'd often get a lunch special like avgolemono soup with wontons or kung pao chicken moussaka. They'd had a special for years that they called "Yeanling Clay Bowl" and no one could say for sure what was in it.

But the main thing about Lou's was that the place was close to the Hall of Justice, you could hang there and not be bothered, there weren't many citizens around, and known reporters and other members of the media didn't seem to get the same personalized service from Lou as law-enforcement personnel did—just one of those hard-to-explain flukes of nature.

"They were all there," Ridley Banks said.

Glitsky and his men were nearly alone in the place, and the lieutenant was still having a hard time keeping his patience. Of course they—the witnesses they'd interrogated—had all been there. They all admitted *that* much. But not during the lynching. The inspectors' job was to put them on the street *during* the violence and it didn't look to Glitsky like that would be happening in the near future.

"I say we just arrest them and put the squeeze on." Carl Griffin was the least sophisticated homicide inspector on the force, but that didn't mean all his ideas were bad.

"We got a problem with arrests," Glitsky said.

"Which is . . . ?" Lanier, sardonic, leaning back in his flight jacket, was drinking a glass of red wine.

"Which is enough space upstairs," Glitsky said. He took a sip of his tea. "Boles says we're full up and getting worse. He's trying to get Rigby to agree to give citations for everything up to and including armed robbery."

Griffin raised bloodshot eyes. "Are you serious?" Humor was lost on Griffin, and Glitsky explained that he was exaggerating but not by much—only about the armed robbery part.

Ridley Banks spoke up. "But we *are* talking 187 here . . ." Section 187 of the California Penal Code is murder. ". . . if these guys were in the action, it was murder."

Glitsky sucked his teeth. "Well, that's the other thing. It's why we're down here at Lou's instead of my plush private suite. I don't want to get overheard and misconstrued." His subordinates waited. "You might have noticed we've also got a political situation developing."

Lanier sipped wine, made little swirls out of some vagrant drops with his index finger on the table. "The Kevin Shea thing."

Glitsky nodded. "The official line is that he's the only one who did it."

Banks, the young red-hot, sat forward. "But there . . . I mean, it was a mob . . ."

"We got any witnesses saying it was?"

"O'Toole. Didn't he?" Banks looked at Lanier, who shook his head no.

"O'Toole never went outside." Lanier kept his face straight. "Stayed in the bar. Poured drinks. And the other clowns, Mullen and McKay, they went home before it started, isn't that right, Abe?"

"The facts as we know them."

Griffin spoke up. "The photographer, what's his name?"

The lieutenant inclined his head a quarter inch. "Okay, him. One guy. Westberg. Point is, the mob's too unwieldy or something. God's mouth to the chief's ear, boys, they want Shea and only Shea. Symbolism or something like that. The mayor wants him, Rigby's going along, Locke's leading the charge. We get Shea and the whole problem is solved."

Lanier continued his doodling. "Okay, so? We bring 'em Shea."

"We can't find him. Guy's got any brains, he's gone anyway," Glitsky said. "The thing is, if we do come across some hard evidence that any of these yo-yos—McKay, O'Toole, any of them—were part of it, I'm not much inclined, personally, to just let it slide, and I wanted to convey that message to all of you." He looked around at his inspectors. "When things cool down, *after* things cool down, I don't much cotton to the idea of getting called on the carpet because we didn't pursue our investigations thoroughly. This is the kind of political"—he paused, seeking the right word—"machination that has a way of coming back to bite at you, and I just wanted to bring it all up front, out on the table. Okay?"

Lanier raised his finger. "You don't think Shea was in it?"

"I'm not saying that. I've got no reason to believe that. I've seen the picture, too. It's just when things get this convenient . . ." He shrugged. Everybody knew what he was talking about. "It was probably him and all the others, so yeah, we break him and we get the rest. But I'm a little worried none of our boys back in there seemed to know him."

Banks put in, "Mullen said he knew him to nod at."

Glitsky's scar stretched between his lips. "I heard that, Rid. I wouldn't build my house on it after today, the whole city knows him to nod at. Also, either of you guys"— he motioned to Banks and Griffin—"did either of you get an offer to take a look at the cuts on Mullen and McKay? You might want to talk to their doctors. Maybe pay a call on McKay's house and see about that sliding door."

Lanier shot the remainder of his wine, swallowed. "You saying go after these guys, aren't you, Abe? Whatever anybody else tells us?"

"We got, say, a minimum of ten guys who had to be accessories here. Let's say I'd like to find at least a couple of them."

"And Shea?" This was from Griffin.

"Sure. Shea, too. See you all upstairs."

24

Finally, the wind came back up, the fog was rolling down Bryant Street and it had gotten back to the usual—cold. Glitsky pulled his jacket closer around him to keep it from blowing open. His eyes were bleary from fatigue, his head heavy.

In the lobby of the Hall of Justice, Sheriff Boles had set up a makeshift area for processing arrests—they were in fact giving out citations, just like parking tickets, to some of the scores of people who'd been arrested in the civic disturbances since the day before—for looting, mayhem, trespass, battery, whatever. Boles had persuaded Dan Rigby, the police chief, to let him sweep for outstanding warrants on other charges, after which—if the person being charged had none—they were to be processed on the citations and released.

The place was bedlam and Glitsky pushed his head further down within his jacket and made for the elevators. He had to get upstairs to his office, call Rita again, check on his boys. He also had to get some sleep sometime. He had no idea when that would be. He knew that the strands of his temper were beginning to fray, and soon his judgments would begin to suffer. The fatigue was weighing him down.

But the elevator opened and there, facing him, stood Elaine Wager. "I was just in your office, Abe. Nobody knew where you were." Was there a rebuke there? A warning? Was someone really watching? "You got a minute?" she asked. "We can ride back up."

"Sure." There was no point in arguing it. He'd do later what he'd felt he absolutely had to get done now. He couldn't call his sons. He had to come when bidden. It was the job.

He squeezed in next to her as the usual press of bodies piled into the eight-foot-square box—perhaps twenty people of all races, a microcosm of the city outside. The doors closed and all sounds from the lobby vanished, exaggerating the silence in the elevator. There was a palpable tension in the enclosed space, suspicion and mistrust choking off the usual chatter.

When the door opened on the third floor, Elaine nudged Glitsky. "My office." He'd thought they were headed up to Homicide on the fourth, but Elaine was making the call and he tagged along behind her.

Her room was the standard cubicle used by the assistant district attorneys—two desks, as many ancient file cabinets as would fit, a coffeemaker, two grimy windows with Charming View of Freeway Overpass #4. Elaine waited at the door for Glitsky to pass her, then closed it behind them.

Glitsky parked his rear on Elaine's office mate's desk. Whoever normally sat at that desk wasn't there now. Elaine turned, slumping slightly, and to ease the tension, Abe found himself asking if she'd had as much fun on the elevator coming up as he had.

Elaine gave him a weak smile. Like him, she was exhausted and the fatigue was showing. "This is so unreal," she said. "San Francisco just doesn't have this kind of problem."

"You know how many unions we've got? The PD? I'll tell you. Three. We've got one for white cops, one for women cops, one for black cops. Even as we speak, the gay cops are lobbying for another one."

"But you all work together, I mean like we do, you and me. People get along, do their work, right?"

"Generally. Things spill over."

"But not like this."

"It's a logical enough extension. People stop being just people first, well . . ." Glitsky shrugged, standing up, stretching his back. "But you didn't look me up to talk about this."

Elaine sighed. For an instant Glitsky saw her mother in her eyes, something almost more familiar in her expression, in the shape of her face. He rubbed his own eyes while she

agreed with him—she hadn't looked him up to talk about
the general situation. She paused, considering. "Can this be
off the record?"

"What's to be on it?"

Glitsky was vaguely aware of his reputation as a hardass.
He supposed it wasn't totally undeserved since he tended
to make a point of being straight with people. At least he
didn't sugarcoat or dissemble, and with the right look on
his hatchet face, he knew he could say that he loved and
cherished someone and come across as abrupt and cold. It
had happened with Flo.

But Elaine had thicker skin than he'd supposed. She gave
him a look, the start of another smile, this one with a few
more watts, and he finally nodded. "Okay, sure. Off the
record. What?"

"My mother . . ." She stopped. "Well, no, not . . . not
her. I don't want to bring her into this." She bit her lip,
looking beyond Glitsky out through the windows.

"Isn't she already?"

"Not exactly. That's not what I want to talk about. What
I guess I mean is this whole thing."

Glitsky nodded again. "It's unusual, I'll give you that."

"It's my career," she said.

"It could be. You're right."

"I've got to know if there's no case."

"Elaine, you're making the case," he told her.

"I know. I'm supposed to be. I'm assembling the facts."
Silence.

"I just want to keep the door open between us."

Glitsky took in a breath and walked over to the windows.
The fog was thin and he could see some spires of smoke
still rising across the Bay in Oakland and, he supposed,
Richmond. Suddenly, seeing Elaine's direction here, he felt
his anger rise again—it seemed to be on a steady slow
simmer, ready to boil at any time.

He turned to face her. "You know, Elaine, you're a
charming person and I think you're probably also trying to
do the right thing here, but I really hate getting bullshitted
and especially today I don't have much stomach for it."

Her eyes went wide. "But I'm not—"

"You're covering your ass, Elaine, and okay, we'll leave
it off the record, but my door has always been open. We

don't have to make special arrangements to keep doors open."

"This isn't a special arrangement."

"No? Funny, then, that here we are in a locked room and off the record."

"I just didn't want to be interrupted. I didn't want Chris . . ."

Glitsky pointed a finger. "*Now* we're getting somewhere. You didn't want Chris . . . ?"

"But he's my boss. He gives me my assignments."

"So *do* them. But don't come around me playing both sides. Either you're on his agenda—maybe your mother's, too, I don't know about that—or you're being a righteous DA. Whichever one you pick is your call."

"I don't want to make a mistake, Abe. I *can't.*"

Glitsky's scar stretched white through his lips. "I wouldn't worry about it. I make them all the time. But I'll tell you one thing that makes life easier."

"What's that?"

"Do things in order. There's a way it's supposed to get done so everybody's time doesn't get wasted." Glitsky turned the doorknob, then stopped. "You know, for what it's worth, I got no bleeding heart for Kevin Shea. I'm just more comfortable doing things by the book. You go different, you see too many bad guys walk when the smoke clears."

"You *do* think he's it, then?" This seemed to hearten her.

Glitsky, risking a charge of assault, sexual harassment and general political incorrectness, reached out a hand and rested it for a moment on Elaine's shoulder. "I'm not trying to get him off. What I want is what you want—a righteous case on him. And my door's always open. Period."

25

"Is anybody with you?"

"Kevin, is that you? Can you talk a little louder?"

"Yes, it's me, and no, I can't. Can you hear me?"

"Enough, I guess. Where are you? Are you all right?"

"I asked is anybody with you?"

"No."

"Are you sure?"

"Kevin . . ."

"Because I need some help, Melanie. I need serious help, and I don't need Cindy Taylor or anybody else—damn."

"What?"

He whispered even lower. "There's a guy upstairs. He's moving around again. I just heard the door close."

"What?"

"Wait. Just hold on. I can't talk. Just a minute."

He heard the steps approach again, saw the faint shadow of feet under the doorway. The good neighbor upstairs was a model citizen, no doubt about it, keeping an eye on the empty apartments when people went on vacation. There was another knock on the door. "Hey, anybody in there?"

In the phone, Melanie's voice. "Kevin?"

He didn't let out a breath. Melanie would either hang up or not. He'd told her to wait. Maybe she would.

Finally, after maybe two minutes, the shadows under the door disappeared, and he heard the retreating steps. He waited another ten seconds, made sure, whispered into the phone. "You still there?"

"Yes. Kevin, what's happening?"

"Can you come get me?"

A pause. "Sure. Where are you?"

A problem. He didn't know where he was. There were

a couple of magazines on the table in front of the couch and he risked rising and walking a couple of steps. The tiny noises he made—a spring giving in the chair, a squeaky floorboard—might as well have been bombs going off. He read the address off one of the magazines. "One forty-eight Collins Street, number three. You know where that is?"

"No."

Great.

"Western Addition. A block or two south of California. You might have to go around. There's some National Guard . . ."

"All right, I got it. I'll find you." It surprised him. She was being all business. No panic in her voice. Who was this Melanie? She repeated the address.

There was another knocking now, urgent, behind him. Kevin turned, holding the phone. There, seven feet away from him, looking in through the ground-floor window, was, he presumed, the good neighbor from upstairs, still pounding on the window, yelling.

"Mel!" Thank God, she hadn't yet hung up. "Forget Plan A. Don't move. Stay home 'til I call you. And don't call anybody."

"Kevin, what's . . . ?"

"Just stay home and wait, Mel. They found me again."

He wondered where the cold had come from. It was the one thing about San Francisco he just hadn't been able to assimilate, how one minute it could be beautiful, sunny, clear, and ten minutes later, or three blocks away, you were freezing. Now, suddenly, it was in the fifties, the wind whipping wisps of fog through the depressing rows of apartment buildings.

On this street, whichever one it was, three adjacent buildings had burned, and the acrid smoke hit him with every turn of the wind, making him cough, tearing at his poor sore ribs.

He had no idea how far he'd run—maybe five blocks, over three fences. The good neighbor wasn't much inclined to give up the chase, but finally Kevin felt like he'd lost him. The chase had had the salubrious side effect of bringing him closer to USF, through the worst of the Addition.

But so what?

He doubted Wes Farrell had waited all afternoon for him there—but he would check. Certainly he hadn't been back home. Kevin had called Wes's place when he'd woken up after crashing in the borrowed apartment—it had been going on five o'clock, and there'd been no response, no answering machine.

Ergo Melanie.

A truly last resort but she'd have come through for him on that last call if he could have stayed in the apartment and waited. He was sure of it. And that was a good sign. It could be the entire world wasn't lined up against him.

But for now his lungs ached from the run, pinched from the coughing. He wondered if one of his ribs was broken, if a broken rib could puncture a lung, if a punctured lung could suddenly collapse, bring on a coma . . .

He was coming up to a bigger cross-street, with traffic flowing. Geary? Was normal life going on someplace in the city? He found it difficult to believe but there was evidence of it right in front of him.

Shivering, coughing some more, he crossed with the light at Masonic, found another phone and called Melanie again, telling her where he was. It was only another couple of blocks up to Saint Ignatius. Melanie knew where that was. She'd meet him there in fifteen minutes.

He sat in a pew in the back of the church, pretending to pray. He hadn't prayed much in the past five years, since the Houston diocese had refused to bury his father—a suicide—in the family plot in which *his* father, Kevin's grandfather, had been buried. Kevin's faith, never particularly strong, wavered after that. In the army, in Kuwait, after Joey, cleaning up on the Road of Death, it disappeared entirely.

But his hands were folded. He was on his knees. A priest came up the center aisle and nodded at him, blessedly without recognition, then he stopped, paused—about to say something?—thought better of it and moved along. Kevin let out a breath.

The door opened again. Please, he thought, don't let it be the priest coming back. He was too weary to run any further.

Melanie Sinclair slid in beside him. It startled him. Underneath her concern, the fear in her eyes, she looked radiant, alive, beautiful. Had he really dropped her? He must have been out of his mind. But she'd been, had *seemed,* such an uptight pain in the ass. He thought he remembered that—was sure he did—but the plain fact was that right at that moment he had never in his life been so glad to see anyone.

Ever.

"I think you ought to get out of here."

She was driving and he was slumped in the passenger seat, his face below the window line.

"I might do that," he said.

"Kevin, you *should* do it . . ."

He glanced over at her, a look she'd seen before. "Let's give the *should* a rest, huh, Mel. What do you say?"

Biting her lip, she almost, instinctively, corrected him again, telling him her name was Melanie. Not Mel. But she found she really didn't care if he called her Sweet Sue. She half-smiled at that, almost said it to him, could just see herself saying, "Hey, Kevin, why don't you just call me Sweet Sue?"

"What's funny?" he asked.

"Nothing."

He didn't pursue it, but Melanie wanted to make sure the air was clear. "I didn't mean *should* like I knew, Kevin. I meant *should* like it seems like it might be a better idea to get away until this blows over a little. You're just too visible here. I could drive you right now. Just keep going."

"You'd do that?"

She looked over, biting her lip again. "Yes, I would."

He took that in, satisfied. "Except then I'm really on the run. If I'm caught . . ."

"But you're on the run now."

"This is true."

They stopped at a burned-out streetlight where a policeman was directing cars through. "Don't keep too low," she said. There was more National Guard presence here, camouflage trucks lining the street, the traffic coming down to single file.

Kevin straightened up slightly. "You're right." He waved,

smiling at a few of the soldiers. "We're having some fun now."

"Don't overdo it, okay? Please."

He came back to her. "You remember Farrell . . . ?"

"Yes." Wes, another unrepentant partyer, had been a sore point between them. "Well, I figure my only decent shot is to get the story out on what really happened. Anything else—running, turning myself in, whatever—anything else and when they do get me I'm totally screwed."

"What can Wes do?"

"Wes is a lawyer. He can get through."

"He's not anymore."

"Sure he is. He knows the ropes. He can do it."

"Will he?"

"Sure. I'm sure he will."

"And then?"

"Then at least I figure I've got a chance. I just didn't do this, Mel, you know."

She reached across and laid a hand on his, pulled it away. She wasn't pushing anything. She was helping him. He didn't need complications. "I do know. I'm just saying I think it's a big risk, that's all."

He shrugged. "At this point, everything's a risk. This whole thing's gotten so out of hand. And then, if I run . . . anyway, I don't *want* to run."

"It would look like an admission that you'd done it?"

"Yeah, that, I guess. But more because it just feels wrong. I mean, I know the truth. I know what happened. I was there, Mel. And that's got to come out. What really happened. It's not just me . . ."

"And you think Wes Farrell is the man who's going to get you in a position to clear yourself?"

"I think Wes Farrell's a pretty good human being for a lawyer."

She couldn't help herself. "A lawyer who drinks too much and has a pretty low view of life, including his own."

Kevin almost snapped back but held himself. This wasn't the time to get into it with her. She was there for him now. What was more important than that? He took her right hand from the steering wheel and held it on the seat between them. She looked down at it, smiled and took his hand firmly.

*   *   *

"Not here," Kevin said.

They had swung by Wes Farrell's place and the "pretty good human being for a lawyer" still wasn't there. Melanie was of the opinion, and Kevin couldn't deny it outright, that he was out getting drunk someplace. He had tried joking her out of it—"Doesn't mean Wes isn't a nice person"—but Melanie wasn't much in the mood for jokes, and truth be told and though it had been his own protective reaction to stressful situations for as long as he could remember, Kevin wasn't either.

Small wonder that he couldn't shake the feeling that the whole damn city was after him. The elderly lady in whose doorway he'd huddled had recognized him earlier. The cruising cops had also seemed to. Maybe the guy upstairs from the apartment he'd borrowed.

Isolated occurrences? Maybe. Maybe not. These things had happened to *him*. It wasn't as though somebody *might* know who he was. Somebody—random and disinterested— already *had*.

And now Melanie was turning them into the drive-thru lane—into a line of cars—front and back, get *out* of there— at a hamburger place off 19th Avenue.

"Not here!" he repeated. "What are you doing?"

"We've got to eat," she said. "We're not going inside."

"Inside isn't the point. We've got to—"

All at once it was too late to back out. Somebody had pulled in behind them. Now it was either sit in Melanie's car or get out and make a run for it. But a run for what? And what were the odds on going unrecognized out on the street? Were they better than here, where he was a sitting duck? Did he want to bet on it? Bet his life? Hers, too?

It was not yet dusk. There was no problem with visibility. He honestly didn't think he'd get two blocks.

Twisting his head from side to side he saw a seemingly endless procession of faces everywhere—in the car in front of him (the backseat folks turning around—why?), behind them, crossing at the intersection, up and down the sidewalk—and all of them focused on him.

Casual glances or studied stares—they were all directed at him. Melanie had picked a popular place on a crowded street close to the dinner hour. It had to be only a matter of time before somebody recognized him.

He slumped down, far into the seat. Melanie rolled her window down. "What do you want?" she asked.

"I want to get out of here, that's what I want."

She glanced into her rearview mirror. "Not possible," she said. "What's your second choice?"

Her window was still open. "You know, Melanie, I'd like to, but I can't seem to get myself feeling too casual about all this—"

"I'm *not* casual," she said. "But we have got to eat and the fact is that nobody's looking at you, not here."

"Everybody's looking at me!"

The driver behind them honked and Melanie waved a conciliatory hand out her window, then ordered two double cheeseburgers, fries, shakes. She pulled forward. "I can understand how you'd feel that, Kevin, but I don't think it's true."

They were still in the line, hemmed in, the cars edging forward slowly. It was going to take at least five minutes to go around the building and get to the service window. "It's heartening you don't think that, Melanie, but if you're wrong, I'm dead."

"I'm not wrong. You have to trust me—"

"I have to trust my instincts. They've gotten me this far."

She looked over at him. "For the record, Kevin, I've had something to do with getting you this far. I understand . . . you saw a man get lynched last night, for God's sake. Who wouldn't be scared? *I'm* scared, too. But I think I'm seeing things a little more clearly."

He had to admit he was on the edge of panic and she seemed almost creepily calm. "Maybe you're right, but—"

"I'm only sure that right here is as safe for us as anywhere in the city, and you're the one who wants to stay here and make your stand, so I'd say the best advice is get used to it."

They inched forward. Honks behind them—people talking loud, laughing, yelling—off to the side out Melanie's window, but no one seemed to be moving toward them. Kevin looked down and put a hand to his forehead. "How are we getting out of this?" he asked.

"It'll look better on a full stomach," she said.

*   *   *

Melanie had been right. She had played a major role in getting them to where they were right now . . . no one had recognized him, the drive-thru burger joint had been an inspired choice, and, right or wrong, things did look better on a full stomach. He took in this woman sitting across from him and was washed with intense gratitude.

Most importantly, she had believed him, believed in him.

He had always suspected there was more to her—much more—than he'd seen when they'd been "dating," but something about their chemistry, or his own guilty conscience, or both, had made it all, finally, futile. The relationship wasn't going to work, not under the ground rules they'd tacitly established, so he'd decided he had to move on.

But now his dire situation had shifted the balance between them. They were partners, equals. And this realization suddenly made him feel like a cheat. He'd been unfair to Melanie by not being up front with her when they'd been going out, by not telling her that before they had gotten together he had slept—once, one night only—with her friend Cindy Taylor. Now he felt he at least owed Melanie the truth—both about him and her supposed "best friend." She hadn't just "come on to him," as he had said.

So he told her.

And now Melanie, who had weathered his flight and panic attack with stoic calm, now Melanie had balanced her half-full milkshake cup on the steering wheel and was, quietly, crying.

The early-evening sun peeked through the low cloud layer, highlighting the red in her dark hair, the glistening wetness on her cheeks. "I don't believe it," she said. *"Cindy?"*

"I thought I ought to tell you."

"I don't know why . . . why didn't you feel you should tell me before, when we were . . . I mean when I thought we were together."

"We *were* together, Melanie."

She almost laughed. "Sure. God, what a fool I was. You must have both been laughing at me the whole time."

"No. It wasn't like Cindy and I were an item. It was one night, before you and I got together."

"But she said . . she *told* me—"

"She lied, Mel."

She turned toward him. "Why didn't *you* tell me?"

"What would that have done, Mel, except hurt you? Besides, I half-figured Cindy had told you anyway and you knew and decided it wasn't that big an issue."

Melanie threw him a long glance. "Nice try, Kevin . . ."

"No, I guess that wouldn't have been your response."

"I guess not."

The windows were down a quarter inch, the wind whistling through. "Besides," Kevin said, "I wanted you. If I told you about Cindy, I figured no chance."

She looked at him again, not knowing quite what to believe. "Maybe you just wanted somebody—"

"If I'd just wanted any old body I would have hung with Cindy or somebody else who might, frankly, have been a little easier to deal with."

"Oh, that's nice. Thanks very much."

Kevin turned toward her. "Come on, Mel, what do you want me to say? I thought you were great. You think I felt *anything* about Cindy? Not likely. All right, so you and I didn't work—that doesn't mean it wasn't honest. I tried, we both tried, we just didn't fit."

"But we *did*, I thought we did. We could have." Melanie made a fist and banged it against her thigh. "Oh damn, why are you telling me all this now?"

He reached out to her, grimacing at the pull on his ribs, touched her shoulder across the car seat. "Because you're *here* now, Mel. I don't think you would have been here six months ago."

"That's not true, I would have . . ."

"No. You would never have really believed I wasn't part of this madness. You wouldn't have questioned what you saw with your own eyes. You would have written me off, for the guy who never took anything seriously. But hey, at least now you already know all about my bad character. And I'm the same guy and you're still here in spite of it. *That's* different."

He grabbed the dregs of Melanie's milkshake off the

steering wheel. She was allowing a half-smile. He needed that.

"So now," he went on, "I thought it would be better if I laid it all out—Cindy, the whole thing. No surprises. This is who I am. Maybe, when, if this thing ever blows over we can, you know, like go on a date or something."

Melanie sucked at her lower lip for a moment, then said she'd consider it.

26

Glitsky had come home just before five and had slept nearly four hours. Rita had gotten him up for dinner as he'd asked, all of his boys furious, stir-crazy and squirrelly at their long day indoors, wanting answers, thinking their dad was a paranoid who'd been a cop too long and the older ones telling him so.

Now, dinner finished, the boys sat facing him across the kitchen table, the three of them en bloc, sticking together (which he thought was good), bonded against their old man (not so good). Even Orel, whose gangling body Glitsky had held snuggling in his lap as recently as six months before, was working on his eleven-year-old interpretation of the evil eye—and though not as developed as the glare of his brothers, Jake and Ike (*ave atque vale* Jacob and Isaac), Orel was the one who most favored Flo, and so his hard look cut Abe the deepest. Which was not to say that the two older guys, who had it down to an art, were any easier for him.

Rita had her arms folded across her more than ample bosom. She was frowning. Glitsky was frowning. The kitchen windows were steamed with condensation—they'd had spaghetti for dinner and outside it was now dark and blustery. The dishes remained on the table.

Tonight's issue (as though there had never been a riot, as though life outside the windows was blithely proceeding in some kind of reasonable fashion): back in the spring, Glitsky had planned a camping trip for the following week-end in Yosemite. The Glitskys had always camped—it was one of their family "things." Flo had favored the wilder-ness, but they'd also done their share of site camping and the boys, even Orel, had jobs they excelled at, favorite things to do—putting up the tent, tying mantles on the lanterns, the fire, fishing, backpacking, finding edibles, cooking. So they'd called and reserved their spot and sent their deposit.

But one of Isaac's friends had invited him (and Jake, if he wanted to go) up to a cabin on a lake in the Sierras for the same days. Glitsky was hearing about it for the first time and told Isaac he'd have to make it another weekend. Ike countered by proposing that they not cancel the family camping—he'd just go with his friend and the rest of the family could go to Yosemite and do their camping thing.

Glitsky told him he didn't think so.

So here they were having a rules committee meeting because now Jake had been enlisted and he, of course, would rather go up waterskiing with the big kids than sweat and hike and look at waterfalls in Yosemite. And—now, while they were at it—if the two older boys weren't going to Yosemite, why would Orel want to go with just his father, alone?

"Guys," Glitsky said, "we reserved a place. We made a commitment."

"Who cares?" Isaac.

"Somebody gonna fine us or something if we don't show up?" Jacob.

Older than Methuselah, Glitsky persisted. "The commitment is what it is—they've kept other people out because we're in."

"So they'll let somebody in at the last minute. Big deal, they always do." Isaac was leading the charge so Glitsky thought he'd try to defuse him first.

"Look, Ike, we've paid our money. We said we'd be there. That's the end of it. You just tell your friend thanks, you'll do it another weekend. A deal's a deal."

Jake pushed some spaghetti around on his plate. "Mom would've let us."

This was below the belt as well as beside the point.

"Mom isn't here, Jake. We're here. So how about we vote and get it settled?"

Isaac pushed his chair back. "That's the other thing."

"What is?"

Rita spoke up for the first time. "They don't want me to vote."

Isaac took the floor. "It's not *wanting,* Rita. It's just not fair."

Glitsky hated "not fair." Especially today, he hated people blaming everything but themselves for what was wrong with the world, for the troubles they had. That was Philip Mohandas's platform—in his own kids, it made him crazy. The fuse was burning, but Glitsky kept his voice low. "What's not fair, Ike?"

At the refrigerator, he turned. "Rita gets next weekend off, whatever happens, right? I mean, isn't that why we pick the dates when we do things? So she can get some of her own time? She's not going either place with any of us."

"Okay. So what?"

Jake picked it up—they'd obviously gotten their strategy down. "So she's not involved . . ."

"So why should she get to vote?" Ike finished for him, and even Orel chimed in. "Right."

Glitsky looked sideways at Rita. She was still frowning. "What they say is right, I'm not involved." She didn't even begin to like it, but she was a fair and honest woman, one of the reasons Glitsky was delighted with her. In general.

Isaac jumped right on her admission. "See!"

Glitsky could do a pretty fair evil eye himself. Beaten, and knowing it, Glitsky threw one around the room at them. "All right," Glitsky said, "Rita doesn't vote this time."

So they put it to the vote and, no surprise, it came down three to Glitsky's two, the boys over dad. Glitsky lost.

He listened to the telephone ring in his ear, heard the answering machine of his best friend, Dismas Hardy. He thought he could use a few minutes of easy camaraderie with an adult male friend, somebody to talk to, who spoke his language, or he would lose his mind entirely.

The television in the divided living room droned in the background, more news about the fires, the riots, Kevin Shea. Where was Shea? he wondered distractedly. Maybe fled the jurisdiction?

Dismas Hardy, Abe's pal, was informing whoever the caller might be that he and his family had gone away for the weekend to Ashland, Oregon, for the Shakespeare Festival, where they would not have access to a telephone. Would the caller please call back after next Monday?

He remembered—the Glitskys and the Hardys had gone up to Ashland together two of the past four years. Camping (that dirty word). Frannie, Hardy's wife, had even begged Abe to bring the boys and come up with them this year. But, somehow, without Flo, Abe hadn't felt right about it. Ashland had been more Flo's thing, he'd told Frannie, although that wasn't really true. Glitsky loved Shakespeare, theatre, had even taken a shot at opera and found it fascinating. He took a lot of grief at work about this stuff—these were supposedly non-cop interests—but he was comfortable with them, with who he was.

Nevertheless, he'd told Frannie they couldn't make it this year. So the Hardys were up in Ashland now and he was here in a burning city losing rules committee meetings with his children.

Glitsky left his usual terse message on Hardy's machine, then forced himself up, back through the kitchen. Everybody was in the larger bedroom of the two younger brothers, watching the other television, some inanity with a laugh track. Isaac and Jacob were sprawled across the floor. Orel slept openmouthed, leaning against a sleeping Rita.

"Hey, guys," he said, and the older boys glanced and said, "Hey," waiting, resenting the intrusion.

"Nothing. Just checking in."

They shrugged and went back to the program and Glitsky gave up the effort of making an effort and headed for his bedroom, falling across the bed with his clothes on.

Isaac was shaking him. "Dad! Dad! Come on!"

He forced an eye—it weighed the proverbial sixteen tons. "What?"

"The phone." His son seemed truly concerned over his lack of response.

"Phone didn't ring, Ike." Glitsky didn't hear the phone, and it was right next to his bed. He *always* heard the phone. It was his primary wake-up medium. He rolled over again, closed his eyes. He was nearly back asleep.

"Dad!"

God, why wouldn't the kid let it rest? "What?"

"The phone. Some emergency. They need you. Some senator or something."

That got through. A shiver of adrenaline got him up, his son handing him the receiver. "Glitsky," he said.

He listened a minute. It was Marcel Lanier, pulling a late one. He needed his boss downtown. Immediately or sooner. All hell was breaking loose again. Chris Locke, the District Attorney, had been shot. Killed. Someone in another mob. Senator Wager, who was in the same car, had barely escaped herself. She was down at the Hall now, in shock, waiting in one of the interview rooms, asking for Glitsky himself.

Glitsky put a hand to his throbbing head. "Lord."

Isaac was still standing there, watching him. "What, Dad? What?"

Into the phone. "I'll be right down, Marcel. See if there's a black-and-white nearby, send them here to pick me up. Call me back if you can't."

The connection went. Abe laid the receiver back down and noticed Isaac striking an I-don't-believe-this pose. The boy said, "You're not goin' out again."

Glitsky swung off the bed. "Got to." But he softened his voice, reaching a hand to bring the boy nearer, give him a little physical contact. Isaac ducked again, glaring.

"What are we supposed to do now, Dad? When are you coming home?"

Glitsky checked his watch. A little after ten. He must have hit the bed and died. He wondered what time Locke . . . then it struck him again.

Jesus. Chris Locke *dead*.

Isaac was still glaring, breathing hard with emotion. Glitsky's mind was racing, covering too much territory, losing track of where he was. He tried to focus on his son. "I'm sorry, Ike, what?"

Isaac's eyes filled with tears, then fury. Swiping at his eyes, he turned, swore and ran from the room.

"Isaac!"

Glitsky was up, following, but before he'd gotten out of the room he heard Isaac's door slam on the other side of the house. Rita, hair tousled, wrinkled smock askew, rudely pulled out of her own sleep, faced him in the doorway to the kitchen. "I've got to go out again," he said. "Please keep them inside, I don't care what they say or how you do it."

She was shaking her head, a deep frown creasing her face. "I don't know, Abe. Orel, I can keep him, but the other boys . . ." She motioned back with her head. "What do I tell them?"

She was right and that, too, was terrifying. Beyond any consideration of the disorder out in the streets, the realization suddenly that the older boys were old enough—they could just disobey and walk out and Rita would be powerless to stop them.

He nodded. "I'll tell them." And they'd either obey him or go out into the streets. Authority—he either had it or he didn't. He was going to find out.

He gave Rita a weak smile and walked past her toward the back bedrooms.

27

Another Irish bar—the Little Shamrock, oldest one in the city—on a slow Wednesday night. Nobody out at all. Streets dark. Curfew in half the town and the rest content to stay indoors, which was probably smart.

Wes should be in himself. Probably would head back after a couple more, but this was pleasant, sitting here. These Sambucas kind of put him in mind of his days in Italy when he'd been an exchange student, nights under the stars with Lydia, back when she'd loved him.

Sambuca Romana. Pretty much the same stuff as Pernod, or ouzo in Greece, which they drank with ice all over Europe, the clear stuff turning milky with the ice and water. Here, he'd asked Moses McGuire to put the Sambuca on ice and got a full second of hesitation before he'd said okay.

McGuire was around the same age as Wes, a simpatico guy, if a bit of a purist about his drinks. That was all right. Wes considered himself a kind of purist, too, regarding his drinking. If it didn't have alcohol in it, he didn't drink it. So there was a bond there.

He smiled, took another sip, watching the television, which normally wasn't turned on in this bar. But tonight was real slow, and it was just Wes and a couple of hard-core darts players and McGuire, bartending. Besides, since last night every television in the country was going full time. He didn't blame McGuire. The country was coming apart and everybody wanted to see it live on five.

Wes had missed the opening volleys, the lynching, the first riots, the fires, Kevin's problem. He'd slept in (as he did every morning). Last night he'd been out in North Beach, did a little Brasilia Club cha-cha and tango and the parts he remembered had been fun. He woke up at home on the futon in the living room, his brain, by the feel of it, about two sizes too large for his skull.

He'd had some vodka and orange juice. Not too much vodka—a little hair of the dog was all. And then Kevin had called him before he'd even read the paper, which he still did out of some perverse sense that something might happen that might make a difference or that made sense. About four months ago he had made the decision that he wouldn't cut his hair again until something made sense—the mane had reached his shoulders, graying but still thick on top. He sported a ponytail from time to time, but mostly let it hang free, as it did tonight.

When Kevin hadn't shown up after an hour's wait at the church at USF, Wes drove out through Golden Gate Park, had a Foster's Lager, then took a nap in the Shakespeare Garden, getting away from the tent cities they seemed to be erecting in any area bigger than a softball field. He then treated himself to a piroshki dinner at a fast-food place on 9th before finally putting in his appearance at the Shamrock a little before seven. He was riding a slow buzz, wearing a T-shirt and a pair of loose-fitting khaki shorts, which now that the fog had descended was decidedly the wrong attire. He would freeze his nuts getting home, if he wound up staying unlucky and going home after all. The T-shirt said "Ask Somebody Who Cares."

Wes Farrell was fifty-three years old. He sipped at his Sambuca and was gently tapping on the bar to get McGuire's attention when the television interrupted its own news report with a fast-breaking development:

"We've just received a confirming report that the flare-up in the civic disturbances south of Mission has in fact claimed the life of District Attorney Christopher Locke. Earlier reports that Senator Loretta Wager had also been shot, perhaps killed, appear to have been mistaken.

"The two had driven to the neighborhood together to analyze the situation at the scene. Both Locke and Wager are African-Americans and the largely white crowd was in full riot before they arrived. Details are unclear at this time but it seems that as their car pulled away, some shots were fired. We'll take you there now, live, with Karen Wallace, who's been working around the clock for two days now. How bad is it down there, Karen?"

"It's pretty bad, Tom . . ."

And in fact it looked pretty bad. Karen was backlit by another rash of fires, and with the wind picking up, the place was an inferno. Most of the people had disappeared, with the occasional shadow rushing behind the newscaster. The cameras caught some of the National Guard, braced for action, moving through the shining streets. Overhead, several contiguous buildings burned.

" 'Nother one?"

Wes turned away from the television. DA Locke killed! Well, it wasn't his problem. And neither was Kevin. The guy hadn't shown up after he'd called *him*. He nodded at the bartender. He'd been coming into the Shamrock pretty regularly for the past year and he and McGuire were almost friends. "Sure, hit me. Get you something, Mose?" Wes had his pockets emptied out on the bar—bills, change, keys. He pushed the pile toward McGuire.

McGuire said he wouldn't mind a McCallan and Wes told him to pour himself a big one. Then he pointed at the screen. "You see that? They killed the District Attorney."

McGuire stopped pouring to look up and listen for a moment. He shook his head, setting loose his own thoughts. "I should have never had a kid. How are you supposed to raise a kid in this?"

"How old's your kid?"

"Three months."

Wes had nothing to say to that. They might be almost friends but that didn't mean they'd exchanged ten words about their personal lives. Wes figured, given McGuire's age, he might have teenagers. But a three-month-old infant? The bartender was staring at the screen. "You think it's going to escalate? All this?"

Farrell nodded. "I think it just did." He tapped his glass. "You know, my first kid was born in sixty-eight. You remember sixty-eight, Mose? Martin Luther King, Bobby Kennedy, Chicago, middle of Vietnam, Nixon gets elected. Worst year in American history, am I right?"

"I was over there. Nam. I missed a lot of the stuff at home."

"Yeah, well, believe me, it was the shits. I remember me and Lyd, we asked ourselves the same thing. How could we bring a baby into this world? Now, here they are, my kids, mid-twenties and doing the same thing themselves. Everybody does—it's the Baby Blues, is all. They get to be three or four years, you stop asking. Three months, though, that's tough."

Wes didn't want to say that the mid-twenties wasn't a cakewalk either, especially when your kids didn't have a lot to say to you anymore, but that was another thing he wasn't thinking about. He was here to party—that was his mission, his goal, his quest. But McGuire was on his own tangent.

"We got another black guy dead, it's gonna go up for sure. I ought to shut it down here for tonight, get home to my wife and kid." He sipped at his scotch. "Correct me if I'm wrong, but black guys kill white guys every day and nobody has a riot about it."

"Yeah, but I don't think they lynch 'em." Wes kept it laconic. There was too much hate in the city already, everywhere—he wasn't going to add to it.

"You're right. Hey, listen to me, turning into some kind of a bigot. Next thing, I'll be wanting 'em to find this poor bastard Shea and lynch him, call it even."

"I think that's the plan, don't you? That's what I keep hearing."

"Well, if he did it, I got no problem with that."

"*If* he did it . . ."

"That's what I said, but I don't think there's any doubt about that."

Farrell brought his glass to his mouth. "There's always a doubt."

"You seen the picture?"

Wes nodded. "I know. But I also know Kevin Shea. He's been in here, you've seen him. He didn't do it."

McGuire was trying to place the face now. "So who did?"

"I don't know."

Two of the dart throwers came over and ordered some more beer, but McGuire told them he was closing up early. Coming back to Wes, he leaned over the bar. "Call you a cab?"

"Nah, my car's just around the corner." Wes reached down, looked down in mild, anaesthetized surprise. His glass had disappeared from the bar in front of him. So had his keys.

"I'll call you a cab. Even pay for it." McGuire lifted the Sambuca from below the gutter and put it back on the bar. "It's my ass you get pulled over. We live in a litigious age. Enjoy your drink. I'll make the call."

"McGuire, I can drive."

"You know what, Wes. I personally have poured you seven stiff drinks in a little under three hours. You are legally drunk, which normally I wouldn't pay much attention to, but tonight seems like a bad night to be driving around under the influence. Cab'll be here in ten." He yelled across the small room. "Okay, guys, suck 'em up. We're closing."

But twenty minutes later the cab hadn't arrived. McGuire called again and learned that they wouldn't drive Farrell to his address because the route passed through an area that had been placed under curfew.

"So just give me the keys and I'll go the long way."

McGuire wasn't having that. His mind was made up. "You can stay at my place, crash on the couch. It's two blocks. Pick up your car in the morning."

"McGuire, I'm *fine.*"

"Whatever," McGuire said. "That's what's happening."

28

They finally gave up on Wes Farrell's return and agreed that Kevin's apartment was too likely to be under surveillance. Lexi—Melanie's roommate—had taken a summer job as a camp counsellor, which left the two-bedroom apartment all to Melanie for the summer. It was the next most logical spot to hide out, not too far from Wes Farrell's place.

Getting there—Cecilia Street, on the way up from San Francisco State, between the Sunset and Parkside districts—they ran into a National Guard blockade and had to go all the way around, out to the beach and back. With the other traffic, it took them nearly an hour. Melanie drove carefully, occasionally looking over at Kevin, his seat back, arms crossed, eyes closed. His face was set—he was hurting, not wanting to betray it but every bump gave him away.

She was still upset about Cindy.

Cindy! He'd been with Cindy, and then her supposed best friend had gone on pretending and just plain lying to her the whole time—but at least, as Kevin admitted, it had happened before they'd started going out. What was he supposed to do, tell her the details of everybody he'd ever slept with in his life? She couldn't expect that, didn't even want that. Maybe he *had* been trying to spare her feelings. Maybe whatever he'd done with Cindy didn't matter that much to him, although she couldn't imagine sleeping with someone and not having it matter.

It was also possible that the other reason he'd given was the true one—that he'd have lost any chance to get together with her if she knew he'd been with Cindy. Well, at the time, he may have been right about that.

She pulled the car off 19th, which always had traffic, but

didn't tonight—most of the other cars had been diverted or had taken the hint. The streets were nearly deserted. Her own block was illuminated by streetlights and, as usual, the parking was impossible.

Luckily, she noticed somebody who might be pulling out. Whoever it was hadn't turned on his headlights yet, but somebody was sitting in the driver's seat, and she slowed.

"We there?" Kevin slowly eased himself up in the seat.

"I just want to ask this guy if he's leaving . . ." She'd stopped, leaned over to roll down Kevin's window. "Excuse me," she said, "are you . . . ?"

The man's own window was down and suddenly there was a bright light shining in their faces. Kevin put a hand up, shielding his eyes or trying to hide, but she had no time to react before there was a forceful knock right at her ear, on the window on her side. A man standing there, holding a badge.

"Kevin . . . !"

"Jesus . . . jam it!"

"I don't know, I—"

"*Melanie* . . . !"

And her foot was down and her little Geo Sport actually got some rubber, squealing on the fog-slicked street.

"What am I doing . . . ? I can't do this . . ."

"You're doing it. Just keep going, drive!" He was turned around, looking behind them. In her rearview she saw headlights come on, then the terrifying red-and-blue flash of the police, which must have reminded Kevin . . .

"Turn off your lights!"

It was a short block, and as she turned the corner she saw them pull out, thought she heard another screech of tires, the sound of a siren winding up. No more looking back. She had a block on them. She would whip the next corner before they'd even come into view.

"Damn streetlights . . ."

"Don't hit your brakes."

"I know, I know."

Their pursuers had to slow at the corner to see where they were. Melanie took the next turn, back onto Santiago, coming up on Hoover Junior High. "Which way? Which way? Are they back there?" Screaming.

"Nobody yet. Oh yeah, here they come."

"Shit shit shit."

Kevin looked at her, pleased and surprised in the midst of it all. "Well, will you listen to that?"

"Shut up, Kevin, where are they?"

They had turned back onto another of the abbreviated streets. As long as they had short blocks so the pursuers couldn't pick up speed, they had a chance, but they were fast running out of them. Taraval was a fairly main thoroughfare, running up toward Twin Peaks, and if they got stuck on that the other car could catch them in two minutes, less.

Still, there wasn't any choice. They couldn't continue straight, couldn't go back the way they had come. She turned left, running dark. *"Watch out!"* A delivery van nearly smashing her, honking, swerving. A batmobile-turn onto the next immediate left, a street dead-ending in half a block at the entrance to the school, a pedestrian walkway with a three-foot-high metal post in the middle of it, on either side a six-foot maximum clearance before you hit fences. She was heading directly for it.

Kevin, turning back: "What are you doing?"

"Stay down!" she yelled. "I'm jamming it!"

"Shee-it!"

"They back there?"

"Not yet."

"All right. *Now.*" There's no way, she was thinking.

But it was the only way. Aiming the car at the dead center of one side of the walkway, she slammed her foot to the floor. She didn't realize that the screaming she heard was her own.

The side mirror snapped off with a pop, and they were in the school's open asphalt playground. She jerked the wheel as hard left as she could, hoping they were out of sight of the street behind them.

"They there?"

"No."

She kept moving, along the fence, seeing her spot, streaking then across the lot to the corridor between the low buildings, finally daring to use the brakes—lights or no lights, she had to stop—pulling up, killing the engine.

They both sat, breathing heavily, Kevin's attention still glued to the gate they had barely cleared.

Ten seconds passed.

Twenty.

They'd lost them.

"How did they know where you lived? Cindy?"

"I think so. Must have been."

They waited a couple of minutes in their hiding place between the buildings at the school, then turned on their lights and exited at the main entrance parking lot, getting back out to 19th and turning south, away from the city.

Melanie needed to spell it out for herself. "She must have told the police about us, that you might try to get in touch with me."

"She's a sweetheart, that Cindy. What do you say we go by her apartment and kill her?"

Melanie shook her head. Almost, for a minute, took him seriously. "I think we should break her kneecaps first," she said.

Kevin chuckled, going with her. "Her kneecaps are already astoundingly ugly."

"All of her is ugly."

"Hideous. Grotesque. The ugliest woman on the planet. And you did good."

"I'm prettier than her, that's why. You're as ugly as her, you can't drive straight."

He reached a hand over and touched her hair, spoke softly. "No part of you is as ugly as the prettiest part of her."

She brought her hand up to cover his.

"So what do you think we ought to do now?"

"I think," she said, "we've got to get you out of town, for a while, at least."

A small hesitation, then Kevin nodded. "Okay, one night. You call it, Melanie, you're doing better than me."

It was a little after eleven. She took the first turnoff into Brisbane, home of the Cow Palace and little else. There was a row of strip motels, and Melanie pulled into the third one down on the right, the Star, because it had an interior courtyard invisible from the street. Kevin waited while she went to the office, his shoulders hunched, his ribs aching, unmoving.

"You know I've never done that before?"

"What?"

"Registered at a motel. I told the man it was just me. I think he was hitting on me a little." She was whispering, turning on the television for background white noise, turning the channel to avoid news programs until she came to a rerun of *Land of the Giants* and left it there, turned low.

Kevin had come in from his scrunched-down position in the car, which Melanie had parked directly in front of the room's door. Now he was making sure the drapes were closed all the way. Turning, he sat on the one double bed and looked across at Melanie sitting with one leg crossed over the other on the room's single, mostly green upholstered chair.

Kevin thought that even though she had spent the better part of the day under tremendous pressure in the driver's seat of her car, Melanie was likely the best-looking female the night clerk had seen in a lot of days. No doubt he had tried to hit on her, an unattached young thing staying alone in a place like this.

In the room's dim light her dark hair still managed to shine. She wore a man's white shirt tucked into a pair of jeans that fit ideally. The shirt still looked ironed, its top three buttons undone and beginning to reveal the shadowy swell of her breasts. A glimpse of white brassiere with a lace border. He had no idea how she managed to retain her freshness under these conditions, and where before it would have bothered him that she was so perfect, tonight he thought it wasn't so bad.

Her shoulders seemed to settle. She let out a small sigh. "Are you all right?" she asked.

"I don't know," he said, the effort at speaking almost too much. "I guess I should try Wes again." He staggered over to the phone and listened to it ring eight times before he hung up. He didn't ask Melanie where she thought Wes might be—he knew what she'd say and he was afraid she'd be right, that Wes was somewhere getting himself into the bag.

He eased himself onto the bed, closed his eyes, letting his head fall forward, then raising it again, his expression tortured. "I keep seeing it," he said. "I close my eyes and I keep seeing him . . ."

"Arthur Wade . . ."

"I think if I'd just *known*. I mean, it was like I didn't believe it was going to go that far, so maybe I didn't—"

"Kevin, you did everything you could."

Shaking his head, Kevin forced it out. "No. It wasn't enough, Mel. If I'd just—"

"How could you have?"

"That's just it. Don't you see? I could have. I *should* have seen from the beginning. I was too damn slow."

"But you *did* get to him."

"I got to him. Then they got to me."

"That isn't your fault."

Again, he shook his head. "I kept believing it would stop. After I got to him I must have eased up a minute. I didn't want to kick and punch and yell and stab at everybody around me. I mean, just five minutes before I was drinking with these guys. I thought once I got to holding him up, then everybody would realize, like, 'Hey, wait a minute. This has gone far enough. We can't do this.' But it didn't happen. I just wasn't prepared for that much *hate*. I let them beat me, and it killed Wade. Now it might kill me, and you . . ."

Melanie came up off the bed onto her knees in front of him. "You know what this is, Kevin? This is fatigue. This is total exhaustion. You don't have *anything* to be ashamed of."

"I keep seeing him . . ."

She nodded. "And you probably will for a long time. You tried to save him, *that's* what's important."

"It didn't work, Mel."

"Lots of things don't work, Kevin. That doesn't mean they weren't worth trying."

He took in a breath and looked up at the darkened ceiling. "How about if *nothing* works? Ever? How about that one?"

She held his arms tightly until he looked down into her eyes. "That's a tougher one," she said, "but that's not you."

*   *   *

She went into the bathroom and when she came out Kevin was stretched out on the bed, his breathing labored and heavy. When she sat on the side of the bed he opened his eyes. "Thank you," he said.

She brushed a finger over the side of his cheek. "How bad are the ribs? Let's see."

"I'll show you mine if you show me yours first." She ignored that and started to pull the UCLA shirt. "Easy, *easy,*" he said. Another heavy breath. "I don't know if this is going to work."

"Can you lift your arms?"

"A little."

He raised them as high as he could, and Melanie tugged at the shirt, gently, until it cleared. "Oh my God, Kevin." The right side of his chest seemed to be encircled by a rope of bruises—black, red, purple. The skin was broken in half a dozen places, looking infected. "We've got to get you to a doctor."

"I don't think that's a great idea."

"Then what are we going to do?"

"I think we should get some sleep and think about it in the morning. I don't think I've got much left, Mel."

"Okay, you lay down." She took his shoulders and carefully helped him lower himself. "All the way up, head on the pillow," she directed. When he was settled she saw the physical relief flood through him, his eyes closed, his body relaxing. Covering him to his waist with the thin comforter, she turned and went into the bathroom, got a washcloth and ran warm water over it.

By the time she was back to his side, perhaps one minute had elapsed, and Kevin was asleep.

She tested the washcloth against her arm, then with great care wiped the bruises on his chest, drying it with one of the bathroom towels and bringing the comforter up to cover him to the neck. Going around the bed, she turned off the television, then the lights by the door, and stepped out of her shoes. Otherwise still dressed, sliding in beside him, she lay down on her back, hands at her sides, hardly daring to breathe.

The knock was barely audible. "Ms. Sinclair? Melanie?"

What? No one knew she was here except . . .

She parted the drapes a couple of inches and was staring into the face of the clerk from the office. Not a young man, his deep-pitched gravelly voice seemed to make the window vibrate against her hand. "I thought you might be lonesome, want a little company?" The look in his eyes chilled her, and she glanced quickly at the thin chain that, in theory, protected her.

She let the drapes fall, stepping back. Another knock, quietly. "Ms. Sinclair?" A pause. "Okay, then, no offense."

She waited as long as she could bear it, then tried the drapes again and looked. He was gone.

Getting into the bed again next to Kevin, she pulled the comforter up around her, but after a short while suddenly lifted it off and sat up.

She walked around the bed, picked up the telephone, and punched in some numbers. It was after ten and she'd been trained not to call anyone after that time, but this time she was going to make an exception.

The tired voice answered. "Hello? What time is it?"

"Cindy?"

"Melanie? Where are you? Are you all right?"

"I'm fine. One thing, though . . ."

"Sure, what, anything . . ."

"Fuck you, Cindy."

And she hung up.

29

Glitsky went straight up to homicide, but Marcel Lanier, the inspector who had been on call in the office when Loretta Wager was brought downtown, had decided it would be wise to move the senator to avoid the media circus and had chosen a place he thought would be less likely to be used for the next couple of days—Chris Locke's office. He had borrowed a couple of uniformed officers and asked them to wait, standing guard in Locke's reception area until Lieutenant Glitsky arrived. The way things were going he just didn't know—the senator had almost been killed once tonight, and Lanier wasn't about to have anything like that happen again while he was on duty.

Glitsky dismissed the two men in the reception area, closed the door behind him and for the first time in almost twenty-five years was alone in a room with Loretta Wager.

She raised her head. She'd been sitting with her back stiff, one foot curled under her, on one of the couches in Locke's office. Her profile was to him and she held it there. He remained by the door a moment, struck by the control in her posture, the unexpected vulnerability of her face.

"Hello, Loretta." He stepped toward her. "Are you all right?"

Her voice had a mechanical quality—shock. "I don't know how I am. I don't . . . they tell me a bullet missed me by less than six inches." She uncurled the leg that had been under her, stood up and faced him. She was barefoot, shorter than he had remembered—an inch over five feet. Her shoes and a small clutch purse that matched the color of her blue suit lay on the floor by the end of the couch.

"But Chris . . ." She shook her head wearily, lapsed into silence. "This isn't how I would have chosen to see you again." She let her posture slip, something giving in her shoulders. "But then again, you'd chosen not to see me at all."

Glitsky ignored that, still standing at the doorway. "You want to tell me what happened?" She cocked her head to one side, some expectation verified. Glitsky felt he should say something, explain himself, though he couldn't say why. Not exactly. "I run the homicide department. Chris Locke is a pretty important homicide. I gather you're the only witness we've got. I'd like to hear about it."

Loretta closed her eyes, sighed. Glitsky knew she must have been through it tonight. "I told my story upstairs to several officers and a tape recorder. I'm sure they're writing it all down."

"I'm sure they are."

"But you want to hear it again?"

Glitsky shrugged. He didn't understand why she'd asked for him, but he did know why Lanier had humored her. Well, he *was* here now, and this is what he did. "If you want to humor me I'd appreciate it. I understand you asked for me. Here I am."

There was the start of a smile, but Glitsky couldn't read it. "When you're bidden . . ."

"That's just the way I am, Loretta. I'm trying to do my job. You know that."

A pause. Then: "I remember." Unexpectedly—he'd crossed over to her now—she reached a hand up to the side of his face. But no sooner had the touch registered than she pulled it away. "All right," she said, "but God, I am so tired."

Glitsky nodded. "I've heard of tired. You want to sit down?"

Her voice sank. "*Sit* down? Sugar, I want to *lay* this ol' body down." But then she was back, her senatorial self. "Just teasing, Lieutenant. Let us sit down."

He turned on his pocket tape recorder and let her talk.

"Chris and I had dinner with Philip Mohandas and some of his people—I've been trying to coordinate our efforts so that we're all concentrating on the same way to end these problems, so we're not stepping on each other's toes. And

Philip doesn't see things exactly . . . well, exactly as Chris Locke did. Or me either, for that matter. I keep trying to get the message to him . . . separatism is not the way. Segregation is not the way. We have to work together, all of us.

"Maybe it was naive, but I thought if Chris and I—two black people working and getting things done in the system—I thought if we could somehow make Philip see, to *moderate* just a little, we'd have a better chance of getting the city under control.

"Philip can't seem to stop looking on these . . . these tragedies . . . as something he can *use*. He sees this as a time to demand concessions across the board. So he spent most of the night lecturing Chris and me on his *positions*, as he insists on calling them. It got pretty tedious.

"Now I knew I was going to take a lot of this up later with Philip, try and get him to see a little of the light, so I gave Chris a kick under the table and reminded him—didn't he remember?—we said we'd go out to the Dolores Park tent city, which—you probably heard—some genius had decided to segregate. De facto. Keep the tensions to a minimum.

"Lord, the stupidity of bureaucrats.

"Chris didn't know exactly what we thought we were going to do out there, I told him I thought—still do—that it was maybe one of those times when you can make political points and do some good at the same time. That argument speaks—I'm sorry, spoke . . . to Chris Locke, as you probably know.

"But by the time we got down there, things had flared up. I think it got around—of course, none of the city planners had realized its implications—that this was about two blocks from the spot where Michael Mullen had been shot. So the white half—can you believe this, the white half—of the tent city decides to name itself Mullentown, and in retaliation or whatever you want to call it, someone put up a sign in the other area—the so-called African area—calling it Jerohm Reese City. Which, as you can imagine, lasted about five minutes."

"Which got people to burning again."

Loretta leaned back against the couch, closing her eyes, sighing. Straightening herself up, arching her back, she visibly steeled herself to continue. Her red-rimmed eyes met Abe's and she smiled wearily. "We are so blind," she said. "We are so goddamn blind."

Glitsky turned off the recorder. "You really care that much?"

It stopped her, seemed to hurt her, but she simply echoed what he had said earlier: "That's just the way *I* am, Abe. I'm trying to do *my* job."

The scar between Glitsky's lips ran lighter for an instant and he looked down.

She didn't pursue the moment. Instead, taking a breath, she motioned to the tape recorder. He pressed the button and she was back at Dolores Park. "Chris had had some wine with dinner so I was driving. We stopped but didn't get out of the car. Things had begun to spill into the streets. They'd pushed over a police car, put it on fire. It was just getting dark.

"Then, suddenly, I don't even know how it happened, it was so fast. Or I wasn't paying attention enough, but there were people behind us, on the car, and Chris was saying roll the windows up, let's get out of here. But there really was no getting out—I mean, all at once the mob was in front of us, blocking the street, the people behind starting to try to bounce *our* car, so I put it into reverse and decided to try to get out that way. Chris and I were both turned around. We're backing through this crowd, people are slamming the windows, screaming at us. Some rocks hit the car, something, I don't know, but I just kept going, not too fast, I didn't want to run anybody over, but we had to get out of there . . .

"And then we were through them, or I thought we were. I was still backing up, faster now with nobody in the way. We got to the end of the block and I stopped, figuring we could now go forward. Chris was still turned around, still looking behind us to make sure we were clear, and then, I don't know what—all of a sudden his window exploded and there was this man and I see he's pointing a gun at me now, so I jam the accelerator to the floor just as he fires again and I'm turning up Guerrero. Chris is slumped over. After that I guess I . . . I don't really know. I drove until I saw a police car, then I stopped."

Glitsky sat forward on the couch. His face was impassive. "Could you identify the man, the shooter?"

She thought a long moment, then shook her head. "I don't think so, Abe. It was dark, I was mostly looking at the gun. He was white and if I had to guess, probably under thirty . . ."

"You see what he was wearing?"

"Some kind of jacket—it was open, I noticed, it flapped—maybe a T-shirt, jeans, nothing really distinctive."

"Hair, beard . . . ?"

Again, she shook her head. "I really did tell all this to the inspectors upstairs, Abe. They said they'd look, they'd try. Try to find the gun, match it with something, see where it leads, but the man himself . . . he could have been anybody."

A lengthy silence. Loretta Wager leaned back into the curve of the couch. Glitsky remained hunched over, hands clasped between his knees, eyes on the floor. He flicked off his tape recorder.

When he finally spoke it came out husky and strained with fatigue, not unlike the tone he used with his boys. It wasn't his cop voice. "I didn't mean to be so abrupt today. When you called. I started to apologize but you'd hung up."

"I was . . . you were right. I shouldn't have intruded." She seemed to pull herself back, farther from him, waiting, reading his posture.

Their eyes met. Both of them looked away.

He had gotten up, gone over to the window, was rewinding his tape player. Then that was done and he still didn't move. Time passed. From across the room, she asked it so quietly he almost didn't hear it: "You haven't talked about your wife yet, have you? You haven't told anybody . . ."

She wasn't prying. Anyone else, maybe even Loretta at any other time, he would have snapped off some answer that would have ended that kind of personal inquiry, but right now he was drained, empty, without even the strength to lift his guard.

She'd read something in him. He could at least explain why he wouldn't explain. "It's not something you talk about."

He never had, not since the diagnosis. His role had been

to tough it out, support Flo in her own struggle, keep the boys from breaking . . .

"All right," she said.

If she'd pushed at all, he would have pulled away. He didn't turn around, spoke into his reflection in the window, kept it matter of fact. "She had ovarian cancer. By the time they discovered it there wasn't anything they could do. It took nine months."

"Oh, Abe. I'm so sorry."

"It's funny," he said at last, "all the planning we did, I mean so we'd be prepared, so Flo wouldn't feel so much like she was leaving us in the lurch. I think we really convinced ourselves that we were doing something. But then when . . . when she wasn't there, I looked at all these lists we'd made, all the things I'd have to remember to do with the boys, all of this . . . *activity* that was supposed to do something, keep us on some kind of even keel. I didn't have a clue."

He lifted his head, took in a breath, stared at the black space outside.

"How many boys do you have?" she asked.

"Three."

"Has it been a long time?"

"Sixty-four weeks Saturday." He looked at her. "I don't know why, I just remember it in weeks, like I don't want to admit it's been months, or a year. I mean, you can handle a week. A week isn't that long. How it feels is even less than that. Sometimes I . . . it seems like an hour ago, she was here. She's just gone an hour and she'll be right back. It's stupid, really. Denial. Just a way to handle it."

"Not so stupid."

His shoulders moved. "The only thing is, you run up against real time, against how nothing is the same, it's all changed. That's how you know how long it's been. Everything about your kids, how things work with them, that's all different. How you work with yourself." Winding down, stopping. "Sorry. Running on."

"Hardly that."

"Well . . ."

After a beat, she rose from the couch and walked over to him. "I was luckier with Dana. He died when Elaine was almost seventeen. And he was so much older. He'd lived his life." She looked up at him. "And still it took me a couple of years. You do whatever works." She touched his arm. "Would you mind driving me home, Abraham? I truly am exhausted."

He'd been driven down to the Hall by a squad car, so he had to check out another city-issued vehicle, the same model car Loretta had been driving with Chris Locke earlier in the night. They didn't do any more talking as Abe filled out the requisition form for the car or on the walk down the outside staircase so they would avoid the media still and always clustered in the lobby of the Hall of Justice.

Now as they pulled out of the city lot she sat all the way across the seat from him, against the window, still silent, the intimate discussion upstairs now a barrier between them.

Glitsky was all eyes on the road. The previous driver of the vehicle had left the radio on and some bright-voiced deejay was telling whatever audience might remain in the traumatized city that it was exactly midnight, the first hour of Thursday, June 30. One more day until the official start of the Fourth of July long weekend and Happy Birthday, America. It was sure going to be some fun if we just make sure we load up on the beer and hot dogs and . . .

Abe reached over and snapped it off. "That guy broadcasting from Mars or what?"

"They all do," Loretta said.

Thursday, June 30

30

They were in her circular brick driveway in front of the colonnaded white mansion at one of the city's high points in Pacific Heights, overlooking the entire world, less than two blocks from where Kevin Shea had rested at the top of his climb earlier in the day. The landscaping around Loretta's house had been done before either she or Glitsky had been born, and now stately maples folded their branches over them, enclosing the space, ensuring its privacy.

The ride had continued quiet, tense, laden with all that was still unspoken. Glitsky was angry at himself for what he considered self-indulgence. And, unreasonably, at her for giving him the opening. Then seeing where Loretta lived—the involuntary comparison with his own physical setting, his cramped duplex—seemed to ratchet everything up another notch.

Between the fatigue and the unfamiliar rush of emotion, he knew he was in a dangerous mood—he should just open her door, help her out and say good night. But he didn't, he wanted to settle something. He'd waited long enough. "Well, you married the right man after all, didn't you?"

She shot a look across the seat. "Do you want to hear about Dana?" Glitsky didn't trust himself to say anything. "Because I know you didn't understand. I don't know if I did."

The words spilled out. "What was to understand? You went with him, it's all right. If you hadn't I wouldn't have met Flo, so it all worked out. It was long ago, it doesn't matter now."

"It does, Abe, I think it does."

Suddenly, he slapped the steering wheel. "Jesus, what

was *he* then, forty-five? What could he have . . . ? That's what I guess I never understood."

She nodded her head, understanding the question. It was the crux of it. Her voice, like Abe's had earlier, remained flat. "He had *money,* Abe. He had prestige and power and he was *there.* He wasn't working for it like we were. He wasn't hoping. It was all there, already part of the package. And I could be part of it. He *wanted* me to be part of it."

"*Everybody* wanted you back then, Loretta. Probably still do. Why do you think you get elected? People respond to you, close up or far away. As you said, that's just who you are. I just thought, you and me, back then . . ."

He trailed off and the time lengthened in the car.

"I loved you, Abe, I really did."

His hands gripped the steering wheel, something to hold on to. "You left me, Loretta. You couldn't even be bothered to say good-bye."

She couldn't deny it—it was true. She herself had avoided it for twenty-five years. "I . . . I couldn't decide. I *asked* you, don't you remember?"

"You asked me what?"

"If you were ready, if you could commit . . ."

"And I said I needed a little time, I didn't say no. Hell, I wasn't yet twenty years old, not even out of school. It wasn't you, it was the idea. Marriage? A few more months, maybe. I would have been—"

"But I didn't have a few months." She paused, cornered, her eyes flashing. "Dana was ready *right now.* Don't you understand that? He was asking and he was going to *leave* if I didn't decide."

"You could have decided not to."

"No, I couldn't. Not without you. Not if you wouldn't be there. I couldn't give up what Dana had, not if I wasn't going to have you either."

"We might have—"

"*Might have* wasn't good enough. Dana was my chance and I had to take it. He had what it would have taken me years to get on my own."

So that was the answer. But there was one more question, maybe the most important one.

"Did you love him?"

"I came to . . ."

Glitsky slammed the steering wheel again, harder, biting out the words. "Did you love him *then*, damn it? Were you stringing us both at the same time . . . ?"

"*Stringing* you . . . ?"

"You know what I mean, Loretta. Sleeping with us both at the same time."

The question seemed to rock her. "No, Abe. I never did that. I left you before . . . oh, my God, is *that* what you've thought all this time? I never would have done that."

"It wouldn't have mattered. Leaving was what mattered."

"I know," she said. "I don't know if I was wrong. I was young. I just didn't feel like I had a *choice.*"

"You did and you made one. You can't make a choice if you don't have one."

"I wasn't smart or wise enough to see that then," she said. "I thought everything was easy back then, would be easy. That whatever I did would work out and Dana was a way to guarantee it."

"And it's worked, see?"

She didn't answer, staring at him. So much bitterness there, so much anger. Where had it all come from? Could she have caused all of it? Avoided all of it?

He looked at her and could almost see the question written across her face.

She nodded. "Yes, it's worked, but at what cost?" She reached for his hand and took it in hers, squeezed it tightly, then moved over and held it in her lap.

They'd gone from Dana to Elaine. Twenty-five minutes, maybe more. There was no time. His hand was in her lap. The cold was creeping into their bones. Now somehow they had moved to Kevin Shea, Loretta's plan to calm the city.

Glitsky thought he should bring up some of his reservations, not so much about Shea's guilt as the whole issue of due process and how once you started screwing with that you compromised the whole idea of keeping the law, which was his passion and his job.

But he also wasn't a child and wasn't kidding himself—they were both too tired for heavy philosophy. And like it or not, reasonable or not, the air was also thick with import—something was happening with them. She asked if he wanted to come inside, have a nightcap. He didn't drink more than five times a year, but he used the excuse to himself that he'd talk about Kevin Shea, about his work.

They were in a book-lined room. Glitsky sat in a red-leather armchair, his feet planted flat on the oriental rug. Loretta was pouring amber liquid into snifters on a side-board next to a fireplace. "You ask somebody in for a drink, you ought to pour them a drink at least."

She had taken off the jacket to her suit. Her blouse was purple silk. Glitsky had removed his own leather jacket and hung it on a peg by the hallway near the front door.

Now he sat mesmerized by the angle, the view, as she leaned over, striking a match and laying it against the gas log in the fireplace, the silhouette through the sheer blouse. Some memory stirred in him. He should get out of here.

She turned off the other lights in the room and brought the snifters over, handing him one, then opening his knees and kneeling between them. They touched the snifters—a clear ringing bell from the crystal—and drank. Resting her forearms along his thighs, she whispered to him. "Hold my glass."

He took it, chained.

Her fingers moved to his belt. She looked up at him then, confident. Her eyes came up and stayed on his. Slowly, the belt came undone, the zipper pulled, hands still burning where they rubbed him through the fabric.

She leaned forward, over him, and brought herself down, her hands holding him, around him, almost as if she might be praying.

He surrendered to the moment, the touch, the ecstasy.

31

Carrie, Jerohm Reese's live-in girlfriend, did not want him going out, not now, not so soon after he had just been released from jail. But Carrie was young. Unlike Jerohm, she didn't have an intuitive understanding of how things worked. Jerohm knew that you did what you did for one of two reasons—either when you were forced to or when it was easy. And tonight was going to be easy.

The times you were forced were when you were most likely to get caught. If you didn't plan, didn't take a little time, that's what happened. As it had with Mike Mullen.

Jerohm had been a mule for running dope for nearly three years and making a nice clean life of it, with a steady income, the occasional woman. He had learned about the dangers of spontaneous action, and tried to avoid it whenever possible, but with what turned out to be Mike Mullen, suddenly he had had to act and act immediately. He had had no time, no real choice in the matter.

It came down like this—

Jerohm's supplier and partner, Carlos, was expecting *his* supplier, Richard, to be delivering three kilograms of Chinese white heroin that had, supposedly, recently arrived in the city. Carlos, in turn, had arranged to unload his supply to a local bar owner named Mo-Mo House, who would then step on it and get it moving through its normal channels.

Which was how it always had worked in the past. Except on the day this delivery was due—the day before Mike Mullen died—Richard did not appear. There was no product. This made everyone more nervous than they normally would be—Carlos, Jerohm, Mo-Mo—looking over their shoulders, thinking their mothers might be undercover narcotics officers.

But Mo-Mo had worked a long time with Carlos, so he

gave him a chance, with the condition that if the heroin wasn't delivered to Mo's place, the Kit Kat Klub, by sundown the next day, the deal was off. Mo-Mo would take his delivery from somebody else.

Which alone would have been all right, perhaps a hassle to reestablish Mo-Mo's confidence in the Carlos/Jerohm supply line, but nothing too serious. As it turned out, Richard finally did arrive near the end of the next day as the sun was sinking. Carlos had a commitment to buy the drug, but without the sale to Mo-Mo, he wouldn't have anything to pay Richard with, and the last man who didn't pay Richard didn't see any more mornings.

Now Jerohm, by the time Richard showed up, had figured he wasn't going to have any work today, no run to the Kit Kat, so he had helped himself to a little PCP, and suddenly he found he had to go steal a car off the street in the time it might take him to blow his nose. And, with angel dust driving his engine, paranoid over Richard and Carlos and most everything else, Jerohm took his .38 Police Special from the place he kept it stashed under the stairs.

There had been no cars on the street. Nobody had parked and left their keys inside, he couldn't get the use of any wheels. And Jerohm was out of time.

Which turned out to be the worst bad karma for Mike Mullen, who was sitting, window down, bouncing along to some tune on the radio. Jerohm couldn't *believe* he had come all the way to Dolores Street already, which seemed as though it were halfway across town. He had to make his move. The sun was going down and if he didn't get his hands on a car, he was dead meat.

So he shot Mike Mullen, pulled him out of the car and took off. There wasn't any remorse, any particular thought involved at the time or later. Jerohm's feeling was that everybody had their allotted time and this had been Mullen's. It could have been anybody. It was nothing personal. He was merely the agent of blind fate.

Jerohm got the car, got it back to Carlos, took the heroin to Mo-Mo. Everybody was happy.

But though that episode had worked out fine from Jerohm's perspective, generally speaking he had been forced to do what he did, and in that direction lay trouble.

The other way, why he was out tonight, was when it was easy.

Jerohm was wearing black nylon warm-up pants, a black turtleneck under a black sweater and a pair of Converse black tennis shoes. There had been riots earlier in the day not far from his house on Silver Avenue, and then later tonight up in the Mission District, Dolores Park. Jerohm reasoned they'd pull the National Guard up from Silver, leaving the place deserted, hoping most everybody would stay in because of the curfew.

He smiled to think of it. Citizens were so lame.

He was in good shape. The few days in jail hadn't hurt him any. He could have just run up to Silver but he needed something to carry the stuff away in, and he thought he'd wait a while before trying to score another car off somebody new. Last time hadn't worked out the best.

So leaving his apartment a little after one in the morning, he took his under car—the throwaway he used for business—and rode with the lights out all the way up to Silver, where he slowed down looking out at the playground, although nobody was playing.

He kept driving, running dark, until he came to the row of storefronts, then pulled over in front of the second building—Ace's Electrics—and got out, his sneakers crunching the broken glass under his feet. A few steps over the sidewalk and he was through the broken window, into the shop. He took out his flashlight and checked the shelves. More than he thought there'd be—the Guard must have been doing good, keeping out the looters, until they left.

The problem was that the stuff in the shop wasn't high-end—it was the wrong side of town for that. Only radios, clocks, whatever the hell else Mr. Ace thought he'd call "electrics." But Jerohm didn't waste any time moaning about it. Whatever was here was here for the taking. It would bring him something. Lifting a few of the fancier-looking radios, he came back out through the broken window and put them in his backseat.

Three doors down was Ratafia's Body Shop—a lot better, though he had to break his own window to get himself in. They had a couple of pretty good-looking toolboxes jammed to the top with shining gear. They weighed a ton but it would be worth it to carry out—bring some real cash.

Across the street was the liquor store, window broken but bars, and he had to make do reaching through, pulling maybe twenty, thirty bottles out, the ones he could reach by hand or hook with his tire iron.

He kept moving steadily up the street, seeing no one, hearing nothing but his own footfalls over the broken glass. The thrift store was hanging open, but who wanted anything in there? He just lifted a couple of suits that might look good for himself, two or three dresses for Carrie and threw them into the car. Then, thinking about it, he reentered and grabbed a large toy truck for Damien, some scary-looking guys with swords, couple of realistic submachine guns. The kid would think it was Christmas.

It wasn't much of a street, but hey, he wasn't complaining. It was all his. Couple more shops—bulk grains and canned goods that he piled in the trunk, a whole passel of what looked like good food stamps in the cash register.

Eighteen minutes. That was enough. He got back into the car, rolling back down Silver, turned onto Palou. Hadn't seen a living soul, which is what he'd told Carrie would happen. Curfew, he told her. People hang inside. Scared of getting shot at, which he wasn't.

But she worried. That was her. Let her. She'd be glad enough to see it when he got it all home.

He knew better, how it worked. You did things when you had to or when it was easy. And tonight was easy.

32

Wes Farrell had vague memories of no sleep.

If he recalled correctly, and he thought he did, Susan—Moses McGuire's wife—wasn't enthralled with the idea of her husband bringing home from his bar a drunk guy she didn't know to spend the night on their couch.

The baby woke up at least three times, although that assumed that she'd been asleep to wake up, and you couldn't have proved it by Wes. He had kept hearing noises all night, one or both of them shuffling around, opening the refrigerator, arguing—"Would you *please* bring her in here? I'm not walking around in my nightgown with *your friend* out there on the couch." To say nothing of the baby's cries.

As rosy-fingered dawn had lightened the sky, a bleary-eyed Moses McGuire had come into the room and dropped Wes's keys on the floor by the side of the couch. Subtle.

Lydia—Wes's ex-wife—had wanted the dog for companionship because Wes spent so much time away from the house, in the courtroom, and once the kids were gone she did not want to be all alone in the big house. A dog would make her feel safer, too.

But during the divorce negotiations, Lydia had decided she didn't want the dog anymore. Well, Wes didn't want the boxer either. He'd never wanted it in the first place. It was always Lydia's dog—Bartholemew D. (for "Dog") Farrell, Bart for short. Bart the sixty-five-pound dog-doo machine.

And Lydia had said, "Okay, then he's going to the pound." It amazed him how Lydia could cut things like

that. Had she always been able to? He just didn't know
anymore, maybe had never known.

Wes couldn't let that happen. Too many other things had
fallen apart in the short years after his youngest—
Michelle—had moved out. For some reason he found himself incapable of allowing Bart to go to the pound.

This particular morning he figured that Bart would be
pissed off at him. After all, he had been gone close to eighteen hours. He turned the key and there was Bart, whining.

"Hey, guy. Sorry." He gave him a scratch between the
ears. The dog, tail between his legs, leaned into him for a
few seconds, then led him to the kitchen. Wes had to be
proud of him—Bart had pulled yesterday's *Chronicle* onto
the floor from the table and used it properly. But Wes
could tell he was embarrassed.

He really wasn't in the mood to take Bart for his walk in
the trolley tracks that ran down 19th Avenue, but he felt it
was his duty. His care for Bart was somehow his psychic life
raft—his connection to the person he'd been when there had
still been a home, kids, wife, a job—responsibilities that had
sustained him and given him some day-to-day meaning. Now
there was just Bart, and Wes knew he was just a dumb dog,
but he wasn't really ready to give up on taking care of him.

Not that he was especially good at it—as the past hours
had proved. But he hadn't been particularly successful at
the earlier efforts with his family either.

Bart, turned loose, ran ahead, found a likely spot, took
care of business. Shivering, still in his shorts and T-shirt,
Wes walked on the black asphalt path along the tracks.

There had been feeble sunlight while he was driving back
from where he had parked near the Shamrock last night,
but as the earth turned, the sun had hidden itself behind a
lowering cloud cover. Now no one else was out. There were
no shadows because there was no sun. No wind. The place,
the normally humming thoroughfare—the whole city, come
to think of it—seemed unnaturally, eerily silent. Wes
stopped, listening. Bart reappeared from somewhere and
sat beside him.

Turning, he caught a flutter of white in the corner of his
eye and left the path and went over to it. He tore the
makeshift wanted poster down from where it had been
tacked to a telephone pole.

Maybe Kevin hadn't intentionally blown him off, after all. Maybe he hadn't had a choice. He stared at the poster—that was Kevin, all right. The boy was in some deep shit.

Back in his apartment, Wes took a hot shower, put on a pair of heavy flannel pajamas and—congratulating himself for his self-control—drank down two large glasses of Tabasco-spiked Clamato juice without any vodka. Then poured himself a third.

He was in what he referred to as his living salon, waiting for Morpheus to call him, drinking his Clamato juice, absently petting Bart behind the ears, across his neck. He hated to admit it, but the damn dog gave him a great deal of comfort.

Part of him didn't really want to hear from Kevin. Probably the boy had just been out tying one on, got confused, then figured out what he was going to do all by himself. That was probably it.

But, as of late last night, he was still at large. What if he was not only in trouble but really did need him? Wes looked again at the poster he had brought up with him—there wasn't any doubt Kevin was in big trouble. The only question was whether or not he deserved to be. Wes was reserving judgment, but the fact remained that Kevin's call yesterday wasn't just some youthful confusion, some drunken delusion. The poster was real enough, scary enough. And the young man clearly was under the impression that he might need Wes's services, that Wes might be able to help him . . .

Well, now . . .

Wes drank some juice and thought that *if* that were the case it was a whole different can of worms, wasn't it? Because the little whispering voice inside him had been nagging for weeks now—since the semester had ended in June—that he didn't care all that much about getting a doctorate in history. That had mostly been something to fill up the time while he tried to chart a new direction after his wife's, Lydia's, departure and his best friend's, Mark Dooher's, betrayal.

He and Lydia had been sweethearts when they'd been

young, then partners-going-on-strangers through the child-rearing years. And then, after Michelle had moved out, the silences in the big house had lengthened and deepened into trenches that neither of them could easily have crossed even if they had wanted to. And it turned out that they hadn't.

He had been a lawyer for so long, going to court, hanging around the Hall of Justice, occasionally chasing the ambulance, while she had been a mom, a PTA person, then a real-estate broker who had started her own company. In the end there wasn't anything much to talk about. He had put on twenty pounds, she had lost almost thirty. She saw her life as beginning a new phase—exciting, challenging, filled with freedom. And Wes . . . ?

While all this was going on with his wife, Lydia, Wes had been consumed with something else altogether removed from his domestic life . . . the trial of his best friend Mark Dooher, who had been charged with murdering his wife. Wes was Dooher's attorney, and it had been the trial of his life.

He leaned back on the couch. Why the hell wasn't sleep coming? He didn't want to think about this now. Not ever, in fact. Maybe he would go and pour in a shot or two of vodka, take the edge off.

But he didn't move.

The truth was, after everything had shaken down, Wes was left with the bereft conviction that he had lived his life and it just hadn't panned out all that well. The child-rearing years were behind him, and he felt he hadn't been much of a dad, hadn't spent enough time on the personal stuff, and now the kids were gone and he didn't know them and they didn't care to know him and he didn't blame them.

And the law—the god he had worshipped and served for all of his adult life—the law had proved to be a sham.

When Lyd had said she wanted to leave him, what had shocked him the most was that after twenty-seven years he had felt only a mild regret that he'd spent so much time in the charade if the only place it had taken them was to here.

But it was the nature of his best friend Mark Dooher's betrayal that had shaken his faith to its foundations. And he had gradually come to realize that he had just stopped caring. The natural skepticism that he had cultivated as a protective device for working with venal and dishonest clients had turned to a profound cynicism about humanity in general.

It was why he had started to drink and why he kept at it so religiously. To keep himself numb. To keep things on the surface. You move fast enough on thin ice and it won't crack. But he also felt himself slipping further and further out, away from everyone else, away from any sense that anything had meaning.

He wasn't any closer to cutting his hair.

It was why he'd taken and kept and continued to care for Bart. It was also why he was suddenly so ambivalent about what might well be a stark reality—Kevin Shea could be counting on his legal help.

Potentially, another line to the raft. But also another opportunity to hope, and he was not inclined to listen to its knock, especially where the law was involved. The law—the once sacred beautiful law . . .

No. He couldn't let himself be drawn back to it. He wasn't going to try to help Kevin Shea or anybody else. Maybe he'd refer him—that was as far as he'd go. He wasn't going to open himself up to getting betrayed again. If that happened, he held no illusions—it would destroy his soul, if he had one, and then there would be nothing at all left to save.

He stood up. A little vodka—tasteless, odorless, colorless—would hit the spot after all, thank you. Hold the Clamato.

A telephone seemed to be ringing somewhere. Underwater. Which proved it was a dream. He didn't have to acknowledge it, do anything. Just roll over and it would stop.

He knew he couldn't have been asleep more than an hour, and for a change of pace he'd made it into his actual bed, under the comforter, before he'd crashed. Pulled down the blinds. It was dark as night in his bedroom, warm and secure. He wasn't moving and that was that. He needed at least six more hours before he could face the day.

He turned over, pulling the comforter over his head. Two more rings. Three. Then silence again.

See? A dream.

33

At seven-forty in the morning the mayor of San Francisco, Conrad Aiken, stood looking out over yet another tent city, this one in the Civic Center Park, directly below where he stood partially hidden behind the flags of the United States and of California on the ceremonial balcony area over the magnificently carved double-doorways of City Hall.

As had been the case for the past day and a half, he was having trouble assimilating the information before him. Here he was, the executive in charge of the billion-dollar-plus budget of one of the world's most well-loved and beautiful cities, the destination of thousands of tourists every year, one of the convention capitals of the country, a mecca for gourmets, a center of liberalism and the arts, with the sixth greatest opera house in the world, a haven for the have-nots, homeless and homosexuals of the rest of the country, and he felt as though it had all fallen to pieces around him in a matter of hours.

Through the thin morning fog, smoke from cooking fires was rising in wisps over the tents. In his mind's eye it recalled the image he had seen in photographs since his childhood—San Francisco struggling to rise from the ashes of the Great Quake of 1906, until today the city's darkest hour. Before, the image had always struck him as hopeful—the citizens pulling together to rebuild their lives and homes—but today, looking down over the tents, hearing the *thrum* of boom boxes, the sporadic voices raised in frustration or anger, the reality was anything but hopeful.

Aiken was meeting with the eleven members of the Board of Supervisors in fifteen minutes and he had no idea what he was going to tell them. Worse, in spite of his best efforts with selected staffers whom he had cultivated as moles, he had no real sense of what they might recommend to him. Experience told him that whatever they came up with was unlikely to be productive, although it *would* vastly increase his workload, undermine his authority and dilute whatever substantive efforts that might be called for or were even already in the works.

He'd put the Board off all day yesterday, hoping the situation would somehow blow over quickly, but with the assassination the previous night of the city's district attorney, Chris Locke, which had sparked a new wave of nocturnal riots, there was no longer any pretending that this was going to go away.

Donald, Aiken's administrative assistant—a tall, well-groomed single man of thirty-five—appeared at his elbow. They both stood unmoving for a full minute. "If you'd like an opinion . . ." Donald ventured.

Aiken, still in his thoughts, nodded. Donald was an asset—ears always to the ground, open lines of communication with everyone at City Hall and blessed with a keen sense of politics, positioning, strategy. "I'll take anything you can give me."

Donald was holding a folder that Aiken hadn't noticed. Now he opened it and handed the poster of Kevin Shea to his boss. Aiken had seen it a hundred times. He was sick to death of it, but he'd listen to Donald. He looked over and up at him, thinking not for the first time that Donald would be the perfect assistant if he weren't so damn tall.

"Okay? What about it?"

"I spent all day yesterday walking these hallowed halls, and my sense is that if you don't immediately take charge of the meeting this morning with the simplest possible message you are going to have an unqualified political disaster."

Aiken had come to this same conclusion on his own. The members of the Board of Supervisors in San Francisco were elected in city-wide, non-district elections. No one person represented any geographical area—a Nob Hill or a Hunter's Point or a Castro Street. In effect each member of the board represented—*embodied*—an *agenda*. Aiken's experience was that this tended to make consensus very difficult on many issues.

Further exacerbating the problem with the Supes—as

they were called when not referred to as the Stupes—was their salary structure. The San Francisco charter provided that each supervisor made twenty-four thousand dollars per year. (Which meant that their own clerks and secretaries made twice what they did.) In other words, anyone who needed to work to make a living could not be a supervisor.

So many individuals—including Conrad Aiken—had come to hold the view that the members of the board were for the most part abysmally ignorant of the rudiments of the workplace. This failing was often combined with a disdain for compromise, an almost sublime disregard for reality, at least as Aiken knew it.

What the Supes did have, in general, was time, personal financial security that ensured isolation and sycophancy— and opinions. Positions. Attitudes. Ideas. Yes, these all were present in spades, clubs, diamonds and, mostly, hearts. Ideas abounded on the board. And, although they had no executive power, they could *recommend* action to be taken by the mayor. Police action, for example. Or declaring Ho Chi Minh City in Vietnam to be a Sister City to San Francisco. Or holding off on freeway reconstruction after an earthquake until an environmental impact report could be prepared on the danger such reconstruction would pose to the indigenous frog population of the China Basin.

The mayor didn't have to take any of their recommendations, but if he chose to ignore them he did so at his political peril. Somewhere among these dilettantish positions— white, Hispanic, gay, Asian, African-American, feminist— there resided an absolute majority, and that was what it took to get elected mayor.

Aiken took the poster from his aide. "And this is going to help me take charge, Donald?"

"I think Senator Wager was right yesterday about this. When she was here?"

"I remember, Donald. With what exactly?"

"And especially now, with Chris Locke's death. I think what we've got to do is go in there and up the ante. Every one of the Supes is going to be pushing in his or her own direction. There are a thousand cameras in the chamber already—everybody's going to want to make a speech, decry the violence, pass their own resolution . . . well, you know."

Aiken knew. "So what's this about upping the ante?"

"March right in there, take the podium and admit that we—all of us—the whole city has obviously and for too long been ignoring the racial tension that has been here among us. We've been hiding our heads in the sand. Especially here at City Hall."

Aiken smiled grimly. "Well, that's true enough."

"No, listen. There is a point here. We have been negligent—ignoring the truth that inequality still exists here, that there is justified rage out there in the streets among the regular citizens, especially among the black community. It is obvious that we are—all of us—to blame for the deaths both of Arthur Wade and now of Chris Locke. We have a debt—we have a debt to repay."

"Donald, this is getting a little thick."

"True, but when the silver-tongued devil speaks . . ." A look of conspiracy.

"By that you mean, of course, my own self . . ."

Donald nodded. "This is only the general idea, sir. In your words, it will not come out heavy-handed . . ."

The mayor was accustomed to the flattery, but he thought Donald was probably correct—he knew he did have a gift for oratory. And one thing the Board was usually receptive to was an appeal to their collective liberal guilt. If he started by telling them how they'd all caused this problem themselves, or contributed to it, he just might be able to get something past them. "All right," he said, "what's the rest of the general idea?"

"That *before* we consider any of the Board's proposals, *before* we do anything else, we must take immediate measures to integrate the alienated black community back into the mainstream of decision-making and public life. To reach out to them. Something symbolic."

"Symbolic is always good," Aiken said.

"So to demonstrate our commitment, to show that our first priority is to bring the city back together . . ."

"We hand up Kevin Shea."

Donald nodded: "He's guilty. Look at the pictures. We offer, say, a half-million dollars, which is cheap indeed if it stops the rampage."

Aiken ran a hand under his tired eyes, over the port-wine stain. "I don't want Chief Rigby to think I'm pointing

the finger at him, Donald. For not having arrested Shea
yet. They're doing all they can."

"No one's saying they're not, sir. You can even make
the point overtly. But we need—you need—the gesture, the
assurance to the black community that the city *is* trying,
that we're all in it together. It might even—all by itself—
throw some oil on the waters for a while."

It was all right, Aiken thought, because it could work.
And it was justified. A rare combination. "In other words,"
he said, "the order of business this morning is to rally the
Board around this reward, around apprehending Kevin
Shea, make a resolution to that effect . . ."

"You lead them there, sir."

"And then walk out?"

Donald gave it a moment, then nodded. "Essentially.
Yes."

Aiken, too, bobbed his head. "I like it," he said. "Let's
go make it fly."

When the door closed after Aiken had left the room to go
to the Supervisors' Chamber, Donald sat at his desk for a
very long five minutes, timing it. Often, Aiken would rush
out, get halfway to wherever he was going, then turn
around and burst back into the office, grabbing whatever
it was he'd forgotten, giving a last-minute directive that he
had overlooked.

But since Aiken was only heading to the opposite side
of City Hall—a one-minute walk—Donald thought that if
he were going to return it would be almost immediately.
Still, Donald was cautious by nature. It was wise to give
yourself twice the time you needed. What if the mayor got
stopped by the media out in the hallway and then remembered something and ran back in here? One couldn't be
too careful.

That thought in mind, Donald got up from his desk,
walked the long internal panelled corridor to the reception
area, then out through the public door, number 100, that
admitted the public into the mayor's outer office.

There was no one in the hallway. Donald walked over
to the balcony overlooking the vast rotunda—across the
way, in the opposite hallway, he saw the edges of a crowd

trying to see inside the Supervisors' Chamber. Something— he imagined Aiken's arrival there—had set off the crowd.

Satisfied, he turned and made his way through the office. At his desk he removed a white piece of paper from his wallet. It was blank except for seven numbers—no name attached.

At the receiving end a pleasant female voice asked him to leave his message.

After identifying himself, Donald told the machine that the mayor was in fact going ahead with the alternative they had discussed, and Donald predicted that the Board would pass the resolution within the next few hours.

When he hung up his hands were unsteady. Well, what did he expect? He had never done anything like that before—naturally it made him nervous. But the funny thing was that it was probably actually helping Conrad Aiken. It was a good idea.

Still, he did feel a small sense of betrayal. It bothered him, as though he had somehow switched loyalties. But after this catastrophe, and it hadn't even played out yet, Aiken was no certainty for reelection in five months and then what was Donald going to do if he didn't watch out for himself?

He had to broaden his base, make himself valuable to other people who might need his help. He had no doubt now—after this call—that Loretta Wager would remember him if he called on her. He wouldn't have to say it—she would know that she owed him. And she would deliver. That was how it worked, and the senator well knew it.

He'd heard. Mutual acquaintances.

34

Senator Wager's daughter, Elaine, had finally slept—soundly and long, waking up a little after dawn. Out through her living room window, under the cloud cover, there was considerably less smoke than there had been the day before. She allowed herself a moment's optimism—things might be getting better, the city's wounds would heal after all.

Then she had opened the newspaper . . .

In one of the oversized men's T-shirts she used as a nightgown she was sitting on the hardwood floor just inside her door, where she had been when she saw the headline and her legs had gone. She remembered reaching out to the wall for support and then deciding she was just going to have to sit down. She must have lost control of her bladder, the floor under her was wet. She was sucking her index finger. Time must have passed.

Her stomach was growling and she tried her legs again. It was a long way to the bathroom.

She could not believe no one had called her. But then she remembered she had unplugged the phone and turned down the answering machine—there were some times when you had to get some sleep.

Chris Locke's voice was on the answering machine.

"Oh God," she said, a new wave washing over her.

He'd called before . . . before . . .

Her hand clutched at her stomach, kneading the unyielding knot, mesmerized by the words, the voice, the last time she'd hear it.

He loved her, he was saying. He needed her, they had

to talk. Was there any chance she could meet him tomorrow—oh Lord, that was this morning—before work? He was going out with Mohandas and her mother for dinner, and that should run late. Maybe he'd drop by her apartment before going home. She could beep him and let him know.

Then here was her mother, with her voice of controlled calm she used in moments of greatest stress, calling from the police station. Someone had almost shot her, had shot Chris . . . Please, honey, she was saying, don't go out until you get this message, until you've talked to me.

Next on the machine was her officemate, Jerry Ouzounis, but that was information only, the start of office politics, and she fast-forwarded through part of it, then let it play, not listening, her eyes glazed over.

Somehow she had gotten dressed. Was she actually planning on going to work? She didn't know. But here she was, her hair was up, makeup on. Shoes. No hose. She took off her shoes, then forgot what she was doing. She knew she was sitting on the bed and she'd wanted to remember to do something, and here were her pantyhose on the bed next to her. But the connection wouldn't come.

There was the telephone, next to the bed. Was it somebody she wanted to call? She'd tried her mother but there was never any telling where she might be. The phone had rung fifteen times. She punched in that number again. Maybe that was it. Trying again.

There was always a line of black-and-white police cars parked along the curb in front of the Hall of Justice, but this day they clogged four of Bryant Street's five lanes.

Elaine Wager had to take a cab—her usual bus wasn't in service this morning. She stood at the corner—Seventh and Bryant—again with the overriding sense that reality had shifted in some fundamental way. A parking and traffic enforcement meter minder was casually writing out citations on the *police cars* as though they were normal vehicles, writing down license numbers and sticking his handiwork under wiper blades as though someone had told

him this was a reasonable use of his time amid all this
madness. And he had *believed* it . . .

The crowd inside the Hall had thinned, no doubt as a
result of the curfew—fewer bodies getting hauled in during
the night for processing. Elaine spacewalked through the
metal detector and came around one of the columns, the
cavernous lobby opening out before her.

There were maybe a dozen officers in uniform, standing
loose guard over their charges. Why, she thought, were
there so many police cars in front of the building? Where
were the rest of them? The disconnected observation struck
her like a message from a half-remembered world. She had
no idea.

The men in the line this morning were the usual unkempt
and motley collection, shuffling along, exhausted, blank-
eyed. As she was waiting for the elevator one of them
caught her attention.

She had been planning to take the elevator up, get to
her office, close the door. Maybe try calling her mother
again, talk to Jerry Ouzounis or to Chief Assistant DA Art
Drysdale . . . somebody upstairs . . . find out what had
happened, what she could do. She had to do something.
Do something for Chris.

Walking to the yellow tape that delineated the temporary
booking area, she stepped over it and got a better look at
the man.

"Excuse me," she said to an officer talking to another
uniform.

"Yes, ma'am." Then, seeing she was a civilian: "I've got
to ask you to go back over there. You're not supposed to
be behind the yellow tape."

There weren't any cordial smiles left in Elaine. "I'm with
the DA," she said, flashing her ID. "Elaine Wager."

If either of the two cops in earshot put together any
relationship between this attractive young woman and the
senator from California, they hid it well. But the DA was
the DA, and if this woman was part of that office, she could
talk to them and they would listen.

"Yes, ma'am," the officer repeated, "how can I help
you?"

Elaine gestured with her head. "Isn't that man Jerohm
Reese?"

*   *   *

"Hey, hey, this ain't right. Hey. I'm talking to you. You hearing me. I am *talking* to you."

Elaine ignored him. The officer, with J. Dealey on his name tag, was between her and Jerohm, and he told Jerohm to shut up. They were riding up in the visitor's jail elevator, which was faster than the public elevator and stopped at the sixth floor only—the entrance to the jail.

"No, I mean it, 'cause hey, this is no shit. They got no warrant on me. I just got sprung. This is bullshit, man; just a pure hassle. I didn't do nothing . . ."

Dealey turned to Elaine as though they were enjoying a stroll in the park: "We pulled him over in a curfew zone, in a stolen car loaded with merchandise he'd looted from—"

"Hey, now, hey . . . that wasn't no stolen car, that—"

"Did I mention shut *up,* Jerohm?" Dealey gave a jerk on the handcuffs, almost lifting Jerohm off his feet.

"This is brutality! Po-lice brutality. You seein' it, sister. This is it, now. Hey, c'mon, this guy—"

"I'm not your sister," Elaine told him, meeting his eye and staying with it. "I am your worst nightmare."

Art Drysdale, the chief assistant district attorney, was *living* his worst nightmare. It wasn't yet nine in the morning and he'd been up all night, getting downtown by five-forty. He refused to work even temporarily in Chris Locke's office— he didn't want any misinterpretation, he wasn't angling to become the new DA—and his own space wasn't even marginally close to big enough for the parade of humanity he'd been entertaining this morning, everybody wanting answers or consolation or decisions he wasn't empowered to make.

Normally Drysdale had a carefree style, often juggling baseballs behind his desk—he'd been a major league player for several weeks in his youth—while he discussed office policy or negotiated plea bargains with defense attorneys. Today he wore a white shirt, his tie loosened, arms resting on his desk and hands folded in front of him, knuckles whitened.

"All right, send her in."

Elaine came through the door and stood in front of him.

"I hope I didn't hear this right," he began. "You've got Jerohm Reese . . . the same Jerohm Reese we released two days ago without charging him with murder—*that* Jerohm Reese we've got back upstairs?"

"Yes, sir."

Drysdale brought a hand to his forehead and rubbed. He squeezed his temples. "On the same charges as everybody else we're letting go with citations?"

"A few more," she said.

"A few more. Enough to make an arrest mandatory? From downstairs in the GODDAMN LOBBY! Excuse me, I don't mean to yell, but we can't have this. We don't need Jerohm Reese here right now."

"I'm sorry—"

"I'm sure you are." He shook his head. "Elaine, why did you feel you had to do this?"

"I thought . . . I thought if word got out that we'd arrested Jerohm Reese again and let him go again—"

"I know, I know. But now we've got him in jail. And we're not keeping anybody else in jail for doing the same things he's done."

"But we can't let him go now. We can't just give him a ticket and let him walk."

"No, I don't think we can. Not now." He sucked in a breath, let it out in a whoosh. "Goddamn it."

"I just felt I had to do something. I wasn't thinking clearly. This thing with Chris, Mr. Locke . . ."

Drysdale held up his hand. He was sensitive to the realities of this situation. Elaine was the daughter of Loretta Wager. She was black. In the real world she couldn't be seriously reprimanded, much less suspended, for something like this, possibly not for anything. She was as bulletproof as Kevlar. And he had Jerohm Reese upstairs, which maybe he could somehow keep the media from discovering and exploiting. But meanwhile there was nothing of substance to charge him with, beyond, of course, the usual crimes that Boles was letting everybody else walk on.

"This thing has us all upset, Elaine. I don't know what *I'm* going to do and I don't know what's going to happen to this office. But our job is putting on trials, not facilitating arrests. We're supposed to think clearly before we take any action like this, you understand that?"

"Yes, sir."

"I know you do." Drysdale's hands were back together, the knuckles white again. He'd make some decision on what to do with Jerohm Reese. Legally, the DA had only two days to charge him, but Drysdale was getting an idea that with the Fourth of July weekend coming up he might be able to finagle putting off an arraignment until the following Tuesday, which might be long enough to avoid continuation of this disaster.

He brought himself back to Elaine. "You're on the Arthur Wade case." It wasn't a question. "You're working with Homicide on this, right? Closely?"

She wasn't, but she remembered talking with Lieutenant Glitsky at length about it just yesterday, so she wasn't strictly lying when she said, "Yes, sir."

"Just see that you do, all right. If you need any help, come to me, ask for it. You don't have to do this alone."

"Yes, sir. Thank you."

"Right. Don't mention it. And send in the next victim." He didn't smile when he said it.

35

Glitsky was in the police lot behind the Hall of Justice inspecting the last car Chris Locke had ever ridden in.

It was the same year, make and model of the car he had driven back to the Hall this morning, the same one he had taken Loretta home in the previous night, or, for that matter, the same as the one he had driven home earlier last night and sent a patrolman to retrieve and return to the city lot this morning.

The colors were different, that was all. The city had bought a fleet of twenty-seven Plymouths for the convenience of its employees and guests—plainclothes policemen, assistant district attorneys, the occasional visiting dignitary.

Inspector Marcel Lanier, putting in yeoman's hours building up his comp time, was giving Glitsky the grand tour of the crime scene. It was cold and foggy and some wind had come up. The two men wore heavy flight jackets, and Marcel kept his hands in his pockets. Glitsky, into feeling things, had the front-side passenger door open.

Halfway bent over, Glitsky squinted at the passenger's window. It had been rolled up when Locke had been shot and what was left of it was a cobweb of safety glass with a fist-sized hole in the middle of it.

"Forensics got all the glass?"

"All we found."

"It's a big hole."

Lanier checked it out. "Two bullets, Abe. Point blank."

Glitsky nodded. "You find the second slug?"

"Other side."

They walked around the car, Glitsky stopping at the back fender for a moment.

"What? You see something?"

"Nothing. I don't see a damn thing."

Opening the driver's door, Glitsky went down to one knee, examining the bullet hole in the car's upholstery, then slid in behind the wheel, eyeballed the hole in the window across from him and traced the trajectory of the second bullet with his hand. "She is one lucky lady," he said. According to his trajectory the bullet would have scraped the front of his chest; Loretta, of course, wasn't as thick as he was, and so it had missed her, but not by much.

"She must have got lucky with the ride home, too. Last night." Lanier kept his face straight, but he was jabbing.

Glitsky should have expected it—homicide cops tended to know everything and comment on it with a minimum of respect. Evidently the word was already out that he'd spirited Loretta from the Hall in the middle of the night.

"Give me a break, Marcel. The woman's a senator. It was on my way."

"Another lucky break for her."

He could feel the scar in his lips getting tight and fought to control his face. He had to take this without a sign— any response at all would tip a guy like Marcel. "Where's the rest of the blood?" he asked.

Lanier leaned over him. "You're looking at it." There was a small, perhaps three-inch circular stain on the seat next to him. "We're talking .22, maybe .25 caliber here. They'll have it this morning. Small hole, not much pop. No exit wound even. Lucky for her again. She didn't even get splattered."

Glitsky itched to give his inspector a few choice words about the amount of luck it took for Loretta to get herself shot at in the first place, but this, again, would be too much reaction—an admission of something out of the ordinary. So he held his tongue, except to say, "Okay," as he slid out of the driver's seat, carefully closing the door. They started walking back toward the Hall.

"So what's she like? You talk to her?" Lanier asked.

"Not much," Glitsky lied. "She was close enough to shock, pretty exhausted. I think it hit her pretty hard."

Their footfalls crunched on the gravel.

*   *   *

Nat Glitsky was sitting in one of the plastic yellow chairs in front of his son's desk when the lieutenant reappeared in his office. Seventy-six years old and the man was still cooking. As always, a yarmulke covered his wispy white crown. Hiking boots, a multicolored woolen sweater, old-fashioned and paint-stained khakis. He had draped what he called "the classic men's blue sports coat"—he wore it everywhere—over the back of the chair.

Word had gotten out about Jerohm Reese being back in custody upstairs, and Glitsky, who had heard about it coming down the hallway, was trying to fit that information into his matrix of How Things Worked. It wasn't exactly tongue and groove.

He stopped in the doorway. His father did not show up every day, even most days. Hardly ever, in fact, so something was up. Nat had come downtown a little more often during the months of Flo's illness, taken his son out to lunch once in a while, but since her death Glitsky couldn't remember a single other time.

His dad, never predictable, tossed at him a plastic-wrapped bagel filled with cream cheese. Glitsky spied some lox peeking out, too—the combination being his favorite thing to eat in the known universe. He had not treated himself to one in so long he'd forgotten.

Six inches shorter than Abe, Nat came over and gave him a kiss on the jaw, which was how he had always greeted his son and always would, convention and embarrassment be damned. Glitsky had hated it from kindergarten through the police academy, but now it didn't bother him at all. People didn't like it, that was their problem. He was becoming his dad. There were worse fates he could imagine.

"We've got to talk, Abraham."

But this wasn't the best time. In the homicide detail behind him, he could see Lanier, Banks, two other inspectors looking in, waiting for him to be free so they could get some direction. He also wanted to see the coroner, John Strout, regarding the autopsies on both Arthur Wade and Chris Locke—something he liked to do with every homicide in the jurisdiction.

On top of the stack of phone messages he was flipping through he noticed one from Greg Wrightson, one of the city's supervisors—a rare pleasure. Chief Rigby wanted to see him again. Unrelated to the riots, there had been a run-of-the-mill domestic-disturbance homicide last night in North Beach.

Not to mention Loretta Wager—what all *that* meant.

But this was his father, who wouldn't be here if it wasn't important in some way—Nat was no hysteric. "Should I close the door?" Abe asked. Of course, there was no door.

Nat pointed an index finger. "Eat your bagel, sit down."

Which Glitsky was doing, enjoying the hell out of it. "So?" he asked. "What?"

As always, Nat got right to it. "You know Jacob Blume? You do. He's my rabbi and would be yours you start going to synagogue again." He held up a hand. "This is not what I'm here about—you. I'm here about Blume. A good man."

"Okay."

Again, the hand. "Don't rush. Chew. I'm getting there. So a couple of nights ago—you know this—the riot is not two blocks from the temple . . ."

Abe did know it and was surprised that it hadn't occurred to him before. His father's synagogue—Beth Israel—was at Clement and Arguello, around the corner from the site of the lynching. "I'm sorry, say that again . . ."

"This is not your old father railing away, Abraham. This is your work here. Put your mind on. Pay attention." Nat waited, got a nod from his son—Abraham was listening. "This woman Rachel with some last name you don't believe, she is here maybe three months from Lithuania or the Ukraine or whatever they call it now. She comes to Blume, who comes to me."

"What about Rachel?"

"She is scared and confused and comes to Blume and he talks to her two hours yesterday—her English, *oy*—but better than my Ukrainian, I suppose—and it comes out she was on Geary, going home from temple, when the mob starts coming out . . ."

"Out of the Cavern? She saw that?" This was what Abe needed, a credible witness who had been there and could say what had happened. It could be a wedge to get some truth out of the barkeep Jamie O'Toole, among others.

Nat nodded. "But she is scared, Abraham. A Jew, the

police. This is not something to comfort her where she comes from. She has seen something. She knows she should tell. But she did nothing to stop it. So is she guilty of a crime? It's a *shanda,* certainly, taking no stand. What does she need to do? She doesn't know. She wants no trouble here in the U.S. So, finally, a day goes by, she sees what's happening in the city. Maybe she has a duty—she wants to do right . . . So Blume comes to me, asks me will I talk to you, see if this can be . . . if you need this. Which I must tell you there's no guarantee Rachel's going to go through with."

The telephone was ringing. Glitsky stuffed in the last bite of bagel and worked it to the side of his cheek. "Set it up, Dad, I'll be there." He picked up. "Glitsky, homicide."

It was another one of the assistant district attorneys, Ty Robbins, asking him where the hell he was—he was supposed to be testifying in Judge Oscar Thomasino's courtroom today in *People* v. *Sully,* a trial for Murder Two in Department 34. Had he forgotten?

Come on, Lieutenant, life was going on. The judge had given a ten-minute recess but he'd better get his ass down there in a New York minute if he didn't want to get slapped with contempt.

Nat Glitsky tapped his son's cheek, said it was nice chatting with him. He'd call.

The ten-minute recess found itself transformed into a day-long continuance—Mr. Sully's defense attorney had developed a migraine and pronounced herself unable to continue, and neither Judge Thomasino nor Mr. Robbins had had any objection.

This did not sit well with Glitsky, who had thrown on the tie he kept in his desk drawer for just such an occasion and run down to Department 34, wishing he had thought to borrow his father's all-purpose classic men's blue blazer. All he had was his flight jacket—the judge might ream him for a poor sartorial showing just to vent his displeasure at the delay.

Except that now the original delay meant nothing. The entire exercise had been futile and the day was too full for this idiocy. Abe was starting to decide that he was going to mention as much to Ty Robbins when Ridley Banks crabwalked into the pew next to him and sat down, beginning without preamble in a low, insistent voice.

"Couple of things. One, on the Mullen thing, I think we might have a bite. I drove out to McKay's after our little soiree yesterday at the Greek's. Poor guy—McKay—can't seem to find work, just sitting around the house. Wanted to talk to me on the stoop. Actually, didn't want to talk to me at all. I'm a trained investigator, I could tell."

"It's a useful skill, Ridley."

"So I mentioned the word 'warrant' . . ."

"You got a warrant? What for?"

"I didn't. I just mentioned the word and said he didn't have to let me in, but if he didn't I'd probably come back and it wouldn't be so friendly."

"The broken sliding door," Glitsky said.

Ridley Banks looked up to Glitsky, the only other dark-skinned inspector in homicide. In some ways he viewed the lieutenant as his mentor. He nodded. "The broken sliding door or lack thereof."

If there wasn't a broken window in a sliding door at McKay's house, there went his story that he and his cousin Brandon Mullen had cut their arms when they fell through it during their fight.

"Did you mention this to him?"

"I believe I neglected to."

"Okay, good," Glitsky said. "Let's get both those guys down here today. Start in again." Then, thinking of his father's information, he added that they might even want to hold Mullen and McKay for a lineup—there was a chance they had a witness who wasn't involved in the mob and who would talk about who she had seen there.

Banks took that in, scanned the courtroom, holding Glitsky in the pew while the assistant district attorney who'd called Abe down, Ty Robbins—the last man besides themselves in the courtroom—closed his briefcase with a snap and started up the center aisle.

Robbins raised a hand feebly. "Sorry, Abe. Maybe tomorrow, huh?" He kept walking, not waiting for any reply. The huge double doors shushed closed behind him, and Glitsky and Banks were alone.

"Something else?" Glitsky asked.

Banks appeared to be having some trouble making up his mind. He made sure again that the room was empty, then took in a breath and, letting it out, said, "I want to tell you a story. Maybe a little personal."

Impatient in any event with today's interruptions, Glitsky almost stopped him—it wasn't a good time, could they get to it later? But something about the young inspector's tone . . .

"Out on Balboa there's this restaurant called the Pacific Moon—small place, been there twenty-five, thirty years."

"Sure, I know it. I've eaten there."

"Everybody has."

"Food's not very good, if I remember."

Banks grinned. "That's the place, which is why, I don't know if you noticed, but you almost never see the place crowded. You go there on a Saturday night, eight o'clock, there's only like twenty tables and you get seated right away."

Glitsky sat back on the hard bench, not knowing where this was going. "Okay?" he said.

"So before homicide I did eight years in white collar, and when I first got in there, there was an ongoing investigation about money laundering at the Pacific Moon."

"Money laundering through a restaurant?"

"Sure. In the old days before electronic transfers, it was pretty common. You have yourself a ton of dirty cash and you deal in a perishable like food, it's custom made. You write up receipts for meals that never got served and presto, there's the cash in your till, clean as a whistle, just like magic."

"Okay. So the Pacific Moon laundered some money."

"A lot of money, Lieutenant."

"Okay, a lot of money. You get any indictments?"

In his own years on the force, Glitsky had heard a lot about "ongoing investigations"—he had conducted a few himself on people he didn't like, didn't believe, wanted to nail. Few of them panned out because evidence got cold faster than scrambled eggs. If you didn't get it the first time you looked it was unlikely to turn up later. If white collar couldn't bring any indictments against the Pacific Moon, the principals either had done nothing wrong or were very good at covering their tracks, most probably the latter. Either way, in the police department manpower was always at a premium, and if there wasn't some vein in the ore, the on-going investigation would have to stop—most often sooner than later.

"Nope. Place came up clean."

"Well . . . ?"

"Well, I was young and a red hot. I started eating dinner there every couple of weeks, staying for drinks, hanging out, counting people."

"Counting people?"

"There wasn't ever more than twenty people in the place. Ever. You know what the Pacific Moon grossed that year, this was eight years ago?"

Glitsky shook his head. "A million dollars?"

"Two-point-nine million dollars."

A minute of pure silence. Glitsky said, "Twenty tables?"

Banks's voice took on an edge. "If they filled every table every night five nights a week and turned them over three times each, and if every dinner averaged fifteen dollars, you know how much they would have grossed? I worked it out, Lieutenant, I'll tell you—three hundred thousand tops. Three hundred thousand. And they admit a gross of almost three million."

"They must have sold a lot of drinks." Glitsky scratched his cheek. "You couldn't get an indictment on that?"

"Can you believe . . . ? Nobody wanted to reopen the case. Evidently we'd blown a wad on it, the place had receipts like it was Chez Panisse, the books looked clean, white collar lost its papers on it and the DA didn't seem to save anything, but I'm telling you, nobody goes there to eat."

"Not twice anyway."

"That's what I'm saying."

Another dead minute. Then, Glitsky: "Well, it's a good story . . ." Meaning, but-so-what?

One last look around the courtroom. "So what is that—this was a few years before I got into it, but still—the word was that Dana Wager was a heavy investor in the place."

"Dana . . . ?"

"Right, the senator's husband. He filed for bankruptcy in 1977, all his real-estate investments had gone belly-up. He was done. Then he caught the rebound on the economy, reinvested, got lucky. All the sudden he's back on the high seas, and the Pacific Moon is his flagship."

"People get lucky, Rid."

"People also get money in ways that aren't legal. And then launder it."

"You think that happened with Wager?"

Banks wasn't coming right out with anything. He wasn't sure where his lieutenant stood on it, didn't want to dig himself too deep a hole. "There was some talk . . ."

"There's always talk."

Another pause. How far to take it? "This talk was about his wife, now our senator. How the rumor was that Dana's money came from Loretta, that she'd brought like a million dollars home with her from South America."

Of course, Glitsky had heard about the incident: Glitsky had followed it closely at the time. It had been all over the place, reported in the media. He couldn't very well have missed it, even if he'd been disposed to, which he wasn't.

In 1978 Loretta had been an administrative aide to California congressman Theo Heckstrom, and the two of them, among others, had gone down to Colombia on a fact-finding mission before the "war on drugs" had been openly declared. On a flight from Bogotá to Quito, Ecuador, their small plane had gone down deep in the Colombian jungle. Among the six people in the aircraft, including Heckstrom, Loretta had been the sole survivor.

Badly hurt herself, with a compound-fractured leg, she had remained in the plane's wreckage with the dead for four days, living on candy bars and plantains, before she was finally rescued and airlifted out and back to the United States. Most believed that the publicity associated with the tragedy had made her a household name in San Francisco, and had helped fuel her first successful run for Congress.

After she had won, Glitsky had also begun to hear the rumors about the million dollars—although the amount always varied—about the suitcase full of cash that Loretta had supposedly found on the plane and somehow spirited back into the country.

Now Glitsky was shaking his head. "The small problem with this phantom money, Rid, is customs."

Banks was ahead of him on that. "There weren't any customs. Everybody seems to forget this. They sent a special plane down there to pick her up, get her out in a hurry. Diplomatic airlift direct to Mayo." He repeated it. "No customs."

The room was getting stuffy, the air unmoving. Glitsky pushed his back against the bench, stifled a stretch. "You think Oswald killed Kennedy by himself, Rid?"

Banks shrugged. "Conspiracy theories, right?"

"Do you honestly think that if there was anything to all of this—and I'll admit it's a neat story—but do you think there is any way it wouldn't have come out? The woman's run—what?—four campaigns for office, two of them state-wide, against people who I'd bet have some knack for finding dirt. Anything was there, it would have come up."

Banks didn't answer.

"You think I'm in denial here, Rid?" But there was a tone in it—half-joking.

"I'm telling you what a lot of guys working the street believe down to their toes, that's all. You know a lot of 'em. They're not generally into conspiracies." The younger man slapped his hands on his thighs, took a short, sharp breath. "Anyway, for what it's worth . . ."

The lieutenant pushed himself up and next to him Banks stood, too. "It's worth knowing," Glitsky said. "Although this particular time, I think the senator might be doing some real good."

"Okay." His duty done, Banks nodded. "I'll go put a call out to McKay, follow up on these guys, get 'em down here. You hear anything about Kevin Shea?"

"*Nada.* Guy's got any brains, he's in Scandinavia."

They were at the double doors and Glitsky grabbed one of the handles, then stopped. "Hey, Rid, I appreciate it, but you don't have to worry."

"Okay, Lieutenant, I won't."

Glitsky had wanted to protest to Ridley Banks that all he had done was drive the senator home. Except that wasn't all he'd done and he didn't want to start with small un-truths. They tended to grow large and unruly.

As earlier with Lanier, he was hamstrung by the possibil-ity that he would come across as saying too much. Banks was a good cop, and no group hung together like cops.

Functioning as early warning, protective of his lieutenant, Banks was putting it out that people might be watching pretty closely. *Were already* hanging on the nuances. That maybe, on some level he couldn't define, Loretta Wager could be trouble for him.

And this—if he was honest with himself, and he tried to be—constituted a message Glitsky wasn't ready to hear.

He had given her his home telephone number and she had called him before he'd had his morning tea. Isaac had picked up the call and, handing it over, the expression he'd given Abe could have frozen a flame. Some instinct had told Ike that this wasn't a business call—it was a woman and his dad cared about her. And it was too . . . damn . . . soon.

When Glitsky heard her voice, all that went away. She wanted to see him again, needed to, could they arrange something for today?

Which wasn't reasonable, probably not doable, but they were going to try.

She had gotten a hold inside of him, where he'd told himself he wasn't letting anybody in ever again. He didn't know what worried him more—that it was happening at all or that it might end.

36

"Well, here I am, a grown-up at last, wanted by the police and all, and I guess if I want to call my mom and dad, no one's going to stop me."

Kevin shrugged at Wes. "She's just got this way in the last day or two, I can't really figure it out." But he knew he liked it.

Melanie gave them both a smile. "Adversity," she said, moving toward the kitchen's wall phone.

Wes slumped on the couch in the living salon. His long hair was down and he wore a pair of khaki shorts similar to the ones he had sported the day before, and he had his bare feet up on the footlocker that served as a coffee table. In his right hand was a can of Coors Light, stuck into a holder that read: "Beer—it's not just for breakfast anymore." Bart had his face resting in Wes's lap.

Kevin was trying to find a way to get comfortable.

Wes's furniture leaned to the austere—there was a large shaggy lime green bathmat doubling as a throw rug, two canvas-and-wood director's chairs, two straightbacks. The "couch" was a futon on a plywood frame set a foot off the ground. What with the other amenities in the salon—a television on the floor, a small extra refrigerator for beer, a brick-and-board bookcase, the beanbag chair Bart slept on, various grocery items whose expiration dates had expired—Wes's apartment might manage to look homey only to someone who had grown up in, say, the Senegalese bush.

"You haven't heard then?"

"Haven't heard what?"

Wes had been living with the television all morning and filled Kevin in on the mayor's initiative this morning, the

city stupidvisors' show of solidarity with the rage of the
black community. In one of the director's chairs, Kevin
shifted. He was afraid he was going to have to see a doctor,
but this was more immediate. "Two hundred thousand
dollars?"

The mayor had not been able to get his half-million.

"Round it off to three hundred if you include the original
hundred thou—that's a good hunk of change on your poor
ass. I'm thinking of turning you in myself, retire to Costa
Rica."

"You're already retired."

"But I'm not in Costa Rica." Wes smiled, took a slug of
his beer.

In the kitchen Melanie raised her voice. She had been
on the phone for fifteen minutes. "He is *not* lying. He just
did *not* do it, Daddy."

Wes made a face. "Somebody believes you at least."

Which brought a frown. Any hint of defensive banter
was gone. "You don't?"

Wes tipped up his beer can, found it empty, made a small
show of getting himself another from the fridge, offering
one to Kevin, who shook his head. And then, his inflection
rising with each word, said, "Hey? You hear me? You
don't believe I didn't do this?"

Melanie again, from the kitchen. "NO, I AM NOT." She
slammed the receiver against the wall box and it popped
out again, smacking on the floor.

Wes settled himself back on the futon, no reaction. The
kid had better learn the cold facts of the world.

"Goddamnit, Wes . . ."

Bart didn't like threatening noises made to his master
and although he knew Kevin, his back hairs went up and
a low growl began. Wes patted his rear as Melanie appeared back in the kitchen doorway.

Kevin was laboring out of the chair. "Let's go, Mel."

Wes's voice was flat. "What do you think you're doing.
Sit down."

Melanie, from the doorway: "What?"

Kevin threw her a look. "He doesn't believe me, either."

"Yes, he does. Of course, he does. Wes?"

"It doesn't *matter* what I believe, that's *not* the issue—"

"That is the *only* issue, Wes. That's the reason I'm here."

Wes didn't reply, nipped at his beer. Which heated Kevin up another notch.

"Well, what *do* you think? What the hell you think I'm here for?"

"Hey, listen, you want to yell, you'll strain yourself. I got an old bullhorn in the bedroom, maybe we shoot some flares out the window, let everybody know there's a party up here."

Holding his ribs, Kevin was collapsing back into his chair. Melanie went over to him.

Wes leaned forward, his eyes dark. "For the record, Kev, the real reason you're here? You got me. You called me, remember? You think I'm somehow putting my foot in this mess. I am done with that. I am not turning you in, and that right there is three hundred thousand dollars' worth of good faith. And though it's none of your goddamn business, I've got absolutely every reason in the world not to get myself involved in this, in you, in any of it."

Melanie was on her knees by Kevin, glaring at Wes. "What a great man you are."

Wes drank some beer. "I am who I am."

"Come on, Mel, let's go." Kevin was trying to get up from the chair again, his breath coming in short gasps.

"Where are you going?"

Melanie turned on him. "What's it to you? What do you care?"

The tears in her eyes were anger more than anything, and for an instant Wes was reminded of his daughter Michelle. Something twisted in his gut and as a cover he forced another slug of beer, which was suddenly warm, stale. "You're right," he said, "what's it to me?"

"I'm going downtown," Kevin said. "End all this."

"Kevin! You can't do that!"

He shrugged her off. "That's what I'm doing. Screw this. I'll do it on my own."

"Kevin, somebody will kill you . . ."

Wes was standing. "Why don't you just get out of here, out of the city?"

Melanie clearly didn't want to side with Wes, but she had to say it. "That's what I've been telling him."

Wes pointed a finger at her. "And you've been right."

Kevin was up now, limping toward the door. His face

was drawn. He stopped. "I'm going down and telling them the truth—"

Wes laughed. "Oh, that's great. That's really great, Kevin." His expression withered Melanie. "Would you two get *real*? You think anybody really cares about the truth at this stage?"

"I do," Kevin said.

"Pretty fuckin' stupid, you ask me."

"Yeah, well, thanks. That's really good to know."

Wes, a couple of shots of vodka and two beers in him, was heating up. He moved closer to them, his own volume rising. "And what are you getting downtown in? Melanie's car? Which every cop in town is looking for? Or are you going to walk, limp, whatever the hell you're up to?"

Melanie came between them. "He's got a point, Kevin. The car, I mean. We can't—"

"I'll give you my car," Wes said, "but for God's sake, use it to get out of this town." His tone softened. "Kevin, they will kill you. Somebody will put a knife in you, believe it. You won't last two days in jail. Sit *down,* will you?

"I'll ask for a private cell."

Rolling his eyes, Wes turned in a full circle. "You think you know how it works? You don't have any idea how it works."

Melanie, stepping in. "And you do, I suppose . . ."

"Yeah, as a matter of fact I do. And you know how it works? It doesn't. Which we're seeing a good example of now out the window." He faced Kevin. "You want to put yourself in the middle of that?"

Kevin had gotten to the wall by the door and was leaning up against it, obviously weakened by the outbursts. "That's why I came to you . . ."

"And what'd you think I was going to do? What miracle was I supposed to perform?"

"Forget it, Kevin . . . let's get out of here—"

"I thought you were going to help me, Wes. You know the ropes, you're a lawyer, get somebody to listen—"

"People listen all the time, Kevin, they don't hear a damn thing."

Kevin reached for another breath. "Well, I want you to hear *me,* Wes. This is not right. I did not do this. I tried to save him. You hear me? You hear me?"

Wes simply shrugged. "If you say so—"

"Goddamnit . . ." Kevin lurched forward and swung for Wes's chin, grunting with the pain.

Wes stepped back, Kevin's fist missing him by half a foot, as Kevin's forward motion crumpled him to the floor. Bart jumped forward with a bark.

"Bart!" Wes cuffed at him and the dog slunk to the side.

Kevin was trying to get up. Melanie was down to him, cradling his head in her arms. "You bastard."

He backed away. "I didn't . . ."

Melanie's eyes stuck with him. "I don't care *what* happened to you," she said. "There's no excuse to explain somebody turning out the way you have."

An hour later, about noon, Kevin was passed out in Wes's bedroom, the windows drawn. Wes had a supply of Motrin and Tylenol with codeine and they had pumped Kevin full of the stuff, washed down with a clam-tinged Bloody Mary.

Barefoot, Melanie looked in on him after she came out of the bathroom. She had had a shower and changed into another pair of Wes's khaki shorts, held up with a length of laundry rope and one of his white shirts, much like the one she had been wearing during the last twenty-four hours.

"He's passed out," she said.

"He'll be okay as long as he doesn't operate any heavy machinery." It was an attempt. Feeble, he knew.

But she understood and even appreciated it—the atmosphere had been uncomfortable for the last forty-five minutes. She sat at the opposite end of the futon running a comb through her wet hair.

Wes was watching the news. It was another banner day for the media—we may go down in flames, Wes was thinking, but at least we'll have commentary on it—with the continuing investigation into the death of Christopher Locke, the increase of the reward for Kevin, then the, to Wes, startling news of the rearrest of Jerohm Reese, which in turn had galvanized Philip Mohandas into previously un-scaled heights of rhetoric.

Mohandas was on the screen now, carrying on about racism and calling for the ouster of Acting District Attorney

Art Drysdale for approving the arrest of and allowing the charges against poor Jerohm, who had done nothing more than the other four hundred and sixteen citizens who had been cited with various violations over the past few days. No, he was saying, it was because Drysdale was white and Jerohm was black . . . that was why Jerohm was in jail. The *only* reason. No charge had ever been brought against him for Mullen's death.

"Hey, Phil!" Wes was yelling to the television. "Here's a flash for you. Two hundred and eighty-six of the other guys were black, too." Then, to Melanie, in a different voice. "I hate that guy. I really do."

One of the commentators was giving "deep background," dignifying Mohandas's charges—a recycling of Drysdale's past that presumably proved him unfit to serve in any capacity in the city and county. Seventeen years before, when asked about his stand on affirmative action in the DA's office, Drysdale had ventured the notion that perhaps there shouldn't be quotas used in hiring experts—for example, trial attorneys—that the people getting hired should be the people who could do the job, be they black, white, chartreuse, polka-dotted. "Hell," he'd said at the time, "if monkeys could do it, I'd say hire monkeys. But they can't, so I wouldn't."

Naturally, this was interpreted as meaning that Drysdale had called all black people monkeys, and saying he would never hire a black person. The misunderstanding had marked the end of any political aspirations Drysdale might have had (which were few in any event), and over the better part of the next two decades he had gone on to become the rock of the DA's office, a counsellor to anyone of any color or creed who needed his help.

And now Mohandas was on him like yellow on a lemon. "Poor Art," Wes was saying. "He's done."

"You know him?"

"Everybody knows him. He's the fairest man in the Hall of Justice."

"But—"

"You watch. He's gone."

They stared at the picture for another few seconds until one of those "why-ask-why?" commercials made Wes mute the screen. He liked all kinds of beer, but he'd asked why too many times about too many things to have any idea of what the damn ad was about.

He sat, then, his bare feet flat on the floor, his elbows resting on his knees. "Want a beer?" Although he didn't move to get one. Finally he sat back, patted the sofa, and Bart jumped into the space between him and Melanie, settling again with his head on Wes's lap. "What did your parents say?" he asked her.

Here was an unpracticed moue. "About what you'd expect." Then: "What happened to you, Wes?"

The abrupt segue wasn't clear, and he supposed he could have finessed it for a round or two, but of course he knew exactly what she meant. He had talked Kevin—both of them—into staying a while, into thinking through their strategy a little more carefully. At least get some rest.

And why had he done that? Why hadn't he just let them go? Maybe it was time to find out what *he* was made of, what *he* was going to do. Maybe open his battered soul's door a crack and take a peek inside, see if there was anybody there he wanted to get to know.

He wasn't very optimistic about it, but Melanie was here, listening—once again she reminded him of his daughter Michelle. All right, he could at least start, see where it went.

"Mark Dooher. I met him in seventh grade. One of those guys the light always shines on, you know? Great-looking kid, he smiled at you and everything was possible. A little like our friend Kevin in fact. In that way.

"And, lucky me, there's a chemistry. I'm not really in his shadow because I'm nothing like him—I've got to work at things, for example, and I swear to God Mark had it all without any show of effort. He once told me, said he didn't understand life—people working so hard to get someplace. To him, it just came. He told me if he had to work he'd probably fail at everything, but it just wasn't that tough for him—you believe that? And there was no arrogance about it, that was just who he was, some guy that everything broke for the right way.

"And I mean *everything*. Brains, looks, personality, talent, even luck—everything. I should have hated his guts. But a guy like that thinks *you're* his best friend, thinks *you're* cool, and that's the way it stays your whole life? Guess what? You figure in this one way maybe you've grabbed a little of his luck—for some reason, the gods like you too. You take it—figure it doesn't have anything really to do with you. Greater forces are at work.

"So we go through life, Mark and Wes. We play ball together—he's shortstop and I'm second base. We go to the Babe Ruth World Series together and damn if he doesn't win the thing with a home run in the bottom of the seventh . . . and who's on base in front of him? *Moi.* A sweet moment."

He paused, scratching Bart absently. One of his feet was curled under him and Melanie thought that, in spite of the gray field of stubble, the long unkempt hair, he suddenly looked younger. He smiled, embarrassed. Perhaps there was something in Kevin choosing him as his friend.

"Anyway," he went on, "Mark went to Stanford and I went to Cal, but we stayed close. He met Sheila, and Lydia and I got together—thank God we didn't go for the same type of women, never did—and we both started law school in the same boat down in LA—pregnant wives, living if you can believe it on the same street in Westwood. It was a good life in spite of no money . . . LA in the seventies." He did the first few bars of "I Am, I Said," got to the feeling being lay-back, and raised his eyebrows.

"Naturally, Mark doesn't crack a book and somehow is law review and clerking with the majors and I'm living at the library pulling B's. This story too long?"

"No."

"So after law school he gets on the partner track here in the city starting in the high thirties. This is 'seventy-five or so, remember, and that was a ton of money then. I hang up a shingle and start hauling it in in the large hundreds doing low-rung criminal stuff. But that's okay. It's Mark and me, it's who we are. No sweat. We're still best friends. We've got kids the same age—baseball and soccer—we play bridge with our wives and the families do stuff together all the time. It's like we're all one family. My kids call him Uncle Mark and I'm Uncle Wes. It was nice, it was perfect, like everything with Mark. We both eventually wind up back here in the city, and even if he's in St. Francis Wood and we're up the Richmond—so what? We're all happy, what's the problem?"

"So what happened?"

"Well, wait, there's one other thing." Wes stood, stretched, went to the salon's small refrigerator and took out two bottles. He twisted the top off a Mickey's Big Mouth and gave it to Melanie, who took it without thought. She couldn't remember any time she'd had beer in the afternoon. Well, first time for everything . . .

Wes was back down, half-turned to her, one bare foot curled under him. "There was the law. I don't think it's the law as you or Kevin think of it. Or too many other people. Maybe only me."

"And Mark?"

He chuckled, and it seemed to her both brittle and bitter. "And Mark, of course. You work in it long enough and I suppose it gets like anything else. You burn out, get cynical. But Mark and I . . . and this goes back to early high school, maybe before that . . . I don't know what started it, but we got into this, this *attitude*. It was like a deal between us." He sipped his beer, taking a minute, then added, "No, that's not nearly it. It was more a sacred pact."

"What was it?"

"It was that we wouldn't lose faith. That sounds stupid—"

"No, it doesn't."

"Yes, it does, believe me. We saw it happening with everybody around us in the law—how the hours would eat you up, the clients who lied or who were just plain guilty, the crap you had to put up with to survive.

"But Mark and I stuck to our pact. He had this . . . this *vision* . . . don't laugh . . . that life had to mean something. That that's what made people successful—not what they did but how they did it, how they felt about it, that they didn't stop trying. And we're not just talking monetary success here—no, this was Mark Dooher, this was Life Success, What It Was All About, The Big Picture. So twice, three times a year, I don't know, one of us would get down on the whole thing and we'd take this retreat—go fishing, whatever—reaffirm, get back to What Counted . . ."

Melanie was sitting forward, entranced. "Everybody should do that."

"You're right. It was great. It worked."

"So?"

Wes let out a long breath. "So one night three years ago—both of our youngest kids had just moved out—a burglar breaks into Mark's house, rapes his wife and stabs her to death."

Melanie's beer stopped halfway to her open mouth.

"And after about four months, *Mark* is charged with the murder."

The bottle, untouched, was back in her lap. She was tempted to ask if Wes was kidding her. It seemed the only thing possible. But she knew he was not. This had happened, and as the truth and portent of it began to sink in, she muttered, "Oh my God."

"No kidding."

"He didn't do it, did he?"

"Get real. This is Mark Dooher, senior partner in his law firm, major philanthropist, dedicated family man. Give me a break. But he got charged. It was, I thought, an extremely weak case, *all* circumstantial. His fingerprints were on the knife—but he was the cook in the family, *of course* his fingerprints are on the knife. Could be his blood type from the sperm samples—right, him and a thousand other guys. But no solid alibi—he'd been out late driving golf balls at Lincoln. Mark and Sheila had just raised their insurance, stuff like that. And he asked me to defend him. And of course I did."

"And?"

"And I won. Fight of my life, case of my life. And I won it. Got out of the trenches. Mark was megahigh profile, put me on the map. Got two murder referrals in the next year and it looked like I was going to start making some money."

Melanie nodded. "But he did it, didn't he?"

He blinked back the dim shine in his eyes. His voice thick, he had to begin twice. "The . . . the son of a bitch . . . the son of a bitch *told* me, said he didn't want *the fact that he had killed his wife* to get between us, we were still . . ."

He wiped a hand over one eye, swore.

"So that's why," she said finally.

He nodded. "Yeah, that's why."

37

After the speech and its aftermath—the supervisors unanimously recommended the two hundred thousand dollar reward for Kevin Shea—Mayor Aiken thought his post-lunch meeting with Philip Mohandas would be smooth sailing, a photo op. Black leader, white leader, solidarity, ya ya ya.

He was wrong.

Mohandas, accompanied by his bodyguards Allicey Tobain and Jonas N'doum, were lounging in his outer office, having either intimidated or flattered Donald to get in. So at the outset, to Aiken, there was an odd dynamic—his natural turf had been usurped. Wondering where Donald had gone, he stopped in his doorway.

"Mr. Mohandas." Recovering, smiling, striding forward, his hand outstretched. "Good to meet you in person at last."

Aiken's eyes took in Mohandas's two aides, but they stayed seated, apparently awaiting instructions. Mohandas was not here to be friends. He got right down to it. "Mr. Mayor, I'm here speaking to you only because our mutual friend, Senator Wager, asked me to be. I'm frankly appalled at this city's official response to the situation we're now all facing."

Aiken, moving around behind his desk, felt the heat rising in his face. "Well, sir, we've just gone a long way toward addressing that. The city's official response so far, besides trying to keep itself from burning down, has been to raise the reward on Kevin Shea. No doubt you've heard . . ."

"No doubt *you've* heard, Jerohm Reese is back in jail, and Kevin Shea isn't. That's the reality *I'm* seeing. I'm

seeing a white man, a murderer, walking the streets and an
innocent black man being held in jail for no reason."

"Kevin Shea isn't exactly walking the streets—"

"How do you know that?"

Aiken didn't, of course. These were bad cards and he
didn't want to play them. "In any event, Jerohm Reese is
not an *innocent* black man, either. Not as I understand it."

"He's no more guilty than five hundred people you let
go with tickets—"

"Which doesn't mean he isn't guilty, does it?"

"We're all guilty of something, Mr. Mayor. What it *seems*
is that Jerohm is not getting the same treatment as white
folk. It means you got a bigot acting now as DA and he
saw his chance—"

"Art Drysdale's no bigot."

Mohandas took that for a beat, turned on a heel and spoke
to Allicey and Jonas over his shoulder. "This man don't want
to help." His people rising, Mohandas was halfway to the
doorway, and Aiken was half-tempted to let him go.

But if he did it would be worse.

"Mr. Mohandas. Wait a minute." He came around the
desk. Mohandas stood impatiently by the door. "What
would help? I don't want to argue small points with you, I
want to help. I thought I'd done something very helpful
this morning with the supervisors. Perhaps it wasn't enough.
You tell me."

There was a quick gleam of triumph in Allicey's eyes,
just as quickly quashed. Mohandas saw it, though, and let
go of the doorknob. "Alan Reston," he said.

"Who?"

"Alan Reston. The deputy state attorney general. San
Francisco born and bred. Former prosecutor in Alameda
County. I've spoken to him this morning. He is available."

"Available for what?"

"Appointment to District Attorney." The mayor was too
stunned to respond. Mohandas breezed right on. "Alan
Reston has the credentials, the expertise and the political
acumen to help pull us through this difficult time. And"—
Mohandas shot a finger for effect—"the fact that he is an
African-American will go a long way to balance the lack
of minority representation in city government that has been
created here with the death of Chris Locke."

Suddenly Allicey Tobain stepped forward, her imposing presence dwarfing the mayor. "Sir," she said mildly, "appointing Mr. Reston at this time would not just be a gesture. It would have real meaning. It would demonstrate that the city is with us in a tangible way. And I'm sure that the community would respond in a similar fashion."

She didn't have to say, "Votes"—Aiken heard her.

But the mayor was not stupid—he understood that if you appeased too much you antagonized everyone else. He didn't know what precise position this woman enjoyed with Mohandas, but she was obviously in his inner circle, and Aiken felt he could talk her language. He looked up at her, smiling, appreciating the view.

"I'm sorry, I don't believe we've met."

She extended her fine hand. "Allicey Tobain, sir." Turning to Mohandas, she said, "I apologize for speaking up, Philip." But clearly her role had been discussed, maybe even rehearsed.

Mohandas smiled. "Allicey and Jonas"—he acknowledged the other man—"they keep me on the pulse." D'houm's face was a stone mask, but Allicey was flushed with the compliment.

Aiken spoke to her. "I know of Reston, of course. But bringing him on for the express purpose of releasing Jerohm Reese is not going to fly."

Mohandas glanced at Tobain—for approval, direction? She nodded, almost imperceptibly, and he said, "That would, of course, be the District Attorney's decision."

But Aiken wasn't giving away the store without a guarantee or two. "Once he got to be District Attorney, yes. And whomever I chose would need to reconcile himself with Mr. Drysdale."

Mohandas nodded. "I know Alan Reston and I know he'll do what's best for the city."

The mayor nodded back. "I'd be interested to hear what his plans would be," he said.

Allicey Ibbain stepped even closer. "May I use your phone, sir? I know where he is right now."

38

Loretta Wager was alone at home.

After the events of the day before, it would be unseemly of her to be out on the streets. She also wanted to make herself available to Abe Glitsky, in either his professional role or personally. This was no time to lose track of her priorities.

For all the comments she had heard making light of it the first day she'd been out here, she was in fact glad of her decision not to have brought any of her staff with her. They had important work in Washington, and there was too much she had to do here on her own—this was one of those times when her actions didn't need any "spin."

She was doing what needed to be done.

She was awake early, her mind filled with Abe Glitsky. She had wanted—needed—to call him before he went in to work. Then she was on one of her phones to her Washington office. On the private line the other calls had been steadily coming in: Donald from the mayor's office had called. The wire services. Alan Reston and Philip Mohandas. The whole world wanted her. Well, it would have to wait. She in turn waited until she thought Elaine would be downtown, then called her.

Her poor daughter was suffering badly, but that would pass. Suffering passed—she knew that from her own experience. She wanted to tell her—though of course never could—that she was much better off, that Chris Locke never intended to leave his wife and children, ever—not for Elaine, not for anybody. Loretta made it her business to know things, and this she knew with a certainty.

And then Elaine—the only truly precious thing in Loretta's world—her beautiful and sensitive daughter Elaine would find her spirit broken. She'd become what her mother was.

God knew, Loretta had made enough compromises in her life, but the one constant had always been preserving Elaine's—what was the word?—innocence? Idealism?

Loretta had lost hers long ago, maybe even before her four days in the Colombian jungle, thinking she was going to spend eternity there, clutching a suitcase full of the dollars that the Colombian businessman on the plane had carried aboard as hand baggage, contemplating the money's uselessness to her, living day and night with the lizards and bugs and the decomposing bodies of five dead men. Now she was a pragmatist, what counted was what worked. She was a woman of stature and accomplishment, but the idealist she had once been—back, say, when she had been with Abe Glitsky in college—that person was gone forever. And God, how she missed her! How she wished she could return! But, of course, that was life, wasn't it? The taking of one road that foreclosed the possibility of taking any of the others . . .

Well, now that part of it might not happen to Elaine. At least not because of Christopher Locke. It was a shame that it had to happen, but it wasn't the end of the world—her daughter *would* get over it.

She wished she felt worse about Locke, a powerful black leader cut down in his prime. But on the other hand, he had lived his allotted time and his death was going to save her daughter from a terrible trauma, whether she realized it now or not.

At first she thought Mohandas was expending useless energy on the Jerohm Reese matter, but on reflection realized that her daughter had unknowingly delivered a trump to their hands, and Mohandas was holding it. The problem was that Loretta wasn't sure Mohandas knew how to play it for best effect. So she was going to do it for him and then tell him what she had done. And in exchange for . . .

Well, there was always that—Philip would have to be made to see that he'd have to deliver, too. Nothing was for free.

The passage of the increased reward on Shea was a sign

that things were going her way. Once the river of appease-
ment started flowing, it tended to take on a life of its own.
Even better was the fact that the mayor had come to focus
on Philip Mohandas as the symbol of the outraged black
community. It was a reaction she had helped engineer; she
was playing Philip in her own game of chess.

But she had to remind herself not to underestimate the
man—he was no mere pawn. In calmer times she knew that
Mohandas managed to retain only a small following in the
voting community. But when flare-ups occurred, when the
general perception got to be that the essence of American
black life itself was under threat from the white majority,
even moderate blacks—her constituents—flocked to him in
large numbers, significant numbers.

The blinds were drawn throughout the house. Dressed in
a black woolen outfit suitable for mourning, Loretta sat
at a cherry secretary in her small office at the back, looking out and down to the Presidio, the decommissioned
army base that had recently been converted to a national park.

The last place of decommissioned and deserted prime
real estate in San Francisco was the Hunter's Point Naval
Reservation, and, waiting for Abe Glitsky's arrival, Loretta
was putting in more phone time to Washington. Her idea
had been percolating for months, and she had been patiently waiting for the time to set it in motion. And now
that time had come. Whatever the outcome of this crisis,
she was confident that her plan would deliver her nearly
every African-American vote in the Bay Area.

He arrived in another unmarked Plymouth, parking in the
circular driveway by the front door. Nervous, he had called
fifteen minutes before from downtown, and she had been
waiting for him, watching his car pull up, then the man
himself get out, stretch his back, catch her looking in the
window and break a small smile, knowing.

"The last thing I want to do is argue with you."
    Somehow, an hour had passed.
    Glitsky, dressed again, sat with her at her breakfast nook,

drinking a mug of Constant Comment tea with extra lemon. There was an island separating the nook from the kitchen, and, her bare feet swinging slightly, Loretta sat up on it, wearing her dark skirt and blouse.

"Disagreeing isn't arguing."

"Come visit the Senate sometime. The two are kissin' cousins, sometimes twins."

"Not now."

"All right, not now." She slipped off the island, pulled a chair up next to him. "But right at this minute, I don't even want to disagree, okay?"

She was right there, next to him, and he was surprised that she seemed almost timid, afraid to touch him now that the fires had been banked for a while. To some degree, he found himself relieved about it. He couldn't say why, but a casual touch from her—right at this moment—would have struck him as inappropriate, something she might do with almost anyone to drive home a point. He didn't want her to use that trick. Or any trick.

But, this close, he had to touch her. He reached a hand out and rested it on her forearm. "My agenda is different than yours, Loretta, that's all I'm saying. Your job is politics. Mine is homicide. I want to find who killed Arthur Wade."

She spoke quietly. "We know who did that, Abe. We've got a picture of it."

"I'm not denying Kevin Shea—"

"Then you've got to get comfortable with us using him . . ."

"But we know for a fact that there were others, we don't know if Shea was the leader of anything, what he was doing there at all."

"I think it's clear he was doing enough."

Glitsky was silent.

"Abe, listen. Doesn't this make sense if you think about it? Forget police procedures. You've said my job is politics, and this is political. It's trying to get to some consensus, get people thinking some solution—it almost doesn't matter which one—is going to *work*. To stop this thing before it destroys the whole city, maybe the country."

Glitsky swallowed some tea. "And you honestly think arresting Kevin Shea . . . ?"

"I think *as a symbol,* that could end it, yes."

Glitsky searched her eyes and discovered something he recognized as crucial—at least Loretta believed it.

"So what about Jerohm?"

Loretta sighed. "That might be a blessing in disguise if we can get the right spin on it."

Glitsky, a thin humor. "I don't know from spin . . ."

"Jerohm appeases the angry whites, Kevin appeases our angry brothers and sisters . . ."

"Half brothers and sisters," Glitsky corrected her, "if you want to get technical."

Loretta took that in. "One drop of blood," she said.

"What's that?"

"That's the law of our land, Abe. If you've got one drop of black blood, you're black."

"If you say so . . ." But he didn't want to fight, he didn't want to have a *discussion.* He was moving his hand up and down her arm, and she leaned her head down and kissed it. "You know," he said, "it may be different with the people you deal with, but I don't think about my color all the time, about where *we're* going as a *people* . . . it's more everybody, the world . . ."

"Going down the tubes together?"

"Fast enough. And choosing up sides over who we're gonna hate doesn't seem to be making it any better."

"Why, Abe Glitsky, you're still an idealist, aren't you, in that heart of yours?" He had to laugh . . . he considered himself the greatest skeptic he knew. She moved up, closer to him. "Maybe it'll get better."

"Does it seem like it's getting better?" he asked.

"On any given day, maybe not. Today, certainly not. But sometimes . . . sometimes . . . I mean, somebody like me, twenty years ago a black woman is not a U.S. senator. I've got to think that in the long view things have changed for the better. It must mean something."

"It might mean that people believe you, Loretta. It might be just you, who you are, what you give people."

This brought her up short. She bit her lip, straightening, then put her arm around Glitsky and held herself against him. "How did I ever let you go?" she whispered.

*   *   *

He got beeped and found that his father had succeeded in cajoling Rabbi Blume's reluctant witness to the riot—Rachel from one of the former Soviet republics—into talking to him. He wasn't fifteen blocks away, he could be there in ten minutes.

At the door he told Loretta that he wasn't going to get in her way over Kevin Shea. That was her bailiwick. It wasn't his habit, and it wasn't in his job description, to go public with his investigations. Actually he had few if any substantive doubts about Shea's involvement. But he did want to get the whole picture, a verifiable sequence of events so that when the time came any charges brought against Shea would stick.

"And you know," he said finally, "you might want to talk to your daughter."

"What about Elaine?"

"From her perspective what counts is to prove Shea guilty. If we arrest him and she can't prove he did it, she's going to take the fall for it. If I were you, that would be a concern right now. That she gets it right."

Glitsky was starting to walk to his car but Loretta held his arm. "Abe?"

He stopped.

"Would you help her, too? Not let her get hurt?"

He nodded. "I'll try," he said. "It's my job."

39

What Glitsky's father Nat had not told him was that he had picked up the boys—all three of them—and was taking them first out to Tommy's Joynt for sandwiches and then down the coast, maybe to Monterey, where there weren't any riots, to see the Aquarium, do something constructive with their summer.

It was ridiculous to keep them cooped up in the house all day every day. What did Abe think he was doing, being a good father?

"I'm trying to protect them, Dad. I don't want them hurt."

Father and son were in Rabbi's Blume's office, the boys visible outside the window shooting some hoops in the synagogue's playground, which was otherwise deserted. Blume and Rachel were waiting in the attached residence, and Abe was not in any hurry to see them until this got settled with his father, who was not exactly breaking down in the face of his son's wrath—"What's going to hurt them, tell me that?"

"How can you even ask that? You look around lately? You see what's happening?"

Nat Glitsky shrugged. "I drove downtown to see you. I drove back to Rachel's. We walk together here, on the street, from her house. Nobody bothers us. Nobody's out."

"You might want to ask yourself why that is."

"I know why that is, Abraham. Sit down, would you? You're overreacting."

"I don't want to sit down. I'm not overreacting! These are *my* children and *my* responsibility and I'm not exposing them to . . . to this. I'm not going to lose any more of my family."

In spite of saying he didn't want to, Abe sat heavily. Nat hesitated by the rabbi's desk, then walked across the room and pulled up a chair next to his son.

"You can lose them this way, too. Holding on too tight, Abraham."

"I'm trying to protect them, I'm trying to do what's best."

Nat nodded. "Always. I know this. But I called this morning, trying to get you, and Jake answers the phone. I never hear him talk about you like this . . . 'Dad's losing it, Pops. He doesn't have a clue.' This kind of talk. And from Jacob, who you know worships the ground under you. It worries me."

"It worries *you* . . . ?" Glitsky barked a laugh, cut short.

"I know, I know, it worries you, too. Hey, who doesn't worry a little? And you, since Flo . . ."

"It's not *me*." His voice was sharp. "It's not *my* fault this is going on here. And it's not about Flo. It's me and them. Flo's not part of this."

Nat put a hand on his son's knee. "Flo is the whole thing, Abraham. Don't be kidding yourself."

"That's bullshit, Dad." Then more strongly, "That's pure *bullshit*!" He swatted the hand away, standing, striding across to the window, breathing hard, his face set.

"I think this is the first time you swear at your old man, hunh?"

Abe tried to focus on his sons, the game outside. They were doing precision drills, the two older boys taking rebounds and feeding layup shots in to Orel. The patter was barely audible, though clearly loose and playful. "I can't lose any more, Dad. I can't."

Again, Nat crossed the room to his son. He stood behind Abe, much shorter, seeing the boys outside. "We cannot hold on to anything, Abraham. It is not in our power and that is God's truth."

Glitsky turned. "All right, but what if—?"

Nat cut him off. "That is what you are thinking and it doesn't mean anything." Putting a hand on his son's arm, he went on. "Abraham, think. What if they are locked in at home all day and someone decides to start a fire on your street? This is not in your control, none of this. There is nothing you can do here except second-guess yourself to death. Let me take them. We go have some fun, come back when this is over."

Glitsky's shoulders slumped as he let himself down onto the corner of the desk. "When's life going to start feeling real again, Dad? I don't know what the hell I'm doing."

"I know. When Emma . . . well, you remember."

"You never changed."

A short laugh. "Abraham, I don't think I ever changed *back*. What I tried not to do was change how I treated you, how I acted. I kept up the motions, the habits, so how I was feeling wouldn't affect you, that's all. You had lost your mother. That was enough for you to deal with."

Glitsky motioned outside. "Like them now. That's the message, right?"

His father nodded. "There are similarities. So now, you do your job, you keep at it, things get to feel normal in a new way maybe. It never does go back to the way it was. That's over." He paused. "And that's the hard part to accept. It isn't going back. So what is it going to be now?"

Glitsky brought a hand to his eyes and rubbed them. He stood again, walked a few steps, looked outside. "If you go to Monterey, stop by the pier and pick me up some saltwater taffy, would you? I love that stuff."

40

"You guys again?"

Ridley Banks stood grinning on Peter McKay's stoop. "You know, Peter, you're hurting my feelings, that kind of talk. This is my partner, Marcel Lanier. Say you're glad to meet him, would you? He's sensitive."

"Yeah, glad to meet you."

Banks turned half-around. "What did I tell you? You ask nice, you get a response. This is the kind of witness we should get to interview every day, make life sweet. What do you say?"

"What do you guys want this time?"

"We want to talk to you a couple of minutes, discuss your statement of the other day . . ."

"Who's that, Petey?" A young woman with lank blond hair appeared behind McKay in the doorway. A worn, flesh-colored tank top barely concealed boyish breasts. Skinny white legs under cutoff jeans, white socks and tennis shoes.

"Oh, excuse us," Banks said. "I didn't realize you were entertaining."

McKay backed up a step. "This is my wife, Patsy."

"Your wife? I didn't know . . . how do you do, ma'am? How's the arm, by the way, Pete?"

McKay twisted his wrist, flexed his fingers. He was wearing a flannel shirt with long sleeves. "Better every day," he said.

"Bandage off?"

"Not yet. Couple more days."

"Is Petey in trouble?" Patsy asked. She had a smoker's voice. She'd moved forward a step into the light—Banks didn't think she looked fifteen. But, he noticed, there was a gold band on her finger.

"No, ma'am, not now. We're just double-checking a few things he said last time he talked to us."

"Like what?" She got in front of her husband.

Marcel Lanier spoke from behind Banks, over his shoulder. "Like how he hurt his arm, for example?"

"He cut it on a door," she said. "The glass broke."

"Well, that's what he told us." Marcel was jockeying for position on the stoop, stepping up now behind Banks. "But the thing is, we went back—well, actually, my partner Ridley here did—he is some kind of thorough, kind of like Colombo, remember him? Always that 'Uh, just one more thing.' Drives us all crazy sometimes but there you go. Anyway, how the arm got cut . . . You mind if we come in? It is definitely not warm, and you look a little chilly yourself."

Accompanied as it was by a glance downward, Lanier was being more antagonistic than he sounded—Patsy McKay's nipples were protruding like gumdrops, poking at the thin fabric of the tank top.

"Why don't you go put on a shirt, hon," McKay said. "You guys got a warrant or we can talk right here. What about my arm?"

But Patsy didn't leave, so Banks spoke over her. "About your arm is that your cousin Brandon Mullen said you both cut yours falling through your sliding back door and when I was by here yesterday I happened to notice that the door isn't broken. You get it fixed right up? Got a receipt for the repair?"

But Patsy was shaking her head. "That was at Brandon's, not here."

Banks half-turned, glanced at Lanier. "Brandon said clear as a bell that you both came back here to have your own private wake for Mike Mullen. To Petey's, is what he said."

McKay moved forward. "First—"

"Shh." Patsy held a hand out, spoke gently but firmly to her husband. "Hush now." Back to the inspectors: "I had a bad headache. They kept waking me up so I asked them to please go over to Brandon's, which is what they did."

Banks begged to differ. "Brandon said they came here."

"They came here *first*. Then they went there. Why don't

you go ask him again? We'll even go over there with you. Petey didn't do nothing wrong. We got nothing to hide."

Brandon Mullen was home and acted for all the world as though he had been expecting them. He lived in a lower duplex on 22nd Avenue in the Richmond District, five blocks from the McKays. The sliding glass doors that led to his tiny patio were brand-new. And why, yes, Inspectors, he did just happen to have a receipt right here for it—two days ago, isn't that right, signed and all? Reardon Glass and Screen.

"I'm going to go bust some chops."

"Can't do it, Rid."

They were sitting outside of Brandon Mullen's place, waiting—for nothing. Marcel had the driver's-side window down, his elbow on it. "McKay told Brandon about you coming by his house. Somebody put it together about the window."

"The wife."

"Maybe. Anyway, they figured they better break *some* window."

"I already figured that out. Thanks."

"You want to go talk to Reardon of Reardon Glass and whatever the fuck else it is?"

"See if he made the repair yesterday or two days ago, the date on the invoice? No. I don't think he'd be honest with us."

"I'm shocked. A good Irish Catholic boy?"

"Welcome to police work," Banks said. "Shocks abound."

Working by himself, Carl Griffin took another tack.

He knew he wasn't going to get squatola from any of the other good ol' boys—O'Toole, Mullen, McKay, Shea—the black Irish pulling close 'round their own men.

His first thought had been to try the emergency rooms at the various local hospitals, but one or two calls had disabused him of that notion—with the city's upheavals, the emergency rooms were, if anything, more swamped than the Hall of Justice, and there weren't many people with the time, inclination or memory to be of much help.

So—methodically, doggedly—he started cross-working a map and a telephone book, phoning every private doctor's office within a two-mile radius of the Cavern Tavern, identifying himself as a homicide inspector and asking if any of the doctors had seen anything remotely resembling a knife wound during the last three days.

Doctors' records were not protected by the evidence code in criminal investigations. In fact, in some cases—such as incidents with gunshot wounds or sexual assaults—doctors were mandated to report to authorities.

It was at the tail end of an eggplant parmigiana submarine sandwich. Griffin had parked his beefy frame at his desk in the Homicide detail. Leaning back, the heels of his black brogues on the pitted desk, he balefully contemplated the new jail, the slice of clouds and blue above. He was on "E." Flipping the pages labelled "Physicians," he realized he had another five pages to go.

This was Carl Griffin's brand of police work—you did it by the numbers, you were not inspired, you slogged it out, and eventually, if you covered everything, once in a while you hit it. He considered going to the end of the listings and started backward from "Z." But then, he knew, the one he'd left off on at "E" would turn out to be the jackpot. So he dialed the number for "Epps."

Miss Manners would have disapproved of the last bite he took of his sandwich. The telephone was ringing in his ear and when it picked up he had to swallow without chewing and for a fleeting instant thought it wasn't going to go down, that this was his last moment.

"Hello, doctor's office," the voice repeated.

He swallowed again—saved—and cleared his throat. It turned out that Dr. Epps was having her own lunch in the coffee room and she listened without speaking while he gave his spiel. "Since when was this?" she asked when he had finished.

"Tuesday night."

"Just a minute."

Griffin was suddenly elated he hadn't jumped to "Z." She was back on the line. "I had a rather severe Achilles tendon slash that I sewed up on Wednesday morning. The patient was a young man who said he'd gotten tripped up, then fallen over a shovel in his backyard, one of those freak accidents, but I don't think it was a shovel . . ."

Griffin waited.

"The wound looked like a suture cut—clean and straight."

"I see. And did you mention this to him?"

"I asked about it, yes. But he said, no, it was a shovel. Brand-new, never used, edge like a knife. He didn't blink and I guessed it was possible. I sewed it up."

"How old was the man?"

"Just a second. Colin Devlin. Twenty-four. Do you want his address?"

41

The waiting area of the bowels of the San Francisco morgue, on the other side of the heavy door that leads to the examination room, was drab and windowless. Plastic yellow chairs, sagging with age and perhaps the accumulation of grief, hugged the shiny light green walls. The two plastic rubber trees no longer looked remotely real, but no one had removed them, no one had noticed. The people in this room were thinking of other matters.

As the assistant district attorney handling the Arthur Wade homicide, Elaine Wager had been called down to the morgue by John Strout, San Francisco's coroner, to go over the forensic report, which, due to the crushing workload over the recent days, had been a little slower coming than usual.

Knees pressed together, hands clasped in her lap, Elaine waited in the anteroom. Strout had told her when he had called upstairs that it would be at least an hour, but she had picked up her folders and gone down immediately, content to be in hiding.

She had spent a good deal of time in the morning fighting herself, keeping busy doing background work on her suspect—his friends, workplace, history. Anything to avoid thinking of Chris, of what had happened . . . The police had forwarded to her the name of the woman who had provided Kevin Shea's name in the first place—Cynthia Taylor—and while she had picked up very little in the way of evidence that would be useful in court, the picture of the man had begun to emerge.

According to Ms. Taylor, Shea was a half-step up from white trash. He came from a broken family somewhere down south (which fitted perfectly with what he'd done, she thought). He was one of those hangers-on at SFSU, drifting from class to class, drunk a lot of the time. Though Ms. Taylor believed he worked part-time in some kind of telemarketing ("No way could he hold a real job"), he also bragged about using the GI Bill to buy his booze, didn't have any friends to speak of, although he'd had a relationship with one of Ms. Taylor's friends for a couple of months, and now appeared to have hoodwinked that hapless victim into becoming his accomplice in escaping. Ms. Taylor had ended the interview with the statement that she thought he was "really dangerous, unstable. You never know what he's going to do."

And then the coroner had called, and Elaine realized that she had had enough. The walls were closing in. She needed time to let her emotions flow, to be alone. The room outside Strout's lab gave her that opportunity.

Suddenly—any movement in the dead room appeared sudden—the big door swung open and Strout's lanky form was pulling up a chair next to hers. Strout had a strong deep-South accent and no enemies on the police force or in the DA's office. A true professional, he lived for his forensics. He also had a sly humor and a skeptical eye that had many times discovered a homicide in what at first appeared, even to the police, to be an accidental or benign death.

"I'm gettin' real tired of lookin' at dead people," he drawled. He had his latest ME forms on a clipboard that he held on his lap. "Couple of days seems to be my limit. Get up to four, five, gives me a sour stomach."

Elaine didn't react. This was how Strout always was. It wasn't personal. "Is that Arthur Wade?" she asked, motioning to the clipboard.

He nodded, enough with amenities. "No surprises, not that I expected any. Cause of death was asphyxiation, which you'd expect gettin' pulled up—must have taken some minutes. Poor man. Long time to hang. Hey, let me get you some water."

"No, I'm all right."

But she found herself resting her head back against the wall, closing her eyes. This was too much. She couldn't sit and listen to someone talk about Arthur Wade hanging for a long time like this—at Boalt, Arthur had seemed to be one of those wonderful people, not that she'd known him all that well. And now, four years later, his future was the past and that was all.

And Chris Locke . . . no, don't start, she told herself. Don't open that up.

More time had gone by. Strout was back with lukewarm water in a paper cup. "Y'all want to lay down a minute, there's a couch in my office?"

But she couldn't help herself. "Chris Locke is in there, isn't he?"

"Yes, ma'am." Strout sucked some air between his front teeth. "Sometimes . . ." His voice, with a sudden guttural quality, trailed off.

She put a hand on his knee, took it away. "I know."

Back in her cubicle—ancient desk, stacks of files, smell of paper and dust—she closed the door behind her. Since an hour ago when she'd left to go to the morgue, someone had come by and dropped a large yellow envelope in the center of the desk. She sat, dropped her Arthur Wade files on the floor by her feet and opened the envelope.

It was another copy of the original Paul Westberg photo that was in the newspapers and everywhere else. But then, about to slip it back into the envelope and throw the whole thing into the file folder, she stopped. Something had caught her eye and she pulled the photo all the way out.

With everything that had happened since then, she had forgotten that she'd asked the photographer—a request, not a demand—to send her the other picture that he had developed. Which he had now done.

It was very close, as Westberg had said, and he had been right, too, that the likeness of Kevin Shea was a little better in the picture everybody had seen. It was obvious why he had gone with the one and not the other.

But there was something strange about the second one. She picked up the file folder, dug for the first picture, and held them side by side. She was struck by one detail—in the second photo Arthur Wade was clearly holding the knife that, in the other picture, was in Kevin Shea's hand.

Well, so what?

Lots of people—professionals even—carried small knives in their pockets. She herself had a penknife in her purse.

She closed her eyes, trying to imagine the moment, the threatening crowd, Shea in the center of it, deciding—now that Arthur was hanging and helpless—that he would take a stab at him as well, put a knife in his ribs, and Arthur had somehow managed to see it, to reach down with one hand, grab for it, a last moment of struggle, captured here in Westberg's photo.

Or another explanation—weaker but, she considered, still possible. Arthur had somehow managed to pull a knife of his own before they had lifted him from the ground, realizing he'd have to try to cut the rope. It would be his last chance to survive. And then Shea, reaching up, had grabbed it from him, wresting it away. It didn't change any of the basic facts of what had happened—in fact, it made the picture clearer.

But something else.

And it came on her in a wave, a revulsion that nearly doubled her over, then straightened her back up with rage. There was Kevin Shea, grimacing with the efforts to pull down on her old classmate, setting off the chain of events that had killed Chris Locke, her boss, her lover . . .

It was intolerable that this man—this bigoted Southern schoolboy—was still at large. Her mother was right—so were the supervisors, the mayor, even Philip Mohandas. One man *was* responsible for all this. It may have been a mob, but this *one man* had led it. This *one man* had driven the city to its knees—and he had to be taken. He had to be taken now. The madness wouldn't stop until he was. He had to be found.

Elaine pushed out from her desk. She had to make people see this, she had to make them hate Shea for what he'd done the way she hated him.

There were procedures and there were levels of hierarchy, but she also knew who she was. She could go outside channels, direct to the people. Art Drysdale might reprimand her but the reprimand would have no teeth. No one would dare touch her.

*   *   *

The city provided the media with two rooms—one for print and one for radio and television—on the third floor of the Hall of Justice, both of them just outside the frosted doors that led down the hallway to the District Attorney's office. Both of these were now full to overflowing, with tables set up in the hall—coffee containers, donuts, half-eaten sandwiches.

Over the past days Elaine and most of the other assistant district attorneys had avoided this hallway in an effort to skirt the schools of piranha journalists who had been in a perpetual feeding frenzy over any scraps that fell into their waters. She had ascended and descended by any of the several internal stairways that connected the floors of the Hall.

Now, her anger high and clear and overlaying the exhaustion in her face, she was hip-deep in the main hall, laying a trail of chum.

"I don't believe this."

"I do," Wes Farrell replied. He had not moved. He looked typically slob-like in his khaki shorts and his "On Strike From Major League Bull———" T-shirt, bare feet up on a milk crate, another can of beer in his hand, Bart's head in his lap.

They were all fixed on Elaine Wager's live interview. "This is how they do it. Get it on the tube, it becomes fact."

"How do they find out all this stuff?" Kevin whispered. Talking in his normal voice was painful. He couldn't shake the feeling that he was getting weaker rather than improving. His left arm had a constant throb, and at every breath his ribs pinched at him. When he had gotten up, the consensus had been that what he needed was a hot bath. He'd taken one but it had seemed to make everything hurt even worse.

He was drinking coffee. "What is she talking about, 'unstable'? 'Despondent over the death of his brother'? 'Liable to do anything'? Where does all this *come* from?"

Melanie was—force of habit—cleaning up in the room behind the men. She had already washed two loads of dishes and now was stacking the piles of newspapers, arranging the paperbacks in the brick-and-board bookcase in alphabetical order by author—she stopped moving for a moment.

"Cindy," she said. Then, to Wes: "One of Kevin's earlier conquests that didn't work out so well." But then she softened it, coming up behind Kevin, planting a kiss on the top of his head. "A lesson for us all."

On the tube, Elaine—indignant—was answering another question. "Well, the fact that he's gone this long without contacting the authorities argues compellingly that he has no reasonable defense. This office is proceeding on the assumption that he is dangerous . . ."

Slumped, Kevin said, "Yeah, a major threat."

". . . and I urge any citizen who thinks they have seen Mr. Shea to get in touch with the police or the District Attorney's office immediately."

Farrell was shaking his head. "Ah, the temperate voice of sweet reason . . ."

"I've got to go in," Kevin said.

"You've got to go in to *that*? Are you listening to this, Kevin? To what's happening out there?" Wes shook his head, finished his beer, number three. "We need to have ourselves a talk, you and me."

The image on the screen had changed, and Farrell pointed his remote and turned up the sound. A man with a forbidding countenance was standing on the steps outside the Hall of Justice, collar up against the wind, obviously not enjoying the camera or the microphones in his face.

The male voice-over was explaining that ". . . Lieutenant Abraham Glitsky, the chief of the homicide detail, apparently doesn't share Ms. Wager's certitude."

And then Glitsky, terse: "We continue to gather evidence. We're trying to get to the truth. That's all the comment I can give you."

Glitsky was trying to get by but the reporter was in front of him again. "What about Kevin Shea, Lieutenant? Shouldn't he be your focus? With the mayor's increased reward and the—?"

The camera closed in, and Glitsky said: "Shea's a suspect. We want to question him, get his story. The end."

"His story? But Ms. Wager says . . ."

"Ms. Wager is doing her job and I'm doing mine—collecting evidence."

"But don't you have evidence?"

"No comment."

"What about the picture?"

Glitsky appeared to consider his question. "Pictures are open to interpretation. Now if you'll let me . . ." Pushing the microphone away, he brushed by the reporter through the Hall's swinging doors.

At the cut to the commercial, Wes Farrell turned off the television. Scratching Bart's ears, he twirled his empty beer can on the arm of the futon and cursed.

"What?"

He turned to Kevin. "Glitsky." He gestured toward the TV. "That guy."

"What about him? You know him?"

"We've done some business."

Melanie came around in front of him. "So why does that bother you? He sounded to me like he wasn't sure . . ."

"You got it. That's what he sounded like."

Kevin sat up. "So what's the matter with that?"

"The matter with that," Wes replied, straightening up, "is it means we got a chance. We go to him, we might even get a listen."

"You mean you'll . . . ?" Melanie glanced at Kevin and he raised a hand, slowing her down.

The room went silent. Wes twirled his beer can some more.

"Does that mean you'll help?" Melanie asked.

Wes looked at Kevin. "Kevin, if it comes out you had *any* part in this, I'll kill you. I will personally kill you. I will hunt you down and kill you like a rabid animal, except slowly and painfully. Am I making myself clear?"

"I didn't," Kevin said.

Wes swore yet again, shook his head, tried his empty beer can. "You better not have."

42

Glitsky was studying the second photograph, asking some questions of his own. The homicide detail was empty. Blessed peace. There was a note from Carl Griffin that he had gone down to interview a potential knife-wound victim. Good. Glitsky's didn't have an alternative explanation yet for the cuts and bandages. But they were there and something had caused them. Perhaps it had been a knife. His father's friend Rachel had mentioned a knife. There was a knife in both pictures. Until he knew what had gone on with the knife he wouldn't have the whole picture, couldn't know for sure what had happened. So knowing would help. Knowledge always helped. No word yet from Banks or Lanier.

The telephone rang. "Homicide, Glitsky."

"Ashland, Hardy."

The lieutenant pushed his chair back, put his feet on the desk. His best friend, Dismas Hardy, was calling him back from Oregon. "I liked your message," the voice continued.

Glitsky's entire message had been "Hardy, call me."

"My favorite part was when you did that falsetto part from 'Duke of Earl.' A lot of old guys like you can't go that high anymore. I thought you were great."

Glitsky reached for his cup of tea and sipped. "You picked a good weekend to go away," he said. "How are things there?"

"In Ashland? Pretty good. *The Tempest* was awesome. The pinot noir's good, too. Oregon's nice. Frannie sends her love."

"You know that the world as we know it is ending down here?"

"I've heard rumors. It hasn't all gotten here yet." Then, more seriously, "How are *you* doing?"

"I get some time, I'll ask myself. You'll be the first to know. You hear about Locke?"

"I wondered if that was the silver lining we hear so much about." Hardy and Locke had been professional enemies. Locke had fired him from the District Attorney's office, and then Hardy had gone on to embarrass Locke by presenting successful defenses in a couple of high-profile murder cases that Locke had been prosecuting. So there was no love lost between them. "I'd be lying if I said the news broke my heart, but I didn't want the man dead, Abe. That's too close to home."

"I know, Diz. The thought had occurred to me. I sent the kids away with my dad."

"It's that bad?"

"I guess as long as we don't run out of water we'll survive. It feels like half the city's on fire. I'm trying to put 'em all out."

"You need some help? I mean personally. You okay?"

"I'm hangin' in. I've had better weeks."

"You let me know. Leave one of your scintillating messages. We'd come home if we had to."

"It's not getting to that."

"All right, but if it does . . ."

"I hear you. Thanks. Kiss your wife for me."

"Okay. Where?"

Glitsky found himself chuckling and didn't want to give Hardy the satisfaction, so he hung up.

During the past forty hours Chief Rigby's office had taken on the flavor of a war room. A couple of tables had been moved in and pushed together, and on top of them had been taped a large map of San Francisco. A half dozen staffers were moving around, pushing and pulling pins in various locations, answering the several ringing telephones.

Outside the windows there was a drift of smoke to the south through what Glitsky knew to be a cold-blowing thin haze of eye-burning smog. The afternoon sun broke through intermittently. Summertime, and the living was easy . . .

Rigby was standing behind his desk in serious conversation with Alan Reston, a man Glitsky knew slightly as a Sacramento politician with a formidable ambition. The deputy state attorney general had chaperoned Abe the couple of times he had gone up to the state capitol to talk to the legislature on some crime bill or other. Polished and well-spoken, he was about Glitsky's size and five years or more his junior. Now he was here in Rigby's office in a suit and tie. Glitsky had no idea what that meant, but he had been summoned here for a few minutes after he had gotten off the telephone with Dismas Hardy, and when he was summoned by Rigby he came.

Glitsky knocked at the open door, came around the double tables and over to his chief's desk. "Sir?" he said. Then, to Reston. "Alan."

"Abe, good," Rigby said. Reston barely nodded, which Abe thought was a little strange, but these were tense times. People weren't themselves. "Let's go on outside a minute where we can talk."

They paraded out in silence into the hallway, Rigby leading the way, Reston bringing up the rear, past a couple of doors to a deserted interview room. Without preamble Rigby was turned around facing Glitsky: "This is more in the nature of a friendly discussion than a reprimand, at least at this stage. I want you to understand that, Abe."

Glitsky swallowed. Friendly discussions that began this way weren't typically his favorite. Reston had moved up, and Rigby included him in his gaze. "I believe you know Mr. Reston, our new District Attorney."

"Sure, but I didn't know . . ." He put out his hand. "Congratulations, Alan." The handshake was perfunctory. Glitsky turned back to Rigby. "Is something wrong? What's this all about?"

"This is about the television news," Rigby replied. "Specifically, you being on it."

"But I wasn't—"

The chief stopped him with a hand. "Listen. I know. We saw it. We heard you. I've ordered a tape if you'd like to see it. You know we've got a community-relations person, Abe. Someone who gets paid to do this."

"I'm still not sure I know what I did."

Rigby told him. "You went public questioning our investigation, which is complete. The man's been indicted."

It took a minute to digest that. "With respect, sir, some reporter stuck a microphone in my face and I think I said maybe twenty words."

"Eighteen too many," Reston said.

"The District Attorney is correct," Rigby said, and Glitsky noticed the formal tone. Rigby, too, was being played here. Jobs must be at stake, including his own, the one he had worked his life to get to. Okay, then, if they wanted to do it that way. "The correct response," Rigby went on, "is no comment."

"I believe that was what I said." But Glitsky knew the truth—if you were accused like this, it was no-win. The more you denied that you'd done something wrong, the more it proved you had.

And Reston picked it up. "I know this comes across like we're a couple of hard-asses, Lieutenant." In Sacramento, Glitsky had always been Abe, Reston had always been Alan. Now, clearly, things had changed. "But there has been a great deal of effort expended on a lot of fronts trying to create a . . . a consistent direction in controlling this situation. We don't want to confuse and stir up things more than they already are."

"I'm not confused," Glitsky said. "I must be ignorant of some basic facts about the evidence we've got . . ."

"Facts aren't at issue right now," Rigby said.

"That's what I keep hearing. But I'd be interested to find out the District Attorney's position on that when he takes Kevin Shea to trial."

"By *then* we'll have all the facts . . ."

Glitsky wasn't going to escalate this. He needed his job, and he also felt he was doing it right. "Let's hope they're the right ones," he said mildly.

Reston seemed sure enough. Maybe he didn't want to fight either. Not yet. "They will be," he said.

His message delivered, Rigby had other business to attend to. "Just so it's clear, Abe. This whole thing is on a higher level than you or me. The public needs a . . ."

Glitsky helped him out. "A spin?"

"Exactly. A spin."

Reston smiled, and it seemed genuine enough. He put out his hand again, and this time it was firm. "I knew you'd understand, Abe. We just can't afford to mess with this. Shea is the villain here. We don't want to muddy the waters. Right now he is the best solution to this crisis. He did it. We get him . . . he *is* guilty . . . and the city can move on, start the healing process."

His face straight, Glitsky looked to his chief, then to the new district attorney. "You got it," he said to both of them. "No problem."

Next to John Strout in the chill air of the forensics lab, Glitsky was shivering. The body of the late Christopher Locke lay, mostly under a blanket, on a gurney in front of them, his head protruding. Strout put a gloved hand under it and raised it a couple of inches. "Back here," he said.

Glitsky forced himself to look. It was a small hole, clean and round, behind and a little under Locke's left ear. It might have been invisible had not Strout shaved the surrounding hair. He focused on the spot alone, trying not to see the face, trying not to recognize in it anyone he'd known, talked to, shared jokes with, even if he hadn't been all that fond of the man. He wasn't entirely successful.

"Anything funny?" he asked. "Anything you didn't expect?"

Strout shrugged. "Not really. Why?"

"No reason. Force of habit. Maybe I'm just getting in the mood for something funny."

"Yeah, I know what you mean." Strout let the head down gently but did not pull the blanket right up. Instead, turning it all the way to one side, so that the hole was up, he leaned over it. "Powder burns about what you'd expect, maybe a little heavy . . ."

"Glass?" At Strout's questioning look, Glitsky clarified it. "From the car window? Shards around the wound?"

The doctor shook his head. "Shatterproof. It's a city-issue car. I wouldn't expect many, although the microscopic ought to be done any hour now, tell us for sure. You getting at something?"

Glitsky set himself back, flat on his feet. "You know, John, I'm not getting at a damn thing. I don't know what I'm doing, just pulling at every straw I come across, see if maybe it's attached to something. Tell you the truth, I think I'm overworked lately. And seeing people I know dead doesn't seem to help any."

Strout straightened up, pulled the sheet up over Locke's face. "Y'all are sure gettin' that way," he drawled. "You think it's a little cold in here?"

He started leading the way out to his office, a large square room lined with bookshelves and well stocked with a variety of ancient and medieval instruments of torture displayed under glass. He stopped on the way to his desk to blow the dust off a spiked mace that graced a pedestal to the right of it. "One of the DAs was by this morning, handlin' the Arthur Wade thing. Poor girl was a mess."

"Elaine Wager?"

Strout nodded. "Started goin' into cause of death— asphyxiation—that whole thing, and she goes 'bout as white as her genes will allow." He allowed himself a small grin. "Manner of speakin', of course."

Glitsky nodded. "You find any knife wounds on Arthur Wade?"

Strout, by now seated behind his desk, took a moment. "Knife wounds? No. Rope burns, lacerations, cuts and scrapes, but nothing like a clean cut." He raised his eyes. "More straws?"

"Yep."

"You don't mind a little advice, Abe? Little prescription for some peace of mind?"

"Yep."

The coroner folded his hands. "Keep pullin' at 'em," he said. "You just never know."

"Homicide, Glitsky."

"Lieutenant Glitsky, this is Wes Farrell. I'm an attorney."

"Sure, Mr. Farrell, I know who you are. How can I help you?"

"I'd like to talk to you about Kevin Shea."

Glitsky was halfway out of his chair, snapping his fingers, trying to get someone's attention outside in the homicide detail so they could pick up a phone, maybe run a tape, at least be a second party. He couldn't see anyone through his open doors at the moment, although he was sure some-one had been at one of the desks when he'd gotten back from Strout's.

But no one was appearing. He sat back down.

"Are you representing Shea?"

"I think I know where he is." A pause. The voice was slurred, as though Farrell had been drinking. Glitsky looked at the clock on the wall. No, that was unlikely—it wasn't yet three o'clock. Still . . .

The voice continued. ". . . and I'm in contact with him. He's very much afraid and would like some assurances be-fore he turns himself in. He wants his story heard."

"All right, then, Mr. Farrell. I want to hear it."

"Where can I meet you?"

"Where are you? You want to come down to the Hall?"

Another long pause. Glitsky heard some discussion over a covered mouthpiece—Shea was right with him. My king-dom for a tapped phone, he was thinking.

"Lieutenant?"

"I'm here."

"I'd prefer if we could meet personally, alone, you and me."

"Is Shea going to be with you?"

"No. I'm coming alone. It would just be me."

If it would put him in touch with Kevin Shea, Glitsky would meet Farrell naked at the top of Coit Tower. "You know Lou the Greek's, across the street, downstairs place?"

Farrell was definitely slurring. Maybe the guy had a speech defect. "Lou the Greeksh? Ushed to get my mail there."

"Say an hour?"

"One hour."

"Mr. Farrell?"

"Yeah?"

"Drive carefully, would you."

Glitsky moved the police and forensics reports around on his desk. He had been a long time in the business and thought he'd developed a pretty good sense of the moment in a case when the dynamic changed, when you felt you were maybe finally getting to the end of something. He had that feeling now.

He realized that in a certain way Rigby and Reston had done him a favor by reminding him that his role was, after all, specific and limited—he was to bring in a suspect in a murder case. That was all. Find him and bring him in, like Tommy Lee Jones in *The Fugitive*. (Glitsky's all-time favorite moment in movie history—Richard Kimble, the fugitive, at the end of the tunnel on the lip of a mile-high waterfall, says to Tommy Lee Jones, "I'm innocent," and Jones—beyond cool—goes "I don't care.")

That would be Glitsky now. Leave the big picture out of it. Collect evidence as it came in and if things changed, be flexible. But for now, the job was to get Kevin Shea into a cell here in the Hall.

He still wasn't completely confident that Loretta's theory would hold, that bringing Shea into custody would throw any oil onto these roiling waters, but on the off-chance it did, wouldn't that be a nice bonus?

Meanwhile, he would go by the book with Wes Farrell. He would play fair, keep it to himself and meet him alone. A deal was a deal, and he was reasonably certain that Farrell, even if he wasn't sober, was not trying to pull anything. It had sounded legitimate. Farrell was a lawyer protecting his client, and that wasn't necessarily at odds with Glitsky's job. At least, not yet.

He didn't blame Shea for getting a lawyer. Three hundred thousand dollars was ample motivation for someone to cause him serious mayhem. And Glitsky wasn't forgetting the not-so-hidden hundred-thousand-dollar message that Philip Mohandas had delivered—kill him if you have to. Shea must know, and Glitsky thought he was right, that it would be child's play to concoct some story of attempted escape or self-defense that would work as a justification for taking out Kevin Shea.

So it would work out, maybe by tonight. The boys would be gone out of harm's way in Monterey with his father. The city would creak its way back to business as usual, and Abe Glitsky might look forward to a weekend alone catching up on some much-needed sleep. Maybe other things, too.

He lifted the phone, punched some numbers. She answered on the second ring. From her tone she was relieved to hear from him, as though she expected he wouldn't ever call her again.

She would be going back down to City Hall, to her office. Did he have the number there? She couldn't just stay in her house any longer. She had flown out here to San Francisco to make a difference and even if she was devastated by what had happened with Chris Locke, she had to get back to work—people needed her. She had to try to use what influence she had, meet with people on every side of it, find some workable solutions, play peacemaker.

Would Abe make it a point, please, to look in on Elaine? She hadn't been able to contact her all day and was getting sick with worry.

He let her go on, admiring her strength. A powerful woman with an important agenda. It was heady, but somehow natural, that he would be her connection, she his lifeline.

It would help if she knew how close it was to being over. She would be able to assure people that Shea would soon be in custody. He was meeting Shea's attorney at Lou the Greek's, and they would be arranging the details of his surrender. It ought to be done within a few hours, a day at most.

She told him that that was wonderful news.

If Abe got a chance after that, later, she asked him, would he be able to stop by her office at the Hall before he went home? Even a few minutes would be okay. She didn't know what to do with all this, these feelings about the two of them, what was happening. She really needed to talk to him. She needed him.

43

Art Drysdale had been about to make his way over to give Elaine Wager the rest of the week off when he got the news about Alan Reston's promotion to DA. Through connections at one of the television stations he had gotten early wind of Elaine's latest bout of unpredictability and had decided not that she was under too much stress—hell, everybody was under too much stress—but that she wasn't handling hers properly.

Daughter of a senator or not, she was going to take some time off and think about what she was supposed to be doing here. First she arrests Jerohm Reese. Then she spouts to the media about Kevin Shea, apparently sounding very much the official spokesperson for the DA's office, which she was not. Next, she might . . . but that, Drysdale thought, was the point—there was no telling what she might do next. He didn't want her around so they could all find out.

But then had come the call from the mayor's office. Not surprising in itself—after all, the DA's job was a political position and Drysdale was primarily an administrator—nevertheless the speed of turnover and person selected for the job were both unsettling.

So Drysdale had sat a few minutes, juggling baseballs, awaiting the arrival of his new superior. Then abruptly he had stood and gone down anyway to his original destination, Elaine Wager's cubicle. The door had been closed and he had knocked, then opened it, finding her sitting on the floor in the corner, hugging her knees to her chest. When she looked up, her face was streaked and ghostly.

Drysdale had gone down to the bathroom and brought back a handful of wet paper towels. By the time he got back Elaine was up off the floor, sitting in the chair behind her desk. He sat in silence at the next desk to her while she wiped her face, blew her nose, got herself together. She said she was sorry. He understood. It was all right. A couple of words. A few more.

A half-hour later, when Glitsky knocked at the door, they were still talking quietly, sitting at the two desks as though they shared the cubicle and were working. Drysdale stood and walked the six feet around the desk to the door, opening it a few inches. Seeing who it was, he turned and gestured a question to Elaine, who nodded, let him in. The lieutenant was wearing a jacket, as though he were going out somewhere, and he had some file folders in his hands.

"If I'm interrupting . . ." His eyes went to Elaine.

"Come on in, Abe. Pull up a chair." Drysdale closed the door behind them.

"They're looking all over for you, Art. I think you've been paged a dozen times in the last half hour."

"Yes, I imagine they have. I seem to have taken a powder."

"You heard, then, about Reston?"

Elaine came to life. "Alan Reston? What about him?"

Drysdale looked over at her. Their discussion had evolved into a personal one and he hadn't gotten around to the new office hierarchy. "Oh, that's right, I—"

"You know him?" Glitsky interrupted.

She nodded. "He's a . . . he's one of Mom's people. His daddy's rich . . ."

"He's also," Drysdale said, "your new boss."

That stopped her for a beat. "What do you mean?"

They played a few rounds of "what do you mean" until things became clearer, after which Glitsky looked at his watch and said he had an appointment, but Loretta was worried about her, would Elaine give her a call? She was down at City Hall.

Elaine nodded.

Glitsky said, "I also wanted to apologize to you."

"What for?"

"Evidently our little news interviews got played back-to-back and it came across that I was saying you were wrong, which isn't what I meant." He paused. "I meant what we had talked about earlier this morning—that we just didn't know yet."

"That's all right," she said. "Everything I've done today seems to have been wrong anyway. Isn't that right, Art?"

Shrugging, Drysdale said maybe so, and then added enigmatically, "Not that you don't have a reason."

"I don't care about reasons too much anymore. They're all just excuses for doing what you shouldn't have done if you'd thought about it a little longer, which I didn't, or been a little stronger. I'm sorry."

Glitsky bobbed his head. "If you say so."

Drysdale took the ball. "We were talking about . . . about extenuating circumstances. About why people do things, have a bad day. Why Kevin Shea did what he did, all the environmental crap in his background . . ."

"Everybody's got environmental crap."

Elaine was almost pleading. "That's what I'm saying, Abe. I got both of you guys in trouble today and I don't care about any excuses—I just screwed up."

"I thought this was *my* apology," Glitsky said, and it loosened things up a bit. "And I do have to go, but listen . . ." He handed her the folders he'd been holding, motioning down to them. "This is exactly the kind of thing I was telling you about earlier, that's going to kill you at trial if you're not ready for it. I don't even know what it means at this point, but Strout's forensic report shows that Wade died of asphyxiation—that's his ruling."

"Okay. We knew that. That's what happens when you hang, when you get pulled up." Elaine had the folder open, and Drysdale got up and was looking with some intensity at the second picture.

"Yeah, that's what Strout said . . ."

Drysdale straightened up. "So what are you getting at, Abe?"

"I'm getting at the story you guys have developed for Kevin Shea, that these pictures seem to show so clearly. That he repeatedly pulled down on the body . . ."

A moment's silence. They both got it at the same time. ". . . which would have broken his neck."

Glitsky nodded. "Right. Not strangled him, and strangulation is what Strout says he died of. You can bet Shea's attorney is going to mention that when it goes to court and you'd better have an answer for him. That's all I'm saying.

As both of you know, niggling facts can, you should pardon the phrase, hang you.''

Drysdale had the second picture out, studying it more closely. "And what's this?"

Elaine was ready with her answer. She launched into her first explanation, that Shea had pulled out his knife to stab Arthur Wade, who had been trying to grab it from him in self-defense.

Glitsky and Drysdale gave it a courteous listen, which led her to go on to her knife-in-Wade's-own-pocket theory, where Arthur had pulled it out in an effort to try to cut himself down. This time impatience took over. Glitsky didn't want to, but felt he had no choice. He had to speak up.

"You're saying that Arthur Wade is being chased by a crazed mob, they get a rope around his neck, they're pulling him up, and he goes 'Hey, I remember now, I've got a Swiss Army knife in my pocket, I'll just cut myself down.' I don't think so. I don't think a jury will think so. Plus I just talked to a witness not an hour ago—a sweet elderly woman from Lithuania with no reason to lie about it—who says it looked to her like Kevin Shea was lifting Wade *up*, not pulling him down. That he had gotten out his knife and handed it to Wade, trying to get the guy to cut himself down, he just couldn't keep at it long enough."

"That's not possible," Elaine said.

"It's inconvenient if it is." Drysdale was in the business of putting on successful trials, and strategically this was a case-breaker. That the argument could even be made . . .

"If I were you," Glitsky said to Elaine, "I'd get that photographer down here again and find out for sure what order he took those pictures in, if he can remember."

Drysdale swore quietly.

Glitsky looked at his watch again. "I've really got to go."

"There are probably twenty witnesses out there who could testify to Shea pulling down . . ." Elaine was back in a challenge mode, her eyes hard on him, not giving up on anything.

"But they haven't come forward and we haven't found them. And if they were in the mob, they're accessories. Which is why we haven't found them." Glitsky held up his hands, avoiding further confrontation. "Look, folks, I'm on your side, but you better know your cards, that's all I'm saying." One last look at his watch. "Besides good-bye."

"Alan Reston isn't going to like this." Drysdale was back at the desk next to Elaine's. "Maybe I ought to get back and make the man's acquaintance. You say you know him?"

"I met him through mom. I don't think you can tell him anything about this."

"It's trial strategy. That's my job. I've got to bring it up."

"He won't listen to you."

"So you do know him?"

She shrugged. "I've seen things like this enough. If he's got this job already, my mom is somewhere in the picture, and Kevin Shea is her program, so it's going to be Alan's."

"Not if it can't hold up."

"Who says it can't hold up? Any argument *you* make to Alan is going to come out like a rationalization, not a trial strategy. I still don't think there's any doubt Shea did it, but Abe's right—it's going to be a little harder to prove at trial."

"Which is what I should tell Reston, which is what I'm going to—"

"Art, please. Let me. When we know a little more. Maybe my mom . . ."

She let it hang, and Drysdale subsided back into his chair. "We present evidence to a court, Elaine, you know that. That's what we do."

"I know that, Art."

"Whether or not the shitheads get off . . ."

"I know."

"If you don't think *that's* Reston's primary commitment— and say what you will about Chris Locke, that was his— then somebody ought to know about it real soon. I don't care if he's black or in your mother's hip pocket. Pardon my lack of circumlocution."

She waved it off. "I don't know what his agenda is, Art. I don't."

Drysdale got his long frame up out of his chair. "You know, about the only thing I'm *more* tired of than the word "agenda" is the fact that so many people seem to have one.

How we gonna all work together, much less live together, with this shit going on?"

"I don't—"

"I don't either, Elaine. I just pray to God you don't look at me and see a white man first, 'cause I'm not any more a white male first than you're a black lady first. What I am *first* is just a plain old human person." He stood at the door. "Now, I hope you're feeling better than you were, and I know you've got some phone calls to make, and I've got to go do what I do."

"Art . . ."

"It's all right. I'll let you take it up with Mr. Reston. Just remember, this is your case. It's *not* your mother's. That's all."

Elaine placed a call to the photographer Paul Westberg and left a message on his machine that she would like to see him again at his earliest convenience.

She sat and stared at the second picture, then suddenly realized what had not registered when she had heard it. And found herself grappling with the question of how Lieutenant Glitsky knew her mother well enough for her to ask him to pass along the message to Elaine that she was worried about her.

"We were together in college."

"What do you mean, together?"

Loretta Wager let out a sigh over the telephone. Elaine could picture her in the small unmarked office at City Hall, her shoes off, her feet on the ratty old desk. "I think you can figure that one out, honey. He was . . . my boyfriend."

"Abe Glitsky was your boyfriend? Were you serious about each other?"

"For that age, I'd say yes."

"And what now?"

Her mother hesitated. "Now we are friends."

Elaine had some trouble with this. "Mom, I have been around you just a little bit, and I have never heard you mention his name before."

"We lost track of each other, hon. That happens, you know. He had a wife and family. So did I."

"But he *couldn't* have lost track of you . . ."

"Because I have a public life? Maybe not. But there was no reason for him to look me up. Now, since the other day, with this . . . anyway, he interviewed me about Chris . . ."

Elaine was silent.

"Are you there, hon? You okay?"

"I don't know what I'm going to do."

"You haven't told anybody, have you? About you and Chris?"

"No, but I think Art Drysdale kind of has a feeling about it. He was here with me for a long time. We talked."

The words came out carefully. "Let him have a feeling, Elaine, but don't ever admit it. Would you promise me that?"

"Mom, I wasn't going to . . ."

"It will give him too much on you. Anybody, in fact . . ."

"Not Art. He's not—"

"He's your supervisor. If he needs it he'll use it. That's the way the world works. And you, especially—you're not allowed to have a scandal."

"Mom, it's *you* who's not allowed to have a scandal. You're the senator. I'm just—"

"No. This isn't for me. I'm thinking about you."

"Art Drysdale isn't going to say anything. How did we get on this? I don't even care if he does. What matters is Chris."

Her mother sighed again. "Chris is gone, hon. You'll find somebody else." A pause. "Somebody better for you."

"I don't want somebody better for me." Tears threatened again.

"You will, Elaine, believe me. Someday you will."

44

It might have been interpreted as a nice domestic scene—the clean-shaven young man with the bandaged leg sitting around the coffee table with his parents and their well-dressed friend, all of them listening politely to the overweight blue-collar guy with the heavy black shoes, perhaps a repairman telling them all about the leaking water heater, the pros and cons of getting a new one.

It was turning into a much more formal police interview than Carl Griffin had ever intended.

Colin Devlin was twenty-four years old and still lived with his parents in a renovated Victorian on Clifford Terrace in the upper Ashbury. Griffin had called from Dr. Epps' office and reached the young man, asked a couple of cursory questions and got a minimal response, then wondered if he could call on him, have him make a statement about his injury, keeping it all vague. Colin, sounding nervous on the phone, had said okay. Griffin had reasoned he wouldn't have been able to say anything else without creating suspicion, and he was proved right.

On the way to Devlin's, Griffin ran into an area that had been cordoned off by the National Guard and had to detour for half a mile. Then, in spite of the eggplant submarine sandwich he'd wolfed at lunchtime, he also suffered a Mac attack and found he needed a burger. So he set no land speed marks getting up to Ashbury, and by the time he arrived, so had the reinforcements—Colin's parents and their lawyer, a Mr. Cohen.

In its own way, this was the most positive thing that had happened to Griffin in three days, since even in today's paranoid world most people did not feel the need to call their attorney to be present at an informal police interview over a self-inflicted shoveling accident.

Given Cohen's presence, Griffin was surprised to be admitted to the house without a warrant. The man was probably the father's business lawyer, not a criminal attorney. If that were the case he wouldn't be up on the rules, which Griffin hoped would prove to be bad luck for Colin.

After a few moments of awkwardness, they got settled in the tastefully appointed front room. A pale mid-afternoon sun came and went through the ancient curved windows that lined the circular room. In spite of a low-burning fire in the grate, the whole place felt cool, and Griffin left his coat on, leading with his best shot. Why, he wondered, had Colin felt the need to invite Mr. Cohen to this meeting?

The father, Mr. Devlin, was a friendly-looking dark-haired man in a Donegal tweed suit and regimental tie. Clearly, he was in control. Though Griffin had not addressed him, he answered. "Inspector Griffin, let's cut through the malarkey here. As I'm sure you suspect—it's why you're here—my son did not cut his leg the way he told Dr. Epps. We don't want to go through the charade of having to produce the shovel and . . . all that nonsense." He waved a hand.

"All right," Griffin said. If they were going to give it to him free, he was going to take it. He shifted his bulk in the creaking bentwood chair and leaned forward. "What happened exactly?"

The wife, a pretty woman with a lot of jewelry, spoke up. "Colin didn't mean to—"

"Mary, please." The husband's imperious look stopped Mary Devlin. He went on. "We would like assurances that Colin's cooperation with the police . . ." Unsure of the process he was trying to control, he seemed to run out of steam for a moment, then found his rhythm again. ". . . that there'll be some quid pro quo."

Griffin was leaning forward, his hands clasped. "Cutting deals is up to the DA," he said. "Most times, they'll talk about it. How'd you get cut, Colin?"

"I don't even know. Some guy behind me . . ." The boy's eyes were hollow, his face pale as though he'd worn a beard for a long time and had recently cut it. Maybe in the last half hour.

"Colin, just a minute . . . I don't think we should talk any more unless you can give us some guarantees," the father said.

Griffin nodded, stalling. "If Colin here was at the scene of the lynching, his testimony would be very important. I'm sure the DA would recognize that, put it in the mix."

Mr. Devlin chewed on it a moment. "We're not trying to duck responsibility here—any that might fall to Colin— but I don't want my boy . . ." He faltered again. "Being there at all, being part of it, was unpardonable, I understand that . . ."

"Dad, I—"

"Colin!"

The boy shut up.

". . . and I'm sure that we've been too lax, letting him live at home, giving him an allowance, not insisting he go to work, get some job, but his mother . . . well, that's going to end. The boy has to grow up, take responsibility for what he does, but he has promised us that he did *not* touch the man, and I absolutely believe him. He never got close to him."

At last, the lawyer spoke. "Bren, I think that's enough. Inspector, what do you think?"

"I'll have to talk to someone downtown, but I think they'll be . . . receptive."

"What should be our next step?" Mr. Devlin asked.

Griffin stood, pulled down his jacket, which had ridden up over his middle. "I don't want you to take this wrong, sir," he said, then turned to Cohen, "or you either, but I think you might want to get yourself an attorney who does this for a living. You might find it makes a difference."

Jamie O'Toole, jobless due to the loss of his workplace to fire, was bitter and angry. Jamie was a man who had lived in the city his entire life, had gone to Saint Ignatius High School and then done a year at San Francisco State, during which Rhoda (the name alone, he should have known), his girlfriend at the time, had gotten pregnant and he'd *married* her, which had killed five years dead.

Also, it left him without a college degree, which he would have gotten otherwise, he was smart enough. But the breaks just hadn't worked out for him so he could stay in school. So there he was, needing a job—any job—at the beginning of this recession, and he didn't care what they were saying about it in the newspapers, here in California it wasn't getting any better.

So he'd gotten into bartending—decent tips, most of the money under the table, where he could keep it instead of give it to Uncle Sam or, worse, to Rhoda. Guys had told him, "Don't get so you're making any money on the books, the ex will just come and get the judgment upped." And he had listened. Rhoda *would* do that to him, no question. Same as she wouldn't get married, though she was living with some dweeb in Richmond, because then he'd be allowed to stop his alimony. He supposed the child support would just go on forever, more money out of his pocket, another thing holding him down, keeping him where he was.

They were already giving out some federal emergency money and he had read the guidelines and realized he qualified—government always giving something away to somebody, usually not to him. He'd take it this time.

So he was waiting in a long cold line at the distribution place they had set up on Market Street—place was crawling with lowlife. Jamie O'Toole hated it, waiting with all those street people, shivering his ass off.

Then some guy, familiar, walks up to one side, and he's got it, he places him—the plainclothes cop, Lanier, that was it.

"How you doing, Jamie?"

"I'm cold, man. Witch's tit out here."

Lanier was wearing a heavy flight jacket, corduroys, boots. He looked cozy, smiled. "I was just out at your place. Your old lady said where we might find you."

"Well, she got *something* right. Who's we?"

"My partner's parking around the corner. Be here in a minute."

"I can't wait. Make my day. What do you guys want now?"

Lanier was standing almost on top of O'Toole, backing him away from the line. "Same as before, just to talk."

O'Toole went with it, a step at a time. "What are you

doin', man? I been waiting an hour here. This same shit again, Jesus. I'm so tired of this."

Lanier got him to the corner, a distance off from the rest. O'Toole lowered his voice, punched a finger into Lanier's chest. "You quit pushing me."

Lanier smiled. "You strike a police officer, I'll bust your head open. You think you're tired now . . ."

"There a problem, Marcel?" Ridley Banks had appeared behind O'Toole and thought it seemed like a good moment to make his presence felt. Lanier smiled over O'Toole's shoulder at him. "No, no problem. We're in the midst of the age of enlightenment here."

O'Toole whirled around, took a beat noticing that Banks was black, then shrugged. "Yeah, well, we got nothing to talk about. I told you everything I knew last time."

Lanier grinned. "Jamie, a smart guy like you, I figure everything you know ought to take at least an hour. Wouldn't you say, Ridley?"

"At least."

O'Toole twisted his head back from one of the inspectors to the other. "Well," he repeated, "I've enjoyed it. Now I gotta run."

Lanier stepped in front of him again. "There was one little thing, Jamie. The other day you said it was Kevin Shea, by himself, as far as you knew, that had done the thing with Wade."

"I said I didn't know. I wasn't out there."

"Oh, that's right," Banks put in, "I think he did say that."

"Did he? Was that exactly it?"

"I think so. You wouldn't change your story, would you, Jamie? Where'd he get the rope?"

"What rope?"

Lanier smiled, humoring him. "What rope? he asks."

"If Shea was in your bar and left to go lynch Wade, what happened? Did he stop off at his car and grab a rope from the trunk, or what?"

"I don't know what happened. I didn't leave the bar."

Now Banks stepped in closer, also smiling. "He keeps saying that, you notice?"

Lanier nodded. "Sticking to his story. Didn't see a thing. Good strategy."

Banks moved in some more and now they had him surrounded. "We think . . . actually we're pretty sure, Jamie . . . that the rope came from the hardware store next to your bar. What do you think about that?"

"I don't think anything about it. I wasn't there."

"Whew," Lanier, impressed. "This is some consistent story, Ridley. We'd better just give it up and go on back to the office."

"The only thing is," Banks said, "that we found what looks suspiciously like a beer glass, or big pieces of several beer glasses, in the display window of the hardware store, and I think there's a chance one of those pieces is gonna have your fingerprints on it somewhere. We're checking."

O'Toole's eyes were darting back and forth. "I'm the bartender, guys, I would have touched the glasses."

"That's right, Ridley," Marcel said, "he is absolutely correct."

"Gosh," Banks said, "that's right. I must have forgot." He snapped his fingers, as though suddenly remembering something else. "I do wonder, though, about the lawn mower. The one in the hardware store's window? Did somebody take that into the Cavern where you might have touched it—mow some Astroturf or something—and then go put it back in the display next door? What could've happened there, I wonder?"

"Are you saying my prints are on some *lawn mower*?"

Banks shrugged. "We're checking, Jamie. We're just checking a whole load of stuff, you wouldn't believe. You think we'll get lucky?"

"*I* think we will, Rid."

"I do, too, Marcel."

The inspectors smiled at Jamie O'Toole. In spite of the cold, he'd broken a sweat. His eyes were moving, the gears in his brain nearly audible as they turned. "Well, I mean," he said, "there had to be other guys. One guy couldn't have done it himself, could he? I mean, there was a bunch of guys. Everybody was drinking, you know?"

Lanier kept up that smile. "We don't know, actually, Jamie, which is why we're being so . . . I do know . . . pushy. We'd really like to find out."

Banks said: "You know Brandon Mullen and Peter McKay?"

"Sure, I know those guys. I already told you that."

"They were there, they admit it. When did they leave?"

"When did they leave?"

"I think that's what I said. When did they leave? After Shea, before Shea, with Shea, when?"

"I think after."

"That's funny. *They* said before."

"Then it must have been before. Look, guys, it was busy. I can't remember everything . . ."

"Our lieutenant said you told him it was slow . . ."

"I thought he meant afterward . . ."

They kept it up for about five more minutes, then thanked him for his time and sent him back to the line.

Walking back to their car, Banks said, "That was kind of fun. I do believe the man went outside."

Lanier nodded. That was a good idea. "We ought to dust that window. Fire damage or no, we find one of Jamie's prints on anything . . ."

"I hear you," Banks said. "Time comes, it would be a neat surprise."

45

Lou the Greek's was beginning to fill up.

Glitsky stood blinking in the corridor at the bottom of the stairway that led to the bar, letting his eyes adjust to the dimness. An overriding smell of cabbage made him wonder what culinary delight Lou's wife had prepared for lunch that day. Though he often hung out doing some business or other in one of its tiny booths, Glitsky had stopped eating at Lou's a few years back after an unfortunate reaction he'd had to the place's homemade kim chee, which others of his friends swore by.

The cabbage smell now triggered a sense memory of that, and his stomach rolled over. He took a breath, steeling himself, and walked in.

A hand went up at the bar, and Glitsky, after making allowances for the hair (now in a ponytail) and a few extra pounds, realized that he had known Wes Farrell in another lifetime, had testified in a couple of cases that the man had been defending over the years. As he pulled up a stool, Glitsky was further struck by Farrell's attire—most of the people at Lou's worked at the Hall and wore some variation of the uniform. Farrell looked as though he had just come from the beach—he must be freezing, Glitsky thought, and said as much.

"My veins are ice. I don't feel a thing."

Farrell was having a coffee drink, maybe just coffee. Glitsky motioned to Lou that he'd like his usual—tea. "That's handy in this town," Glitsky said, "not feeling the cold."

"I don't know what it is, probably age, like everything else. I used to feel it, chatter my teeth, all of that. On the other hand, it could be I'm just anesth . . . anesth . . ." He broke a weary smile. "Fucked up. Never could say that word, even sober." He sipped his coffee. "Right at this moment, for the record, I'm halfway back to sober, I think. Haven't had a drink in two, three hours."

Glitsky nodded.

"This is not a problem for me, I hope it's not for you."

Glitsky shrugged as his tea arrived in a cracked brown mug to match Farrell's.

"But enough about me," the lawyer said, "I want to tell you a story."

"That's why I'm here." Glitsky sipped his tea.

Farrell started to talk, quietly now, with no trace of a slur.

"That's what *he* says." Glitsky, to be saying something, did not want to come across as gullible, but even wearing his most cynical hat, he still believed every word he had just heard.

Farrell, holding the high ground, did not need to push. "You have any evidence that refutes it, any of it?"

"The picture seems to."

"You got it here?"

Glitsky did not, but there was a newspaper behind the bar and Farrell leaned over and pulled it from the counter. "Let's glance at this puppy a minute, what do you say?"

For not even close to the first time, Glitsky was face-to-face with the ultimate truism of observation—you saw what you expected to see. Now, looking at the picture that was convicting Kevin Shea all over the country, but with different eyes, Glitsky only saw what Farrell had described—Shea was grimacing with the weight of holding Wade up. He wasn't pulling him down, he was trying to save his life.

There were tiny clues, visible if you knew what to look for, if you were so inclined. The manner in which Wade's shirt was bunched, for example. If Shea had been pulling down, wouldn't one expect the shirt to be pulled taut to the body? And the rope, did Glitsky see the actual rope? Not much of it was visible in the picture—a few inches—but what there was did not seem to be perpendicular to the ground, which it assuredly would have been if it were holding the weight of two men.

And then, and most convincingly, there were the knife wounds. This information hadn't been released to the press.

No one had even admitted to having one—Glitsky hadn't yet heard about Colin Devlin and Carl Griffin. They didn't officially exist—the very possibility of someone having a knife wound was part of Abe's mix, not the public's. They were one of his secrets, one of the little tricks that experienced policemen liked to trot out and go "boo" with. And now Farrell had preempted him on them, told him all about them, how they fit the picture.

Kevin Shea had had to cut his way through the crowd. He had slashed at the men closest to Arthur Wade. He was sure he had cut some of them. There had been blood.

And Arthur Wade had died of *asphyxiation,* which Glitsky knew from the coroner. He had not had his neck pulled on.

His tea had long ago gone cold. "Well, Mr. Farrell, I'd say you've got yourself a pretty good story."

"It's not a story, Lieutenant. It's what happened. Kevin Shea is, if anything, a hero in all of this."

Glitsky was thinking hard, not committing. If this were a normal case, if every media outlet in the Bay Area, if not the country, hadn't already run stories on the heinous life and career of the arch-bigot Kevin Shea, he would simply bring Farrell across the street and have a talk with the DA or Chief Rigby . . .

Hell, he was the head of homicide. He'd just be tempted to interview Shea and recommend the DA drop the whole thing right there. If it could be verified, and Farrell's knowledge of the knife wounds came close to meeting his criteria for that.

If this were a normal case . . .

"What's funny?"

Glitsky glanced sideways. "Not much."

"You looked amused."

"Oh yeah. I'm often amused. Do you have any idea how much energy has been invested in your client being guilty?"

"Some. He's a little more on top of it than I am."

"Where is he?"

"I don't know."

Glitsky shot him a look.

"I don't know," he repeated. "He calls me. The boy's got a doubting nature, thinks I might turn him in for the rewards, and he might not be all wrong on the right day."

"I'd like to talk to him."

"I could probably arrange that."

"He should bring himself in."

"That might be a little trickier. He's pretty convinced that if he gives himself up before this gets turned around somehow, he's dead."

"He's being paranoid, you should tell him that. We've got protective custody, solitary—"

"Lieutenant, excuse me. We're doing fine here together, don't start bullshitting me now. You and I know, somebody wants to kill him, and we can assume somebody would for a hundred grand, he's gone. Jail or no jail. And he doesn't want to go to jail period. He didn't do anything wrong. What he wants is to get the word out. He saw you on the tube saying you needed some evidence, he thought you'd be the man."

Glitsky consciously controlled his face. "I'd be the man?"

"Get it to the DA, broaden the net, take it off him."

Thinking of Elaine, Glitsky nodded. "I can try that, but I'd still like to interview him."

"He'd still be under arrest, though, wouldn't he?"

"Well, that's the grand jury, the indictment . . ."

"Can you quash the indictment?"

"Not at this stage. It's not in my province, anyway. The DA's got to withdraw the charges, which, look, you bring him down—backdoor it, I'll get him in to the DA personally. He'll listen, we'll go over the evidence we've got."

"I don't think so. It's not about evidence. Not anymore."

To which Glitsky had no response. Farrell was right.

Lou came around to see if either wanted a refill and both declined. Behind them, the room was close to its capacity, elbow-to-elbow with the trade.

"And meanwhile," Glitsky said, "the city keeps on burning."

"That's not my client's fault, Lieutenant. If he could stop it, he would. He's a good kid."

This was an unexpected direction. "He is? You know him personally?"

"We took some classes together," Farrell said. "He's a regular guy, normal as you and me."

"So what's all this broken family, deep South bigot, unstable personality?"

"That, sir, is quite possibly a young woman that Mr. Shea had the bad fortune to sleep with and then tire of . . ."

Glitsky raised his eyebrows.

". . . either that or the media needing to fill air time or blank paper."

Glitsky had heard both explanations in different contexts too often before to be surprised, but the way they both fit in here—the hand in glove of it . . . He shook his head, nearly gagging on the last of his tea. "How do I reach you?" he asked.

"I don't know when Kevin will get in touch with me, but when he does, I'll call you. Then we'll see where we go from there."

Glitsky stood up. "I'll do what I can."

"You know, Lieutenant, I believe you."

"Elaine."

Alan Reston came around the desk—only yesterday it had been Chris Locke's desk—with his arms outstretched to greet her. She rested her leather satchel next to her feet and stood, close to attention, letting him put his arms around her, raising hers to enclose him lightly because it would have been more awkward not to. He did not press her to him, though, merely held her an instant and let go, as old friends might. Establishing that they were old friends, reminding her. "This is a terrible business."

"Yes, it is."

"And losing Christopher Locke . . ." He didn't seem to have anywhere to go with that and let it hang in the room between them. Another bond. Chris Locke. His face twitched out of nerves or fatigue and he blurted, "I'm glad you've come down. I was going to try to get by your office earlier, say hello but"—motioning to the papers piled on his desk—"as you can see . . ."

"That's all right, Alan. It's okay if I still call you Alan?"

"Elaine . . . come on. Of course I'm Alan." His grin came on and he started to reach out to touch her on the arm but stopped midway. "Can I get you something, anything? You want to sit down?"

During her mother's first Senate campaign, when she had still been a teenager, Alan Reston had been a jerk. In his mid-twenties at the time, and engaged (he was now married to the same woman), with a rich father and an ingratiating manner, Alan had an unshakable belief in his attractiveness to the opposite sex.

On the night of her mother's election, and emboldened by cognac, he had wagged his ding-a-ling in front of Elaine Wager in what he had thought was some kind of charming, harmless, celebratory way. He really seemed to think—or so he acted—that this was an acceptable mating ritual. After all, there was this obvious mutual attraction and they had been campaigning together and there was no reason . . . why, what was the matter? Didn't she know what this was *for*? What it was?

She had looked down and replied that it looked like a penis, only smaller.

It was the last time they had seen each other, until now.

She went to the couch and placed her satchel full of workpapers next to her. He pulled one of the wingbacks around to face her, but before he sat down she was talking. "Have you talked to Art Drysdale? I was just by his office, I thought he might have been here. That's why I came by. I didn't want to bother you."

"And I'm glad you did. It's no bother."

She waited. Then, prompting: "Art Drysdale?"

"That's right, Drysdale. He had a meeting, I believe, with the mayor over at City Hall, something about all this . . . this awkwardness between us. I think your mother was part of it. Smooth the waters."

"Art doesn't want to be DA, Alan. He really doesn't."

Reston lifted his hands, as though all these things were out of his control, they were just happening. "I think a couple of his decisions . . ."

"Jerohm Reese."

"To name one, yes."

"What are you going to do about Jerohm?"

"Well, I just hope they don't go too hard on Mr. Drysdale. From all I've heard, he's invaluable around here."

"He is, and I'm the one to blame for Jerohm Reese, not Art. I brought him upstairs on my own authority . . ."

"And now he's our hot potato."

"Which is not Art's fault."

Reston, now taking his seat, spread his palms. The Art

Drysdale situation was being resolved at higher levels; it was not his problem. If Drysdale came back he'd work with him. If not, administrators grew on trees. "Well, Elaine, in any event, you're here now. Maybe I can help you. What were you going to see Art Drysdale about?"

It would have to come to this eventually, she knew, and as she had said to Art, she was the one to bring it up. "Do you know Abe Glitsky, Lieutenant Glitsky?"

Reston was smiling now, on top of the situation. "If this is about him stepping on your toes I've already spoken to him."

"When? About what?"

"An hour ago, maybe a little longer. It's all taken care of, these opinions he's releasing to the media. Chief Rigby and I told him to—what?"

She was shaking her head. "Not an hour ago. Not that. He was just by my office ten minutes ago."

"The man gets around."

"Yes, he does, Alan. I think he's trying to get it right."

They sat, staring at one another. The criticism—the challenge?—was hanging there between them. Reston crossed his legs. "We all are, Elaine. So what's with the good lieutenant?"

She told him—Glitsky had come straight to her after the meeting with Wes Farrell, supplying her with the gist of it—the details regarding the knife wounds, the revised theory on the second photograph to say nothing of the first, even the explanation that the snitch, Cynthia Taylor, might have been one of Shea's jilted exes.

Reston listened to it all in silence. "Well," he said, slapping his hands on his thighs, then standing. "Well . . ." Stalling, he walked over to the window, stared at it, shifted from foot to foot.

Elaine spoke to his back. "Lieutenant Glitsky asked me if we—if the DA's office—might want to review the charges . . ."

Reston turned quickly around. "We can't do that." And then less severe: "On what grounds?"

"What I've just explained to you."

"Which is what? An alternative explanation by the suspect's own lawyer? This is supposed to be compelling?"

"Alan, Glitsky isn't—"

"I'm not talking about Glitsky, Elaine. We've got a Grand Jury murder indictment on Kevin Shea, pushed through as I understand it by this office not two days ago, a picture of him in the act of committing the crime . . ."

"*If* it's—"

"No ifs, Elaine. The picture is what it is. It's clear to the whole world."

"The interpretation might be wrong, Alan. That's all Lieutenant Glitsky was trying to say to me. If we take it to trial . . ."

Now he was pointing a finger, raising his voice. "But *we* are the ones who take it to court. Not Lieutenant Glitsky. The DA's office. And I'm hearing nothing that remotely challenges my conviction that Kevin Shea is responsible for this . . . for all of this."

"All right, then, how about this?" Standing, Elaine removed the second photograph from her satchel and brought it over to his desk. She moved some of his junk aside as he crossed to her.

"What is . . . ?" he began.

"Taken two or three seconds after the other one. Shea handing the knife to Arthur Wade, giving him a last chance to cut himself down."

She let him study it for a while, then started to put out, fact by fact, the alternative explanation of what appeared to be there—the way the shirt was pulled, the angle of the rope as Glitsky had shown her.

When she finished, Reston flipped some pages from her file, then walked to the window again. "It sounds to me like Shea's got himself a good attorney."

"Or he's innocent, Alan . . ."

Reston shook his head. "No, he's not." He turned again to face her. "Elaine, let's get this straight. We have a case that convinced the Grand Jury. The Board of Supervisors got together to put a reward on Kevin Shea's head. *You* particularly—representing this office—have gone public over the airtightness of this indictment. And now you're coming to me, my first day on the job, and you expect me to call off the whole thing—maybe the best opportunity we have to get the city under some control again? That's not going to happen."

"Even if he didn't do it?"

"You have any *proof* that he didn't?"

"Traditionally, Alan, we're supposed to have proof that he *did*. Remember? Lieutenant Glitsky thinks he can get Shea to come in if you'll talk to him."

"If I'll drop the charges . . ."

"Only after."

"No. It's too late for that now. He comes in, he's put under arrest, we go from there. No deals. Not with him."

"Then he won't come in."

Reston let out a long breath. "Then he's taking that risk, and it's substantial." Trying to close the gap, he stepped closer to her. "Elaine, maybe you ought to talk to your mother about this. She's got her own investment here, you know."

"This isn't about my mother, Alan."

"You may not want to hear this, Elaine, but your mother may be the reason you got the case." He leaned back against his desk. Some of his folders slipped off to the ground. They both ignored them.

Her eyes narrowed. "That's not true. Chris Locke believed in my—"

"No question, but . . ." This time he did touch her arm. "Look, Elaine, no one's saying we're not going to give Shea a fair trial, but you don't about-face from rabid abuse of a suspect on television to letting him go because his own defense attorney for Christ's sake comes up with some reasons that *might,* and I repeat *might,* explain some facts differently. That would make the process and all of us look like fools. It would make your mother look ridiculous."

"I'm not saying he didn't do it, I'm asking what if . . ."

His hand, still on her arm, squeezed it firmly. "And I *hear* you. I don't want this case going south any more than you do, any more than your mother does. But we can't just do what Chris Locke did with Jerohm Reese—say we're giving up on the charges because the evidence suddenly got shaky. That's what started all this, remember? Even if I thought there was significant merit there, I wouldn't do it. I couldn't. Not now. The city would explode. Nobody's ready to hear it." He lowered his voice. "To say nothing of the fact that, personally, I'd be betraying your mother. As you well know."

"So what are you going to do? What are *we* going to do?"

"I'm going to wait, Elaine. There's no reason to do anything, to change direction at all. We don't have any new *facts*. Do we?"

She guessed not, not hard ones . . . well, maybe the lawyer's assertions about the knife wounds, but they weren't substantiated either. She just didn't know anymore. She was too tired.

"Look, Elaine, it's been a long day. Why don't you go home, get some rest, try not to think about Shea for a while."

She realized that there was nothing she could do now, and the possibility still existed that an arrest of Kevin Shea would at least bring some calm to the city. She didn't want to muddy those waters, especially not if it would embarrass her mother. There really was nothing to do but wait it out.

She forced a weary smile. "I'm sorry, it's just been . . ."

He nodded. "It's all right, Elaine. It's all right, I understand." He touched her arm a last time. "My door is always open."

No sooner had the door closed, though, than Reston was behind his desk and on the telephone, placing a call to Chief Dan Rigby, who picked up from his War Room on the second ring.

"Chief, I'm sorry to bother you, but I thought we were pretty clear with this Lieutenant Glitsky in homicide, that he ought to keep a lower profile."

"Yes. Well, I thought so, too."

"Well, I just had a long conversation with Elaine Wager, and he doesn't appear to have gotten the message."

46

Melanie had left Kevin alone upstairs and this made her nervous. She didn't like leaving him, felt that he needed her, that without her he wouldn't make it.

So there was a sense of urgency in her work. Her hands were shaking, and not only from the cold. She was half-hidden behind a large car in the darkened shadows of the parking garage under Wes Farrell's building. Whenever the light would change at the corner, there would be a rush of traffic out on the avenue and she'd stop and wait, looking to the garage's gated entrance. Wes had opened it up for them when they had first gotten here—it had gotten her recognizable Geo Metro off the streets.

People were starting to get home from work. She couldn't be too careful. The problem was that she could barely see the grooves in the screws to unfasten the license plate, and then with the tremor in her hands, the screwdriver kept slipping out. Well, there was only one more screw and it should come loose.

After that, of course, she would have to attach it to her car—take her own plate off and put this one on. She'd do it. She had to do it. They had to get out of here, at least for a while—until they were sure Wes hadn't been followed home.

He had gone downtown to negotiate with the police. And she and Kevin, left alone with their fears, had remembered the unmarked police car parked at the street in front of Melanie's own apartment, their narrow escape less than twenty-four hours ago. It wasn't unreasonable to consider the possibility that someone might follow Wes back home.

They didn't want to risk a cab, even a limo, although Kevin thought that might work—with the tinted windows no one could recognize him. But, she had argued, there would be a pickup and drop address, a paper trail for the credit card.

So she had come up with the idea of exchanging the plates from one of the cars parked in the garage downstairs with her Geo's. It shouldn't take her more than ten minutes—it already felt like an hour.

They would go to the apartment of another of her friends. Ann was gone for the long weekend and she had a key to her place because she'd agreed—it was the kind of thing she did all the time—to water Ann's plants and feed her precious goldfish. Ann's place hadn't crossed her mind last night as they were running from the police, getting their motel, but now suddenly it had strategic value and her brain had retrieved it.

Finally, finally, the last screw began to turn easily. Another line of traffic passed the garage entrance. No one was coming in. Watching the door, she kept turning the screw—and the license plate came off, falling with a clang onto the concrete. She froze. "I hate this," she whispered to herself.

Crossing to where she had parked her Geo, she squatted down again and began loosening the screws that held her own plates on.

She heard the grind of the gate before she had any chance to react. A car had turned out of traffic, waiting as the gate slowly opened. It drove past her down the length of the garage and parked in the last stall on the opposite side.

Holding her breath, she waited, praying he wouldn't look her way.

The man wore a business suit. He got out of his Camry and activated the security system—bu-BEEP. At the internal door, without thinking about it, he kicked away the block of wood Melanie had positioned there to keep the door propped open and then, perhaps realizing that this was unusual, he stopped and let his eyes roam the floor.

Hunched behind her tiny Geo, Melanie was certain the man, even all the way over where he was, could hear the blood pounding in her ears. But his gaze passed over where she hid and evidently saw nothing as he pocketed his keys and went inside. The internal door—the only one she could use to get back inside the apartment building—closed behind him with a sickening click.

*   *   *

The license plates were changed. There was an inside button that would open the garage gate and let her out to the street, but once that closed behind her she would be outside taking her chances, getting around to the front door of the apartment building where she could buzz upstairs.

Of course, being who she was, she had cautioned Kevin not to answer a buzz for any reason. Remember (she had reminded him), Wes had his own key—he'd let himself in when he got back from downtown. There was no reason to open the door for anyone else . . .

God, sometimes she hated herself. Whenever was she going to learn?

She rang the bell. It was her only chance to get back inside before Wes returned, possibly tailed by policemen. What else was she going to do, hang out in the garage all day? She knew it would probably be futile but she rang anyway. Maybe if she kept it up, kept ringing it constantly for five minutes, maybe tapped out an SOS in Morse code or something, then Kevin might be tempted to . . .

Obviously, he wasn't.

She buzzed again. No answer. More time passed. The evening wind had come up, cold-and-fog-laden and swirling her hair in front of her face. She hadn't worn a jacket, either. She pushed the buzzer again, held it, yelled into the speaker. "Goddamn it, Kevin!"

No response. Nothing.

Stomping her foot, she stared at the speaker, her eyes filling with tears.

Then his voice, finally, a whisper from the speaker: "Melanie?"

"God, Kevin. *Yes.*"

And the blessed sound of the buzzer.

A black Mercedes-Benz 130D was parked in front of Melanie's Geo, blocking it, and by its open driver-side door stood a tall woman in a business suit, her arms crossed, impatience and anger etched on her face.

Kevin and Melanie came from inside the building through the internal door to the garage and saw her. She wasted no time. "Is this your car?" The tones were clipped. "In my space?"

"Yes, it is. I'm sorry," Melanie began. "We'll just—"

"You know, I'm so tired of this," the woman said. "I get home from work and then I wait around for whoever has decided on that day to take the place that I pay for."

"Well, we'll just—"

"You don't even live here, do you? Who said you could park here? Who let you in?"

Kevin stepped forward. "We're really sorry, ma'am. We've got a friend in the apartment and he said—"

"Who?"

The two fugitives looked at each other. "That doesn't matter. It's—"

The woman pointed a finger. "You know what? It *does* matter. I've rung the manager and he's coming down and we're going to talk about this. This is the sixth time this month somebody's been in my spot and I am at my limit. So we'll just wait."

Melanie: "Um, we can't. We're expected . . . we've got a meeting."

The internal door opened again and a balding man, mid-forties, in a mouse-colored sweater and khakis, no socks and some decade-old topsiders, was moving toward them. "What's the problem, Maggie?"

"Someone told these people they could park here, Frank, and I want to find out who, and then I want something done about this. *It's got to stop.*"

Melanie spoke to the manager. "Listen," she said. "Frank. We were told we could park here and now we're leaving. It won't happen again, I promise. But we've got to be somewhere right now." She turned to the Maggie person. "We're sorry about the five other times, but that wasn't us."

Maggie was not listening. Life in the city often hinged on finding a parking place, and a lot of other things that were as seemingly trivial and just as difficult. "I'm not paying for this place," she said to Frank. "Not this month."

Now Frank seemed to focus on Kevin for the first time. "Don't I know you?"

"Are you going to do something, Frank, or not?"

Kevin said he might have seen him in the hallway once or twice. He was a friend of Wes Farrell's.

Frank kept staring at Kevin, wondering if that was it.

"Wes Farrell. Okay, then." Maggie, knowing who she was going to go after.

Frank appealed to her. "What do you want me to do, Maggie, call the police? Why don't we just let these people go on their way?"

"*Yes,* that's exactly what I think. I think we should call the police. They're parked illegally. They've stolen my place and they should pay for it."

"We will pay you," Kevin said. He was getting out his wallet. "What do you want?"

Frank spread his hands. "That won't be necessary. Come on, Maggie, please move your car, let 'em pull out."

Maggie, arms still folded across her chest, stared at the three others, tapping her foot once or twice, sighing. "Oh, all *right.*" She slid back behind the wheel of her Mercedes, slammed the door closed, rolled down her window. "This is not the end of this, Frank."

Melanie was heading for her car. Frank fell in beside Kevin and the two of them walked to the button by the gate.

"I'll get the gate," Frank said. "I want to close it up after you're out."

The Mercedes started up, pulled forward a couple of feet—enough to let the Geo out of the space—and Melanie hit the ignition. Kevin jogged a few ragged, painful steps in her direction.

When he got to the car he turned around. The gate was open, Frank standing by the button. Suddenly, just as Kevin was getting into the Geo, Frank snapped his fingers and called out. "Maggie! Back up, quick! Stop 'em."

At the same time, he turned and pushed the button to close the gate again. "That's Kevin Shea! That's who it is! Kevin Shea!"

Melanie yelled, "Get *in,*" and Kevin half fell into the front seat as the car jerked forward. The Mercedes had not yet had the time to react, but the gate was closing and Frank stood in the center of the drive, blocking them as they turned into it. Melanie leaned on the horn.

"I'm gonna have to . . . to run him over . . ."

"He'll jump out of the way! He'll have to."

She pressed down on the accelerator and the tires squealed on the smooth concrete. The gate was nearly half-way closed. She kept her hand on the horn, heading toward Frank, whose hands were up in front of his face.

"I *can't*," Melanie said. She hit the brakes. The gate slammed into Kevin's side of the door. Frank came forward a step and put his hands on the hood.

"Hold on," Melanie said, and pressed her foot down, the sudden movement lifting Frank onto the hood as it went out over the sidewalk. He fell off into the street as she turned into it.

She ran the stop sign at the corner of Junipero Serra, turned right at the next one, then left, then back up to 19th Avenue, where the traffic was lighter and at least it appeared that no one knew who they were.

Melanie was driving north on 19th Avenue. The sun was setting below the clouds, bright red with the smoke in the atmosphere.

Frank's recognizing Kevin built on the closeness of the previous night's escape. Neither said a word for seven blocks, until Kevin pointed. "What's that?" On either side of them up ahead pillars of smoke were rising—new outbreaks beginning to erupt as the day wore to dusk. Ahead of them, the traffic was slowing.

"I don't know."

She changed into the right lane. Ahead of them a crowd of people was visible a couple of intersections ahead. Were they throwing things onto passing cars? That was what it looked like. They could make out people running, coming out into the street. "I'm turning," she said.

Twenty minutes later they had parked at the end of Page and walked around the corner of Stanyan by the border of Golden Gate Park. Ann's apartment building was a U-shaped four-story brick structure that faced the park, with the entrance in the center, behind a smallish courtyard with a weed-filled garden, a waterless fountain and chipped

Spanish tiling. The wind had collected volumes of paper
trash and deposited them in the corners by the building.

Melanie let them into the apartment building with her
key. When the door closed behind them she made sure it
had locked, then something seemed to go out of her. She
stopped and turned into Kevin, pressing herself against
him, shaking. He enfolded her into him and they stood
there a long moment, embracing as the last rays of the sun
slanted through the ancient vestibule windows. Finally he
lifted her chin and kissed her. "We'd better get upstairs,"
he said.

Ann's apartment was on the fourth floor in the front,
overlooking both the scenic courtyard and, across Stanyan,
the lawns and evergreens of Golden Gate Park.

As soon as they had let themselves in, Kevin crossed to
the windows and pulled the blinds. He turned on a couple
of low-watt lights, made a quick tour of the living room.
Potted plants squatted on every available surface—a million
plants. Also a video camera on a tripod—Ann was a film
major—some books and CDs, a television and audio gear
and telephone, botanical posters and prints of Marilyn
Monroe, James Dean, Jim Morrison, Bogart. It was a typical student's apartment, busier and more feminine but not
really so different from Kevin's own place. He lowered
himself down into the stuffed chair.

"Melanie?"

"What?"

She was standing by the entrance to the kitchen and
turned. Their eyes met, and froze with the realization of
what they'd come to, what they were doing . . .

Minutes passed. The room had darkened, the sun now fully
down. Kevin lifted his body from the chair. Melanie was
somewhere in the back half of the apartment. "What are
you doing?" he called.

"Might as well feed the fish since I'm here. And water
the plants," she called back.

Kevin looked around again. "That could take weeks.
How many plants does old Ann have?"

"I've never counted. She's only got three fish. Want to
meet them?"

"It would give meaning to my life. But first maybe we should call Wes, find out how it all went."

"Oh, come meet the fish. Wes is either going to be back or not, and either way we left the note saying we'd call. He'll wait."

That was true enough, but Kevin wasn't disposed to wait. This was his life, and hers too, they were talking about. He made his way through the living room and stopped in the kitchen doorway.

Melanie was feeding the goldfish, her hands passing back and forth over the aquarium. She had taken off Wes's white shirt, which along with her bra was hanging on the back of one of the kitchen chairs.

Kevin stood in the doorway, watching the action of the smooth muscles in her back as she moved her arm over the water. She half-turned, her face betraying nothing, then came all the way around, facing him. "I know we could call Wes right now," she said, "but then again I thought . . ."

He moved toward her.

Farrell was surprised at the note but couldn't blame them for their caution. They'd both had a hairy couple of days and he thought they had earned the right to get cautious. Still, Glitsky had given his word, and even though they were on opposite sides—prosecution and defense—he sensed the man played straight.

"Yo, Bart!"

He had the television set turned back on, had cracked another beer and was opening a can of dog food by the kitchen window that overlooked Junipero Serra when the doorbell rang from down below. At the box by his front door he pushed the intercom button.

"Wesley Farrell?"

Wesley? he thought. Not even his wife had called him Wesley. "That's me," he said.

"This is Sergeant Stoner, a special investigator for the District Attorney's office. I have a warrant down here to search your apartment on information and belief that you may be harboring a fugitive . . ."

47

Glitsky sat at his desk, fingers drumming on the blotter. After meeting with Farrell, his chat with Elaine had left him with the impression—incorrect, as it turned out—that the DA would be open to negotiation regarding the Kevin Shea issue. Somehow he would oversee Shea's technical arrest in the next twenty-four hours and this particular segment of the crisis would be over.

He had returned to homicide to find the place still deserted, which didn't bother him . . . his troops were out there doing their jobs.

He decided to catch up on his paperwork on the chance that the call from Wes Farrell would come in soon. Since the riots had begun, the run-of-the-mill homicides in the city had continued at their usual pace. Predictably, a couple of gang lords had decided to use the cover of the disturbances to mask a few raids on rival turf—last night a drive-by into a milling crowd had killed two children, wounded fourteen adults and left no known gang members even scratched. A typical result, but the case had to be assigned and followed up.

Likewise the Korean businessman who had been killed, and Glitsky had to make sure that his inspectors were trying to identify the killers. There were also the Molotov-cocktail fires and their victims, the North Beach domestic, the boys who had been pulled from their cars. The weight of it all eventually slowed him down. Four more folders to go, and he simply stopped.

For over a decade his life had been the study and investigation of a seemingly endless succession of violent deaths. It had bred in him a profound hatred of violence—possibly because of that, but also because it was part of Flo's protective nature—and he and Flo had never hit any of their children, which, he was convinced, was where it all began. A cuff here, a back of the hand there, the other abuses piling up—verbal, sexual, simple neglect. Nobody paid enough attention—it was a rough road and if you wanted it cleared you pushed people out of the way. You didn't say "May I be excused"—you kicked some ass.

He shook his head. The folders lay there, Post-its stuck on like Band-Aids. Forcing himself, he grabbed the next one, the file on the late Christopher Locke. He opened it and saw that Lanier's taped interview with Loretta last night was first up, transcribed in record time—probably one of the secretaries interested in what the senator would have had to say—grist for the Hall's thriving gossip mill.

The senator . . .

And he'd just been thinking about Flo, about the way they'd tried to raise the kids . . . he still had a picture of her in his desk drawer. Now he opened it, pulled it out. She was blond, smiling, radiant, impossibly dead at forty.

The room, small enough in any event, closed in, finally wasn't there.

Flo had been so different from Loretta—that, he supposed, had been one of her attractions in the beginning. A white woman, tall, athletic rather than curvy, nurturing instead of combative, as Loretta had been before she'd—apparently—mellowed. Flo did not overvalue what Loretta liked to call the life of the mind. Flo valued life. She also wasn't competitive the way Loretta was. And having less to prove, she lived on a different plane—more serene, more truly self-confident.

Loretta had always projected herself as supremely competent and sure of herself, but her life-of-the-party, nothing-can-touch-me persona was, Glitsky knew, mostly a front, a reaction to her roots. She had grown up the third of four children in a low-income section of San Jose. Her parents had been, in Glitsky's view, people of integrity and self-respect who had worked their whole lives, her mother in the same dry-cleaning establishment for over twenty years, her father in a variety of clerical or retail or service jobs—shoe salesman, short-order cook, bus driver, whatever he could get.

By the time Glitsky had met the parents, they had

seemed old and used-up even though they were probably
close to his age now. Their first- and second-born sons, both
of Loretta's older brothers, had been drafted and killed in
Vietnam. Which went a long way to explain Loretta's early
radicalization and identification with, especially, the Black
Student Union. Her main issue when she had first met him
was more that her black brothers were fighting the white
man's war than that the objectives of the war might be
wrong in themselves. Later, of course, the sixties being
what they were, that evolved, too.

Loretta's younger sister Estelle had already had one ille-
gitimate child when Abe met her, and he had read in an
article about the senator a few years back that her little
sister was at that time eking out a welfare existence in Los
Angeles with three children and a succession of men. The
article said that Loretta and Estelle were no longer close
(nor, Abe knew, had they ever been).

Flo had had none of that—nothing to scratch and claw
her way out of. Resolutely middle-class, she had attended
Gunn High School in Los Altos ("Stanford Prep"), then
had switched gears and taken a swimming scholarship out
to the Central Valley—University of the Pacific in Stock-
ton, of all places.

Glitsky had met her in San Francisco at the Jewish Community Center gym, where he went to work out and where
she used the pool. Her goggles had been fogged up and
he'd been swimming laps, and she executed a perfect swim-
mer's shallow dive into him, nearly giving them both con-
cussions. (Later she would say she had noticed him at the
pool and couldn't think of any better way to introduce herself.) At UOP she had majored in child psychology (now
called early childhood learning), after which she had put in
two years teaching preschoolers at the Community Center.
Then, as it turned out, she was ready to have a few children
of her own.

Glitsky and Flo had fashioned a successful existence together. Many of the "issues" that had seemed so important
to him when he had been with Loretta in college faded
from their everyday lives, and he found he didn't much
miss them. Yes, he had dark skin and, yes, he had suffered
the usual prejudice when he had been younger and even

afterward, but though it continued to enrage him when it occurred (and Flo, too, for that matter), they refused to let it become their focus—*that* remained the two of them, the kids, the family. He made no apologies for his priorities—this was who he had become and it was worthwhile.

It was obvious why the world's injustice cut so much more deeply into Loretta's flesh, her psyche, her life. Given her own younger sister, given the way it so often turned out for black women, it was small wonder the senator was so protective of Elaine, her own daughter. Glitsky understood, for the first time now, that Loretta had pulled some strings with the District Attorney to set up her daughter in her position.

He was even starting to see, perhaps dimly to understand, why she might have felt the attraction of an older, white, rich Dana Wager so compelling, more even than young love had been. She wasn't going to end up powerless and in despair, the way her parents had. Good people, but . . . good didn't guarantee anything.

Funny, the differences, he thought . . . Loretta had married white, pretty much against her own politics, to get out of the ghetto, to ensure she would never have to go back. And now she was making her amends, identifying with her blackness, rationalizing that Elaine's figurative one drop of black blood made her one hundred percent black. Glitsky, on the other hand, had married white because he had fallen in love with a woman who happened to be white.

Now whatever was happening between Loretta and him was because of their chemistry, not their color. On her side, did that make it purer? On his, what . . . ?

What if they had stayed together from the beginning?

It was, he figured, better all around that they hadn't. Certainly, Flo had centered his life, took him out of currents that might have washed him away. And Loretta had done very well by herself. To the objective eye, she had reached a pinnacle of the American Dream never before touched by anyone of her background.

But now . . .

Well, now they were both grown, both free. As Abe's father had told him, the thing to do now was look ahead. Loretta already knew—her life had taught her—that it was pretty much all random. Events, basically, could not be controlled. And Flo's death had reminded him of that, rocked him, knocked him off balance.

Maybe now he and Loretta, by their separate routes, had finally arrived at close to the same place. Maybe his own sense of balance could be restored. He didn't know. That, too, might be random.

But he had to find out, keep trying until it got clear.

The room came back into focus. Where had he been?

He looked down at the open file on the desk . . . oh yes, Loretta's transcript, probably the rest of Strout's forensics, the microscopics. He flipped a page, scanning the lines of type. He didn't need to read it again—he'd gotten the story from her the previous night. He'd talk to Marcel Lanier tomorrow. Now she was at City Hall and had asked him to come by on his way home. Just for a minute even, she said.

Pulling his flight jacket off the chair behind him, he closed the folder and left it in the middle of his desk, hitting the light on his way out.

"Hey!"

He stopped. Ridley Banks was sitting at his own desk in the dusky light.

"Sorry," Glitsky said, "I didn't know anybody'd come back."

"You were in a trance. I didn't want to interrupt."

Glitsky flipped the switch and the light came back on. "How'd it go?"

Banks sat back in his chair. "Jamie O'Toole seems to be getting some recollection that there might have been a mob. He might have even seen someone in it. I think it'll come to him in a dream or something real soon. And speaking of him, you know the last two words a redneck says?"

Glitsky shook his head.

With a down-home accent, Banks said, "Watch this!" And waited.

Impassive, Glitsky stood by the door. "That's the joke?"

"I love that joke. 'Watch this!' Think about it. It gets funnier."

"I will." Mystified. "Meanwhile, what about Mullen and McKay?"

"These guys," Banks shook his head. "These guys are just too clever." He told Glitsky about the "mistake" as to whose sliding doors had been broken through.

"See if you can find their doctors," Glitsky said, and went on to explain a little about how the knife fitted into the picture. "If there are knife wounds and not caused by breaking glass, that means they were close enough to Arthur Wade to get cut. If *that's* the case, we've got enough to bring them both down, book them with something. I heard a good story today about what started it all off."

A questioning look. "So what about Kevin Shea?"

"I expect we'll be seeing Shea before too long. These stories I've been hearing, they come from his lawyer."

"He's got a lawyer? He's still in town?"

Glitsky nodded. "Interesting, isn't it? Makes you wonder. And guess what?"

"The lawyer says he didn't do it?"

"Sometimes you do this clairvoyance thing, Ridley—it's spooky. But yes, he does say that. And here's the interesting part—it might even have some truth in it." He came up to Banks's desk and sat on a corner of it.

Banks sat back. "You're not telling me Shea had no part of it?"

"Off the record, I think there's even a chance of that. He might be the good guy, might have tried to cut Wade down . . ."

Banks chewed on that a minute. "Uh oh."

"I know. But we're still bringing him in, let it work itself out. You seen the other guys?"

"Marcel went home. He was talking about getting some sleep. Griffin, I don't know, someplace." He hesitated, and Glitsky read it. "What?"

"Nothing."

But Glitsky knew what remained on his inspector's mind—Banks was tempted to say a few more words about his Pacific Moon theory, that there was something new he had discovered, or remembered, about Loretta Wager and how they said she had laundered money she'd allegedly smuggled out of Colombia in 1978. Banks, eyeing his lieutenant, thought he recognized in Glitsky a warning not to bring it up. Not now. Not, at least, until all this upheaval in the city was in the past.

Neither man said anything else. Glitsky stopped at the door, half-turned. "Watch this!" he said, deadpan, and hit the light switch again.

48

Loretta Wager was sitting in her small office at City Hall. Her desk was covered by a map of the city. She had been letting her fingers do the walking and now she sat back, folded her arms and allowed herself a moment of congratulation. She was proud of what she had accomplished in so short a time.

All that had to happen now to make it complete was the arrest of Kevin Shea, and Abe Glitsky had told her that that was imminent. Perhaps, even without Abe, it had already occurred.

Her eyes went again to the map and she rubbed a hand over it. What a beautiful city! Even the ugly parts . . .

The Hunter's Point Naval Reservation covered almost three times the ground area of all of Candlestick Point—it was nearly half the size of the Presidio. Unlike the Presidio, however, the Hunter's Point Naval Reservation was flat, windswept, nearly treeless. The ground under it was poisoned by toxic waste. Its open spaces were dead or gone to seed; its buildings squat, deserted, crumbling. It abutted the most pernicious ghetto in San Francisco, the nadir of the Bay View District, called home by Jerohm Reese. No one was ever going to make a movie entitled *Hunter's Point Naval Reservation* as they had about the Presidio.

Loretta Wager knew the place well. Its negatives didn't bother her. You took negatives and turned them to your advantage, that was how politics worked. That was how life worked.

Take Alan Reston, for example. Reston was the son of perhaps her largest single contributor, Tyrone "Duke" Reston, who years ago had begun bottling what, in Loretta's opinion, was the finest rib sauce in the world. Alan Reston, his son, had even campaigned for her directly, proving to her that he could be a player of the first order. Then she had supported him in his bid for deputy state attorney general. And then the Chris Locke vacancy had happened . . . She needed a conservative African-American in Locke's position and with enough personal authority to continue delivering the white moderate vote in San Francisco. Alan fit the bill perfectly.

The negative was that because he was a crime-busting prosecutor he was not exactly aligned with the African Nation movement. He had no problem with putting people—be they black or otherwise—in jail. Philip Mohandas did not want to go near him, and Loretta had already positioned Mohandas to be the voice of the current outrage, the one Mayor Conrad Aiken would hear.

Loretta had wanted Reston in the DA's office, and she needed to convince Mohandas to sell the idea to Aiken. After all, she had argued to Philip, it wouldn't be all bad. Reston was African-American, as Locke had been. Mohandas, in pushing Reston, would have an opportunity to talk about Drysdale, get his message out there.

But she needed more. Mohandas told her he wasn't going to "betray my principles," not for just that. Which had made her think of the old line: "We've already determined what you are. Now we're just haggling about the price."

How about if she could somehow deliver to Mohandas control of the huge tract of prime real estate that was the Hunter's Point Naval Reservation? Sitting as it did right on the bay, with some of the best views in the city, in the heart of an African-American cultural enclave, the place was a diamond in the rough, simply waiting for the right vision, the leader who could make its facets shine.

Loretta was in fact a member of the Parks Reclamation Commission and sat on the Committee on Decommissioned Military Installations in the Senate. She knew that the site was a multimillion-dollar headache for the federal government. Estimates on the cleanup of the toxics alone—if it could be done at all, and opinions varied widely on that—ran to over $30 million. After that gargantuan task had been accomplished and the site designated as a national park (as the Presidio had been), the renovations and improvements necessary before it actually could be opened to the public would cost an additional fifty-five to one hundred fifty million. Finally, add to that the cost of administering the park—twelve thousand dollars a day—and the Hunter's Point Naval Reservation had to be seen, in even the kindest light, as a negative.

But Mohandas needed to know none of this.

There were other considerations. First, she was certain she could in fact deliver. She'd been working for months now on some version of what was developing as her final plan. Because it was such a white elephant, Loretta knew that the federal government would like nothing better than to simply *give* the HPNR away, wash its hands of it, good-bye. Naturally, bureaucracies being what they were, this couldn't just happen in the normal course of events.

But that was the very point of the past few days—the normal flow of events had been radically altered. Symbols were needed, drastic action, red tape cut through to get the message across—we're all in this together, on the state and national level, good faith needed to be *demonstrated,* not talked about.

And so, early that morning Loretta had pitched the final draft of her proposal to a couple of her senatorial colleagues, as well as to the president's chief of staff, and it had been immediately embraced as brilliant and even visionary by each of them—the idea of an executive order that would release the HPNR to a trustee who would pledge to develop the site as a camp for underprivileged children. It would be a fine opportunity for the president to demonstrate his sensitivity to the plight of inner-city youth—give them a place to go, to play, to learn. (It would also get rid of a massive two hundred million dollar administrative nightmare.) Of course, sources close to the president would leak that Senator Wager had come up with this brilliant idea.

And who better to be the trustee than Philip Mohandas— a man with a *vision* who had shown even in this crisis a willingness to compromise for consensus? Mohandas had an undoubted commitment to the people he'd be serving, an organization already in place to administer the project. The moderate Senator Wager would vouch for his good intentions.

Finally, she had told Philip, he could expect federal funding (not even including what he could expect in matching or co-payment funds from the state government in Sacramento and the city of San Francisco) in the neighborhood of twelve million per year. A million a month. No taxes. Essentially—cash.

And, like cash, it was nearly impossible to keep perfect tabs on it. No one really even expected it.

So Philip Mohandas had gone to Conrad Aiken and sold Alan Reston to the city of San Francisco as its new District Attorney.

Chris Locke's death, Alan Reston, Philip Mohandas, the HPNR—all potential negatives, and wasn't it marvelous to see how they all seemed to be working out?

"Let me drive. You look exhausted."

Glitsky hesitated briefly, then shrugged and handed his keys over to Loretta. "I won't argue."

"And I'm paying for dinner, too."

"I don't—"

"No discussion. Senators do not brook argument with lesser mortals, which includes everyone except the president, who doesn't brook much argument himself."

Glitsky enjoyed her, no doubt about it. He was crossing in front of the Plymouth, going to the passenger side, smiling. "What about the vice president?"

She gave him a disdainful look. "He's just a senator who doesn't get to vote very often. Definitely a lesser mortal."

"Governor?" he asked.

Opening the driver's door, she shot back. "What state?" Inside, leaning to the side, she flipped up the lock on Glitsky's door.

He slid in. "California."

Loretta thought a minute, reached under the seat and tried to slide it forward. It didn't move. She wasn't big enough. "Help me here, on three." She counted, and together they got the seat far enough so she could touch the floor pedals. "California, I'd say brook."

"Brook? What does brook mean?"

"Lieutenant, what are we talking about here?—the brooking of argument, are we not? And I'd say the governor of California would *brook* no argument from lesser mortals."

He grinned at her, the scar tight through his lips. "Okay, then, how about the governor of Delaware?"

"No brook."

"Louisiana?"

"No brook."

"Hmm. So police lieutenants . . ."

Turning the key—the car started right up—she patted his leg, slipping into the familiar patois she used with her daughter and almost no one else. "Honey, they is only a hundred U.S. senators in the whole world. You got any idea how many police lieutenants they is?"

Glitsky actually laughed out loud, something he did with about the regularity of a lunar eclipse. "So definitely they are lesser mortals? Police lieutenants?"

That disdainful look again, a Whoopi Goldberg glint in her eyes. "Now you tell me, sugar. I don't make this stuff up. The numbers don't lie."

"So I am definitely a no brook."

"In theory, absolutely right on. But you, personally, Abe Glitsky, there might be a loophole . . ."

"Which part, the lesser or the mortal . . . ?"

Her hand was on his thigh again. "Good part of you ain't no lesser than nobody . . ."

They pulled out into Polk Street, into traffic, heading north—bantering, goofing one another.

Kids.

There were no tents in Washington Square. The riots had not yet infringed on the core of San Francisco, the compact and for the most part elegant wedge of pie bounded on the south and east by Market Street and on the west by Van Ness Avenue—thirty-five blocks north to south, seventeen east to west. The city within.

Glitsky was sitting with Loretta at a back corner table in La Pantera on the corner of Columbus at Washington Square. Up the street was the much more tony Fior d'Italia; across the park was Moose's, hangout even in these days of crisis of every bon vivant in the city. But La Pantera was a private place for anonymous citizens and that suited them both. This was a private dinner.

"The rumor that just won't die," she said. She pushed some tubular pasta around on her plate, drank some of her 7-Up, sighed. Glitsky marvelled at the shape and tone of her face—unlined, the skin smooth as fine chocolate. "The Pacific Moon," she said. "Sometimes I wish I'd never heard of the place."

"I'm just telling you what I heard, Loretta. It's not an issue for me personally. It was just one of my inspectors trying to protect me, that's all."

But she didn't seem to hear that. "Now it's three million dollars? Time I'm sixty it ought to have grown to ten."

"Three million is the profit . . ."

"I know, I know." She held up a hand. "Please. Wait. I want to tell you."

He nodded, waiting.

"After . . . after the plane crash . . . you know about the plane crash, right? Colombia? I thought you did, but . . . well, Dana and I were having some problems even before then. It was one of the reasons I have something of my own in case Dana and I split up, which at the time I thought was pretty likely."

"You mind if I ask why?"

She took a long moment deciding. "Dana was one of those men who was great to be around when things were going well, when he had money and things seemed to be under his control. He was all tied up in that."

"Okay."

"But his investments started to go sour. He took a couple of big hits in the stock market, tried to recoup some of that in real estate here in the city and guessed wrong. Notes were coming due and he couldn't pay them and I guess he started to panic. I mean, he was turning sixty by now. His confidence began to erode. I told him that it didn't matter, that we still had plenty. What was important to me was how he treated Elaine, if he loved me, personal things. But to him, if he wasn't a provider he wasn't anything—it was all tied up in that men's macho thing. And then he got so . . . well, we gave up on . . . the physical side, and that of course just continued the cycle."

She sipped at her drink.

"But after Colombia . . . ?"

"After Colombia, after I got back . . . I don't know. Maybe it shocked him awake. He wasn't that old. He wasn't going to lose both me and Elaine. He couldn't let that happen. So when I got out of the hospital we came back home and people started talking about me running for Congress, running for Theo Heckstrom's seat, and suddenly we were both looking forward again. His confidence came back, he took a few risks—one of them was the Pacific Moon."

"And the place made three million dollars?"

She smiled at him. "Abraham. Please. In the first place, it wasn't three million dollars, not even close. And whatever it was got divided up among the investors. In the second, what it did make was based on another risk Dana took—that's the way he always was. When he had the guts he could do anything. He talked the other investors into rolling the restaurant's profits into the down payment on some throwaway land south of Market here that Dana had heard was going to . . . well, a good portion of it now is the Moscone Center."

"My, my, my." The Moscone Center was San Francisco's own multimillion-dollar convention showcase.

"Yes. And as it turned out they only had to make three or four payments before the city bought it back from them. It was a nice windfall, one time only, and then Dana got out of the restaurant business, rolled his share of the profit over to continue in development, which was his first love anyway. He just needed the Pacific Moon to use the other investors' money, to get some leverage so he could make a move on the land."

Glitsky was sitting back, arms folded. He leaned forward. "This isn't somewhere in the public record? Why would there still be rumors?"

A resigned edge crept into her voice. "I think, Abe, first, because people don't understand what Dana did. And when people don't understand an answer, they often make one up. Next, I'm a public figure—there would never have been a rumor if I were some housewife, believe me. But now it might be to someone's advantage to find out something bad about me." She leaned across the table, speaking quietly. "Abraham, listen to me. Dana went to some pains to keep his books . . . private. The investors formed a holding company, which bought the property, then turned the profits back to the restaurant, which is why the restaurant showed so much profit that year. No names. But you can find them—people have found them—if they know where to look. Auditors, for instance.''

"But why didn't he use—?''

"Why no names? Why all the hiding?'' She sat back. "Because Dana believed knowledge is power, so don't tell anybody anything they don't need to know. Also, he thought, probably correctly, that there would be resentment by voters if it appeared that I made money off the city on a lucky guess, which was essentially what it was. We didn't do—*Dana* didn't do—anything wrong, but in this business, my business, politics, appearance is everything.'' It clearly troubled her still. She reached a hand across to him. "That's the story. Satisfied? Can we still be . . . whatever we are? You being a policeman and all?''

"I didn't need all that, but it's good to hear.''

Their hands met in the middle of the table. "I don't need you to be doubting me.''

"I don't. I won't.'' He raised her hand to his lips, held it against them.

It was tempting, though Loretta knew she could never do it, to lay it all out for Abe and the world to see. She'd been listening to the moans and accusations of the self-righteous for most of her adult life, and just once she'd like to go on record so the vast unwashed could really understand what you had to do to get somewhere if you'd started where she had.

She had always wanted to do some honest good, to help raise up the people she represented, to make a difference and be an active part of making her country a better place. She wasn't a cynic—she truly wanted these things. And in her career she thought she had gone a long way toward achieving some progress.

It had not been just for ego or self-aggrandizement—at least not for those alone. She *never* wanted Elaine to suffer the slights she'd had to endure as a child and even more as a young woman. And by God, she hadn't. Power and position *did* get you protection from the worst of the world. And through Elaine, by extension, her protectiveness embraced others—she'd started out her career by representing the disadvantaged, the downtrodden, back when there was a plurality of votes in that stance.

That had changed now, and she'd had to change along with it if she wanted to stay in power to do any good. She didn't believe she was abandoning her principles; she had just had to adapt to hold on to them. She couldn't help anybody, could she, if she didn't get elected first? Perhaps a politician's age-old rationalization, but it was also true. So maybe the message got watered down some, but it didn't get compromised away, not completely.

What would the righteous have done, she wondered, in her place? It was one thing to take the high moral ground and say, "Oh I would have turned the found money over to the authorities," another altogether to sit for four days in the stinking jungle thinking you were going to die and know you had in your possession over half a million dollars in cash that no one could ever trace.

She had never felt any qualms about the fact that she alone survived the crash. No survivor guilt. It was hardly her fault. Yes, the money might originally have come from drugs, who knew? It might have belonged to somebody else, it might have gone untaxed in the United States as income, but certainly the greater good was all it had enabled her to accomplish for her people first as a congresswoman and then a senator.

The ends did justify the means—and anybody who didn't think so wasn't living a reality-based existence.

There was another more personal reason why keeping the money had never bothered her. For her it represented random fate evening out the playing field. She had been a victim of poverty—even though her good parents had always proudly if blindly denied it. They had been wrong—where they ended up verified that. She had felt the pain of it every day, in every situation. She *deserved* some random good luck after the bad that had been the accident of her birth into a powerless family.

Well, finally it had come to her and she had taken it—without apologies, without explanations or guilt. The only ones who wouldn't take it were losers who were afraid to reach beyond where everyone else expected them to stop. That wasn't her. She'd made it and she'd done a hell of a lot of good in the process.

God had sent her that money. All the powers on earth would never persuade her otherwise, or could have forced her to give back even a penny of it.

Not back then, not now, not ever.

49

"I'm sorry. You must have the wrong number."

"Wes . . . ?"

The phone went dead in Kevin's hand.

"What was that?" Melanie asked. She was combing her hair at Ann's bedroom vanity—eighty-one, eighty-two . . . She hadn't gotten around to putting her clothes back on.

"That was Wes being cryptic. I'll call him again." He started to punch the numbers.

"No, wait a minute. What did he say?"

"Melanie, he always does stuff like this. Says I've got the wrong number, then hangs up." He started pushing buttons again. She was up from her seat, threw herself over him on the bed, grabbing for the telephone. Landing across his ribs.

"Ahh!"

"Oh, I'm sorry. I'm *sorry,* Kevin, I didn't mean . . ."

He, also naked, was on his side, half-rolled into a fetal position, moaning. She took the phone from him and placed it in its cradle. "Are you all right?"

He shook his head, trying to catch his breath, struggling with it. "You want to call him so bad, okay, you call."

"I don't want to call him. Tell me what he said."

Rolling over, flat onto his back, Kevin gingerly pushed at his ribs. "He said, this is a direct quote, get ready. He said, 'Sorry, wrong number.' "

"Somebody was there. He *was* followed home. We were right to get out of there. It's true. You know it's true."

He poked gingerly at his ribs as she sat beside him on the bed. After a minute she lifted the receiver. "What's his number?"

Closing his eyes, he leaned back again and mumbled it

to her. She pushed the buttons. "This is your mother, Wes. Say, 'Oh, hi, Mom.' Now, if the police are there, say, 'I don't know. I might be busy that night.' "

She nodded. "We'll call you later. Do you think they'll be gone within an hour?"

A small pause. "All right, now say, 'Okay, sorry. 'Bye, Mom.' "

She hung up and put a hand on Kevin's belly, shaking her head.

He covered her hand with his. "Now what?"

Dressed now, hair as neatly combed as Melanie could get it—she thought it might make a difference—Kevin sat rigidly in an easy chair in the living room surrounded by plants, the blinds drawn at the window behind him. They had all the lights turned on, some dragged in from the bedroom, all the lamp shades stripped from them. Ersatz klieg.

Melanie had moved Ann's tripod and video camera around—it was loaded with tape and ready to go—and pointed it at Kevin. She pushed the button, the red light came on, and Kevin tried to smile at the camera, though it came out forced.

"I'm Kevin Shea," he began, "and I did not . . ."

They stood embracing by the inside of the apartment's front door. "There's no other way to do it. I've got to go. I'll be back in less than an hour, then we'll call Wes again."

"Maybe you could go by his apartment. *He* could deliver it."

She shook her head. "I'm not going by there. They've probably got the National Guard surrounding the place." She kissed him. "Look, Kevin, I'm not the one in danger, I'm the only one who can do this. I changed the plates on the car. We got over here, didn't we?"

"Barely."

"Barely counts," she said, kissed him and was out the door.

*   *   *

He thought it odd that he didn't want a beer. Ann had four perfectly good Rolling Rocks in the refrigerator and instead he poured himself a glass of orange juice from the large pitcher. Drank it all down and poured another one.

Back in the living room he tried to estimate the time it would take—Melanie was bringing the tape down to KQED, the public television station, the closest one to the apartment. Assuming she wasn't arrested and didn't get in a wreck, it shouldn't take her an hour. But there was always traffic, and, the last couple of days, the curfew areas she'd have to avoid.

His stomach was cramping. What if something happened to her? Now, when . . .

When what?

He realized he was more worried about what might happen to her than he was about himself. He should never have let her go alone. He should have gone with her . . .

Wes Farrell was answering Kevin's question about the police presence. "They're gone. What are you doing?"

"I've been counting seconds for the last seven minutes. There were four hundred and twenty of them I think. It got a little boring so I thought I'd call you. How's Bart?"

"Bart's fine."

"So your meeting downtown . . . ?"

"I thought it all went along perfectly until the cops showed up here."

"How did that happen?"

"I should have known. Gets to be a lot at stake, they lie."

"Who?"

"The cops. In this case, Lieutenant Glitsky. Said he'd keep it to himself but he obviously assigned somebody to follow me home, figuring you were staying at my place, although I said you weren't. He probably figured it was worth a try. If you'd been here he could claim the arrest, maybe even get the reward. Anyway, imagine my surprise and relief when it turned out I was inadvertently telling the truth about you not being here. It also probably kept me out of jail. So what are you counting seconds for?"

"Until Mel comes back."

"Where is she?"

Kevin explained. "We figure we get me on the air, the media picks it up, maybe we get a swing in public opinion. Something changes. At least the *truth* gets out there."

"I've got one for you, Kev. Why do you persist in thinking that anybody's going to believe anything you have to say?"

Kevin took that in, waited a beat before answering. "I *am* telling the truth here, Wes."

"*I'm* not arguing with you. We've been through that. But I told Glitsky *your* truth—at least as I understood it. He even seemed open to it. And yet there's something about this Grand Jury indictment . . . that's a formal document, Kevin. You are *charged* with this crime. I don't think a videotape of you saying you didn't do it is going to win many hearts and minds. People are going to be cynical about your motives. Trust me. It's going to take a jury now, unless we can get to the DA, get him to drop it, which even Glitsky thought was unlikely. And, incidentally, so do I."

"I'm not going to trial for this—"

"I'd take a reality check on that one, Kevin."

"There's no way, I'm going to—"

"Then why are you staying in the city? I thought you wanted to tell your story, get the truth out."

"Yeah, but not at a damn trial, Wes. I go to trial I'm a dead man, you know that. Hell, that's what *you* told *me*. It can't get to that. That's why I came to you. Get it straightened out behind the scenes."

Farrell couldn't say anything.

"Wes?"

"Barring an act of God, Kevin, a trial is what's going to happen. We'll have to arrange your arrest, then get you out on bail . . ."

"I thought there wasn't bail on a murder charge."

"A *capital* murder charge—that's something we'd have to negotiate."

There was a long silence, then Kevin's voice, noticeably weaker. "Wes, it just can't have come to this."

"That's what I'm trying to tell you, Kevin. It's *already* come to this. It's going to have to play itself out at trial . . . unless they kill you first."

Another long pause. "Gosh, you cheer a guy right up."

"You asked."
"Do me a favor, would you, next time I ask?"
"What?"
"Lie."

50

Allicey Tobain was in the storefront's inner office with Philip Mohandas. N'doum was outside standing guard. In spite of the insistent hum of the voices—some of them raised—of the other people in the front, N'doum could clearly hear Allicey through the door . . .

She was pacing in the small room. "You are losin' sight of the reality here, Philip. You are being manipulated by that . . . that *politician*." She spit out the word, stopped pacing, faced Mohandas. "You tell me this—what we got out of all this? We got one of *her* people in the DA's job. We do that for her, in exchange for something . . . right? But where's the exchange? Where's the something? We get a promise, that's all, but I'm not seeing any something. And in the meanwhile we're losing sight—"

"You keep saying that, Allicey, but what of? What am I losing sight of? And we will get the something. We get a million dollars a month." He spoke quietly, gestured to the door. "That buys a lot of pamphlets, girl, a lot of advertising time, a lot of everything—you hear what I'm saying?"

She wasn't buying. Bringing her face up to his, she said "I ain't running no *day-care* center. This isn't about no *underprivileged youth.* This is about *our people*, Philip, about how we're really treated. We got a man lynched here three days ago and so far *not one person* has been arrested. Far as I can tell, nobody's even lookin' anymore. You call that justice? You call that progress? That what you want?"

He was silent.

She crossed back to Philip's sleeping couch, stopped, turned to him again. Her tone softened. "She's playin' you, Philip. She takin' your teeth out. Don't you *see* that. It's a game for her. You get caught up in the game, you forget what you're about, who you are, who you can trust."

"I don't forget that. But she's offering something important we can use, something—"

"*Goddamn*, man, *listen* to yourself. You talkin' about her *offer*, you playin' her game . . ." Coming back to him, she put her hands on his arms, holding them. "Let me ask you this—is Jerohm Reese out of jail? Is that man Drysdale still working? If you remember, that's what we wanted this morning—those two things—when *Senator* Wager gives us the call. You remember that? We got either of them?"

"You were with me, Allicey . . ."

"I got sucked in a minute, too. I thought we were getting something. But ask yourself, what do we got now? Alan Reston? Who's he? We got the mayor upping the reward on Kevin Shea, but I don't see no Kevin Shea. You see him? You see anything really happening?"

She let go of his arms, smoothed the fabric of his shirt. "We got brothers and sisters fighting out there, Philip. Losin' the streets. Ain't nothin' make them feeling any better until a certain justice comes down here. That's what we gotta be calling for—some simple justice. And I think in the heat of all this . . . this *negotiating* with the *senator* . . . we losin' track of who we are, what we all about. That's all I'm sayin'."

Philip Mohandas kept his face impassive. He backed up a couple of steps, came up against one of the folding chairs and lowered himself into it, his back straight.

Flanked by Allicey and Jonas, Philip Mohandas was out in the front of the store surrounded by perhaps forty of his followers. Even at this time of night, there were a half-dozen microphones, a representative (with telecam) from one of the cable TV stations, a female reporter from the *Bay Guardian* who'd been hanging at his headquarters all day. Mohandas, aware that he was being taped, was orating:

". . . most emphatically are *not* satisfied with what you're calling the progress of the city, the situation as it stands today. All that we have seen, and continue to see, is lip service, that is *all*."

The *Guardian* reporter spoke up. Behind Mohandas, Allicey and Jonas frowned. "But what about Alan Reston? Wasn't he your candidate? He's black, doesn't that show some kind of—"

Mohandas let his voice out a bit. He partially raised his fist. "Whoever it was, the new DA had to be an African-American. The mayor realized he had no other option. Any other choice would have been . . . gratuitously inflammatory. Mr. Reston himself was acceptable under that minimum criteria, but we remain adamant that Jerohm Reese is an innocent victim as well as a continuing example of white oppression, that Mr. Art Drysdale is a racist who must be retired from any public position. So no, to answer your question, we are *dis*satisfied."

"What about the increased reward? Doesn't that—"

Mohandas pointed at the stringer for the cable network. "Now I'm glad you raised that question because it's more of the lip service I've been talking about. It's an empty gesture, designed to lull my community—my outraged brothers and sisters—into a belief that the power structure, that people of non-color are *concerned. Concerned!* But we don't want concern. Concern isn't enough. We want *results.* What good is a reward—be it fifty dollars or five million dollars—if it does nothing to produce the man?" He pointed to The Picture taped to the wall. "We got to have the man."

He turned to the camera, focused and intense. "Let's not get lost in rhetoric, in so-called good intentions. Let us not forget what has happened here in San Francisco, what continues to happen. Arthur Wade has died and nothing has changed. Jerohm Reese is in jail and Kevin Shea walks the streets, and until that gets corrected, until these facts get turned around, we cannot rest. We will not rest."

His voice had hoarsened somewhat, and Jonas N'doum handed him a glass of water, from which he drank. "That is why I am calling for a solidarity march—a *peaceful* solidarity march—on Saturday morning, presenting these demands to the city once and for all: that there is *action* on Jerohm Reese, that there is *action* on Mr. Art Drysdale, that the city employ *all* its resources, *all* its power to find Kevin Shea and begin the righteous task of bringing him to justice."

The room exploded in a chorus of "Right ons" and "Amens" and Mohandas half turned, received an approving nod from Allicey Tobain, then faced the camera with an expression of fixed resolve.

51

They were walking on the cold sand of the beach below the Cliff House, Loretta barefoot with her shoes in her hand and wearing Glitsky's flight jacket against the slight chill. There was no wind. He was holding her other hand, pretending to be immune to the weather. They had gotten out here to the ocean, Loretta still driving, along the northern edge of the city, through the Presidio and the Seacliff neighborhood, bypassing anything resembling a curfew area.

"So when are you going back to Washington?"

"I don't know exactly. I'd like to see this . . . this whole thing resolved, at least stay until that. If it's not too long, which I gather it won't be."

The night had been all personal—both Abe and Loretta were under the impression that Kevin Shea would be in custody by sometime the next day. The madness would be dissipating. They didn't have to discuss it—it was moving toward its conclusion.

She was continuing. "I do feel I'm part of that, of all of this. I'm still very worried about Elaine." Her steps slowed and she stopped walking, turned to look up to Glitsky. "And then there's you."

He kept walking, step after step. His factual voice. "Yes, there is."

"I don't suppose you get to Washington much."

"That's a good guess."

She stopped then, studied the sand, drew a few lines in it with her toes. "I'm here at the recess, couple of times during the year, mostly campaigning."

Over her head the breaking waves had a phosphorescence. Glitsky thought he saw the lights of a tanker out at the horizon. Behind him rose the faint wail of a siren.

"Okay," he said.

Her arms were around his waist. "Would you mind very much hugging me a minute?"

She was holding him tight, her body pressed against him. He felt a shiver pass through her. "Are you cold?"

Her head shook. "That's not it." He kept holding her. "You tell yourself you don't need this," she whispered, almost as though it were to herself.

"I know."

"You get good at it. You have to."

Glitsky didn't trust himself to say much. "Yep."

Gradually, her arms let him go, fell to her sides. He released her and she stepped back. Even in the dim lights from the moon and the street behind him, her eyes were liquid, shining. The hint of a smile fluttered and died. "Senators aren't allowed to cry. It's in the oath."

He touched her cheek.

"I want to ask you to stay with me."

He shook his head no. "You said it yourself. You've got to give Elaine some time. She needs you. And I've got to check in. If Farrell's called . . . to say nothing of the fourteen messages which my trained police eye sees blinking on your answering machine. And tomorrow looks to be another long one."

They were just inside her front door. "Are you always this responsible?"

"Yes, ma'am. Like yourself, I'm a humble servant of the public."

"All right," she said, pulling him down and kissing him. She opened the door, looked out theatrically, back and forth. "All right, it's all clear. No reporters." She faced him. "Come to think of it, maybe I should start getting a little worried about no reporters. Where have they been? They should be here."

"Staking out your house . . . ?"

She hugged him again. "I'm teasing you, Lieutenant. Now get out of here. As it is, I'm going to need a cold shower before I'm going to be able to get my head back into my work."

Glitsky's scar stretched a little. "Now you didn't say anything about a shower . . ."

She pushed him outside. "Git . . . but tomorrow."

He pointed a finger at her. "Tomorrow."

He walked to the car and stared back at her mansion, which was, he thought, far more intimidating than the woman herself.

It must have been Dana's. It was strange to think of her living here, so close to him, all these years. Of course, for most of them, he'd had Flo, he hadn't been looking, told himself he wouldn't have seen it if it had danced in front of him.

Another siren, this one not far away. He turned and looked at the orange glow of more flames somewhere in the eastern sky. Come on, Mr. Farrell, he thought, let's get this over with.

It was still early enough—not yet ten. And he knew no one was home chez Glitsky. It was literally the most free that he'd been in probably fifteen years and he was going to go check back in at work. Somebody might need him.

He got in the car. The seat was still jammed up under the steering wheel where Loretta had needed it. He smiled to himself and said, "One two three," pushing it back to where he could drive. Small packages, he was thinking. What was that expression? What was it that came in them—good things? Or was it dynamite?

This late at night Glitsky's first inclination was to pull directly up to the front of the Hall on Bryant Street and park along the curb. He was aware of heavy traffic even north of Market, and by the time he got where he worked he was barely crawling. Black-and-whites were double- and triple-parked along the entire length of the block. Near the center of the street, by the entrance to the Hall, where he'd been interviewed earlier in the day, the television vans had staked their turf. There was a line of busses for transporting people. He could see the traffic backed up both coming off the Freeway at 7th and down from the lower Mission on

Bryant, and he knew at least one of the other side streets was a parking lot. Finally, turning into an alley jammed with what he knew were unmarked police cars parked on the curbs and sidewalks, he crept through the one open lane to the city lot behind the Hall.

A long, partially covered corridor ran between the new jail and the old morgue and led to the back door of the Hall. Although it had grill-covered lightbulbs spaced infrequently, at this time of night the walkway had a spacey, almost eerie dimness. Maybe it was in contrast to the startling brightness visible through the tall windows in the Hall's lobby or just the sense that you were entering some kind of cave that happened to abut where they stored dead people, but when it was dark out, this walkway always gave Glitsky the creeps. He half-expected bats to be scared out of their resting places when he passed, exploding by him in a flurry of wings and squeaks.

So he was hurrying and didn't even notice John Strout until the man said hello from the shadowed entrance to the morgue.

After Glitsky landed, the coroner smiled genially. "I didn't mean to startle y'all."

"You're working late." He gestured toward the main building. "So's everybody else."

Strout nodded. "I don't suppose you're down here just to take the waters, either, Lieutenant."

"I don't suppose so."

"Anything specific?"

This was an unusual question from Strout. It could be he was making conversation, but Glitsky suddenly didn't think so. "Not really," he replied. Then, on reflection: "Why?"

Mr. Noncommittal, Strout shrugged, considered, raised his eyebrows. "No reason, just—"

"Just what?"

"Just Art Drysdale was by here near closing time, wanted to pay his respects to Mr. Locke. Also probably wanted to hide out a while, everybody bein' on his ass for everything he did or didn't do the last five years." This was a justified beef—Strout and Drysdale had worked together a long time with great mutual respect. "Mr. Locke's death hit him pretty hard."

Glitsky hadn't been much of a Locke fan, but he understood Drysdale's reaction—the two had been on the same team, fought the same battles together. It was natural that a bond would develop.

"All the events of the day, I think he was finally gettin' around to the story on what actually happened with Mr. Locke. Asked me who was handlin' it and I told him you'd been by."

For the usually laconic Strout, this much conversation qualified as a philippic. Glitsky thought he was probably going somewhere with it and waited for him to continue.

"Well, he went on up to your place and one of your men told him he didn't think Mr. Locke's had been formally assigned, something like that. It was on your desk but—"

Glitsky straightened up. "John, Marcel Lanier and I *both* interviewed Loretta Wager, who was our only—"

Strout had his hands up. "This is not me, Lieutenant. I'm not in the middle of this. This is Art's reaction, that's all."

"All right."

"Art seemed to think that some inspector might have gone out and spent the day down by Dolores Park"—the riot location where Locke had been shot—"and put a little effort into finding this shooter, done some door-to-door in the neighborhood . . ."

"You know, John, it's not exactly been a slow news week. Maybe Art hasn't noticed."

"I think he has, Abe. I really do. I think he just knows how fast these trails get cold. Now a day's gone by an' nobody seems inclined to do the routine. Mr. Locke bein' the District Attorney an' all, he thought it might have gotten itself a little more priority, the investigation, I mean."

"There were other—" Glitsky didn't mean to snap. He stopped himself. Drysdale, of course, was right as far as he went. Glitsky *should* have assigned someone to go canvass the area of the shooting, wherever that had been exactly. But that was the point—he should have that knowledge, should know for a certainty that there wasn't any forensic evidence at the site. Maybe there was a strand of fabric, a bloodstain, a shoe print, a bullet casing (although Glitsky knew that the caliber of the bullet that killed Locke didn't come from an automatic so it wouldn't have ejected). Still, something . . .

Drysdale *was* right—his boss and buddy Chris Locke had

been killed and Glitsky, the head of homicide, was neglecting to investigate the death thoroughly. No wonder Art had come down and mentioned it to Dr. Strout.

But damn—Glitsky's blood was rushing—he couldn't do everything. He had every one of his inspectors, including himself, triple-assigned—hell, quintuple-assigned—and he knew that the odds of getting even a long-shot lead to finding the man who had shot Chris Locke—on a dark evening in the midst of a riot—approached absolute zero.

This was the kind of extra helping of the unexpected personal stuff that made his job so frustrating. Not that Drysdale didn't have a point. Not that he wasn't justified that his best friend's death wasn't getting the priority he felt it deserved. But that no matter how hard you tried, no matter how responsible you were—he remembered Loretta's remark—you could never do enough. You were going to piss off someone, hurt someone, let someone down.

And Drysdale, whom Abe worked well with, was having a tough enough time. In fact, he knew, he should have assigned it, long shot or no. Many—most—murder investigations were long shots. The simple, galling truth was that he'd gotten distracted and hadn't entirely been doing his job. And that made him furious at himself, at Drysdale, even at the messenger right here.

But there was no point in losing it with Strout. The person with whom he was really put out lived closer.

"You see Art before I do," he said evenly to Strout, "tell him I realized the same thing, thought I'd come down and correct the oversight."

Just as he entered the building someone started yelling in the cavernous, packed lobby.

The person manning the metal detector at the back door was a former street cop named Jimmy Mercy who had been hit on the head with a tire iron years before and appeared punch-drunk ever since. A sweet guy.

"Been like this all night, Sergeant." Mercy would need another year or two, if ever, before he got used to Glitsky being a lieutenant. "Everybody's in real bad moods lately."

"Everybody includes me, Jimmy." He was moving forward, into the noise.

Which was escalating quickly.

A pair of uniforms came out the double-doors of the hallway—the downstairs of the Hall of Justice contained a regular administrative police post, Southern Station, out of which a small contingent of cops worked. Glitsky also knew that the police assembly room on the sixth floor had people on call the last few nights, ready for "disturbance" assignment. He hoped some of them were still up there now because it looked like the party was coming here tonight.

One of the uniforms turned around and yelled to the area behind him. "WE GOT SOME SHIT HAPPENING OUT HERE!"

A shrill emergency bell started to ring in the building.

In the lobby Sheriff Boles had continued with his make-shift booking procedures. And in spite of the National Guard presence and Mayor Aiken's orders, looting was continuing throughout the city. From Glitsky's perspective, basically nothing was working.

They had more than a hundred people in the lobby and had just unloaded what looked like another bus from another scene. Thirty-five city policemen were roaming around inside and outside the Hall, herding in the new group, another twenty-five or so sheriff's deputies, all inside, were guarding the lines and doing paperwork at the desks. In the line itself mingled a complete set of San Francisco's ethnicities, some of them bruised, some crying, *all* pissed off.

And after the procession, Boles was simply letting these people go. And there was nowhere to go. Some people wanted to get away as quickly as they could, but most were turned loose downtown in the middle of the night—no cabs, no friends picking them up, a loose mob of recent rioters and looters milling on the steps and environs of the Hall of Justice.

Another fight seemed to be breaking out in the ranks of the new arrivals. Inside, the line of detainees, unruly at best, swelled toward the entrance, pushing. A couple of men went down. A woman screamed.

The bell kept ringing and more policemen appeared from the hallway, out of the elevators—probably from the sixth floor.

A burly white youth broke from the inside line, ran at

the three cops at the front door, took down one of them, punched at another. Glitsky saw him go down in a flurry of nightsticks—echoes of Rodney King—kicking, refusing to be subdued.

More cops, and as they ran to the outbreak, leaving their guard posts, more detainees began rushing for the door, a stampede where the line had been breached. Some of them making it outside. Whistles blowing, that damn bell just going on and on, and over it the sound of explosions outside. Was some idiot firing his gun in all this?

Jesus, all hell breaking . . .

Forty minutes later Glitsky was behind his desk. They had finally subdued the riot—two hundred and fifteen police, and by the time it was over they had recorralled one hundred and four rioters. The rest of the potential arrestees had either seen or made their chance and taken it. The sheriff's tables that had been in the lobby were tipped over, torn apart. There had been a small paper fire. The earlier records of citations, for the most part, were gone.

Sheriff Boles and his deputies had packed the remaining detainees into the commandeered busses and were taking them to Alameda County, where they would discover what a real jail was like.

It was eleven-fifteen.

Adrenaline was surging through him.

This thing wasn't going away, wasn't even getting any better. For some reason his mind turned to the French Revolution, to a truth he'd only realized for the first time earlier this summer when he'd read about it in one of his continuing self-improvement programs. It was about the storming of the Bastille Prison in Paris on July 14, 1789. (He reflected on the fact that revolutions always seemed to happen in July, which was now only forty-five minutes away.) At the time the Bastille event hadn't seemed to mark the end of the monarchy. For weeks afterward Louis XVI had made his rounds, giving speeches, doing damage repair, the usual. But from Bastille Day onward he was doomed. He just didn't realize it.

Glitsky wondered if they were all in the same boat here

in the City by the Bay. Three days in and, if tonight were any indication, on a roll.

The pile of messages on his desk had grown exponentially, Chief Dan Rigby's message labeled "URGENT" on top, but the first thing Glitsky did was go through the whole pile on the chance that Farrell had called.

Nope.

Why the hell not? What was going on with that guy?

Next he called Rigby's office, only to hear the extension ringing and ringing in the War Room. It wasn't really any surprise—Rigby had probably gone home, along with his staff, for at least a few hours. If he had been in the building during the riot Glitsky would have seen him. He would check back with the chief first thing in the morning, find out what was so urgent.

Supervisor Greg Wrightson had called him again. Although a nominal liberal, like every other supervisor, Wrightson was one of the few members of the Board of Supes who at least pretended to care about the mostly so-called right-wing issues that concerned the police department. He also was in the bad habit of believing that he, as a city supervisor, somehow had a mandated authority to order police action whenever it suited him. He had been known to call up Rigby himself and ask him to start enforcing the violations on parking meters around City Hall. Important stuff like that.

Glitsky knew Wrightson wouldn't be in his office in the middle of the night, but he moved the message onto the center of his desk, under Rigby's. If Wrightson had called twice in one day, he had something on his mind.

Glitsky's father's message was that he had also left a message at his home—where was Abraham, anyway? He and the boys were at the White Sands Motel in case he got this message. Monterey was quiet, idyllic. Abraham ought to get away himself on the weekend if he could.

"Sure, Dad," Glitsky muttered. "Great idea."

Then the informal correspondence from his inspectors. Carl Griffin's note about a Colin Devlin who was going to come in tomorrow with a lawyer and make a statement about the Arthur Wade riot. And, by the way, Griffin wrote, Glitsky was right about the knife-wound connection.

Devlin had been cut—that's how Griffin had found him. This brought a measure of satisfaction.

But the emotion was short-lived, because looking up brought his stack of folders into his consciousness, among them the reminder of Art Drysdale's complaint to Strout about the Chris Locke investigation, or lack thereof. He reached over and pulled the entire pile over in front of him, digging down through the first four or five until he came to Locke.

All right, this will be on top, too.

And back to his guys—a crisp and cryptic few words from Ridley Banks—"Re: PM, Mo-Mo House, Watch This!" Glitsky wrestled with it for a minute, squinting into nothing. Mo-Mo House was the proprietor of the Kit Kat Klub, the place where Ridley Banks had arrested Jerohm Reese lo these many days ago. Had Mo-Mo called in the late p.m., after Glitsky had gone? But why wouldn't he have spoken to Banks? And what was "Watch This!" beyond a reference to Ridley's redneck joke.

He worked it some more—maybe Banks had been on his way out of the detail and in a hurry. Was he saying that Glitsky himself should go by and question Mo-Mo about Jerohm? Some evidence might have turned up? But then Ridley would have pursued it, wouldn't he? It made little or no sense as he'd written it. Glitsky would need to have an administrative chat with the guys about this kind of thing. A message that didn't convey any information wasn't much use to anyone.

The sound of more sirens came up to him as he put down Ridley's note. He got up and crossed the darkened room, looked sideways and down where the jail did not block the view. What he saw was not the aurora borealis flickering orange out there. The city was still burning.

52

Melanie's fantasy had been that she would ride like the wind up to the television station, where a handsome young receptionist who perhaps doubled as a crusading news reporter would grab the tape and hustle into the studio—herself in tow—and interrupt whatever program was in progress for what would be an important flash news bulletin.

The reality was more prosaic.

She skirted riot areas in the Panhandle and lower Twin Peaks before she got lost and wandered in what she supposed must have been Noe Valley until she found herself on Church Street, from which she knew she could get down to Army (two more miles or so out of the way), then over to the freeway and up again into the city.

Figuring that her best exit was Bryant Street, which she could then take back south ten blocks to Mariposa, she got off the freeway at the Hall of Justice. A mistake.

A fugitive driving a vehicle with stolen license plates, she pulled off not only into a substantial traffic problem, but into a convention, a gaggle of—she estimated—roughly seven million police cars. Acutely aware of the lack of the sideview mirror, which had been sheared off the night before during her high-speed chase, she had to get across four lanes of this traffic to make her turn to the south. She was also positive the entire time that some cop would pull her over and issue her a ticket for the missing mirror.

None of her worst-case scenarios developed. It took her nearly five minutes to go the one block but she made the turn, came around out of the traffic and headed south. At last, having arrived at KQED, she found the station dark, evidently closed for the night. The parking lot was fenced but there was an open entrance, which she drove through, stopping six feet from a dimly lighted doorway. A fat, jowly security guard sat inside, feet on a desk, reading a comic book.

She buzzed at the door and the man looked up, sighed, slowly straightened, got out of his chair and walked to the door, gesturing to her to indicate what she wanted. It didn't appear that he intended to open the door.

Tentatively, she held the tape up. "Tape?" she yelled through the glass.

He nodded.

"I've got a tape I'd like to leave for the newsroom. It's very important."

Another nod.

"Please."

The guard only pointed to a box by the side of the door, yelling something through the glass that sounded like "Stickney's got the pox," but it was probably more like "Stick it in the box."

"It's really *important,* somebody's got to see it right away."

He continued to nod. She had a vision that maybe he had springs implanted in his neck. Maybe it was a physical impairment. Maybe he belonged to the Constant Nodders of America Club. He was also pointing at the box, yelling, "Box, box!"

She couldn't just leave it like this. After all the hassle getting here, Kevin finally getting to tell his story, and finally she had to entrust it to this Neanderthal with neck palsy.

But what else could she do? She'd already been driving over an hour and a half. Kevin would be worried sick. She didn't remember the addresses—or even the approximate locations—of any of the other stations. She couldn't just drive around all night and she couldn't go home with the tape, not after all this.

All right. She placed it against the wide slot and pushed. It was inside. Winkin and Blinkin's buddy leaned over, picked it up, shook it, listened to it.

"It's not a bomb," Melanie whispered. Then, more loudly: "It's a *tape.* It's a VCR *tape.*"

Bobbing his head randomly, the tape now in his hand,

he seemed to be waiting for something else. But she had nothing else. Pointing at the tape one last time, Melanie yelled at the glass, "It's really *important*. Okay? Really."

The guard nodded.

Kevin was up out of his chair as soon as he heard her key in the door, opening it before she could, pulling her to him, gathering her into his arms. "What happened? Are you all right?" Kissing her, his hands over her back, through her hair, pulling away enough to see her face.

She just held him. Held on to him. Both.

The two of them embracing there in the open doorway, the hall yawning behind them. Finally Melanie remembered where they were and got them both over the threshold, closed the door behind them. "You know, I think I could use a drink."

"You? Melanie Sinclair? That's my girl."

"I could use a *big* drink. What's a big drink?"

He thought a minute. "Mai Tais."

"Okay."

Holding hands, they went to the kitchen. She was telling him her adventures while he rummaged in the closets, through the refrigerator.

"So after all that, we're not sure it's even going to get seen?"

"I know. I mean I don't know. I feel like such a failure—"

"Don't," Kevin said. "Wes says nobody would believe it anyway. He says I shouldn't have run in the first place. I should have—"

"But you couldn't . . ."

"I could, I guess, but I didn't. But now that we've gotten to here, he says it's going to come down to a trial." He tried to drop it casually, even followed it with a little riff on drinkmaking. "Apparently Ann doesn't have any orgeat syrup. You can't make a Mai Tai without orgeat syrup." But it didn't get by Melanie.

"Exactly what would they try you for?"

"What? Oh, murder, something like that. Wes thinks they might even prove it with the picture, public opinion, me being white and Arthur Wade black, all that. I told him

I don't think . . ." He looked up, noticed she had started to cry, crossed to her. "Hey, hey," gathered her to him. "It's not that big a deal, she doesn't have One-Fifty-One rum either, so we couldn't have Mai Tais anyway. You really need a float of Meyer's One-Fifty-One if it's going to be any good. Actually, she doesn't have *any* rum, so the whole Mai Tai idea turns out to be kind of lame."

She didn't laugh, didn't even smile. Her body continued to tremble against his. He didn't know what to say.

Melanie was in one of the overstuffed chairs, hands folded stiffly on her lap, staring straight ahead. She had continued to cry for a while—she still held a handkerchief tightly.

Kevin came into the living room carrying two glasses in one hand and in the other a large pitcher of liquid with a head on it. "This," he said, "is going to elevate the good-time quotient on what I must admit has been a somewhat dishearting evening."

"What is this?"

"What is it? she asks. But, I notice, without a really convincing show of interest. When at her very elbow is the very first rendition of a drink that may be to the nineties what the Margarita was to the eighties."

"I'm tired, Kevin. I'm scared. This isn't going to work."

He pointed to the pitcher. "Whatever else may transpire on the roads of our lives," he told her, "*this* will work." He poured into one of the glasses and handed it to Melanie.

She took a sip. "I don't really need a drink anymore. I want to know what we're going to do."

"When?"

She slapped the arm of the chair, the new drink overflowing. "Damn it, Kevin! Now! What are we going to do *now*?"

Back on his heels, Kevin pondered. "You're right," he said seriously. "We're going to have to think about this for a while. I propose we don't say a word for fifteen minutes."

He drank from his glass, refilled the top inch of hers. She wasn't really thinking about it at all—she was too scared, angry, upset. She took a drink.

*   *   *

"This isn't bad, what is it?"

The pitcher was half-gone, three glasses each.

Pouring again for himself, Kevin was on the floor, legs crossed. "You've put your finger on the one problem we face—a name. Every great drink needs a name."

She took another sip. "Fred," she said.

"Fred, the drink?"

"Yep. Fred." She took a bigger sip. "It's pretty good," she said. "What's in a Fred?"

"Fred, hmm. It can't be a guy's name."

"Why not?"

"I don't know. You just don't name drinks after guys. I mean, look at all the drinks with girls' names—Margarita, Tia Maria, Bloody Mary . . ."

Melanie was holding her glass out. "Kahlua, Manhattan, Rusty Nail. . . . in fact, Rusty Nail . . ."

Kevin pointed a finger. "Watch it . . ."

"Besides, it's a guy kind of drink, it ought to have a guy's name. A Fred. What's in it?"

"Well, aside from the obvious beer, orange juice, vodka, cranberry juice, Coke . . ."

"Coke?"

"Diet Coke, actually."

"Okay."

"And port. And some brandy."

She took another sip. "Fred. It could be colder."

"See," he said. "Now we're into the marketing campaign. No, listen, this could be really big. *Fred, it could be colder. Fred, it could be sweeter. Fred, it couldn't be bolder.* I like it. I *love* it."

"Kevin," she said, "he couldn't be a bigger horse's ass."

He grinned at her. "Where was this Melanie Sinclair when we were dating?"

"You weren't smart enough to handle the real me back then."

It set him back a beat. "You know, I think you're absolutely right."

She softened it, coming forward, kissing him.

*   *   *

They were both on the floor, blankets under and over them, pillows piled about, Melanie's head on his chest. The pitcher was empty. The television on low.

The news had aired. Again and again, every channel until they got too sick to watch anymore. The increased reward on Kevin, the appointment of Alan Reston, the night's new fires and disturbances, the continuing problems in Detroit, DC, Los Angeles, the Mohandas call for the solidarity march on Saturday, and now, just an hour before, the riot at the Hall of Justice. All of it, and no hint of Kevin Shea's videotape.

Nothing but what he had started and now he would have to pay.

He stared blankly at the screen. Melanie breathed evenly on his chest, her arms thrown over him. Pulling the blankets up—the room had become cold—he had come around to believing his best chance, finally, was to run. He could never take the chance of a trial in which even Wes thought that the best result might be *some* degree of murder.

He would have to run.

But to where? And how? And could he take Melanie with him?

Friday, July 1

53

Ever since he had been a child Glitsky had taken a perverse pleasure in keeping an eye on water as it heated, giving the lie to the old adage that a watched pot never boils. He stood over the stove now and waited, eyes trained on the simmering liquid—any second now it was going to begin to roll and he intended to be there to see it.

The house felt strange with no one else in it. He had given Rita the weekend off after Nat had absconded with the boys. She had a sister—Glitsky suspected perhaps even a child, although she hadn't mentioned one when she'd come to work for him—somewhere else in town and she would always disappear when Glitsky made the offer. She had moved the screen in the living room aside, and when he had first walked out in the morning he had almost felt he was in the wrong house. It wasn't that there was so much room, but that there was so much *more* of it.

Gotcha! The water was boiling and he'd seen it.

He made his tea—Earl Grey Morning Blend—in a pot with an old-fashioned silver-plated tea bulb. He poured the water in, covered the pot and took it two steps across to his kitchen table—there was no "dining room." He often felt lucky they could fit five chairs around the table in what space they did have.

There were two hard-boiled eggs on a small plate in front of him and he absently cracked the first one while he opened the folder he had brought home the previous night—Chris Locke.

The first problem was going to be to determine exactly what street corner they had been at when the attack had occurred. If he didn't know that, he was going to have a hard time locating trace-evidence there. Loretta knew the city well enough, but he wanted to keep her out of it as much as he could—the experience had been traumatic enough without bringing her back to the scene.

When she had told him the story she'd said that she and Locke had been driving out near Dolores Park, the site of the dual, segregated tent cities. But what route had they taken from downtown to get there?

Reading through Lanier's questions and Loretta's responses he was beginning to doubt that he could get any real answers without Loretta. He flipped some more pages of text, scanning. The officers in the squad car she had pulled over near Mission and 19th Street—already some blocks from the murder scene . . . If the uniforms who had filed their report had been doing their jobs, one of the first things they should have done was drive back with Loretta to pinpoint where the shooting had occurred, but they had evidently been unnerved, shaken out of their routine—as everyone else had been—by the state of siege the city was in, the sight of the fatally wounded District Attorney and the presence of a U.S. senator.

So the ambulance had been called out to Mission Street, forensics had come there and begun their process of going over the car. Marcel Lanier's primary concern had been protecting Loretta, getting her out of harm's way as quickly as he could. In this Lanier had been successful but he hadn't done squat-all about moving the investigation forward. Nor, Glitsky reflected ruefully, had he.

Checking the clock on his kitchen wall—it was six-forty—he decided it was still too early to call Wes Farrell, which he had intended to do as his first order of business this morning. Get that out of the way, or at least moved to the front burner. Enough was enough. He had given Farrell plenty of time to make the first move, to beep him wherever he might have been all of last night, but once in a while you had to make your own timetable. He'd get some action on this; he had the leverage—something to offer Kevin Shea as an inducement to come in—so long as Elaine had been able to convince Reston, which he was sure she had.

Still, he remembered, he'd better call her first. Make sure.

He poured his tea out into the surprisingly dainty porcelain cup—one of the service that Flo had given him for their twelfth anniversary. He finished the last bite of the first egg, started cracking the second and continued his waltz through the rest of the paperwork—Locke's admission to the emergency room at SF General (where he was pronounced DOA), Strout's late lab microscopics corroborating his earlier assessment of the cleanliness of the entry wound—the car's safety-glass window had spiderwebbed, preventing any tiny glass shards from spraying inward. Other preliminary and follow-up reports: the trajectory of the bullet that had barely missed Loretta—across and slightly downward, just what you'd expect from a man standing outside firing in. The bullet itself—.25 caliber— the same size Lanier had predicted; also a match with the one taken from Locke's brain. Glitsky had entertained a small hope that there might have been fingerprints on the shattered window, perhaps even a shoe print on one of the fenders. Some hairs or fabrics. Something. But there were no surprises at all.

Which meant, unfortunately, nothing new to start with, no handle to wedge something open. They'd have to go back to the beginning, which meant bothering Loretta, locating the scene of the shooting, assigning someone to go cover the area, talk to neighbors, do forensics all over again.

He almost laughed. Assign some staff who would get to it exactly when?

Closing the folder, he noticed the clock again—not yet seven. Time was creeping, which he supposed was a clue that he wasn't having much of a good time.

He called Elaine on the stroke of the hour. She told him that Reston wasn't offering Kevin Shea as much as the time of day and that was the end of that. Shea could turn himself in, but then he was going to be treated like any other murder suspect. Maybe worse.

"I thought the priority was getting this guy behind bars, Elaine. So we could at least say he'd been apprehended."

"This isn't me, Abe. This is Alan Reston." She hesitated. "I got the feeling he didn't necessarily want him behind bars."

"As opposed to what? On the street?"

Elaine stammered, getting it out. "I . . . I thought about this last night, what Alan might be doing."

"I'm listening."

"I explained to him everything you showed me yesterday, showed him how the second picture might be . . . anyway, all that. And he hinted that maybe it would be better if Shea didn't get to tell his story, if something happened that would keep everything, as he put it, clean and uncluttered."

"Something like what?"

"Well, I mean, Alan never said any of this outright. It was just, he wasn't going to give Shea any real chance to come in, any reason to. Make it a no-win situation for him. Then, if it came to some kind of showdown, if he just got shot or something by a mob or by resisting while he was getting arrested . . ."

"Shot *or something* . . ." This was not possible, Glitsky thought. Then again, neither was anything else that had happened during the last few days. But Elaine must have misinterpreted something—there was no possible explanation for this as a remotely reasonable prosecutorial strategy. "Listen, are you on the way downtown? Would you mind if I stop by your place and pick you up on the way in?"

"Well, I'm not going in. Not right yet." She paused. "The funerals."

Glitsky had forgotten about the funerals. The information had crossed his brainpan sometime during the day yesterday, but he'd filed it someplace and hadn't retrieved it until now. The mayor had prevailed in his personal appeal to the families of Arthur Wade and Chris Locke to have their funerals at the same time and location (and thereby reduce the possibility of two separate riots)—at Saint Mary's Cathedral.

True, that had meant that Locke would not lie in state at the Rotunda of City Hall, but his wife had agreed. She didn't care about that. Not anymore. If it would ease the mayor's burdens, she would do what he asked.

"I'd like to stop by, anyway." Glitsky had to get some answers, get a *take* on Reston, on what was happening. He had to push.

She hesitated, then said "All right" and gave him her address.

Wearing a two-piece dark charcoal suit with a light maroon shirt of raw silk, Elaine Wager opened the door to her apartment. Glitsky followed her into the living room with its view of the western half of the city. The furniture was green leather; there was a glistening ficus, a teak entertainment center with books in the bookcase. The tasteful young Spartan look. A framed picture of Loretta smiled at them from the bar counter that divided the room. He glanced at it.

"You look a lot like your mother," he said. "I guess I never really noticed it before."

She smiled. "Taller," she said. "Not as pretty, really."

Glitsky let that go. She wasn't fishing for compliments. Then she surprised him. "My mother told me about you two." He tried to think of something to say. "In college. Just so you know I know."

"It wasn't a secret," he said. "It just hasn't come up much recently. Does it bother you?"

"No."

"Good."

"But she's coming by to get me in"—she checked her wrist—"about forty-five minutes. I just didn't want it to be uncomfortable."

Glitsky suppressed a smile. "I'll probably be gone by then anyway. But I could see her and handle it. It was a long time ago." He sat down on the front six inches of one of her chairs.

She took the couch, settled back a bit, closed her eyes and he recognized a pallor. "How are you holding up?"

She let out a little mirthless sound. "Fine. Great. Except I'm obviously in the wrong field."

"Why do you say that?"

She gestured, dismissing it. "What I said about Alan, it was mostly only a feeling, but I couldn't think of any other reason he wouldn't offer some kind of deal. Can you?"

Glitsky shrugged. "He just came on the job. Doesn't want to get a rep as soft. The situation's pretty explosive . . ."

"That might be it."

"But the point is, you don't think he's going to change his mind?"

She shook her head. "No. I think what bothers me is that he says it would be betraying my mother."

"How's that? She's the one pushing for Shea's arrest since the beginning."

"I know. But Alan's her protégé. He's got a vested interest in protecting her interpretation of the lynching, Kevin Shea, everything she's been pushing for. And if the charges don't stick . . . anyway, it's the same theory I told you before. If Shea doesn't get to refute it, nobody made a mistake . . ."

Glitsky sat back in his chair. "He can't be saying he doesn't want Shea to have a trial?"

"No. In fact he specifically keeps saying he does. But what's he going to say? I'm just not sure that I believe him. He's not acting like it."

"Maybe I ought to talk to your mother. Maybe you should." He slapped his knees and started to get up. "And maybe we should get going, get this thing moving along. Even without a deal the odds are decent I can get Shea downtown. His lawyer talks the language. I'll call him as soon as I get downtown. You mind if I use your bathroom?"

She motioned. "Down that hall, just off the bedroom."

The bedroom blinds were pulled down. His eyes weren't adjusted and the light switch wasn't where it should have been next to the door, so he stood a moment until he could see, then crossed the room. The bed was made. Next to it, on the end table, was another framed photograph, something familiar about it even in the low light. He leaned over, picked it up. Chris Locke.

Next to her bed?

The pallor, the fatigue, the confusion . . . he stood, rooted to the spot.

The light came on overhead. Elaine at the door. "I keep forgetting, they put this switch . . ." Then, seeing him with the picture: "Oh . . ."

A long silent moment. She crossed to the bed, sat, smiled weakly at him.

"Yeah. Me and Chris."

"Does anybody else . . . ?"

She nodded. "Just my mother. I had to tell her."

Glitsky finally put down the picture and went into the bathroom. When he came out she was in the same place on the bed, staring at nothing. He came around to her, paused, then turned around and walked to the bedroom door. "I'd better get downtown," he said.

She drew a deep breath. "I don't know . . ."

"You and me and your mother," he said. "It doesn't go anywhere else. It stops right here."

Glitsky broke through the cordon of functionaries outside the office, opened the inner door to the War Room and strode up to Rigby. "We've got to talk."

The days had taken their toll on the usually genial chief of police. He straightened from where he had been hunched over his desk and raised his voice. "I'm not in the habit of taking orders from my lieutenants. Or in tolerating that insubordinate tone of voice from anyone. AM I MAKING MYSELF CLEAR?"

The room died behind them.

"And you're right," the chief continued, booming, "we've got to talk. BUT IT'S MY GODDAMN CALL. AGAIN, LIEUTENANT, IS THAT PERFECTLY CLEAR?"

Glitsky hadn't been formally dressed down since the Academy—it startled him. "Yes, sir," he said. "Sorry, sir."

Rigby—Marine brush-cut, bulldog face—looked every inch the police chief. He glared at the minions in the room. "You people," his voice boomed, "the lieutenant and I need five minutes. Exactly."

The two men waited while the room cleared, Glitsky at attention, Rigby apoplectic while still appearing to hold himself back. "Where the *hell* have you been?"

"When, sir?"

"Whenever the *hell* I've been trying to reach you, is *when,* Lieutenant. You get a message from me? Urgent?"

"Yes, sir, last night."

"Well?"

"I called immediately, sir. No one was here."

"That's impossible. What time was that?"

"I'm not sure exactly . . . eleven o'clock, midnight."

The chief slumped a fraction of an inch, lowered his voice a decibel. "Goddamn it, Abe, what the hell?"

Glitsky waited.

"You remember the chat we had yesterday with our new District Attorney? Where we requested you not meddle in the DA's internal affairs?"

"Yes, sir. Although that wasn't—"

"And then, not an hour later, you're pleading the case for Kevin Shea's *innocence* with Elaine Wager, who then goes to try and sell it to Reston?"

"That's not—"

"I don't care, do you understand me? I count on you. You run one of my departments and, until this week, you've done a goddamn fine job." He came down to a whisper. "You are a homicide inspector. You don't argue for somebody's *innocence*. Don't you understand *that*? In fact, you don't argue for anything. You're not a lawyer. You don't make deals. You arrest people. Period. The end. Goddamn it."

Rigby pulled at the collar of his shirt, suddenly sucking in air. Glitsky began to move forward, but the chief stopped him. "I'm fine, goddamn it, but I am about at the end of my rope here." The heavy breathing slowed down, the voice modulated again. "Now, I have promised Mr. Reston to take care of this situation, and here's what I'm doing—you are *off* Kevin Shea. You are not investigating the riot or any part of it. The FBI is in on this now and they're taking it under their federal jurisdiction as a civil rights matter."

"A murder?"

"That's right, a murder that deprived Arthur Wade of his civil rights—"

"But it's also under our jurisdiction, no matter—"

"Are you hearing me, Lieutenant, or do you want to hand me your badge right now?"

Glitsky almost bit through his tongue. "Yes, sir. I hear you."

"Then you're dismissed. Thank you."

Rigby looked down immediately, back to whatever he was studying on his desk. Glitsky turned and walked to the door, opened it and marched through the suddenly silent crowd hovering in the outer office.

54

There was little that any civic leader could do about the funerals. No one was about to suggest to Arthur Wade's grieving wife Karin that for the sake of civic peace they postpone putting her husband in sacred ground. She did not object to the mayor's idea of a "martyr's funeral" to include Chris Locke and his family.

Arthur Wade had been a practicing Catholic and the high mass had already been moved from his parish church, Saint Catherine's, out in the Avenues to the expansive reaches of Saint Mary's Cathedral on the same Geary Street that—down at the corner of 2nd Avenue—used to be the location of the Cavern Tavern.

The Most Reverend James Flaherty, Archbishop of San Francisco, had originally intended to preside at the Mass but the Archdiocese had soon found itself in rancorous deliberations with, among others, Philip Mohandas, the Board of Supervisors, the mayor's office, the National Organization for Women, and the National Council of Churches.

These negotiations had ultimately altered the format for the mass, which would be celebrated by what was viewed as a more appropriate, more ecumenical triumvirate of clerics of color, two of whom had been flown in—the female from Philadelphia and the native African from Kenya—under one of the city's emergency budget provisions.

It was nine-thirty on a clear and still morning, half an hour before the service was to begin, and already the concrete open area in front of the cathedral—the size of a football field—throbbed with humanity, mostly well-dressed, mostly African-American, clustered in groups of five to fifteen, moving toward the church's doors.

The limousine door opened and Senator Loretta Wager reflexively reached over, protecting her daughter from the curious who had crowded around the tinted windows to see who was pulling up. On the way to Elaine's apartment and then again on the short ride here the limo had passed armored trucks on the back streets they had been able to drive on.

Elaine stepped out first, then her mother. Around the square, policemen patrolled on foot and on horseback. Overhead, two helicopters circled just low enough to be annoying.

Loretta firmly shooed away the swarm of reporters. This was not the time for a comment. She and her daughter were here to pay their respects to two martyrs of civil rights. It might be a better use of everyone's time, Loretta said, if the reporters put their microphones away and went inside and prayed for the future of our great city and country. Astoundingly, Loretta thought, a couple of them nodded, gave their equipment to their assistants and fell in behind them.

Mother and daughter walked arm-in-arm across the concrete, moving with the flow of the crowd. Inside the high modern cathedral a gospel choir filled the air—beautiful and appropriate, Loretta thought. Tears had broken on Elaine's face. The two caskets were up front at the altar, side by side, and she and Elaine continued their walk until they came to them, kneeled, lowered their heads in an attitude of prayer.

Elaine slid into the ribboned section reserved for them three rows back, but Loretta took another moment. Walking to the front of the first pew, she held out her hand to Margaret Locke, who was sitting with her four teenaged children, all of them looking stunned, vacant.

"Margaret," she said. Locke's widow stood and the two women embraced. "If there is anything I can do . . ."

Then, crossing the center aisle, she paused. The front pew on this side held a dozen mourners—she supposed they were Arthur Wade's parents, brothers, sisters, his wife's family. It was obvious which one was Karin, Arthur's wife. Attractive but without expression except an attitude of rigid control, her gaze straight ahead and unseeing, the young woman sat flanked by her toddler twins. Loretta walked over to her.

"Mrs. Wade?" She introduced herself, striving to sound like a person and not a senator. "I just want to tell you how terribly sorry I am. I know that it can't be any help. Not now. But if you find you do need anything or if there is anything I can do . . ."

It did seem to matter. A little. In a surprisingly strong voice, Karin Wade thanked her, introduced her to the twins—Brenda and Ashley—and then to Arthur's mother and father, both of whom shook her hand in dignified silence.

A glance back at her daughter, sitting rigidly next to Alan Reston, who must have just come in. In front of them, braving the censure of the crowd, was Mayor Conrad Aiken and his wife. He had to be here, and to his credit, she thought, he was.

In the same row on the opposite side—Arthur Wade's side—sat Philip Mohandas with his two bodyguards.

Loretta was in a quandary over Philip's latest calls for action, his march tomorrow, his verbal attacks on Art Drysdale, his demand for the release of Jerohm Reese. But as soon as she got her executive order on Hunter's Point signed she would have secured her political base for the next election and then, even if Mohandas went off the deep end and proved himself unworthy of the public trust of administering the project, it wouldn't be her fault. She had tried. She had reached out to his people. She had other friends who wouldn't have Philip's problem with the twelve million dollars. Who would appreciate it more.

In fact, in a way, she had been relieved to hear about Philip's latest move. With her own small but vocal constituency he could prove to be very difficult to control. He had decided he could make an end run around her and still get his hands on Hunter's Point. Well . . . she already had Alan Reston positioned. That had been *that* trade. Philip Mohandas would soon enough find out how power worked.

For now let him have his little march. Let him foment things even further. So long as Kevin Shea remained the focal point for a little longer—and Philip's latest strategy seemed guaranteed to accomplish that—she was going to get what she asked for in the name of racial harmony.

Of course, if it turned out that Shea was not the pure symbol of hatred she had helped set him up to be, and if that fact came out too soon, it could all backfire. She had been so certain that Shea was guilty, had set up her whole structure on that foundation, but some of the things she had been hearing from Alan Reston, from Elaine, even from Abe . . .

Well, those things just couldn't come out, not until Hunter's Point was settled at the very least, maybe not ever. *If* Kevin Shea in fact was *not* guilty, it was going to be clear she'd reacted before she'd been in possession of or even considered all the facts (which was true). Worse, she was going to look like a fool. And no matter what, she wasn't allowing that to happen.

She inclined her head politely at Mohandas, took Karin Wade's hand in hers one last time and made her way back to Elaine's pew just as the assorted ecumenical ministers came out to begin the service.

55

Too angry to feel safe about returning to his office in homicide—he thought that at the very least he would deface some property, throw a chair through a window, something—Glitsky took the internal stairway down to the lobby of the Hall.

Walking through the same outdoor corridor where he had been rebuked last night by John Strout about paying too little attention to the Chris Locke investigation, he decided to stroll through his city.

Really pushing his luck, he turned up 6th Street, where in the first block up from the Hall of Justice you could be stabbed to death for bus change. Hands in his pockets, he stalked up the block with his edge on, making eye contact with everybody, silently daring one of the lowlifes to try something. He was just in the mood.

The walk took him all the way down to the Ferry Building at the end of Market Street, where he was calmed down enough to get another cup of tea, drinking it out of a paper cup, sitting on one of the pilings as the flat water lapped under him.

It occurred to him that now would be a good time to call Supervisor Wrightson. It was the only thing he could think to do that would, he hoped, not involve Kevin Shea in some way and would keep him out of the office.

Yes, Wrightson would still like to see him and if this morning had opened up unexpectedly for Lieutenant Glitsky, that would be fine. The supervisor would make the time for an appointment at ten o'clock sharp.

Glitsky's experience with the Board of Supervisors was limited to scurrilous rumors and to the *Chronicle*'s political cartoon that had been on the bulletin column outside his office for five years, showing the door to the supervisors' chambers, the motto over the lintel reading: WE WILL NOT BE CONFUSED BY REALITY.

But the Supes did pay Glitsky's salary. To be more precise, they approved the city budget and the salaries of city employees, so they were not a group to antagonize gratuitously, and Greg Wrightson was the *éminence grise* of the Supes. At sixty-two, he had been around City Hall for nearly twenty years. Glitsky knew that the supervisors made twenty-four thousand dollars a year. As recently as fifteen years ago their salary had been only six hundred dollars a month. And yet Wrightson, a man from a middle-class background who had been drawing down this piddling wage for most of his adult life, was a very wealthy man. Abe had been making more than Wrightson for longer, and he was still a wage slave punching a clock.

Having pondered these imponderables on his walk back across town, Glitsky's mood had not improved by ten sharp when he walked into the reception area to Wrightson's office.

Wrightson's administrative assistant wore a tailored suit. The inscribed nameplate on the front of the desk read "Nicholas Binder." (Glitsky was a department head and he didn't have an inscribed nameplate anywhere.) If Nicholas had gotten this job randomly by taking a civil service test, they had upgraded the pool of applicants considerably from the last time Glitsky had looked. Somebody's cousin had pulled a string.

"Mr. Wrightson will be right with you, Lieutenant."

Glitsky waited. Nicholas went back to his computer, occasionally stopping to pick up the telephone, make a note. Were there riots going on outside? Was the city falling apart? No sign of it here. Clearing his throat, Abe checked his watch. It was nine minutes after ten.

"Are you sure I can't get you something, Lieutenant?"

Glitsky's patience had disappeared. "You can get me inside that door there by ten-fifteen. How about that?"

Nicholas tried one of those "What can you do?" shrugs, but it was the wrong day for it. "I've got this fifteen-minute rule I'm pretty strict about and I'm either in there talking with Mr. Wrightson in six minutes or we'll have to do it another time."

"Sir?"

"My appointment was for ten o'clock?"

"That's right."

"Okay, then, ten-fifteen."

Nicholas seemed to decide the lieutenant wasn't kidding because he got up, crossed the office, knocked on and then disappeared through Wrightson's thick, solid, darkly stained wooden floor.

"Lieutenant Glitsky, sorry to keep you waiting." Wrightson was striding forward, hand outstretched. "I'm afraid I got involved in one of those conference calls and lost track of the time. Come on in, come on in. Can Nicholas get you anything?"

"I'm fine."

Glitsky was standing, shaking his hand, taking his measure. The thumbnail sketch put him at five-ten, one seventy-five, nearly bald, piercing gray-blue eyes.

They went, Glitsky following, into an enormous, elegantly furnished office that resembled Abe's in no conceivable fashion. The view looked out through some clean windows (how did *that* happen?) over the six square blocks of the Civic Center Park—now a tent city. But usually, out this window, would be expanses of lawn, sculpted shrubbery, the pool and fountain, cherry and flowering pear trees. This was the face San Francisco put out for the world, and it was a beautiful one, laid out at the feet of Greg Wrightson.

He did not go to his desk, as Glitsky expected he would, but led them both to a sitting area—a couch and two stuffed chairs around a polished coffee table on a South American rug. Glitsky took one of the chairs, sinking deeply, and Wrightson started right off.

"I wanted to thank you for making the time to come and see me. As you know, we're faced with some tough decisions this year on the city's budget, and in the past we've been forced to try to cut back—trim the fat so to speak—on some vital services . . . such as the police department."

There was no sign of irony, though there was good reason for it. The supervisors had just voted an extra two hundred thousand dollars for Kevin Shea's reward (Glitsky didn't even know about the twelve thousand five hundred dollars in airplane tickets and other accommodations for the ministers who were presiding over the funerals at that very moment), and Wrightson had picked now to talk about the police budget?

Glitsky wondered if he should mention his missing door to Wrightson but he kept it straight. "There isn't much fat anymore. It's pretty lean down at the Hall," he said.

Wrightson nodded. He was leaning forward in the chair now, hands clasped in front of him. "Well, with these riots and the perception that San Francisco is not a safe place anymore I think we've got a window of opportunity here. We'll be able to free up some money for police services."

Glitsky sat, listening to him go on, stifling the replies he would have given if he were getting this kosher baloney from anyone else, wondering why he was here at all. Finally Wrightson wound down. ". . . which is why I thought I'd talk with the individual department heads."

"Okay."

"I'd like to know what you really need to do your jobs."

"That'll be easy." But if Wrightson was asking him for specific examples of how short money had hampered investigations, he'd be talking until Christmas.

Wrightson clapped his hands once. "Good. We might as well start with the personnel breakdown in homicide. I could look it up but—"

"What do you mean?"

"You know, how many people, ethnicities, genders . . . ?" At Glitsky's look, he hurried on. "That's what's going to loosen the purse strings, Lieutenant. You know that."

"I thought it was the lack of funds hampering our ability to perform."

Wrightson waved that off. "Oh, sure, there's that, but let's be realistic. Your best shot at beefing up your department is increasing your head count. That increases the overheads all around and, presto, suddenly you've got money for a new coffee machine."

"A new coffee machine? How about a lab that's open on weekends? How about overtime instead of comp time? How about guys getting paid when they stay late writing reports?"

Wrightson was shaking his head. "No, no. I mean, all of that's important, don't get me wrong, but nobody's going to vote money for that stuff. It's just not sexy, you know what I mean?"

"I guess not."

"Well, I do. You tell me about your department and I'll tell you what it needs."

Glitsky ran it down—twelve inspectors, all male, of which four were African-American, two he thought probably qualified as Spanish-surname.

"You really ought to know that kind of thing for sure," Wrightson said. "It's in your best interest." Then: "What about women?"

"No. We don't have any women."

"Asian?"

"No."

"Gay?"

"Doubt it, don't really know. Does this stuff matter?"

"Native American?"

"I didn't realize we had an appreciable percentage of the city and county that was Native American."

Wrightson gave a conspiratorial grimace. "You're going to be in good shape. You'll need at least three, maybe five new inspectors."

Glitsky sat forward. "Mr. Wrightson, we don't need more inspectors. We need more support."

"Yeah, but you won't get the support, Lieutenant. What you need is to get closer to compliance . . ."

"But isn't that for the PD as a whole . . . ?"

"Well, yes, originally, but this was the idea I took to Chief Rigby. He liked it." Wrightson was pumped up about his role in all of this. "Look, the force needs money and this is the way it's going to get it. The quotas—we don't call them that, of course—we amend the compliance-factors language so that it applies to each individual detail instead of the department as a whole."

"But homicide is . . . it's the top of the pyramid. I mean, you don't just plunk people into homicide and make them inspectors to fill some quota . . ."

Wrightson's eyes were shining now, his color high. "Where have you been, Lieutenant? This is San Francisco. Of course, that's what you do."

"But—"

"This should make you happy especially . . ."

The scar in Glitsky's lips was white with tension. He could feel it. He didn't want to react angrily to Wrightson. Not personally. Not this morning. Not with all the other thin ice he was walking on. Maybe Wrightson was right—he was out of step and should be delighted at lowering the admissions standards for his detail.

But he couldn't stop himself. "It makes me puke," he said.

So much for the first two items he had left in the center of his desk the night before—Rigby's urgent call and the two messages from Greg Wrightson. Glitsky flashed his badge at a black-and-white out on Polk in front of City Hall and bummed a ride back to the Hall of Justice.

All these Halls and no shelter to be found.

Rigby had told Glitsky he was off the Kevin Shea matter, but on reflection Glitsky realized that he hadn't been specifically told to stop supervising his troops. Had that been on purpose, he wondered, Rigby covering his own ass in case Glitsky was on the verge of coming up with something? At the very least, that interpretation gave Glitsky an argument in the event he got called in front of the Police Commission.

In ten minutes he was back in his office, Carl Griffin sitting across from him, as angry, if that were possible, as Glitsky was. The inspector had a gooey-looking red stain on the front of his shirt. Either the remains of a jelly donut or he'd been wounded in the line of duty and hadn't noticed.

"So I caught Feeney"—this was another assistant district attorney, Tony Feeney—"last night before I went home, got a tentative okay on immunity for him being in the mob if Devlin testifies. I got everybody down here this morning, eight sharp. Devlin, his dad, his lawyer, the whole gang, and Feeney comes in and announces no deal."

"No deal at all?"

Griffin popped a couple of sticks of gum. "*Nada.* Alan Reston isn't giving deals. New policy. How's he gonna get any witnesses, I ask, if he don't trade for nothing? So Colin

Devlin's lawyer says why you wastin' our time, and they all
go out, get a nice breakfast someplace."

Glitsky was sitting all the way back in his chair, fingers
templed in front of his mouth. "What was this Devlin going
to say?"

"Well, you had us looking for guys in the mob—"

"I remember, Carl. And Devlin admits he was there?"

"Not only there, he was part of it. His version—what he
told me yesterday—started coming down to being that he
got swept up in the mob, couldn't get out of it, and got
between Arthur Wade and whoever was trying to get to
him."

"Did he say why somebody might have been trying to
get to Wade? Trying to cut him down maybe? Did he see
who it was? Kevin Shea, for example?"

Griffin was shaking his head. "None of that. Sorry. I tried
but the guy got his Achilles tendon cut in half, Abe. He
went down like a sack. It never got beyond that, at least
for him. But how we gonna—?"

"I know, I know. Wait a minute." He brought his feet
down. "If Devlin was in the mob he'd be an accessory . . ."
Glitsky was thinking that without a deal they could still
arrest Devlin on that fact alone.

"Sure, that was the plan, but nope. I ran that one by
Feeney, too, before everybody'd even left, while Devlin's
lawyer was still there. I told him, 'Look, you don't cut him
a deal, what are you gonna want me to do, arrest him?'
and Feeney looks at me and says what for? So I tell him
'cause he was in the mob and he tells me without Devlin's
confessing to it there's no proof of that, so *I* tell him he
did confess, more or less. Admitted he was there, at least.
The guy just shrugs. Doesn't necessarily prove intent, he
says. Christ! Whose side these guys on downstairs? Who is
this Reston asshole anyway? Where'd he come from?"

"Devlin might have compromised their case on Kevin
Shea," Glitsky said. "They don't want any of that on the
record."

"What record? We got no record."

"That's right."

Carl Griffin fixed his belt, scratched, frowning at the stain
on his shirt. He wasn't going to waste his time trying to
pretend he understood all this. He had just spent yesterday

finding a guy with a knife wound, which had been that day's assignment. So what did the lieutenant want him to do today?

Glitsky sighed, still in his head with the other questions, "I'll tell you what, Carl . . ."

The orders now were to go out to Dolores Park, try to locate the exact corner where Chris Locke had been shot—someone in one of the tent cities out there would have heard it, perhaps even seen something. Lots of people had been demonstrating, something would turn up. And when he found the spot, call forensics out there and run the battery, see what they came up with.

This was the kind of work Griffin did well. It gave him something to do and it would keep Abe from having to put Loretta through another round of trauma.

Griffin wasn't out of his office before Glitsky began punching Wes Farrell's number into his phone. Enough of this waiting—Rigby or not, he was going to make something happen.

56

Wes Farrell had stopped all drinking early the previous day and hadn't resumed after Sergeant Stoner had left at night. He had decided he had slipped up the day before with Lieutenant Glitsky, reading the man all wrong by trusting him. He thought that today he'd better be a little sharper if he was going to do any good work for his client, and while he wasn't ready to admit that his alcoholic intake had slowed him down or affected his judgment, he didn't want to take any chances.

He had been watching the television ever since he had gotten up and there had been no sign of Kevin's tape. Whether or not anyone would believe it, Wes had a hard time imagining that a news station wouldn't run it. True or not, they had to see it as a development in the case of the most wanted fugitive in the United States. It should have appeared on every station from here to Bangor, Maine, within minutes of its arrival at the station. What could have gone wrong?

He realized he had also erred in neglecting to ask Kevin for the phone number where he was, so he was reduced to waiting on the off chance . . .

And after his lecture the previous night about the probability of Kevin being the defendant in a murder trial, Kevin and Melanie might have decided—at last—to change their names and get into a witness protection program. In Brazil. Or something.

Bart was whining by the door, running around in little circles, needing to go relieve himself. Wes hadn't wanted to leave the apartment, thinking he should be there if Kevin or Melanie called, but the dog was giving him the guilts. It was nearly ten-thirty and he wasn't acting in the SPCA-approved manner. He could be fined, even jailed, his reputation smeared, branded as an animal hater. Failing to believe in the anthropomorphism of animals was turning into the next cardinal sin among the PC set.

He looked down at his suffering pet, not wanting to allow Bart to experiment again with the newspapers in the kitchen. Could be a bad precedent—Bart might get so he liked it. "Okay, guy, we gave 'em a chance. Let's roll it out of here."

He opened the door and Bart rushed to the top of the stairs, whining and circling again. Not entirely trustful of the police who had blindsided him only hours before, Wes atypically locked his difficult deadbolt, not that it would do any good if anybody really wanted to get in but it made him feel more secure.

He was four steps toward Bart at the head of the stairs when he thought he heard the telephone begin to ring. He cocked his head, listening over the dog's whine. Second ring. Yep, the phone.

"Perfect," he said aloud, reaching into his pocket for the keys, which had caught on a loose thread in his pocket. He pulled and out came his comb and all his coins, flung all over the floor.

Ring.

The keys were stuck to the inside of his pocket, which was now pulled inside out. Swearing, holding the keys awkwardly, he crab-walked to his door. Bart came running up, barking.

Hey, master! Wes! My man. We're going out, remember? I've got to pee a river! I mean it. I'll do it in the hallway here if . . .

Ring.

He knew the trick. He could get the deadbolt on the first try if he calmly inserted the key all the way and then pulled it out the one sixteenth of an inch . . .

Ring.

. . . and wiggled it just the right amount. There!

"Shut up, Bart."

The other lock was a piece of cake. In, turn, open.

Ring.

Cross the room, running, still holding the keys, which still stuck to the threads in the bottom of his turned-out pocket. Into the kitchen, the wall phone.

"Hello."

Dial tone.

He dropped his hands in frustration and the keys, magically undoing their Gordian knot, fell to the floor. He stepped to the side and saw Bart looking up at him, moaning piteously over a fresh deposit.

His pocket still hanging all the way out, Wes stood stock still then deliberately undid his zipper and pulled out his penis. "I am a fucking one-eared elephant," he told Bart, then tucked himself back in and went for a beer.

"That wasn't you?"

"No. This is the first time I've tried to call. We just plugged the phone back in. We wanted to get some sleep."

"That's nice," Wes said. "So who was it?" He couldn't figure who else might have tried to call him. He never imagined it might have been Glitsky—not after the betrayal yesterday.

"I don't know," Kevin said. "How would I know who called you?"

Wes dropped it. "Anyway, you get your nice sleep?"

"Yeah. We both feel better. Even my ribs . . ."

"Great. So what are you planning to do now?"

A short pause, then: "We don't know, Wes. Maybe just wait."

"You know what for?"

"No. We don't know what to do. Maybe wait 'til tonight and then try to get down to Mexico, then I don't know, call you when things maybe calm down, see if by then something's turned up. I mean, *somebody's* got to be out there who can say what happened. Besides me."

"Don't you think they would have come forward by now?"

"Yeah. But maybe not. Maybe they're scared, too. I mean, all this stuff outside. But after my tape comes out . . ."

"Speaking of which . . ."

"Yeah, I know. We're calling the station right after this. Something went wrong there. Melanie says it must have been the guard."

"The guard?"

"The place was closed up. She left it at the night desk."

Wes bit off his reply. He'd like a nickel for every time a detail like this had cost someone a case. You didn't drop things off with second parties—you delivered them to principals even if you had to wait all night. "You want me to call the station, take it from there?"

"I thought you said it wouldn't do any good."

"On the other hand, as you just pointed out, it might bring somebody out of the woodwork, a believable witness, and you might get out of this yet."

"You think so?"

"I don't know, it's a big if. I wouldn't get my hopes up. But at least it's possible. As things stand now, you either run or you go to trial. It's probably worth doing, that's all I'm saying. I could do it for you, keep you guys out of it."

He heard mumbling at the other end of the line, Kevin discussing it with Melanie, then he was back on. "If you really would . . ."

"I said so, didn't I?"

"It's better than running, isn't it? It's the right thing?"

It was odd hearing someone ask that question nowadays, but Wes thought it very much in character. Kevin was a throwback, a believer in doing the right thing—it was what had gotten him into this in the first place. All the right moves that had turned out so disastrously.

And Wes realized he had no choice either. The way Kevin was now was the way Wes had tried to be, had *believed* in being, before events in his life had soured him on believing anymore.

It was irrational blind faith, but giving solace to Kevin and Melanie, committing to help them, Wes realized he felt a whole lot better about himself than he had in a long time. It was the trick he had forgotten ever since Mark Dooher, since his wife . . . sometimes people *didn't* screw up on you. That was the thing he'd forgotten. You had to take chances. If you didn't you were dead, or might as well be.

"Wes?"

"Yeah, I'm sure. I do think it's your best shot, Kev. If you run and you're caught . . . no telling what would happen." He didn't have to draw a picture. "For now, I'd say lay low. Wait another day. Nobody knows where you are. Maybe something will break in your favor. You can always run, but once you do that, you're committed."

57

Glitsky was home for lunch. He was *never* home for lunch on a workday but he had spent the rest of the morning assigning cases, following up with his inspectors who weren't working Kevin Shea in one way or another, checking over some other autopsies, scheduling courtroom appearances, liaising (an FBI word if ever there was one) with Special Agent Margot Simms on the "progress" of the Kevin Shea investigation. The FBI had decided that this was a civil rights case and that the federal government had at least parallel jurisdiction in the matter. They didn't need to be invited to investigate by the local police anyway, no more than they would if they were looking into the murders of civil rights workers in the deep South. Now, on their own authority, they were on hand, and Chief Rigby seemed inclined to let them take whatever glory the case might provide, or whatever heat. Special Agent Simms was more than happy with this arrangement, although she hadn't been much interested in knife wounds, Jamie O'Toole, photographic inspections, the Mullen/McKay cousins, Rachel from eastern Europe, any of that.

What *did* interest Simms was the personality profile that depicted Kevin Shea as armed and very dangerous. Glitsky thought this had probably originated from Elaine Wager's outburst to the media, then been goosed up by FBI staff researchers who knew what they were looking for, and hence often found evidence of it, even when the data wasn't particularly compelling.

Knowing the FBI and their propensity to shoot first, Glitsky had tried to set Simms straight on that notion. But she clearly didn't want to hear it—this was the kind of high-visibility case a young female agent needed if she wanted to get really equal and make her own bones among the men who hadn't been afraid to use firepower when the situation had called for it. If they needed them—she wasn't telling Glitsky they would, but *if* they did—she had two weapons specialists, including a marksman, at her disposal.

Next she wanted to know what Glitsky thought of Wes Farrell, was he their best bet to make contact with Shea— maybe a federal tap on his phone line? Special Agent Simms was "connected" to a federal judge who, she said, would issue a warrant to her to go look for just about anything "on half a molecule of ten-year-old DNA" when- ever she asked.

Glitsky had said he thought it was possible that Shea and Farrell would telephonically connect. He'd kept his face impassive the whole time.

He had really just been spinning his wheels all morning, waiting to have meaningful discussions with two people— Ridley Banks and Loretta Wager.

Banks had not appeared at the office—not unusual in itself, he was a field inspector—but the no-show left intact the mystery of the Mo-Mo House note, which was the next item of those Glitsky had centered on his desk. Perhaps whatever that was about had nothing to do with Kevin Shea, and therefore Glitsky could officially pursue it. (When Wes Farrell hadn't answered his phone he had had to shelve even his informal hunt for Shea. He had no trail to follow. Maybe Special Agent Simms would put him onto one.)

And he knew that Loretta was at one of the burials and would be neither at home nor her office until the early afternoon, at least. He kept telling himself that he wanted to talk to her so soon, now, again, for business reasons. He could even wait if he had to—it wasn't that he *needed* to talk to her for anything personal. Whatever they had to decide about each other would develop in its own time . . . Finally, he had given up on trying to appear busy and had driven home.

Chopping an onion, he was watching a pan filled with canned chili through tearful eyes now. He'd already grated up the remains of a rock-hard lump of what looked like cheddar cheese that had been stuck in the back of the refrigerator.

He was still worrying the question of talking to Loretta

about all of this; he had been in the bureaucracy long
enough to know that going over your supervisor's head was
the quickest and most thorough way to threaten your position and reputation. But he'd put enough of the pixels together to be getting a fairly clear image of what was
happening, and he realized that the solution to the problem
might well lie with Loretta Wager. It was all, as Strother
Martin had observed to Paul Newman in *Cool Hand Luke,*
"a failure to communicate."

Glitsky would have to go to Loretta, who was undoubt-
edly unaware that Alan Reston, in his zeal to please his
powerful benefactor, was abusing his newfound power, the
authority of his office, to undermine the interests of justice.
Reston (Glitsky reasoned) was going on the assumption
that Shea had to continue to *look* guilty—if he wasn't guilty
it would make Loretta look bad . . . Glitsky didn't think
Loretta gave a good goddamn about that, she didn't want
the guy railroaded. But Reston's position was that he didn't
want to deal, just now, with anything that appeared to
weaken the DA's case against Shea.

It was typical—shortsighted but common enough that it
didn't even mildly shock him. Reston, the new guy, wanted
to deliver his first major case to the person who had managed his appointment. He would be a hero. It would make
Loretta a hero too. Everybody wins. And to a career prosecutor like Reston, it was an article of faith that Shea, like
every other defendant on the planet, was certainly guilty
of something.

Reston figured he was protecting Loretta, and from the
DA's perspective, Glitsky wasn't. Therefore Glitsky was the
enemy. For the time being, anyway. Nothing personal in
it—he'd even warned Glitsky to keep a low profile to avoid
it coming to this. But it had.

Glitsky reminded himself that Loretta didn't know anything about Farrell's information, about Rachel's statement
(Shea lifting Wade up, not pulling him down), Colin Devlin,
Jamie O'Toole starting to weaken—about any of the reasons Glitsky had now arrived at for a formidable state of
doubt regarding Shea's guilt on any level. He and Loretta
hadn't spent last night—or any of their time—rapping down
the intricacies of Kevin Shea's case. There had been more
immediate issues.

But now it had gone too far. He was going to have to bring it up with her, go over Rigby's head, over Reston's. Special Agent Simms, with her sharpshooter, had finally put it over the top for him. He was going to have to talk to Loretta, open those lines of communication between her and Reston, get people back to thinking about how they ought to do their jobs. Pretty basic stuff, not unreasonable.

But what he still couldn't understand was why Farrell hadn't even tried to call him yet. That made no sense unless Shea had gotten some cold feet, which was not, after all, so far-fetched. As far as Farrell knew, Glitsky's offer of a deal still held—that at least Shea would get a listen. In fact, Reston's refusal through Elaine to offer any protection to Kevin had changed all that—the message was that he wasn't going to listen privately to anything Wes Farrell or Kevin Shea had to say. No, Reston was committed—his position was Shea was guilty and that was that.

Now Glitsky had no deal to offer in exchange for Kevin Shea coming in, but Farrell wouldn't yet know that. So why hadn't he called?

He stuck his index finger into the small pan, stirred. Almost ready, and the doorbell rang.

A strip of gauze covered the narrow glass window beside the front door, and he moved it to one side. No one was out on the landing. He opened the door.

"If I were a trained assassin you'd be dead right now. Why are you crying?" His friend Dismas Hardy had pressed himself against the house on the stairway, stepping out when the door had opened.

"I'm not crying, I was cutting onions. I thought you were in Ashland."

"Rumor had it that *Hamlet* could be missed this year. I'd just spent a week in the wilderness, camping with a three-year-old and a five-year-old. We got worried about the house with all these fires you mentioned when we talked. Seemed like a good time to come home."

"Not so good, actually."

They were inside, halfway to the kitchen. "Maybe you don't remember the experience of camping with toddlers," Hardy said. "You ever do that with your guys?"

"Sure. Lots of times. Peace, tranquility, the experience of nature . . ."

"Except for the peace and tranquility part." Hardy leaned over the stove. "Umm, chili. I don't think I've had chili in a year. Smells great."

"You're not having it now, either. This is the only can in the house, the first time I get a whole can of chili all to myself in like fifteen years."

"A whole can? You can't eat a whole can."

"Watch me."

"This is cruel and unusual, making me watch this. Fritos, even!"

Glitsky was pouring Tapatio sauce over a large serving bowl—a normal soup bowl wouldn't have been nearly big enough to hold the mixture of chili, onions and cheese, covered by a whole bag of Fritos that Glitsky had layered over the top. He stopped long enough to point. "The door's where you left it. Close it on the way out." He took a mouthful, providing more sound effects than he would have if he'd been alone.

Hardy sat across the kitchen table. He was wearing his non-lawyer clothes—jeans, a long-sleeved green-and-white rugby shirt, tennis shoes. He had placed another bowl in front of himself, as well as an oversized spoon, but Glitsky had ignored the hint. "You're turning into a mean person, Abe. I hate to see that."

Glitsky swallowed. "You don't know the half of it." He spooned more chili. "The promotion's gone to my head," he said. "That's probably it."

Hardy watched his friend eat for another minute, then—when it didn't appear that guilt was going to work its magic—stood up and went back into the hallway.

Presently, Glitsky heard the familiar drone of the news on the boys' television. He poured a little more Tapatio over the chili, picked a Frito off the mass. The name Kevin Shea came through, and when he heard it a second time he picked up his bowl, stuck the spoon in and walked out of the kitchen back into the kids' hallway.

Hardy was lounging on Isaac's bed, hands crossed behind

his head, catching up on all he had missed. A commentator was talking about the effect Mr. Shea's tape was going to have . . .

"What tape?"

"They're going to play it again. They just said."

"When?"

"Soon. Wait."

Glitsky came into the room, pulled around a wooden chair, sat on it backward and put his chili down onto the floor, by which time Kevin Shea's face had filled the screen.

". . . and I didn't do any part of this. I was in the bar, and when everybody started moving I got kind of propelled outside. I saw what was happening to Arthur Wade and I tried to push myself through the crowd. I took out my Swiss Army knife and cut a few people who were in my way. The police should be looking for people with knife cuts, not for me . . .

"Mr. Wade was already off the ground when I got to him, and I swear to God I was trying to hold him *up*, not pull him down. I gave him my knife so he could cut himself down. But then they . . . the crowd . . . they knocked that away, and then somebody hit me and I went down. Then I got kicked in the head. I don't remember after that, except when I looked up, Arthur Wade was dead. Some guys came and threw me into a pickup truck and got me away from there. They said they'd kill me if I said anything about what happened."

There was a pause in the tape. Hardy said, "Southerner," and Glitsky responded, "Texas."

Shea was continuing. "I have not left the city. I want to tell what really happened, but every time I've tried to contact the police and get some protection they have . . . they have betrayed my trust."

"That's b.s.," Glitsky said.

"Just now—it is Thursday night—my lawyer told me that he had been followed home by the police after going downtown and trying to arrange my surrender. I don't want to run away—that would make me look guilty, *and I haven't done anything wrong.* I don't know what else to do, so I'm making this video. I hope someone listens to it. I did *not* do this. You have to believe me . . ."

As soon as the tape went blank, Hardy answered it. "I don't."

The station broke for a commercial and Glitsky muted the screen. Hardy was sitting up. "Good strategic idea, though, to get the heat off himself. But it's going to backfire. Who's the lawyer?"

"Wes Farrell," Glitsky told him.

"I heard he'd retired. He hangs out sometimes at the Shamrock, doesn't he? I should ask Moses. I'd never let a client of mine do that."

"Why not?"

"'Cause it reeks of guilt, that's why. It's going to blow up in his face."

"It might be true, though."

Hardy shot him a glance. His friend Abe the cop did not often come down on the side of suspects. "What do you mean?"

"Well, the part about Farrell being followed home is bullshit, but the rest of it . . ."

"Hello? If one part of it is false, you can bet the rest of it is. Typical client mistake. They put in too much and then can't take it out." He picked up the bowl of chili and got it grabbed away from him. He scowled. "So how come you think it might be true?"

Glitsky was punching Fritos down with the spoon. "The knife wounds he mentioned—his version is about the only explanation for them. Other things."

Hardy nodded. "Secret police business, no doubt."

"Secret enough."

In the living room now, Glitsky threw Hardy another bag of Fritos. "But," he said, "that's all it said."

The conversation, with a few hairpins, had gotten around to the cryptic note about Mo-Mo House. "So what's the 'watch this' part?"

"It was a joke Ridley Banks told me."

Glitsky repeated the joke and when he had finished, Hardy pulled a Frito from the bag and chewed on it. "That's it? That's the whole thing?"

"It's also an I.Q. test," Glitsky said. "If you don't think

it's funny you're dumb. Try it on your friends, you'll see."

But Hardy was pondering it—the note, not the joke. "I'd wait and ask Banks."

"I would, too, but he's not around. I get the feeling it's not a coincidence."

"So what could it be?"

"Well, you know, I've asked myself that question."

Hardy got up and walked to the window, the early afternoon rays of sunlight beginning to come through. Hands in his pockets, he stood still. "Whatever it was, he didn't want anybody who might read the note on your desk to recognize what it was about. You guys have any office business going on between just the two of you? Maybe whatever you were talking about—you and Banks—when he told you the joke, if you call that a joke? Kind of a memory jog?"

"No. Nothing."

But of course there had been. He wasn't going to tell Hardy about it—he hadn't mentioned his new relationship with Loretta to a soul and wasn't about to start now. But suddenly he recalled the exact moment yesterday with Ridley, the look between them when he'd been about to mention something else about Loretta, something to warn his lieutenant about, but Glitsky had cut him off—he hadn't wanted to hear more slander about Loretta.

Could that have been what the "watch this" was all about? It was way beyond cryptic—that Ridley wanted Abe to reflect not on the joke itself but on what they'd been *about to discuss* when he referred to it. On the other hand, the Byzantine logic seemed to be in the realm of acceptable to Hardy.

Glitsky chewed his cheek. Last night Loretta had quite plausibly explained the reality behind Ridley's whole Pacific Moon scenario. And Ridley's reference to Mo-Mo House in the ambiguous note *had to* be about Jerohm Reese. Didn't it?

And yet if Hardy's theory held—the hidden meaning behind "watch this"—Ridley was in reality advising Glitsky to go see Mo-Mo House about something to do with Loretta Wager. And if that were even the implication, Glitsky didn't think he ought to ignore it.

Glitsky was on his feet, moving to the door.

"Let's go, Diz. Back to work."

"I'm not working today."

He stopped at the door, opening it. "I am. Let's go."

On the way down the steps, Hardy told him he was turning into a really lousy host, and Glitsky told him that next time he should maybe wait until he got an invitation before he came over.

58

Jerohm Reese, sitting within the thirty square feet of the attorney's visiting room on the sixth floor, thought his lawyer Gina Roake was looking pretty fine lately. Lost some weight, maybe put some highlights in her dark hair where he'd noticed her getting some gray strands. She always good with the makeup, looking fresh. Woman must be near forty—time to get serious she wants to get herself fixed up with some man. She doing okay.

It was after lunchtime at the jail and people could say what they wanted, but Jerohm, he'd take meals on the county anytime—today breakfast he got eggs, sausage, potatoes, three slices of bread, juice, cup of fruit. Then, not four hours later, they were bringing up his tray with two thick slabs that good meat loaf, mashed potatoes, country gravy, green beans, three slices bread (they always did the three slices bread), big old square carrot cake with that maple syrup icing, couple cartons milk. No complaints 'bout the jail food—most times better than what Carrie put out.

"*Damn,* girl"—he was grinning at his lawyer—"you lookin' *good.*"

Gina Roake had already placed her briefcase on the floor beside the tiny table. She had been with the public defender's office for eight years and had represented Jerohm three times since his early days at the Youth Academy. She was the one who had gotten him leniency on his "first offense" (as an adult) and who had argued successfully with the late Chris Locke on the insurmountable evidence problems the prosecution faced regarding the murder charge on Mike Mullen.

Seem like every time Gina show up Jerohm walk out of

the slam, so she lately be Jerohm's favorite—Gina didn't quite share the feeling.

"Sit down, Jerohm."

"Hey, I'm sittin', but I tell you, I like that new thing, the hair . . . whachu doin' with color . . ."

She leaned back as far as she could, arms crossed over her suit jacket. "What are you doing with your brains, Jerohm?"

"Huh? Hey, what?" It hurt him when she came down on him like this. Girl got no call . . .

But she was going on. "Not even one week ago we get you out of here, you remember that? We talk and say maybe it be a good idea"—Gina slipped into the jargon like an old pair of shoes—"be a good idea you stayed inside, watch a lot of television, like that. You remember that?"

She got no call talkin' like that at him. He sat back now, mimicking her, arms crossed, sullen. He shrugged. "They giving everybody else tickets. Me they lock up."

She pointed at him. "You," she said, "had two thousand dollars' worth of assorted merchandise which didn't belong to you in the trunk of your stolen car, Jerohm. You see any difference here?"

Another shrug. "They just out to get me. Looking for me, is all. Hasslin'."

She was forward now, halfway across the table, trying to keep her temper in check. "Hey, listen up, Jerohm. Hasslin' is like when they're following you around, bust your chops for jaywalking, you hear what I'm saying?"

"Hey, now, girl, *you* listen . . ."

"AND DON'T YOU *GIRL* ME ANYMORE." The outburst felt so good, she forced herself to rein in. "I'm not your girl. I'm your attorney, and you're putting *me* in a position where I cannot do you any good. Don't you understand that?"

One of the guards who had been standing outside knocked on the door, opened it. "Everything okay in here?"

Ms. Roake nodded. "Everything's fine, thanks." The door closed and with an almost visible effort she brought herself back to her client. "Sometimes, Jerohm, I have to wonder why I want to get you off. I mean what are you doing out there in the middle of the night robbing these stores? This is *your* 'hood, these are your people."

Jerohm rolled his eyes. "Hey shi . . . they leave the door open, who's problem is that? 'Sides, they got insurance, likely. Ain't nobody gettin' hurt." •

" 'Cept if somebody show up, try to stop you."

"Well, nobody did." QED. "Hey, look, you get me off 'cause that's what they pay you for. Weren't for guys like me, you got no work. Maybe you out on the street yourself." Smug and secure, a charmer, he broke a toothy smile.

She sucked in some air. The chain reaction that had begun with the negotiated release of Jerohm a few days before had led Gina to question the very nature of what she was doing. In her mind there had been no question that Jerohm had shot Mike Mullen point blank in cold blood for the temporary use of his car, though of course Jerohm was smart enough (if that word applied) to deny it to his attorney, but that had not been the issue.

The issue had been, as it always was in defense work, does the prosecution have enough evidence to constitute proof beyond a reasonable doubt? And when all the eyewitnesses had gone sideways, she had realized that in this instance there was no case. She had argued that before the late Christopher Locke and she had prevailed.

And look what had happened.

Always before, whenever she'd have these doubts, she'd talked with her fellow public defenders, had a couple of drinks, gotten resold on the idea that her job was to provide the best defense the law allowed. It was the give and take of the law—win some, lose some.

But Jerohm, suddenly and unexpectedly, had made it all more significant, and personal. This was a murderer, a thief, a mugger, a sociopath of the absolutely first rank, and he sits here joking with her as though the whole thing's a lark. She found herself wondering if "doing her job" fell under the general rubric of "following orders" that had been the great rationalization for so much evil for so long. Gina Roake was Jewish and she was intimately familiar with the parallels. And they were shaking her.

But, for the moment, she was here. She was supposed to represent Jerohm again. She folded her hands together on the table in front of her. "Okay, so . . . where do we go now, Jerohm? You're getting arraigned on Tuesday . . ."

"Tuesday? What's this Tuesday?" With attitude now, a bit of the street push, seeing he was getting to her.

"We got a holiday weekend, Jerohm. The courts are closed on the Fourth of July, which is Monday, so it's Tuesday."

"Now wait a minute, can't you get me like *habeas corpus,* something like that?"

It was her experience that a great percentage of the jail's population could spout Latin like Jesuits when they had to. She thought it was a powerful example of motivation being the key to learning.

Gina shook her head. "No *habeas corpus,* Jerohm. And I think we're going to have a problem with a not guilty here. We might have to cop a plea."

"Hey, no way, man. I ain't going down for no jail time on this." He studied her a minute, trying to figure what game she was playin' on him. He didn't see it. "Hey, c'mon, Gina, you know, this wasn't nothin'."

"Well, actually, it was . . . we got stolen goods, Jerohm, we got presumption of looting, resisting arrest, we got breaking the curfew."

"Yeah, but we also got the fact that everybody else doin' this shit is walking out with—"

"It's not exactly the same shit."

"Close enough and you know it is, girl." At her reaction to the second "girl," he held up a hand and said he was sorry. "But you know the truth is it don't matter what I *did*—if that was it you know I ain't in no *county* lockup. They have me up to San Quentin. We gotta say I'm bein' prejudiced against. That the shot."

That *was* the best shot. Gina knew that. She could go down to the new DA's office and argue passionately for that position. She had done similar things many times and sometimes it worked. But this time she wasn't sure she could do it. She felt that at some point you had to draw the line, and she was at hers.

"Jerohm, this time that's not gonna go."

He leaned back, truly sullen now. Frowning. "Well, I say it and you gotta do it, ain't that right?"

"Well, you can always ask for a new lawyer." She allowed the trace of a smile. "Put me out on the street."

Getting his bluff called rattled him a little. "But hey, you and me, we been good together. We done some good shit."

"That may be the case, Jerohm, but I can't go down and argue prejudice here. I don't think it *was* prejudice. I think we're going to have to cut a deal."

"C'mon, girl, you think I white this happen?"

This was a trick question and she avoided it. "The cops that picked you up, Jerohm, they black?"

He nodded. "One of 'em."

"And the DA who brought you upstairs here, she was black?"

"Okay."

"And the new DA himself, Alan Reston, who says he's holding you for trial, he's black, too, am I right?"

"Right."

"So who was prejudiced exactly?"

Jerohm chewed on his cheek a minute, stumped that even the multiple-choice question had no correct answer. "Must of been somebody," he said at last.

Gina took up her briefcase, stood and knocked on the door. When the guard opened it, she turned back to her client. "You figure out who, Jerohm," she said, "you give me a call."

Not seventy-five feet away as the crow flies, Special Agent Margot Simms sat with District Attorney Alan Reston in his new office. The new DA had recently returned from his predecessor's funeral, where he'd had a private discussion with Senator Wager in the cathedral's sacristy after the service.

Three men were in the process of removing Christopher Locke's personal possessions. Since Reston had known he wouldn't be in for most of the morning he had directed them to start early, and they had taken most of the books down from the shelves. Packing boxes lined the walls.

Reston and Simms were discussing Kevin Shea. She professed to having a difficult time understanding why, since the fugitive was still in the city, he had not been apprehended. Reston laid it off on the police department, then offered up his excuse for them—with the disturbances they had been undermanned, overwhelmed. The point was, now the FBI was taking over and what were Simms's plans?

"We've got a task force of fifteen agents attempting to contact every known acquaintance of either Shea or Sinclair—"

"Sinclair?"

"Melanie Sinclair, the girl with him." The expression told Reston he had better pick up in context the allusions he didn't immediately grasp. He should have known who Sinclair was. He had to be careful what he asked about. "We've got Shea's address book from his apartment. Sinclair's got her addresses on the computer in *her* apartment." At his glance she nodded and quickly explained. "We don't have a warrant problem here. This is a priority case. So we're interviewing everybody on either list, and, of course, we've got some people in Texas with the mother and sister."

"What about the tape?" referring to the videotape Shea had made and that had been played on television.

"We've got a couple of specialists analyzing the background. There's some distinctive molding—maybe you noticed—at the windows and ceiling line behind him. Perhaps we can date the building he's in. Long shot, but you never know. Could be one of a kind."

"I'm impressed."

"Yes." Special Agent Simms was accustomed to impressing. She was intelligent, professional and attractive. Shaded dark blond hair fashionably cut. Nice legs. "We also have a team talking to this Cynthia Taylor—she's the woman who originally identified Kevin Shea, you may recall. Melanie Sinclair and Taylor are—were—close, it seems. There's some chance she'll know likely places for the pair to go underground—friends, friends of friends, that sort of thing."

Reston was thinking that manpower was a wonderful thing.

"I did want to run by you, though, just so we're clear on it, that we still believe our best move is a tap on Shea's lawyer's telephone. Wes Farrell. Lieutenant Glitsky expects that the two of them will get back into contact. In any event, you know some of the legal issues that arise over wiretaps, and I wanted to make sure we were kosher on any local rules."

Reston knew that California law made wiretaps functionally impossible, but that the fruits of a lawful *federal* wiretap were admissible. He told her to pick herself a federal judge if she needed to get a tap approved. He didn't think there'd be a problem.

"Good. I'll follow through on that." She clapped her hands together briskly. "Which leaves the question of apprehension."

Reston thought this was, in fact and the law, one of Chief Rigby's areas of responsibility, but he had Simms here now and thought it wouldn't hurt to plant a seed. "Naturally, our interest is in placing him under arrest."

She nodded. "Of course. But I wondered if you had anything that doesn't appear here"—she tapped the folder in front of her—"regarding his state of mind, anything we might want to watch out for."

Reston took a moment getting the phrasing right. "Well . . . we know he's had military training. He knows how to use weapons, although we don't know if he has any with him now. But judging from the high-speed chase as well as the panic evident on the videotape, we know he's fairly desperate by now. And then, he *is* charged with murder. I don't imagine killing someone else if it would help him get away would particularly bother him."

Agent Simms took that in. "That's a good insight," she said, standing up, extending her hand. "Thanks for your time, sir. If in fact Shea is still in the city we stand a decent chance of locating him within twenty-four hours. This kind of limited manhunt . . . this is what we do."

"Excellent," Reston said. "We'd like to get this behind us."

"I understand," she said.

They shook hands again.

59

Despite its location and outward appearance, Glitsky thought the Kit Kat Klub wasn't that bad a place. True, the walls on the street outside were tagged all the colors of the rainbow and both the picture window and the porthole in the door were blacked out and crisscrossed with bars, but the same was true of most of the establishments in this neighborhood.

Inside it was dim and close, but the place smelled of beer and cigarettes, not urine and dope. This, Glitsky thought, was a big difference. The club featured some pretty hot blues on weekends, local guys working on their chops during the week, but at this time of the day it was just a slow bar, a half-dozen people sitting around with glasses and bottles in front of them.

Glitsky still wasn't one hundred percent sure why he was there. He pulled up a stool and waited for the bartender to make it down to see him. Some vintage Clapton grunged out from the box, loud, and Glitsky reflected that while it was a fact that white men really couldn't jump worth a damn, a few of them—Clapton, Robben Ford, the late Stevie Ray Vaughn, a local guy named Joe Cellura—could blow some pretty mean blues.

With a heavy sigh the bartender lifted his three-hundred-pound bulk off the industrial-strength stool he half sat, half stood on behind the bar. "Comin'." It was a good thing he announced it—otherwise it might not have been obvious that he was moving. Glitsky, one elbow on the bar, waited patiently. Here was a man built for comfort, not speed. The wooden slats on the floor creaked beneath him and the fifteen-foot walk seemed to just about tap him out.

"I'm looking for Mo-Mo House." Glitsky had his wallet out on the bar and opened it, flashing his buzzer.

The man looked down as slowly as he did everything else. "You found him." He wore gold-framed round lenses. The shining black forehead was high, the dreadlocks brushed with gray even in the dim light. The voice had wasted itself with whiskey—a talking blues voice—or maybe he gargled with tacks, razor blades. The fat man waited. If you don't ask, you don't ask the wrong question.

"I thought I might run into a Ridley Banks down here."

Mo-Mo shrugged, rotated his head a few degrees. "I don't see 'im. Get you a drink?"

Maybe it was because his friend Hardy had been around. Maybe Flo was hovering somewhere nearby—sometimes before bed she used to pour herself a shot of frozen vodka—but Glitsky surprised himself. "What's in the Stoly bottle?"

Mo-Mo threw a look over his glasses, backed up a couple of steps, and with some effort leaned and opened a cabinet under the bar. Reaching in, he rummaged a minute, grunting, then came up with an unopened bottle of Stolichnaya, the seal still intact over the cap. He placed it on the bar, grabbed a glass, fished some ice into it. "Help yourself. On me."

Glitsky pointed to the other bottle of Stolichnaya on the shelf behind him. "I don't need a new bottle."

Mo-Mo almost smiled. "You with the ABC?"

The Alcoholic Beverage Control would take a dim view of Mo-Mo refilling his premium vodka bottles with piss, but it didn't matter to Glitsky. These were the trades you made if you wanted results on the street.

Glitsky cracked the new bottle and poured a half inch over his ice. "So how's business?"

Mo-Mo held up his hands. "Hey, the blues, you know." He glanced out over his domain. The music had changed, now either Albert or B.B., still loud. No one was paying any attention to Mo-Mo or Glitsky. "This about Jerohm?"

"Should it be?"

Mo-Mo shrugged. "Jerohm," he said, "he some bad nigger. But he old news. He in jail again?"

"I hear."

"Me, too." Mo-Mo settled his bulk against the counter behind him. "So it ain't him."

"No. I don't think so."

Another silence. "Some bad shit going down out there, huh?"

Glitsky nodded. "Not good." He took a small sip and the straight spirits, as always, constricted his throat. How did people drink this stuff every day? He swallowed again, wished he'd ordered tea, dug out a cube of ice and chewed at it.

"So, what?" Mo-Mo asked.

There wasn't really any subtle way to get what he thought he wanted, so Glitsky figured he might as well just out with it. "You know Loretta Wager, Mo-Mo?"

No movement. Not a tic of the eye or a twist of the head. It was as though Glitsky hadn't spoken a word. Finally, the body heaved slowly and Mo-Mo reached for the well in front of him. He poured what looked in the dimness to be some yellow custard out of a bottle into a large glass into which he dumped a handful of ice, then drank off half of it.

"Can't say I really know her," he said at last. "Ain't seen her now in a long time. Girl doin' pretty good for husself, ain't she?"

"Looks like. When you were seeing her, how was that?"

He sucked some more of the pudding out of his glass. "We had some of the same friends, best way to put it."

"The same friends?"

Mo-Mo nodded. "Other day, your man axed me again 'bout this."

"Ridley Banks?"

"That's him. Man who take down Jerohm. He and me, we go back." His voice went down further. Glitsky had to lean halfway across the bar to hear him over the music. "We do some tradin' now and again."

Glitsky knew what this meant. Banks had evidently discovered something about Mo-Mo or his operation here at the Kit Kat that wasn't exactly legal. But it didn't concern any of Ridley's active homicides. The most obvious thing would be that drugs got sold out of here. And armed with that information, Banks would make a deal—he wouldn't drop the dime on the fat man, and Mo-Mo would become an informer. This, Glitsky reasoned, was how Jerohm Reese came to be found here at the Kit Kat in such a timely manner after he had shot—oops, allegedly shot—Michael Mullen.

In his career, Glitsky had himself maintained relations with any number of criminals—prostitutes, drug couriers, con artists, burglars, car thieves. He was a homicide cop, and if these people didn't kill anybody, it wasn't his mission to bust them. They were sources of information you couldn't get at, say, the Lion's Club. So you left them alone if they stayed out of your own personal face.

"Ridley asked you about Loretta Wager?"

Mo-Mo shook his head. "Not direct, no. Not her. But you now axin' me 'bout her, I put it together . . ."

"Put what . . . ?"

"The Pacific Moon, must be."

Glitsky felt a chill run up his back.

"But hey, them statues of limitations, they all gone run out now. Been like fifteen, sixteen years . . ."

"What has? Since what, Mo-Mo?"

"Since them days." He obviously wasn't going to elaborate. "You look aroun' here now. This place is what I do. Straight and legal, got no time for that crazy blow. Got a business here."

"I can see that, Mo-Mo. You got a business now. But what happened all these years ago?"

Mo-Mo put down the last of his custard, belched discreetly and placed the glass on the bar. Holding out his hands defensively, an innocent man: "Ain't none of this no secret now."

"No. All right."

"I mean Ridley, he know all about this."

"Okay, Mo-Mo. I read you. But what?"

"Well, one deal. Last one I done." Glitsky swirled his ice, waiting, and Mo-Mo went on. "Got, like, a load of bread all at once, was like a bean, bean and a half, like that, I don't remember exactly." Mo-Mo was talking about one hundred and fifty thousand dollars. That was a load of bread all right.

"But it was gettin' ugly, people gettin' theyselves killed over that kind of green just layin' around. I figure I stay in the bidness I don't get old. I am not the fastest-movin' man they is, you might have noticed. But the blues, man, I love the blues. I say, 'Mo, get out of this. Put that money down on some dive, make it you own.' But the money needs cleanin' up. You follow me?"

Glitsky nodded. "So you invested it in the Pacific Moon."

" 'Zackly. They take a lot out, mind you, but I get like eighty ninety clean. I put it in this place. Hey, look around. Fifteen years, I still goin' strong."

There was a hole in the blues as another song ended. One of the patrons came up and ordered a couple of longnecks while Glitsky sat there playing with his glass. Mo-Mo got the beers from the cooler, then lumbered down to the end of the bar, got his stool and carried it back with him. He sat with a sigh.

"And Loretta Wager was in this with you? Her husband?"

"Not with me. Nobody in it with me." He lifted his heavy shoulders. "People mind they own business. Her name come up, that's all."

"Laundering money?"

An expansive gesture. "I don't know that. Don't know what she doin'. Her husband either."

"So it's possible she might have had a legitimate investment with the restaurant?"

Mo-Mo balanced himself a little more securely on his stool. "Anything possible," he said.

Glitsky was inundated with more stacks of paper—reports, phone messages, the day's mail—strewn across his desk, three of his inspectors hovering outside in the all-too-visible doorway. He had already made two phone calls, both to Wes Farrell. On the first one, Shea's lawyer told him that he had a lot of nerve and hung up on him. On the next, he got more personal.

With the third call, Glitsky was luckier—his friend Hardy had gone back home after his lunchtime visit at Abe's and was spending the day, he said, planing some windows.

"I've got a question for you." Glitsky was holding up a finger, keeping his inspectors at bay. There were rumblings of impatience.

"And I've got an answer," Hardy said. "Just a second, let me think—the Greyhound bus station."

"Amazing. You got it on the first try. The question was, name a common acronym for the initials TGBS?"

Hardy liked it. "What's the real question?"

"The real question is how well do you know Wes Farrell?"

"Who?"

"Wes Farrell, the lawyer. You said he hung out at the Shamrock sometimes, which is the bar you own, am I right?"

"Oh, that Wes Farrell."

"I just called *that* Wes Farrell and he wouldn't say boo to me."

"You know what, Abe? Sometimes I feel that way, too."

"Yeah, well, yesterday he wanted to talk to me in the worst way and today he's a stone wall. I've got to find out what's going on."

"Okay. Go find out."

"He won't talk to me. Are you listening? Are you hearing me at all?"

"You ring his doorbell, say you're the police, I don't think he's got an option."

"I don't want to do that." He omitted the information that he had been forbidden to work on Kevin Shea at all. He couldn't assign any of his inspectors. The sudden realization that Hardy could help him had been a bolt of inspiration.

There was a silence on the line. "You want *me* to do that?"

"I don't want to alienate him any further. I may need him."

"You may need him?"

"That's right."

"What for?"

"To get Kevin Shea to give himself up."

"Without a deal?"

"If I need to. If I can. At least I've got to know what's going on, and right now I don't have a clue. I'd put off mentioning my name for the first couple of minutes, though. He really doesn't want to talk to me, I can tell."

"What if he won't talk to me?"

"Why wouldn't he? A fellow defense attorney? You guys are all a big happy family, aren't you?"

"Oh, that's right, I forgot for a minute."

"Hardy . . ."

"All *right*, I'll call him. Get the lay of the land. Do I bill you or the city?"

"I'll buy you a can of chili," Glitsky said, and hung up.

For the next twenty-five minutes, the lieutenant put in a few licks on his regular job, listening to the complaints, problems, strategies of his men. They were working on the usual—witness interviews, getting warrants, plans to testify in court, report writing, rebookings (an administrative process whereby after a suspect was arrested for a given crime—in all Glitsky's cases, degrees of murder—the District Attorney's office then decided on the formal charge). It was never ending, especially lately—he discovered he had two more non-riot-related homicides that he needed to assign, families that had to be informed, witnesses to cajole or hassle, legwork, background checks and alibis. He called in two men at random and gave them the cases, told them—a joke—he wanted both cases closed in under twelve hours and went downstairs to the cafeteria for a cup of tea, maybe settle his stomach.

Griffin was eating again—there were two unopened bags of Twinkies in front of him, one of the tiny cakes in his hand, and cellophane and cardboard from at least two more packages on the table in front of him. A quart of milk.

Glitsky stood across from him with his tea. "You on a diet, Carl?" He sat down.

"I was on my way up."

"That's all right. I was on my way down. What'd you get, anything?"

Griffin chewed happily, nodding. "Just a minute," he said, hoisting the milk carton and holding it to his mouth for three swallows. "Okay. Something." He used his notes, pulling a steno pad from somewhere beside him. He brought that, too, up to the table.

"General consensus seems to be that it went down near Dearborn and 18th Street." San Francisco has both numbered streets and numbered avenues—it could be bad luck to get them confused. "There's a dead end halfway down Dearborn."

"A dead end?"

"Yeah. Bird Street."

Glitsky frowned, but Griffin didn't see it. He was con-
sulting his notes. "All this is about a block and a half east
of Dolores Park, where they used to have the tents up."

"What do you mean, used to?"

"I mean they're gone. They relocated after the fire down
there. Moved 'em somewhere else."

"So who'd you talk to?"

"I went door to door. I knew it was on the Guerrero
side so I rang doorbells."

"And . . . ?"

"And the usual. Got one guy . . ." He flipped some of
his pages, searching for names and addresses he could show
his lieutenant. "Says he heard a shot on Dearborn. Another
couple ladies live together"—he flipped the page—"they
say no, it was Bird. Another guy on Bird says it was Bird.
I figure two out of three. But there's apartments all up and
down the block. You couldn't tell where from hearing—
the sound of the shot bounced off the buildings around
the corner."

"But there would have been two shots?"

"Yeah, I know. But I couldn't find anybody who'd heard
two. Nobody recognized two, anyway." He shrugged,
chewed some Twinkie. "Hey, we're lucky we got one. We
can talk to 'em again, the people who heard one, maybe
they'll remember."

"Anybody actually *see* anything?"

"No. It was dark, or just near it. The streetlights don't
work on Bird. A few people mentioned it."

"Maybe some of the rioters?"

Griffin was finishing the Twinkie, shaking his head,
"They were all gone, remember. I got no idea where they
are now, who was there then."

Glitsky didn't like it but he had to take it.

"So I go it must be Bird. Except there's nothing to call
forensics about on Bird. No fresh treadmarks. No accumulation of glass. No big rocks might have gotten thrown. No
nothing. I walk the whole street and I'm just about through
when the old ladies are coming out for lunch, and they say
the riot never came around to Bird—it stayed out by 18th,
maybe pitched a little into Dearborn. So now I'm thinkin'

that it's the reverse of what I thought before—the shots were on Dearborn, they bounced around the corner to Bird."

"So you checked out Dearborn?"

"What I could. You want to come down again, look with me, I'd do it again. But I didn't see anything in the street."

Glitsky took a sip of his tea. It had gone lukewarm. He grimaced—it wasn't turning out to be his day. "But listen to this, Carl. You're telling me there's a riot below these apartment buildings and nobody's looking out their windows, down at it?"

"No. I talked to half a dozen folks saw the riot—"

"But those people didn't see anything, the car . . . ?"

"Somebody might have, Lieutenant, just nobody I talked to. You want, I'll go back tonight. More people home. Somebody will have seen something. Maybe."

Glitsky sat chewing on it for a minute. "You'd better. Why don't you pick one of the guys, have him go out with you. And maybe find out where the residents of the tent city have been relocated to. *Somebody* in that riot killed Chris Locke, and somebody must have seen him do it." Glitsky spread his hands. "Seen something, at least. But it could be a long night."

Griffin was holding his next Twinkie. "Won't be the first one," he said.

60

"Gin." Melanie laid her hand faceup. "Read 'em an' weep."

Kevin folded his cards into the deck.

"Hey, you're supposed to count—"

"You won, Melanie. That's the game. I guarantee I'm over a hundred. I might be over two hundred after that last hand, which was a no-brainer if I've ever seen one."

"You are a bad sport."

"Maybe I'm just tired of gin."

He got up from the kitchen table, where they had been sitting, and went into the living room. The apartment was feeling a little small. They had slept in, then awakened with both of them feeling a bit shaky after the Fred Party. They'd checked the television to see if Kevin's tape was ready for prime time (it wasn't), made love, gone back to sleep. When they'd gotten up the second time Kevin had plugged the phone back in and called Wes Farrell, taken his offer to go see what had happened to the tape, then foraged for food and finally dealt the cards. Two plus hours of gin rummy.

He was standing by the living room window, shades drawn against the light. Melanie came up behind him. She did not touch him but he felt her there. "I think this is really getting to me," he said. "I'm sorry. I shouldn't take it out on you."

"It's all right." She ran a hand down his back. "A lot of people can't play cards very well. It takes a certain kind of mind and you just don't have it. It doesn't mean you're stupid or anything. I mean about other things."

He turned around, his face a blank. Stepping past her, he hooked a leg, reached an arm out and . . . "Hey!" . . .

executed an expert judo takedown, lowering her gently the last six inches to the floor. "Oh. Sorry," he said, continuing across the room, "I guess I didn't see you." He sat in the stuffed chair.

She crawled across the floor on her hands and knees, put her elbows up on his knees, rested her head in his lap. He combed his fingers through her hair. "I wonder if this is what being married is like."

"If what is? You're trapped forever so you play gin to pass the time?"

"Well, that's the romantic view, but I was thinking more about this feeling like you're the whole world, like there's nobody else in it."

She looked up at him, her eyes gone soft. He wasn't teasing her. "I think that's the way some marriages start out. But I don't know too many people who feel like that anymore, who even think you should. Do you?"

Kevin shook his head. "No. I don't know if I ever did."

"Well, your parents . . ."

"No, not mine. It was everybody for themselves in my family. My dad was always preoccupied with business, and Mom was . . . Mom was mostly interested in Mom. And Patsy was just Mom junior. Except maybe . . . Joey."

"Your brother . . ."

"Yeah. He was a good guy." Kevin sighed. "Anyway, what got us on that?"

"I think we were talking about not feeling like you were in it alone. You still miss him, don't you? Your brother?"

Again, a sigh. "You know, the word came and I didn't believe it. I didn't believe it. I mean, it couldn't have been Joey. They must have got it wrong. Of course, they didn't get it wrong. The one time the army didn't screw up . . ."

Her head still in his lap, she held his legs tightly.

"So after that, I just . . . I don't know."

"You and Wes," she said.

"What do you mean?"

"I think I'm starting to see why you two guys get along so well." She told him what she knew of the Mark Dooher story, Wes's loss of faith, the distrust of commitment. "But that really isn't either of you, is it? That's not who you started out to be—"

"I don't know anymore, Mel. I spent the last three

years . . . well, you *know* what I've been, how I've been living. I didn't want to get into any of this"—he gestured vaguely—"this whatever we're in. I sure as hell didn't choose this. This isn't my fight, my story—"

"Maybe it is. Maybe your story is what you wind up doing."

"I don't *want* to wind up doing this."

"Maybe we don't get that option."

"*There's* a comforting thought."

She shrugged against him. "Anyway, it's got us back. That's something, isn't it?"

A long moment passed. He was rubbing gently, moving his hand over her back, her shoulders, her neck. "I was a jerk. I mean before. With you."

"Well, that was me, too. I shouldn't have let you be such a jerk. I should have stood up for myself more but I was afraid you'd leave me."

"I wanted to. That's what I did, see? I left people. I did not feel things, except that I started feeling things about you. I liked you, was the problem. I liked that you were motivated and smart and organized, that you were this quality person . . ."

"You liked that?"

"Do you have any idea how rare that is, Mel? Yeah, I *liked* that. Finally, finally I meet somebody who's not a flake. Who's got some substance."

"I thought you hated that I wasn't any fun . . ."

"You were fun, at first, if you remember, until I—"

"It wasn't you."

"It was too. It scared me—my liking you so much—I mean, what if you weren't really who I thought? Then I'd really be up a creek, wouldn't I . . . so, anyway, I had to see if you were really so tough, so sure of yourself, so *competent*—and my test was that if you continued to like me when I treated you so badly then you couldn't be so great after all. Not if you'd take that . . ."

She shook her head, looked up at him, tears in her eyes. "I didn't just like you, Kevin. I didn't just want a boyfriend. I fell in love with you. I loved you. I still love you."

"I saw that. That was another strike against you."

"Why?"

"Why? What was to love? What do you think I'm hiding

from with all my craziness? No kidding, I don't see how anybody's got any business loving me . . ."

She glared up at him. "Why do you think you're here in the first place, Kevin? Why do you think *we're* here? Because *you*, Kevin Shea and nobody else, tried to save Arthur Wade's life. Because you are probably the one person I have ever known who thinks it's important to stay here and get the truth out, even if no one wants to hear it. Not to run, not make excuses, just to do what you've got to do. And you know what? You're right. You've been right all along. And I love you. Am I getting repetitious?"

"A little. I can handle it."

"And you know, I wasn't so perfect either. Being so controlled all the time. You *were* right about that. I just needed my . . . my bottom kicked."

He patted. "You mean this pretty thing?"

"That very one. And you did it. Kicked my ass good and proper."

"And would again, I might add." He pulled her up the rest of the way into his lap.

"Your ribs," she said.

"Suddenly my ribs are fine."

Melanie lay her head in the crook of his neck as he enfolded her to him.

Melanie was taking a bath. Kevin was in the stuffed chair. He had started to take a look at the News at Four, but one of the lead stories had included a statement by Alan Reston on how the fugitive Kevin Shea's tape was inherently not believable—an obvious ploy to evoke sympathy by taking his case directly to the people. It was not going to work. There was a murder warrant out on Kevin Shea and all efforts were still being employed to bring this dangerous criminal to justice. He'd turned it off then.

What was he going to do now? Wes Farrell hadn't been home. He called three times in the past half hour. The DA's escalation—the words "dangerous criminal"—bothered him. He was beginning to realize a new and scarifying truth: that the longer he hid out, the more irrational the "official" reaction would become. The perception that he had somehow become more "dangerous," more unstable, wouldn't help him if they got close to capturing him, and if they somehow discovered where he was, he was afraid it would come to that . . .

He *couldn't* let it come to that. He also couldn't let Melanie stay any longer if he thought it would. The "dangerous criminal" rhetoric was eating his guts—somebody out there might not be planning on taking him alive.

But he was also distrustful of what might happen to him if he was brought to jail—he believed that there was a too real chance that he would not survive inside long enough to *get* to trial.

He punched the buttons on the phone again. Wes had evidently done a good job getting the tape—finally—recognized and played. But they needed a better way to stay in contact. He hadn't realized that things could move this fast, could cut off his options, take decisions out of his hands. He was getting that feeling now. Events *had* taken things out of his control, and he had to try to stop their inexorable rush, and without Farrell and some legal plan, he didn't have any idea how he was going to do it.

At that moment Farrell was pulling up a chair at the one window table at the Little Shamrock. He had, in fact, gone back to his apartment after his successful mission with the videotape, intent on waiting until Kevin called him again. But ten minutes after he had gotten home Dismas Hardy had called, asking if he could talk with him, off the record, about Kevin Shea. They could meet at the Shamrock.

Word was getting around, all right.

Farrell knew Hardy slightly. He had known him since the days when Hardy had bartended at this very bar. Now he assumed that Hardy, another defense lawyer with a growing reputation on newsworthy cases, was churning the water, angling to get a spot on whatever high-profile murder trial Kevin Shea was going to have. Well, he could go and talk to him—his day wasn't exactly overbooked. Kevin had promised him that he was going to lay low for at least twenty-four hours, so there was no immediate crisis with him, so far as he knew.

Besides, Hardy said he was buying.

So here they were, Moses McGuire coming over from

the bar with two pints of Guinness. Farrell and McGuire had exchanged some pleasantries about the last time Farrell had been in the bar a couple of days before, the evening he had spent on McGuire's couch. And was McGuire's wife talking to him yet?

Neither of the two men—Hardy in his rugby shirt and Farrell in a Pendleton—looked much like lawyers at the moment. They clinked their glasses and Farrell asked Hardy what he could do for him.

"I've heard Kevin Shea is your client."

"Glitsky?"

So much, Hardy thought, for not bringing up Abe in the first couple of minutes. "Yeah, Glitsky mentioned it to me."

"That guy is a shithook." Hardy was silent. Farrell quaffed some stout. "I go down with an offer to bring in Kevin Shea, who by the way is as innocent as you or me in all this." At Hardy's expression, Farrell stopped him. "I know, I know, but this time it's not a bill of goods. The guy just flat did not do what they're saying he did. No part of it."

"You know this for a fact?"

"Let's say to a moral certainty. It's the only thing that could have got me back doing this, believe me."

"So what happened with Glitsky?"

"Glitsky and I have a nice talk. He seems receptive, says he's going to go sell the idea of special protection to the DA, meanwhile keep it all between us."

"And?"

"And next thing I know I'm in my apartment and there's somebody downstairs with a search warrant to look for Kevin Shea. Glitsky had me followed home."

Hardy killed a little time with his glass. "That doesn't sound much like Abe."

"You a friend of his?"

"We talk from time to time."

"He tell you about this?"

"About what?"

"The tail, the warrant, any of it?"

"No. We were talking, he mentioned you had Kevin Shea. I thought it sounded like a good case."

This was the reason Farrell thought Hardy had called in

the first place. Though it might turn out he could use some help if things ever did come to trial—and Hardy might be a good choice in that eventuality, he was starting to get a reputation as a good man in front of a jury—Farrell didn't want to send any false messages. "I'm not sure about that. There's no pockets." Meaning that the defendant had no money.

Hardy shrugged. "Sometimes there are other considerations. You never know. I gather Shea wasn't there, at your place."

"I thought he was at the time. He *was* there when I went out to meet Glitsky. He sent his girlfriend—you know about Melanie? the getaway girl—they got what I thought at the time was a dose of paranoia, except it turns out it wasn't. Now they're someplace else. I really don't know where."

Hardy took it in. On its face it didn't make sense. Glitsky would not—in fact, Hardy was "morally certain" he didn't—order anybody to follow Farrell home. Glitsky had known nothing about any of this—if he had, he wouldn't have asked Hardy to step in and find out why Farrell wasn't talking to him. He would have known.

Not only that, Glitsky knew, morality aside, that this kind of backstabbing did not produce results. It just wasn't Glitsky's style. If Abe had given his word, it simply hadn't happened as Farrell saw it.

"You sure it was Glitsky?" he asked, repeating that it just didn't sound like him. "What would be his motive?"

"Get the collar, the fame of it, maybe even claim the reward. Hell if I know. But he was the only one that knew I was with Shea, and he told me flat out he'd keep it right here." Farrell put a hand to his heart, then drank some more stout. "The guy lied, that's all."

Hardy swirled his own glass. "The warrant was for Shea himself, not documents or papers?"

"It was a search warrant for the premises." Farrell's face twisted in distaste. "Sergeant Stoner was very thorough."

"Sergeant Stoner?"

"Yeah, that was it. I remember I thought the name was a bit . . . ironic."

"Stoner's not with the police department," Hardy said. "He's a DA investigator. I used him when I was a DA."

The District Attorney's office in San Francisco has its own staff of detectives that are not under the jurisdiction of either the SFPD or the county sheriff. Typically, the role of the detectives was to locate witnesses, although occasionally they were used for other purposes.

"So?"

"So it would be odd—to say the least—for Glitsky to assign a *DA's* investigator to serve a warrant."

"So he told the DA—"

"That's not Abe."

Farrell looked at Hardy. "He sent you down to talk to me, didn't he? You guys are pals."

Hardy nodded. "He didn't know why you wouldn't talk to him. He really didn't know."

"Well, he must have leaked it somehow."

"Maybe not. It could have gone down another way. But the point is, he doesn't think Shea did it, either. He thinks he can still help you."

"It might be too late for that. If the DA—"

"He wants to talk to you. I think he's got an idea."

"And what's your part in it?"

"My fee is a can of chili." Hardy put down the remainder of his stout. "Private joke," he said, rising from his chair. "Get you another one?"

Special Agent Simms was back in Alan Reston's office, the door closed behind her, standing at ease in front of his desk. "The subject was one Dismas Hardy, another lawyer in town, do you know him?"

Reston shook his head no.

"He mentioned Kevin Shea and the two of them met at a bar out in the Avenues called the Little Shamrock. We followed Farrell there and both men drank two beers, then went back to their domiciles afterward. No sign of Shea."

Reston was nodding to himself. "Probably just the vultures figuring how they're going to split the pie."

"Yes, sir. That's what we've come to. In any event, it's all we've got to this point, but we're still on-line. I just wanted to keep you informed. We'll get him."

Reston sat up, eyes clear, back straight. "I'm sure you will."

61

Art Drysdale was back at work in his office, juggling his baseballs in a convincing display of *sangfroid*. "I've weathered that whole racist storm before, Abe. It comes and goes. Fact is, I've got no ax to grind here and everybody I work with seems to know it." He smiled genially. "You ought to see what some of our female colleagues have to say about me."

"What for?"

"I took an early public stand against using the word foreperson. You know, like in juries, the foreman. I thought it would be needlessly confusing, poetically uninspired, and—well, how can I put this?—stupid. Let's face it, I can't be trained. I'm sure I'm a menace on some level. Next it's the women's caucus, I'm sure."

The preliminaries completed—they were allies again—Glitsky sat back comfortably. Drysdale actually had upholstered chairs in his office. "I just wanted to stop by to tell you I've got two inspectors assigned to Chris Locke. I'm afraid with everything else I didn't jump on it as quickly as I could've."

Drysdale stopped juggling, squared himself around in his chair, all attention now. "You finding anything?"

Glitsky explained the little that Griffin had come up with, and then went over his plans for the evening—more interviews, more legwork. The talk wound down.

"I'm still having a hard time with it."

Glitsky nodded. "Yeah, I know."

"He was . . . he had a lot of flaws, Chris did. Everybody knows about the woman thing . . ." Even aside from his bombshell discovery of the morning about Locke's relationship with Elaine Wager, Glitsky was not-so-subliminally aware of Locke's many sexual conquests. "But I think his heart was in the right place where the law was concerned. He understood the ones we could win, when we had to drop one. He didn't want to waste everybody's time."

A eulogy on Chris Locke by Drysdale was going to be wasted on Glitsky, but he could listen politely if it made Drysdale feel better. Art had done the same for him enough times. The first months after Flo . . .

"Even the tough calls," Drysdale went on. "Hell, Jerohm Reese. You think it didn't kill Chris to let that scumbag go? But what was he going to do? He had no witnesses. He wasn't going to get a conviction, so what was the point? Waste the people's time and money?"

"That *was* a tough call." Glitsky at his most diplomatic. He really had not liked Locke at all. But the man had been a chameleon—to Drysdale he had remained the loyal friend, the good lawyer, the able administrator. The office had run smoothly, and that was what counted to Drysdale.

"Damn straight, and it wasn't the only one."

Glitsky knew that, too. Locke hadn't been too bad as District Attorneys went—certainly he would not now be pulling the idiocy Alan Reston was attempting with Kevin Shea.

Drysdale was juggling the baseballs again, calming himself. Glitsky was about to get up and go when something else occurred to him, something he hadn't meant to discuss here, but Drysdale's mention of the light evidence on Jerohm Reese had triggered it. Drysdale had been the chief assistant district attorney for almost twenty-five years, since long before Chris Locke's first term. He would have been around. "Art, you ever do any work on the Pacific Moon case? White collar? Maybe fifteen years ago?"

Again, the balls stopped. Drysdale's brow wrinkled in concentration. He prided himself on never forgetting a case. "It go to trial?"

"I don't think so, but I believe it got talked about down here and then dropped. Not enough evidence."

"The Pacific Moon?"

Glitsky nodded. "Restaurant out on Balboa. Got hot for a while with white collar, then died."

"Money laundering." Drysdale had placed it.

"That's the one."

"What about it?"

"Nothing. I don't know exactly. It's come up lately."

Drysdale gave him a look. "It's come up lately—that's a good answer."

"The real answer is I just don't know, Art." He took a beat, then realized who he was talking to. Once he'd brought it up, Drysdale would look over the old files, put out feelers, get it back into the grapevine on some level and Glitsky didn't want that. Better to be up front with him now. "With Loretta Wager in town now, there's been some—"

"That's it!" Art snapped his fingers. He had it now. "Sure, I can't believe it took me this long. It's come up a couple of times with the elections . . ."

"Probably."

"No probably—it has. People digging for dirt. You can imagine."

"So you've reviewed it? I heard some figures kicked around that are . . . provocative. Huge."

"I'm sure you have," Drysdale said. "I remember it clearly now. The numbers were always getting wildly exaggerated." He thought a minute longer. "Because of the profile—black woman, U.S. senator—Chris took it himself. He was the original prosecutor assigned, I'm talking now back in prehistory. The case didn't have any legs then, doesn't now. That was another one, though," he added enigmatically.

"Another what?"

"Another one of the tough calls for Locke."

"What was tough about it?"

"Well, this is between us now, Abe, but Chris did some fancy steppin' getting his hands on that one."

"He *wanted* the case?"

Drysdale nodded, remembering. "It was mostly black people, the investors, although I believe Dana Wager, of course, was one of them. Anyway, Chris was new, wanted to prove he didn't have a color barrier. He *badly* wanted this indictment, make his bones against the brothers, prove he could be a DA for all the people. But believe me, I remember him coming to me about this indictment, asking my opinion, my help—but there was nothing to get it on."

Glitsky let out the breath he'd been holding. "I heard the figure of three million dollars."

Drysdale just shook his head. "My recollection, Abe, is that's not even in the ballpark. I don't think it was even one million back when Chris was looking at it. Somebody got lucky with an investment or something if I recall . . ."

"And it's not ongoing? Not anymore?"

"I haven't even sniffed it, Abe, and I think I would have. And then, of course," Drysdale continued, getting back to his theme, "what made it a tough call for Chris is that when he had to drop it, he had to take flak for dropping it *because* it was mostly a black enterprise. And he couldn't very well come back out swinging, defending himself that he *wanted* to indict these people. Not if they hadn't done anything wrong, and it finally didn't look like they had." He sighed. "The world, huh, Abe?"

"The world," Glitsky agreed.

Loretta was downtown in her City Hall office. It was nearly eight o'clock in Washington, DC, Friday night, the end of the week. If deals were going to get cut, now was the time. They always said "close of business," meaning five o'clock, but in the Capitol the close of business lasted at least three hours. Nobody went home until everything that could be done was done. Still, she thought, checking her watch again, it should be about time.

She was confident. The reports she had gotten during the day—both from her own office and those of her Senate colleagues—indicated that the president's chief of staff had been working and lobbying around the clock to facilitate the transfer of the Hunter's Point Naval Reservation by executive order to the Federal Parks Program, with the stipulation that the land be dedicated to Loretta's idea of a camp for underprivileged youth and administered by an African-American.

Evidently (as Loretta had both hoped and expected), the president had seen it as she had—this was a monumental political opportunity, a no-lose situation that for maximum effect should be done immediately, as a symbol of the president's ongoing commitment to civil rights and in the inter-

ests of continued racial harmony. The telephone buzzed
and she forced herself to wait through two full rings, picking up on the third. It was her secretary calling from one
of the public phones at the Old Ebbett Grill, a few blocks
from the White House.

". . . and I think we can say that congratulations are in
order. The president's going ahead with the order."

"For sure?"

"He's scheduled the signature for noon tomorrow, our
time. Nine o'clock out there. It ought to be ideal for you."

"That is perfect," Loretta said. She had spoken again to
Alan Reston. He was confident that with the FBI's help
they'd have Kevin Shea by then. That would defang Philip
Mohandas and his march on City Hall, which Loretta knew
stood a good chance of getting out of hand. And she didn't
want that to happen—not now, not when a real solution
was so close.

With the apprehension of Kevin Shea and the timing of
the executive order, she was sure things would calm down.
The city would return to normal, or some semblance of it.
And she would be at the crest of the wave of peace and
harmony—a hero to the community at large, not to any
racial segment within it. She had fought for—and won—
concessions for her own people, but she had also proved
again that she was more than willing to work within the
existing white, predominantly male power structure. She
was a pragmatist with ideals intact, she told herself.

"You see the president tomorrow, honey, you tell him
it's Loretta Wager making him look so good. Nice and subtle, though, hear?"

"I hear you."

"I know you do, sugar."

And then there was Abe.

He stood leaning against the jamb, filling the doorway,
half-smiling, the simple enjoyment of watching her. She'd
been making notes on her projected press conference for
the next day, hadn't even sensed his arrival.

"How do you stay so invisible?" he asked her.

"God! Oh, Abe!" Her hand went to her chest. "You
scared me to death."

"'We homicide inspectors are trained to silently stalk our prey. Is it a good time?" Meaning for them to be alone. He stepped into the room, looking a question at her, getting a nod, closing the door behind him. Barefoot as usual, she came around the desk into his arms.

"God," she said again, holding him, "how can I have missed you this much?"

"I know. It's pretty ridiculous, isn't it?"

"Totally."

Eventually they came untangled. "What do you mean, invisible?" she asked.

"I mean normal humans usually only see senators on television surrounded by whatever the technical term is for flunkies . . ."

"Pages."

"Okay, pages. Or at least secret service people."

"We don't have that."

". . . or reporters of one kind of another. *Somebody,* anyway, at least. And here you sit all alone in your diddly little office . . ."

"This is a *nice* office, Abe."

"Well, yes, compared to some, like mine. But still, you're alone so much. It's just never been my fantasy of the power-broker life."

"You think I'm a power broker?"

"I don't think you're anybody's page."

She broke a small smile. "No, I suppose that's right." Boosting herself onto the desk, she sat facing him. "You want to have a lot of other people around, is that it?"

He moved to her again, stood against the desk, between her legs. She was no taller against him than when she'd been standing. "I just don't know how you do it."

"I don't think that door locks." She had her hands around his waist, looking up at him. "Well, believe it or not, when Elaine called—when was it, Tuesday night—and this whole thing looked like it was going to blow up, I just bought myself a ticket and got on a commercial flight to San Francisco. I had to be out here, see if I could help. Sometimes you've got to be free to move. I thought this would be one of those times. And I'm kind of glad I did." She squeezed him. "Are you?"

He went to the door, checked that it did not, in fact,

lock, then opened it and looked out in the hallway. "There's nobody out there," he said, crossing the office, picking up one of the chairs and placing it under the door-knob. Back to her. "It's six o'clock. Place is probably empty." She brought her feet to the floor, slid her hose off and lifted herself back onto the edge of the desk. "We'd better hurry," she said, pulling at his belt, bringing him to her.

"Can I borrow your telephone for thirty seconds?" He was already punching in numbers. She had moved the chair away from the doorway and was sitting in it.

"This is Glitsky," he said after a short wait. "You beeped me." He listened for another moment, checked his watch. "I can be there in an hour." He pulled a pad around, wrote something on it, tore off the page and stuffed it into his shirt pocket. "Good. See you then."

"An hour?" Loretta asked.

Glitsky moved to the other chair and sat facing her. "That was a friend of mine with news about Wes Farrell," he said. "Kevin Shea's attorney."

He couldn't read her expression, though for a moment it seemed as though some of the warmth had left her face. "I meant to ask," she said.

"It's been a busy day, I meant to tell you."

He told her about it—so much to do with Kevin Shea. The last time they'd discussed it—before they'd gone out to dinner last night—Glitsky said he'd been optimistic that he'd be able to apprehend Shea within hours. Now he told her of his difficulties with Reston, with Farrell, Rigby, the FBI.

When he finished, Loretta said, "And you're saying you think Alan's not offering a deal on Shea's safety because of *me*?"

"Essentially, that's it. How I see it."

"Well, that's got to stop," she said. "I'm not out to *get* Kevin Shea. Abe, you know that. I've been pushing for his proper arrest since I got here."

Glitsky nodded. "*I* know that, Loretta, but meanwhile Wes Farrell offers to give him up—just like that—all he needs is some minimal guarantee from Alan Reston, and

Reston won't do it. Then, for some reason, Farrell goes sideways about meeting up with me. Then Shea comes out with this videotape explaining his side of things, which never would have happened if Reston . . . Did Elaine mention any of this to you?"

At the mention of her daughter's name Loretta clearly tensed. "She told me a lot about . . . no, not this. Not specifically." She paused. "She told me you knew."

"Her and Locke?"

"And me and you."

"I kept that vague. In the past tense," he said.

"I'm afraid I didn't."

A hollow of silence.

Then, Glitsky: "Well." He blew out a breath.

"I'm sorry," she said. "But you can see . . . we didn't talk too much about Kevin Shea."

Glitsky stood up, paced the small room. He stopped by the window, looked out into the lengthening shadows. "That phone call," he began. "My friend says he thinks he's got Farrell agreeing to talk to me again. If he does I'm going to need some assurance for Shea, which means Reston."

"And you would like me to talk to Alan?"

"I think it might break the logjam, Loretta. If we could bring him in . . . it would all be over."

One leg curled under her, she sat back on the chair. "Elaine did say there was some indication that Shea might not be . . . that the case might be difficult to prove."

"He's got himself a different version of the events, but that's not exactly unique among defendants. You've got to have a story."

"Do you think—personally, now, Abe—do you think Kevin Shea's story is true?"

At the window, he turned. "What are you really asking?"

"I'm at least in part asking how this is going to affect my daughter, Abe. I picked Kevin Shea as the symbol of white racism, and I believed it, but she's got to live with him. I mean, she's gone public, as a lot of us have, with condemning him."

"I know. I tried to counsel her against that."

"But she's already *done* it. What's she going to do about it now?"

The harsh tone—the note of panic. Glitsky went over to Loretta, down to one knee, his arm around her back. He pulled her to him. "Hey. This is why we're talking, all right?"

She slumped into him. "I'm sorry," she said. "It's not you. I'm just so worried for my daughter. Are you telling me Shea really might not have done it?"

Glitsky nodded. "There's some chance of that, yes."

"And what will that do to Elaine, to her career?"

After a minute he replied, "It'll be better than having it come out after he's been shot down by some overzealous FBI SWAT team."

"I think that's a little extreme, Abe. It's not going to come to that—"

"Have you met Special Agent Simms?"

"No."

"I wouldn't write it off until you have."

Loretta shook her head. "Abe, the FBI agents I know are professionals. They don't want firefights they can't explain or justify."

"That's my point, Loretta. I think Simms wants exactly that—a firefight she could plausibly deny. She'll just say that her information was that Shea was armed and dangerous. She had no choice. But the bottom line to her superiors is she's not afraid to pull the trigger. And believe me— I'm in law enforcement, I know—this is considered a good thing."

Loretta still wasn't convinced. "I just have a hard time believing that the FBI . . ."

"You ever read Chekhov?" At her blank expression he said, "Chekhov says you don't introduce a gun in the first act of a play unless you're going to use it in the third."

"All right?"

"The FBI is here with marksmen. Sharpshooters. Believe it, they did not bring them for a dress rehearsal."

"You can't think they're planning to *kill* Kevin Shea?"

"That's exactly what I think. While everybody has the perception he's still guilty as hell. That's why Alan Reston isn't going to offer any protection. He's setting up a scenario that he figures is going to protect you, Loretta. Maybe Elaine, too, but mostly you, I think."

"Me?" The enormity of it apparently settling on her, she

half-collapsed backward, molding to the chair. "Because I made Shea the center of it?"

"That's right."

"Oh Lord. I do have to call Alan."

Unsteadily, she got up and walked to her desk, to the phone, pushed the faceplate. As she was waiting Glitsky reminded her not to mention his name, he'd been ordered off the case.

No one picked it up. "He's not there. I'll try his home." She pulled her own yellow pad around, flipped some pages and punched more numbers, leaving a message on the service that as soon as he got in, whatever time it was, Alan should call Loretta Wager. It was urgent. She left three numbers—one here at the office, two at her home.

"He'll call," she said. "I'll tell him."

She came back to Abe and put her arms around him again. "Thank you for talking to me." Then, pushing away, "You go see your friend. As soon as I hear from Alan, I'll call you."

62

The way Farrell had left it with Hardy was "Yeah, you can tell your friend Glitsky to call me." Damned if Wes was going to call the lieutenant. He didn't want to say he'd call Glitsky, anyway, because he had no idea for sure when— or even if—Kevin Shea was going to call him again. And he couldn't call Shea even if he had something specific to tell him, which he didn't.

Just cool the heels until something broke.

So he'd gone home, waited, killed time watching the news, waited some more. Story of his life the past few days, waiting. Except this time with two pints of Guinness inside him. He dozed, woke up, looked at his watch.

Was Glitsky going to call him or what?

Finally, he again put a leash on Bart and the two of them almost ran out of his apartment. He didn't want to hear the phone ringing again four steps after he'd locked his deadbolt as he made his escape.

They turned north this time, along Junipero Serra, maybe make it all the way to the shopping district on Ocean. There were places there where he'd eaten at outside tables with Bart.

It was a typical July evening in San Francisco, cool and breezy. He had changed from his shorts and Pendleton into a gray sweatsuit, incongruously carrying with him the super-wide "lawyer's briefcase" (now containing only two pens and a yellow legal pad) that he hadn't pulled from his closet in over a year. Waking from his lethargy, beginning to plan his moves, he whistled tunelessly. Bart, his leash in Farrell's other hand, stopped periodically for territory, enjoying the romp.

Actually, except for the disturbing lack of connection

with the police, things didn't appear to be going too badly. If what Dismas Hardy had said was true about Glitsky not being the one to have sent Stoner with his warrant, there still might be a chance that they could negotiate some terms that would protect Kevin at the same time as it would get him into custody.

In fact, Farrell was already into the next step—the trial. He found he was actually looking forward to it. This was a case he could win! And, unlike the one with his ex-friend Mark Dooher, this time he would be on the side of justice—a concept that until only a day ago he had consigned to the trash heap of ancient history. The thought—that he might play some real role in defending an innocent man—galvanized him. Once he got the case moving into the courts, in fact, he was starting to feel that he could maybe get the charges dismissed before it even came to trial.

Turning onto Ocean, his brain had finally kicked in. The whistling had stopped. Abruptly, he ceased to walk and hooked Bart's leash around the top of one of the wrought-iron fence posts that bounded a manicured landscape of bonsai and sedgegrass beside a gingerbread house. He sat on one of the large square stone steps and opened his brief-case, oblivious of the weather or the scenery.

What was it that had gotten to him? Oh yes . . . the knife wounds. He had to remember when he talked to Glitsky (when? when?—maybe he *would* break down, and make the call) to ask the lieutenant to do a search for people with knife wounds. (Of course, Farrell had no inkling of Colin Devlin or Mullen or McKay.) This was the kind of detail—since it hadn't been released to the public—that a judge might decide constituted a lack of probative evidence to convict Kevin right at the git-go. Oh shit, except that Kevin had mentioned it on his tape. He scratched out what he had written.

But that was just the first significant detail that had occurred to him—he thought of his other arguments to Glitsky at Lou the Greek's. If he could get this client off with an eleven eighteen motion—a directed verdict of acquittal—at trial, now wouldn't that be sweet?

He made more notes—the lawyer back in his element. There were a million things he could do for Kevin . . . call

Glitsky as a witness—a cop as a *defense* witness. He loved it. The theater of it should be persuasive to a jury. He had to get a doctor to look at Kevin, and soon. Make some determination on the cracked ribs, if that's what they were. The lacerations on the face.

Shit again. He'd forgotten to take Polaroids of Kevin, and the scratches were healing. Oh, but the videotape would show them. He hoped. He wasn't sure he remembered. He had to start training himself again. Get sharper. Trials were war and you didn't get into one if you weren't prepared to win or die trying.

Other things? What?

He was chewing on the back end of his pen, some ink leaking out and staining his lower lip. He had to think about the jury—what the hell was he going to do about the racial makeup of the jury? That was going to be thorny, a crapshoot as always. Still, he was getting so he believed he could find twelve people who wouldn't be racially biased, even in a case this potentially explosive.

How many black friends did Kevin have? Okay, maybe it was a cliché, but it also happened to be a fact. He knew there were at least a couple—they'd all been out drinking together. Good witnesses. Kevin would know the names.

But what he was going to need more than anything were a couple of other suspects—hell, not just *suspects*—he reminded himself. The guys who goddamn *did* it.

He tore back another page from his legal pad, scribbling like a madman. Maybe he *was* mad. Here's a long-haired fifty-year-old potbellied man in a sweatsuit, a smudge of black ink emanating from his mouth, mumbling incoherent words. His old fat dog lay curled at his feet—a dog who, truth be told, farted more often than he really should—due to the rich, canned, all-meat (and occasional beer) diet that his owner felt was the proper nutrition for a dog. He hadn't wanted the goddamn animal in the first place, but since he had him, he wasn't going to have the guy live on kibble and meal, not a real man's dog like Bart Dog Farrell. Nosiree.

The streetlights came up—most of them functioned properly on Ocean Street. As it sometimes did, the wind died at sunset. Wes Farrell looked up, surprised not so much at where he was as at where he'd been.

Caught up in it. Alive.

*   *   *

Marcel Lanier had been snagged by Carl Griffin to go with him and look again at the Dolores Park area, so Ridley Banks, who had been teaming with Marcel the last few days, was on his own.

The day had been circumscribed for him by his decision to stay away from the homicide detail. He had every excuse to do it—in their zeal to lay something on Peter McKay and Brandon Mullen, both he and Marcel had allowed their regular workloads to slide a bit, and some time working the street might yield fruit with their other homicides.

But also, Ridley had sensed that if he began any more exchanges with his lieutenant about his suspicions concerning Loretta Wager's past, Glitsky would blow. So he had left his encoded note and things would proceed or not, but either way he felt he had done all he could. He had no more evidence than he'd given Abe, but he still felt that Senator Wager had some skeletons that homicide inspectors ought not to dance with—but he didn't want to argue about it, make a stink. He just wanted to be thorough or, more precisely, he wanted Glitsky to understand what he *might* be dealing with. Whether he chose to do anything with that understanding would be his decision.

Ridley's girlfriend, Jacqueline, worked as a legal secretary in one of the high-rise firms, and he was waiting now in the reception area to see if she would be getting off soon and would want to get something to eat. Though it was full dusk, the workday for the secretaries in Jacqueline's firm ended when their attorney bosses went home—officially there were normal business hours, but anyone who left at five or five-thirty soon found themselves unemployed. Jacqueline's day ended not when her work was done, not when she had put in her time, but when her attorney told her she could leave and not before.

She came into view around a corner down the long muted hallway, and he watched her approach, appreciating her matter-of-fact style. Ridley wasn't into either flash or sleaze, although—actually *because*—he had experimented with both when he had been younger. Jacqueline was a working woman, as he was a working man. She had a good heart, a warm smile, a civil tongue and bone structure.

There was a tension in her bearing, but she greeted him normally. She had, he thought, too much class to display all her emotions. "Good timing," she said. A buss on the cheek. More tension. She was wearing a long woolen skirt and lavender blouse. Ridley was aware of a vague scent of cinnamon. He thought he might marry her before too long, though they hadn't really talked about it yet.

In the elevator, he took her hand. "What's the matter?"

She took a long breath, held it for a couple of floors. "Stan's working all weekend," she said. "He wants me to come in."

This wasn't at all unusual. Stan was Stansfield Butler III, "her" attorney—a thirty-four-year-old married white man with two young children, bucking for partner next year after six years with the firm. Hours meant nothing to him. He lived law.

Ridley shrugged, reluctantly accepting this news. "That's all right," he said, squeezing her hand. "All the troubles, I'm sure I can pull some comp time."

They had tentatively talked about getting away, maybe up to Point Reyes for a couple of days, but this kind of last-minute demand was always a possibility. Jacqueline had been Butler's loyal and highly efficient secretary-assistant for four years. She was under no illusions, however—if she said no too many times (once? twice? she didn't know the precise number), she would be replaced. It had happened to too many of her coworkers. She was black and she was staff. If she wanted to keep this good-paying professional job she should not put any priority on her personal life. That had to come second if she were to survive.

"Well, that's not it, exactly."

"Not what?"

The elevator door opened and they stepped into the enormous marble-tiled foyer. There was a fern bar for young professionals across the lobby and they gravitated, by habit, in that direction. Jacqueline would often take a glass of chardonnay after work.

She stopped walking, turned to him. "I'd hoped to go to the march, Ridley. I'm not sure if I'm going to come in for Stan. Not tomorrow. I . . . I told him that."

Ridley chewed on that for a minute. "And what did he say?"

"When he picked up his jaw, he said that was my decision. If I didn't come in, then I'd have made it for myself. He said that this late he'd have trouble getting another secretary, and if he lost the client because *his* secretary wasn't available, well . . ."

They both knew where that was going. Ridley put his hand gently in the small of her back and they were through the doors into the bar. The taped music was New Age. There were a couple of free tables in the front by the floor-to-ceiling windows.

After they had ordered (Ridley had a ginger ale), they linked hands on the small table. "You were going to the march? With Philip Mohandas?"

"Not *were*." She was matter-of-fact, not defiant. "Am."

"You think it's worth your job?"

"It may sound old-fashioned, Ridley, but I think we've got to take a stand. This has gone on too long and nothing changes."

"And you think standing up there with Philip Mohandas and a few hundred brothers is going to change something?"

"It won't be a few hundred. I don't know anybody who isn't going."

"Yes you do." Ridley detached his hand from hers.

"Don't," she said.

"*You* don't."

"This isn't you, Ridley."

"No? That's funny. Somehow I thought here I was a cop and this march is all about how us cops aren't doing our job, how we're all controlled by a passel of honky trash, isn't that it? That's how I heard it. And you want to be part of that? And then you tell me it isn't about *me*? Give me a break, Jacqueline."

"Don't be mad." She had her hand out on the table.

"Don't be mad. Okay."

"Maybe you're not seeing it . . . like us. I mean, maybe you've been inside it too long—"

"Gone Oreo, huh?" He glared across at her. "You any idea what I been doing the last three days when I haven't had any time to see you or anybody else?"

"I—"

"I'll tell you what. I've been hunting down the people, trying to *find* the people who strung up Arthur Wade. No march on City Hall is gonna help me get any closer to those people."

"You mean *that person*?"

"Kevin Shea?"

"Yes, him."

Banks lowered his head, pulled himself back. His hand went to the table and took hers. "Jacqueline, honey, listen to me. There was a *mob* of people killed Arthur Wade, not just—"

Now it was Jacqueline's turn to react. She slammed both of their hands down on the table. The ashtray rattled. People at surrounding tables looked over. "You don't *feel* it, do you? You don't feel it anymore?"

"I feel it every day, Jacqueline. I'm *in it* every day."

"But it's not in your guts anymore, is it?"

"What does that mean?"

"It means they sold it and you bought it. It means—"

"I didn't *buy* anything, Jacqueline. I walk around with my eyes open, is all."

"No, you walk around being one of the *cops,* one of *them,* Ridley. You think you're on some *team,* like some gang where you're all protected by each other . . ."

"Jesus, Jacqueline, where do you get this?"

"I get it from watching you. I get it from seeing what's changing and what's not. And you're fooling yourself, Ridley Banks. You think you're one of *them* now, you've made it. You're an *inspector,* high-class, can't be touched. But let me tell you something, and this week should have proved it to you all over again. *We* are second class. That's what we're marching for. That's what this is all about."

"Lord, Jacqueline," he began, then stopped. "And you think that's worth your job?"

She banged the table again, glared back at everyone who looked over. "It shouldn't have anything to do with my job! It's a Saturday, for God's sake. It's the Fourth of July weekend. And no warning. What am I supposed to do, drop everything for the rest of my life every time Stansfield Butler the Third wants a goddamn cup of coffee, with skimmed milk yet? You think I weren't black, I'd have to worry over *that*?"

"But you are, girl, and you do."

"And that's what we're marching against."

"But it might also be anger that you're just a secretary, not a lawyer. Maybe black's got nothing to do with it—"

"*Just* a secretary! I . . ."

A man who looked like a young athlete in a coat and tie approached the table. "Excuse me," he said, "I'm the manager here and some of the other patrons . . ." A gesture, not his fault. "I wonder if I could ask you to continue your discussion outside."

Jacqueline gave it back. "And I wonder if I could ask *you*—"

But Ridley had her hand covered, lifting her, pulling her by it. "Jacqueline, come on . . ." Arm strongly around her now, leading her to the door.

Outside on the sidewalk she turned on him. "Get your hands *off* me. Get *away* from me."

"Jacqueline, please . . ."

She struck out at him, turning away.

He grabbed for her again, but she spun, hitting him high on the forehead, the force of it pushing him back a step. "You stay away from me. I don't want to see you. Get *away*." She was backing up, facing him, a hand held up. Then, abruptly, she whirled and ran.

He followed her a few steps, gave it up and stopped in front of the huge windows of the bar. A sea of all white faces stared out at him through the glass.

He didn't feel like one of them. Not even a little bit.

63

"The cupboard, as they say, is bare." Melanie was opening the doors to the cabinet shelves. "I mean, nothing." She reached out and pulled a can of mixed fruit cocktail from the back of the shelf, a tiny tin of Vienna sausages. Kevin appeared in the kitchen doorway.

"What's your friend Ann live on?"

"I guess we're looking at it." She opened the refrigerator. It, too, contained little in the way of food or drink. For breakfast, they'd finished some cheese and stale crackers. Lunch had been two eggs, scrambled, for the two of them, with water.

"I sure feel like a pizza," Kevin said. "I wouldn't mind a beer either."

"Maybe we can order up. Do you have any money?"

Kevin checked his wallet, counting fifty-eight dollars out onto the kitchen table. He placed one of the ubiquitous flowerpots on top of the bills. "Which reminds me," he said, "I haven't called work, told them I wouldn't be in for a while." (He had worked twenty-five hours a week as a telemarketer selling business software to small companies, manning one of a bank of telephones out of a converted home in the Marina.) "I wonder if they've noticed? Probably haven't even missed me." Neither off them smiled when he said it. The banter couldn't cover the tension.

Melanie went back to the living room, flipped pages of the phone book and called a place she knew. When she hung up she said, "They're not delivering, not with the riots."

"Try someone else."

*   *   *

Seven calls later—three pizza places, two Chinese, a Mongolian Bar-B-Que and a piroshki house—and not one was delivering. Melanie was standing by the phone in the living room, starting on the eighth when Kevin looked up from his stuffed chair. "I think I'm going nuts here, is what I think. Are you going nuts, or is it just me?"

She nodded. "A little."

"Hey, it's Friday night. It's dark out. People—normal people—are on dates, into themselves." Her look was not encouraging. "We go out, maybe Ann's got a wig or something, I stuff some cotton balls in my cheeks . . ."

"You're going to eat pizza with cotton balls in your cheeks?"

"Okay, no cotton balls. But maybe a little lipstick, a tasteful touch of rouge . . ."

Melanie was shaking her head. *"Kevin . . ."*

His hands were flat against his sides. "I am truly going crazy here."

"So am I," she said, "but it seems every time we poke our heads outside—"

"Not every time," he reminded her. "Last night we sat in the line at that drive-in for a half hour and nobody recognized us."

"Nobody was looking at us there."

"Or *for* us, which they also wouldn't be at some local little dive, either. In fact, think about it, out in public is about the *last* place anybody would expect to see us. Even if they looked right at us, just sitting casually eating a pizza, they'd go, 'No way. It couldn't be. They wouldn't be that stupid.' "

Melanie sat by the phone, giving it some thought. "On the other hand, look at, say, John Dillinger. Coming out of a movie theater . . ."

"He was set up, Melanie. Nobody knows where we are right now, where we're coming from, where we're going." He was up out of the chair. "I actually think it's a smarter choice than if we just went out to get some food at the store. We go, we eat, we come back, what do you say?"

Ann did have hats, and they each wore one—Kevin's a multicolored ski cap that he pulled to his eyebrows, Mela-

nie's a faux-velvet beret into which she tucked her hair.
They selected accessories, and Melanie applied an extra
coat of fire-engine red lipstick. She also painted two moles
on her face. Kevin had opted for the more natural look,
although he couldn't resist a small golden ear cuff.

The city, when they were out in it, still smelled of smoke,
and contrary to Kevin's notion that people were dancing
all over the place, there wasn't much sign of it. The tent
city in the Panhandle of Golden Gate Park was, after all,
only two blocks north of them. At the cross streets, looking
through, they could see campfires and the harsh blinking
of yellow caution lights on the sawhorses that set off the
campground.

Melanie had her arm around Kevin's waist—the night
was chilly—her hand in his back pocket. He held her tight
against him and they walked fast. Haight Street itself was
not a curfew area, although there was almost no street traffic and fewer pedestrians. Every few doorways homeless
people asked them for money. Kevin dropped his last few
quarters.

As Kevin had predicted, no one seemed to notice. The
street might have been empty, but Pizzaiola was crowded
enough at nine something on a Friday night. Kevin picked
a booth in a back corner.

"Under the Exit sign, just in case."

"That's not funny."

Melanie went up to order—a large combination with an-
chovies, a pitcher of Sam Adams, two glasses.

"Could I see some I.D., please?" The man behind the
bar was an African-American about Kevin's age. He smiled
at her, no threat, waiting.

She froze. She had been twenty-one now for six months
and, especially while she had been dating Kevin, had gotten
used to ordering beer and not getting "carded." Now she
stared, all but openmouthed, wondering what to do. She
couldn't bolt out of here alone, not without Kevin, not
without alerting the whole neighborhood. She half-turned—
Kevin wasn't even looking her way.

"Ma'am?"

"Oh, sorry." Nothing else to do. She took out her wallet and presented her driver's license, which the man held under the light. "Thanks. Who's the other glass for?"

Oh God . . . they were going to get caught. She should just run—yell to Kevin and run. "My boyfriend, back there," she said, striving for control. "He's older than I am."

The man squinted over through the dimness. "That old, huh?" He was still smiling, drawing the pitcher of beer. "Waitress will bring it right over." In a daze, she crossed back to the corner, sat down at their table.

"This was a good idea," Kevin said. "Tomorrow we . . . what's the matter?"

The waitress arrived, put the pitcher down between them, left without a glance. Melanie was trying to control herself, shaking her head so Kevin would stop asking, not call any more attention to them. Kevin leaned over the table, closer to her. "What is it?" whispering. He put out his hand and she covered it with hers and told him.

At the bar Melanie's bartender was a dervish, more pitchers were getting filled. Behind the open counter, one of the cooks was spinning pizza dough in the air. Sting was on the jukebox singing "Love Is Stronger Than Justice." Though there wasn't a dance floor a few people were free-form dancing, apparently immune to the rhythm changes in the tune. Nobody was paying any attention to Kevin and Melanie. Kevin mentioned this.

"I know. But you . . . what if . . . ?"

He patted her hand. "We'd take off. We're getting pretty good at that." He flashed his confident grin. "Hey." He touched a finger to her face. "It's okay, Mel."

"Kevin, I'm no good at this stuff anymore. That guy looked over at you and I thought I was going to be sick."

"But you *are* good at it."

She shook her head. "What's going to happen to us? When does it stop? *Does* it stop?"

He pulled his hand out from under hers and made a show of filling both glasses, stalling for time. "That's what we're going for, stopping this, aren't we?"

"I don't know what we're going for anymore. I'm just scared, that's all I know. Scared to death." She paused.

"Sometimes I think we're not even going to live through this. That somebody's going to kill us before it's over."

He leaned all the way back in his chair. "That's *not* going to happen."

"You want to knock on wood when you say that. Please."

Dutifully, Kevin rapped once on the table. It wasn't entirely to make Melanie feel better. "You know, come to think about it, it's really only me. Mel, *you've* got other options. You could—"

Her eyes flashed. "No way! You think I'm leaving you now, after all this?"

"I thought you just said—"

"I *never* said that. I don't want that. I'm just scared, Kevin. I'm scared for *both* of us. Who in his right mind *wouldn't* be scared right now?"

"What I'm saying is, you could just walk out of here, this minute, take a cab down the Peninsula to your parents' house, get a lawyer . . . ."

"*No.* Shut up, Kevin."

His face was near hers again, his voice low. "Maybe you should, Mel. This isn't fair to you."

She took a sip of her beer, swept the room with a glance. She broke a steely smile, met his eyes. *"Fuck fair,"* she said. "This whole thing isn't *fair.* If the world were fair you'd be getting a medal at the White House . . ."

"I don't know if I'd go that far. I'd settle for the warrant getting lifted."

A nod. "That would be a good start."

The waitress arrived with their pizza, slapped it steaming onto the table, was gone.

Kevin gestured after her. "See? Perfectly safe," he said.

"There's hope," Wes said.

Kevin was talking on the pay phone in the hallway by the restrooms and the emergency exit at Pizzaiola. "We were just talking about that."

"Where are you? What's that noise?"

"Pizzaiola. Pizza place out on Haight." Into the black hole of silence: "We had to get out, Wes. We were going stir crazy. It's cool. Nobody knows who we are—"

"Kevin, *everybody* knows who you are. Maybe, let's hope, nobody's recognized you where you're at right now, but that's not the same thing. Could you please try and remember that?"

"Sure, Wes, sure. Look, we're leaving in a minute anyway, going back to our cozy little hideaway. What about the hope?"

Wes was having trouble with his friend and client—the most wanted fugitive in the city, county, state, possibly the whole country—hanging out in some pizza joint, but there was nothing he could do about it now. "Evidently Glitsky didn't have me followed home," he said. "It was somebody else, the DA, not the police."

"Okay?"

"Okay, so suddenly I think we might have a decent chance to get what we wanted last night—a hearing at least, extra protection."

"A decent chance . . . ?"

"Better than none, Kev. I'm trying."

"I know. I just . . . so you've talked to this Glitsky . . . ?"

"Whoa. Not yet. He's calling sometime tonight. Frankly, I expected it by now."

Kevin couldn't repress the sarcasm. "Gosh, this is heartening . . ."

"It's not bad, really, Kevin. I promise you. At least now we've got a good reason for you to stay put, not take off. This morning, you remember—"

"I remember."

"Okay, then. This time tomorrow, I think we'll have something worked out. I *know* Glitsky's going to call me— he went to some lengths to get me back talking to him. He's on our side—a cop. This is not bad news, Kev."

"Okay, you've convinced me, I'm happy. Jubilant, in fact."

Farrell sighed. "Why don't we just set up a time when you'll definitely call me? You could also just give me your number."

"I would, but I don't know it. It's not mine, after all. Or Mel's."

"All right," Farrell said, "but this not being able to reach you is making me old."

"I don't think that's it." Kevin paused. "Something,

though. Something is definitely making you old. *Has* made you old. Did I ever tell you my cosmic radiation theory as the cause of old age?"

"I got a theory, too, Kevin. Old age is caused by living a long time."

"That's a good one, too. Okay, so when?"

"Nine."

"Nine? Wes, it's Saturday. It's criminal to have to wake up at nine on a Saturday."

"*Saturday*? What's the difference—Saturday, Tuesday, who cares? Jesus, Kevin . . ."

"Nine's all right. I'm kidding you."

"You're a riot, Kevin."

"Don't use that word, Wes. Riot . . ."

"Nine," Wes growled. "Do it."

This was her first job in San Francisco, and Special Agent Simms could not believe the weather—the first day of July and she was freezing. In DC it had been ninety and ninety, degrees and humidity, since the middle of May, and she had figured summertime in California would be close to the same except for the humidity. Previous assignments in LA, Modesto, Sacramento, even as nearby as Oakland had not prepared her for the micro-climate here. Had she been the literary sort, she might have taken some warning from Mark Twain's oft-quoted remark that the coldest winter he'd ever spent was a June in San Francisco, but Margot Simms had not read anything but manuals in six years, and little else before that.

She was around the corner from where the surveillance van was parked in front of Wes Farrell's apartment, her hands wrapped around a tall glass of *caffe latte*. Though there was no wind, the temperature had abruptly fallen to the mid-fifties and she was wearing only a skirt and blouse under a lightweight tailored jacket. During the three plus hours she had spent in the unheated van after she had finally left the Hall of Justice, the increasing chill had worked its way into every cell of her being.

Ten minutes earlier she had given up, leaving her post in the van in a quest for a little warmth, which she had found a block up the street in a mini-mall. A corner diner—

in DC they would call it a diner—except that here it was all angles, high ceilings, dramatic light. San Francisco was into drama, she'd give it that. Substance zero, form ten. California fruit and nuts everywhere you went.

She had come in because the place looked warm and served coffee. Also beer, wine, breads, *sirops* and flavored waters, pretentious crapola—you wouldn't just want a place to grabba quick cuppa, no, not here. The menu—even the coffee drinks—was all in Italian and there was an enormous glass counter under which were serving platters filled with exotic pastas and salads. Simms was only here for the warmth, for a mug of coffee to wrap her hands around. The *latte* was the closest they had.

It wasn't just the cold. She sat there alone at her cute tiny table, still shivering—most of the other little tables were filled with groupings of chattering urbanites her age and younger—it was near San Francisco State, that might have been part of it. Suddenly Simms realized she hated San Francisco with all her heart.

She was seized with an urge to take out the gun she wore under her ineffectual linen jacket and take a few pops at the track lighting, the tinted floor-to-ceiling windows, the espresso machines, maybe a few of the trendoids themselves. Wake 'em up.

What did they think was going on here anyway? The whole sham structure of a melting pot was being dismantled brick by brick all over the city at this very minute—had been all week—and here the intellectuals and bon vivants and liberals and faggots sat with their *lattes* and *sirops* and the occasional white wine—what did they call it, *schmoozing*? Well, they weren't her problem, but God, she hated them. Let 'em eat—she scanned the blackboard menu—let 'em eat *foccacia*, whatever the hell that was.

Her thoughts were interrupted by one of her technicians—Sam the Van Man—scanning through the windows of the place, recognizing her, getting to the door, through the maze of creative floor arrangement to her table. She was already up, coming toward him. "We've got him," he said, nearly breathless from his run. "It's definitely Shea. Place called Pizzaiola—eighteen hundred block of Haight Street."

Forgetting the cold and everything else, she was on her way out, dragging Sam in her wake. "Let's roll."

*   *   *

Kevin covered Melanie's hand again—easy, easy—as the black-and-white police car pulled up on the street in front.

"We'd better get the check." Matter-of-fact.

But before they could catch the waitress's attention the two uniformed policemen walked into the pizza place, chatting, apparently taking a break, filling up—it seemed to Kevin—a lot of the space inside, using up a lot of breathing air.

"Will that be all?" Their efficient waitress.

"Thanks. It was great. Just the check, please."

A quick turn and she was gone.

The cops stood together by the ordering bar, talking with one of the dough throwers. The waitress stopped up front next to the cops, said a few words, laughed.

Kevin and Melanie huddled together in their corner, keeping their faces as covered as they could. "Just keep cool," he said, and she nodded, squeezing his hand.

Not soon—say about the half-life of carbon later—the waitress came back with their check, dropped it facedown, left. Kevin picked it up—$34.65 for a pizza and some beer—and reached for his wallet.

The cops finished with their order and turned to look for a table.

"No. Not here, not here," Kevin intoned.

"Shhh."

"You'd hate it here, there's a horrible draft. Also, I think something must have died in the hallway . . ."

"Shhh! Kevin . . . !"

Moving back through the restaurant, the policemen pulled chairs up less than three feet from where Kevin and Melanie sat at the next table over.

"I'm going to throw up," Melanie whispered.

Kevin opened his wallet. He looked again. There was no money in it. Keeping his voice low, he gripped Melanie's hand. "Where's the money? Did you take the money?"

She looked at him as though he were insane. "You had the money, don't tease like this . . ."

Kevin folded open the wallet, showing her. "I think we left it on the table back at Ann's."

"*We* didn't . . ."

"I put it under a flowerpot on the kitchen table. I don't remember taking it. I must have left it."

Melanie covered her face with her hands. She wanted to run. She couldn't run. The police were *right here*! Looking at Kevin. "Oh God!" It just came out.

Hearing her, one of the policemen—an older guy with a kind face—leaned over to them. "You kids okay? Everything all right?"

Melanie stared at him. Frozen. Finally: "I'm sorry," she said. "My cat, it just died, today." She tried to smile.

Kevin gave them half of his profile—more than half would be inviting disaster. "Murray," he added, "his name was Murray. Had him for six years."

"Gee, that's tough," the cop said. "Myself, I'm not a cat man, but my wife is."

Simms was the only woman on the team. The four men who'd been hanging out in the van were more prepared for the cold than she was—leather jackets, heavy pants. They had already patched a call to the backup unit at the hotel— including the other marksmen—all of them would rendezvous at the famous corner of Haight and Ashbury and move in from there.

In her car, flying now out to Geary, but without a siren. Damned if she was going to let any of the local authorities in on this. The San Francisco police would just screw it up. This was an FBI bust—Simms sat in the front seat on the passenger side, her three guys primed but controlled on the way out. They didn't say much, they didn't have to recheck their weapons, any of that—the weapons would work if they were needed. Her men were pros.

"What I want you to do is just walk to the bathroom."

"Kevin, we've got to pay. We can't just leave . . ."

Kevin was using all of his strength to keep his voice down. "I'm not giving them my credit card. I don't think you should, either. I think you have to go to the bathroom, *don't you*?"

Melanie struggled with it, got up and disappeared into the hallway behind them. Kevin waited as long as he could stand it, then turned around to the policemen—more than halfway around. In the low light he had to take the chance.

"Excuse me," he said. They stopped talking, both of them turning to him. "I'm just going back to see if my girlfriend's okay." He pointed to the unpaid bill. "She's got the money with her. In case the waitress comes, sees we're both gone"—he flashed a grin—"would you please tell her we didn't cut out on the check. We'll be right back."

The nice cop nodded, said sure, and Kevin was gone.

Melanie, white as death, shivered by the back door, which was clearly labelled "Emergency Exit Only. Alarm Will Sound."

Kevin stopped in front of her, studied the sign. "You ready? Let's go."

"What do you mean, let's go?"

He took her hand, bringing her along with him, pushed into the bar that held the door.

No sound. The door opened—quietly—into an alley.

Margot Simms pulled up behind the police car that was parked by the curb in front of Pizzaiola. "What's *that* doing here?" she asked of no one, getting out of her car.

She had already positioned a man each at the opposite ends of the alley that ran the length of the block behind the restaurant. She and the last one—Sam the Van Man—were going in through the front door.

Simms had decided that there would be no point in making a fuss. No sense inviting resistance or worse. Kevin Shea would have no idea who she was—just another customer—until she flashed her badge and, if need be, pulled her weapon.

Standing just inside the door, surveying the room, she did not see anybody resembling Kevin Shea. There were only about twenty tables—and it took that many seconds. One of the tables, back by where a couple of city cops were sitting, had not been cleared off yet but its seats were empty. She turned and issued an order to Sam to check the bathroom.

Back with the policemen, she identified herself, took out Kevin Shea's picture, asked them if they had seen anyone who looked like . . .

A frozen glance between the men. One of them, cattle-prodded, almost knocked the table over jumping up, reaching for his gun, going into the hallway. Simms followed in hot pursuit.

Sam came out of the bathroom. "Nothing," he said.

They were gathered in the narrow hallway. The older San Francisco cop hesitated by the back door, then pushed. Nothing.

He let it swing all the way closed. Pushed at it again. "Alarm must be out of whack," he said.

"I literally thought I was going to die," Melanie said. They were turning off Haight onto Stanyan, fifty yards from the lobby entrance to Ann's building. "What are we going to do about the bill?"

Kevin gave her the eye. "You're worried about the bill?"

"Well, you just don't walk out without paying."

"Sometimes you do. It's called situational ethics, I think."

"We're going to go back and pay them sometime, though, aren't we?"

Kevin squared her around to him and kissed her. "Yes," he said. "That's a very important point and I concur that we should do it at the first opportunity. Which might not be tonight."

She snuggled up against him, the relief flooding through her. "Okay. But let's try not to forget, okay?"

"I won't forget. I've got a mind for this kind of stuff." He kissed her again. "You are such a dork," he said tenderly. "I don't know why suddenly I'm so in love with you."

She came up as though she were going to kiss him back, but instead took his bottom lip in her teeth, held him there, whispering with equal gentleness. "Birds of a feather."

64

Before dinner Dismas Hardy had loaded up about five hours' worth of opera on the CD player and now a male tenor—beyond Pavarotti, Glitsky wasn't too hot on the names—was barely audible, singing to break your heart. His heart.

After leaving Loretta, Glitsky had originally planned on zipping by here, getting the lowdown on Hardy's interview with Farrell, then calling Farrell and moving out on Kevin Shea.

As soon as he had come in he had called Farrell's number but there had been—maddeningly—no answer. Why didn't the man have an answering machine? All lawyers had answering machines—Glitsky thought they had dispensers for them in the bathrooms at law schools.

Then he had come into the kitchen and given Hardy's wife Frannie a kiss hello and Frannie had taken one look at him and said he was staying for dinner and that was the end of that. It was obvious that he wasn't taking good care of himself. Just look at him—what did he weigh anymore? What was the matter with him? He should at least think of his children.

Frannie was Moses McGuire's little sister, a petite woman with long flaming red hair, skin the color of cream, green eyes. More than a decade younger than Glitsky and Hardy and everybody else he saw outside of work, she was idealistic, headstrong, quite beautiful.

When Flo had died, and though the Hardys had two young children of their own, Frannie had taken all of Glitsky's boys for a month while he had pretended he was starting to get his life back together. It was a crucial time—and it had enabled him to find, interview and hire Rita; it had given the boys some sense of continuity when they needed it most. And it had given him an excuse to come someplace and not be alone after work.

So tonight they had fed him—Dismas and Frannie were turning into some sophisticated eaters, but Abe thought there were probably worse fates. They called it risotto, whereas Abe would have said rice and fish, but by any name it tasted good. He even had most of a glass of wine. White.

A half shot of Stoly during the day, a glass of wine at night. He was turning into a drunk. And speaking of drunk . . .

He'd called Farrell again. Or tried. It was frustrating to realize that his own sense of urgency involving Kevin Shea didn't appear to be shared by the suspect's own attorney. Or maybe it was—it could be they were having a meeting, a strategy session. He thought of his meeting with Farrell at Lou the Greek's, Hardy's description of his own tête-à-tête with Farrell in the Shamrock, and had come to the conclusion that whatever Farrell was doing, it was over drinks.

Well, he'd have to be patient.

Over dinner they had covered the riots, Abe's kids and his dad, Monterey, Ashland, the production of *The Tempest*, camping in general, which led to the Glitsky household's rules committee, on to early childhood development (the Hardys' kids were five and three, respectively), somehow over to Supervisor Wrightson, the city's wrongheaded policies on affirmative action, then on to events at the Hall, Art Drysdale, Chris Locke, the future of the United States political system. The usual stuff.

The subject of Loretta Wager had come up as well. As had Elaine. In catching up with the week's events, Hardy had not been thrilled by the role the two women had played—the rush to the indictment of Kevin Shea, the cynical way they had manipulated the media.

But Glitsky—not really wanting to dissemble in front of his friends—had segued to a different topic, saying all of that was just politics. Nothing to talk about. And how about these green beans—how did Frannie keep them so crisp? With all of the other topics they did not get around to the specifics of Hardy's talk with Wes Farrell, the fact that the search warrant had been served by a DA's investigator. It just never came up.

Now Glitsky sat on the low couch in the warm and spacious—compared to his—front room of the Hardys' house. He couldn't help noticing with some measure of regret and envy that there wasn't a large and unsightly changing screen—as there was in his own cramped duplex—separating the living area from the sleeping area. Of course, there was no need. The Hardys didn't have a nanny. Frannie stayed at home with the two kids. Dismas went to work. Old-fashioned, but there it was. The way it had been with him and Flo, and the way it wasn't anymore.

An oak fire crackled in the fireplace and he could hear his friends in the back of the house, the familiar and comfortable chitchat as they got dessert together.

Frannie appeared now from the kitchen—her hair was back in a ponytail and she wore a white "Cal" sweatshirt and Nike running shorts and sandals, no socks. Carrying a tray with two pots and cups and cookies, she set it down on the coffee table in front of Abe, sat catercorner to him in Hardy's lounger. "What do you say? Let's be bold and *not* watch television tonight."

Glitsky smiled, began squeezing some lemon over his tea. Frannie did think of everything. "You mean just talk?"

She nodded. "Unusual but I say go for it." She reached over, grazed a hand lightly on his knee. "We haven't talked about *you* at all. How are you doing?"

Stirring his tea, studying the swirl of the liquid. "I'm fine."

Frannie poured herself some coffee, added a little cream from a carved crystal pitcher. "I think what I like about you most, Abe, is your gushing nature, the way you just spill out everything that's on your mind."

He kept stirring the tea. "I'm fine, Frannie. Really. That's all there is to it."

"Well, you seem, if you'll pardon me, a little run-down."

"It's been a long week." He sipped. "I'm fine, really."

Frannie nodded. "Dismas says if you say you're fine three times in under a minute, you're not."

"Dismas says that, huh?"

"And if you add 'really' at least once, you *really* aren't."

She was leaning forward. "You said 'really' twice. I noticed."

He had to chuckle. "Maybe this is one of your husband's theories that will prove unfounded."

"What is this heresy I hear?"

Hardy arrived from the kitchen through the dining room with a snifter of something. "One of *my* theories?"

Frannie looked up at him. "Abe's fine," she said. "Really, he says."

Hardy nodded. "Good."

"He doesn't want to talk about it."

"Better." Motioning for Glitsky to slide over, Hardy found a place on the couch. "I don't want to talk about Abe either."

"There's nothing to talk about," Glitsky said. "I'm working, life's going on."

Frannie was shaking her head. "You have not had a date in one year and three months."

Glitsky had been through variations of this scene before. His scar stretched through his lips. "That's 'cause you're already taken."

Frannie beamed at him, said to Hardy, "He's so sweet."

"A cupcake," Hardy agreed. "In spite of what everybody says."

"But really, Abe . . ." Frannie didn't want to give it up.

Glitsky slapped his thighs, was standing. "But really, guys, I've got to try Wes Farrell again."

Farrell finally answered his phone. He sounded sober, pumped up. "I just talked to my client, Lieutenant, not twenty minutes ago. He's very anxious to get this thing moving. So am I. Your friend Hardy indicated to me that you had some kind of plan and I'd like to know what you have in mind." Then, more sharply: "I did think you might have tried to get in touch a little earlier."

Glitsky snapped back. "You weren't home. I did try. And I was around all day yesterday. You were going to call me, maybe you don't remember?"

There was a brief silence, then the reply, curt and formal. "I thought I explained that adequately to Mr. Hardy."

Glitsky could feel the spirit of cooperation slipping away. The lawyerly tones were kicking in, the defense vs. the prosecution, and Glitsky was with the prosecution. Hardy had become Mr. Hardy. Glitsky was going to lose Farrell and therefore Shea and everything else if he didn't rein in the general antagonism that was threatening to overcome him, the frustration.

"I'm sorry," he said. "I'm afraid I haven't had any real time with Hardy. His message to me was that you'd talk to me. That's all we got to. I'm glad you are."

Another pause, Farrell perhaps considering his sincerity. "So what's your idea?"

Now it was Glitsky's turn to hesitate. How much did he dare tell? "I've spoken to Senator Wager," he said. "Alan Reston is her protégé and he's our stumbling block, yours and mine. She promised me she'd talk to Reston, convince him to cut Shea the slack he needs, guarantee him some safety."

"You talked to the senator personally?"

"Yes." Then, feeling he needed to explain: "We went to college together. We know each other."

"That's a fortuitous relationship. And she said she'd do it?"

"She said she'd talk to Reston, yes. She seemed confident she could convince him to soften up some, make some guarantees, which is all Shea needs, right? That hasn't changed?"

"Not as far as I know. But that's his minimum, Lieutenant. He still wants to come in, get his story heard. I should tell you, though, I'm going to try very hard to get this whole indictment quashed. It's bogus."

Glitsky figured now was as good a time as any to cement the newly wrought alliance. "You need me to give my two cents to anybody, Mr. Farrell, I'll say what I think."

"And what's that?"

"I don't think your boy did it. I don't think the evidence says he did it. He may even have been the hero here. I think he ought to walk."

Glitsky heard the sigh of relief over the phone wire. "I appreciate that," Farrell said. "Can I ask you another question?"

"Sure."

"You got any leads on who might have been behind it, the mob, the lynching?"

Glitsky decided he could share that information, such as it was. "A couple. Nothing firm, but yes, there are some things, some other people we're looking at."

"I wanted to hear that." Dead air. Then: "So when are you going to hear back from the senator? Or Reston?"

"I'd expect by tonight sometime, morning at the latest. Loret—the senator couldn't reach Reston at the office and left a message for when he got home. No one knows when that's going to be but she said it was urgent. He'll call her."

"I should probably get an answering machine," Farrell said out of left field. "But that timing works. I'm talking to Shea at nine in the morning."

"I should have heard before that. And you'll be around? This number?"

"I'm not leaving. I'll be here."

"Okay. I'll call you."

"All right. And, Lieutenant?"

"Yeah?"

"Thanks. This is above and beyond."

"It shouldn't be, it should be how it works."

"Yeah, well," Farrell said, "if my uncle had wheels he'd be a wagon."

Glitsky cut it short at the Hardys'. Something in their domestic bliss, so obvious and unforced, wrenched at his insides tonight. He didn't know if he was pulling away from the memory of Flo and the life they'd shared, so similar in many respects to the Hardys', or experiencing a kind of foreshadowing of the loss he was *bound* to feel with Loretta.

No question about it—the two of them would never sit, legs casually intertwined on the couch they'd bought after much discussion with the money they'd saved for it. He knew they would never live in *her* house together—in the mansion Dana Wager had built in Pacific Heights. Nor she in his, with the boys. Loretta was a United States senator and her husband had been one of the developers who had helped refashion San Francisco's skyline into what it was today—high-rises and pyramids and glass monoliths to the edge of the famous bay.

Glitsky was a working cop.

It wasn't going to last—no sense pretending it was, and he'd been doing that. Perhaps seeing the Hardys dosed him back up with reality. He and Loretta had a now, but they had no future. He knew he had to face that, prepare for it, accept it—he simply wasn't ready to just yet.

He climbed the darkened twelve steps and let himself into his house. After turning on the light in the hallway he went to the closet, removed his flight jacket, hung it up. The thermostat on the wall read sixty-one degrees—without his jacket on it felt like ten below. He moved the heater lever all the way to the right and within moments heard the heater kick in, felt air begin to move around him. The furnace had a distinctive smell when it hadn't been turned on in a while and it kicked in now, dusty and stale.

He stood as though rooted in front of the thermostat for a long time. Something had stopped him dead. It wasn't a specific thought, or a thought at all. He just didn't move. There was nothing to move for—if everything stopped now, nothing would ever get worse.

Or better.

He was in the kitchen, more lights on, getting more tea—habits, habits. He didn't want to drink any more tea, but all alone now, he found himself afraid—no, not afraid, *nervous*—that if he stopped doing things he would just stop, period.

The water wasn't boiling yet. He went back into the hall and checked the two rooms, the closets, the lock on the back door. In his bedroom, the photograph of Flo was still turned down on his bureau and he picked it up, staring at the once-so-familiar face for a long time.

The light on his message machine was blinking and he walked over to it, pushed the button.

"Dad. Hi. It's Isaac. Grandpa says he thinks we should stay down here another couple days and we were thinking . . . like if you've got the weekend, it's not that far, I mean you could be down here in a couple of hours." A pause. "If you want. I mean, *we'd* like it. Okay?"

Something rushing up at him, Glitsky pushed the stop

button, sat down heavily on his bed, his back bent, holding his forehead in his hands.

He talked to all the boys—Isaac, Jacob, Orel—hearing the difference in the way they talked. Only two days with his father and they were back to the way they used to be with him and Flo, back before he had begun to think only in terms of their protection. He had to stop thinking like that. Had to.

His father Nat came on. They were having a great time. They'd gone to the aquarium again, a minor-league baseball game, bought eight Dungeness crabs . . .

"Eight?"

. . . and shelled and eaten them on the breakwater.

". . . not kosher I know, but, Abraham, I tell you, crabs like these, Solomon would have eaten these crabs, believe me."

Tomorrow they were going to temple in the morning, "since I don't think these boys, they're going so much, am I right? It cannot hurt them." Did Abe think he could make it down to Monterey? It was the boys' idea—they missed him. Nat lowered his voice. "Even Isaac," he said, "he misses you."

He would try. If he could clear up the Kevin Shea thing by, say, noon, there was a chance . . .

Some more tea wouldn't be so bad after all. Get some sleep, big day tomorrow. Back in the bedroom with the steaming mug—no porcelain daintiness this time.

He pushed the answering-machine button again.

"Lieutenant, this is Chief Rigby and this is an official call. I don't know what the hell you've been doing, but I thought I'd made it clear to you this morning that you were relieved of your duties in the Kevin Shea matter. So imagine my surprise when I *just now* got a call from Alan Reston"—Rigby's volume was going up—"and he tells me he has unimpeachable evidence that you're working with Kevin Shea's lawyer, that you're offering Kevin Shea *immunity* from prosecution, that you've even volunteered to *testify* on Kevin Shea's fucking behalf. *Unimpeachable evidence,* do you understand, Lieutenant?"

A brief break while Rigby got his anger under control. Glitsky had the impression Rigby wasn't alone, wherever he was.

"Now, in view of this, effective immediately, I am putting you on administrative leave, as soon as you hear this message. I've left another message just like this one at your office. Paper covering it is on the way. If you want to grieve this decision, you know the channels. I am very disappointed, both personally and professionally, but if you cannot follow my direct and unambiguous orders I will not have you responsible for one of my departments."

After his adrenaline had dissipated itself into his bloodstream, he made himself sit in his lounger in the front room, and there it didn't take him long, maybe five minutes, before he figured out that all of Rigby's information—and none of it was false, although the offer of immunity for Shea was an exaggeration—got conveyed to Wes Farrell during the phone call from Hardy's house. Therefore, Farrell's phone was being tapped. The FBI was on the case—wiretaps were one of its common tools. And Farrell would lead them to Shea as soon as Shea—

Bolting straight up in the chair, Glitsky ran back to the hall closet and pulled on his flight jacket. Down the stairway and into his car, he was at the nearest gas station to his house—four blocks away—within five minutes. At the public booth he pushed some numbers.

The groggy voice answered—it was nearly eleven-thirty—and Glitsky said into the receiver: "There's a tap on your phone. Don't call Shea and don't let him call you." He hung up.

He tried Loretta, each of the three numbers he had. None answered.

If Reston was at City Hall with Rigby he would have gotten the message Loretta had left for him, wouldn't he? And if so, then why wouldn't she have called him immediately, as she'd promised—sworn—she would? It nagged at him. And where was Loretta now?

*   *   *

The other question had come to him driving home. And the more he thought about it the more important it became. Maybe it was the only question.

The last person he could call, who knew, was Hardy.

Back home now, it was after midnight. He still wore his jacket. He didn't know—he might be going out.

A mumbled midnight hello.

"Hardy."

"Abe? What time is it?"

"Why wouldn't Wes Farrell talk to me yesterday?"

"What?"

He repeated the question.

"Because he thought you'd had him followed to his home." Glitsky then heard: "It's Abe, honey. Yeah. He's okay, I think."

"Why did he think that?" Glitsky asked.

Hardy ran the facts for him—Sergeant Stoner, the DA investigator, the warrant.

Now Glitsky was truly stumped. "I didn't send Stoner, Diz."

"That's what I told Farrell. I told him Reston must have. That's why Farrell changed his mind, said he'd talk to you."

"They're tapping his phone."

"Whose? Farrell's?"

"Yeah."

"Why? Never mind, I know why."

How could Reston have sent Stoner? How could Stoner have known who Farrell even *was* to know to follow him? And pick him up from where, Lou the Greek's. *No one* had known of Glitsky's meeting with Farrell, not a soul except the two of them. Glitsky had kept it to himself.

It made no sense. None of it made sense.

Then, like a tinkling bell, came the thought—he'd mentioned it to no one except Loretta Wager.

He had told Loretta, told her he was going to be closing up the Kevin Shea matter, was meeting Shea's attorney at the bar across the street, they could expect the whole thing to be over in a day at the most.

But Loretta wasn't . . .

What she *was,* though, was Alan Reston's ally in this. She could have called Reston, told him about the meeting, directed Stoner to Farrell and brought Shea in before all the evidence about his innocence became public, before she and her daughter, of whom she was so protective, would be made to look so bad . . .

But that was ridiculous . . .

But she was his lover, his . . .

His what?

And where was she? What the hell was going on?

Saturday, July 2

65

The sound of the wind woke him. His watch read six-eighteen.

The television was still on in the boys' bedroom, where he had gone to watch the late news. This morning there was another talking head saying something about Hunter's Point Naval Reservation, about Senator Loretta Wager and the president.

He sat up. Something was happening with the decommissioned navy base, and whatever it was—the details weren't all in yet—it was a major coup for Loretta.

They must have gotten something wrong. If she had been in the middle of these kinds of negotiations . . . She had never mentioned anything about it. He stood up abruptly and smacked the power button on the set, shutting the damn thing off.

He hadn't planned to fall asleep. There was too much to be done—get in touch with Loretta, place a call to Rigby about his job, connect with Wes Farrell, meet with Banks and Lanier and Griffin.

He walked to the bathroom, then the kitchen, put the water on to boil, walked to the east-facing window over the sink and pushed it open.

Smoke. The air looked clear—the sky was a cerulean, Maxfield Parrish blue—but he smelled smoke.

In his bedroom he checked his message machine. He realized that he'd known, without having to verify it, that Loretta hadn't called. Last night—his immobility, the drift off to unwanted and unplanned sleep—his body in denial. Now, suddenly, things were clearer than they had been. Sleep had its place. Patterns had begun to emerge from the chaos. Certain combinations made some sense. Not perfectly yet—all the pieces weren't there—but enough to make it obvious at least where he was certainly, without doubt, going wrong.

The patterns that did make sense—dimly glimpsed as they had begun to shift and sort out the night before—had shut him down for a while, that was all. It wasn't a reaction he was proud of, but there it was. He guessed his psyche, his body, whatever it was, had needed some time out to adjust to the new truths, to get them organized. So he'd drifted off.

He stirred the tea, the phone tucked under his ear. If it came to it, he would need an ally, perhaps even a wedge; but other things being equal, he would rather go for a finesse. He wasn't at all sure that he was strong enough to win a direct confrontation.

Elaine Wager sounded exhausted, but after a beat of hesitation she agreed to see him—he could come over.

Since his discovery of the nature of Elaine and Chris Locke's relationship, as well as her mother's disclosure about the two of them, something personal had developed between Glitsky and Elaine. This was the first time he had ever seen her out of her lawyer's uniform. He thought of her not bothering to dress more formally . . . never mind it was Saturday . . . as something symbolic, she was open to him.

It might also mean nothing.

She wore black baggy pants cinched at the waist with a black nylon cord. She had tucked a purple scoop-neck sweater into the pants. Shades of her mother, she was barefoot. Her hair still wet, she stepped aside after opening her front door, letting him lead the way into the living room. She settled on one of the stools by the bar and crossed her legs.

He stood a moment, looking west out her window. The day was clear and bright, the Pacific glittering in the distance. "Have you heard from your mother?" Glitsky didn't turn around. The clarity of it all out there held his attention. He needed some clarity.

"Yesterday. We were . . . why, is she all right?"

"I think she's all right. Did you see her last night?"

"No, not since the afternoon. Abe, what's this about?"

Now he turned. "I'm afraid it's still about Kevin Shea.

And I suppose before we go on I'd better tell you something else." As he brought her abreast of the change in his own situation, he was relieved to find her at least still listening. You never knew—the bureaucracy was its own environment, and if he wasn't part of it anymore he would cease to exist to most people still in it, but Elaine wasn't one of them—she kept with him.

When he finished she said, "But I'm not clear what this has to do with Mom. We should call her." She was reaching for the telephone on the bar.

Glitsky crossed the room quickly, pushed the button down, took the receiver from her hand. "I don't think so," he said. "Not yet."

"Why not?"

He took a breath. This was the moment. "Because I think she's probably part of it."

"What? What are you talking about?" She was off the stool now, on her feet.

Glitsky kept his voice low. "Your mother was the only person who knew I was meeting with Wes Farrell, Shea's lawyer. The only one, Elaine, the only possibility. She must have told Alan Reston about it and he had a DA investigator follow Farrell home with a warrant."

"And? I'm supposed to think that means something?"

"Then last night—"

"No! I don't care what you say. That just isn't my mother! My mother isn't part of anything! How *dare* you?"

The reaction . . . he knew he'd hit a nerve—Elaine had possibly reached the same conclusion on her own and didn't want to—couldn't?—admit it to herself. She had moved away and now moved back at him. But then the light abruptly went out of her. All at once her shoulders sagged. Backing up, she let herself down into one of the leather chairs.

Glitsky went on quietly. "Right at the beginning you told her I was soft on her Shea theory. She kept me close so she could watch me, Elaine. So she could blow the whistle on me if I got in the way. And that's what she's done."

He saw her swallow, sigh, nod—in agreement, weariness. "She did it to you, too, didn't she?"

"Mom gets what she wants, Abe. That's Mom."

"And what did she want from you?"

Still looking for the words that might excuse or at leas
explain her mother, Elaine said, "It would have been goo
for me, too, Abe. I mean, for my career. This was going t
be the biggest murder case of the decade—maybe as big a
O.J.—and I couldn't lose. Nobody could lose it, at least n
reasonably competent DA, which I am. It would have se
me up." She looked up at him. "It *wasn't* like it was a
just for her."

"Some of it wa̶s, though, huh?"

Elaine shrugged. "Some, maybe. That was always th
way. Mom got something, but she delivered for you, too."

"Not for me," Abe said, "not this time." He came and sa
on the ottoman, pulled it away a bit. "But this isn't abou
me. At least not much anymore. Maybe not even you, excep
I think a little more than me. It's your case and it's gon
sideways, Elaine. Your mom knows it—I told her last nigh
She called Reston, all right, but not to call him off."

"But she wouldn't—"

"I think she would."

"Would what?"

"I think you know exactly what, Elaine." Glitsky me
her eyes and knew he had to go further. Being crypti
wasn't going to cut it. "I think your mother is going to le
something happen to Kevin Shea. You said almost the sam
thing yourself yesterday."

But this, suddenly, was too much for her. It was, afte
all, her mother. "She would *not* go that far, Abe. That'
not my mom, I'd need some *proof* about all this." Sh
matched his own gaze. "That's what we *do,* isn't it? Isn'
that what you've been saying? Well, okay, my mom *mayb*
could be part of some of this. *Maybe* that's who she is. Bu
I need a lot more than you getting put on leave, more tha
the case going sideways."

"I'll tell you some facts, Elaine. Leave your mother ou
of it if you want."

She sat back down.

By now it was all too familiar to Abe—the knife wounds
Lithuanian Rachel and Colin Devlin, the interpretation o
Kevin Shea as hero and victim. And then, even to Glitsk
as he spoke, the last cog falling in. He remembered Hardy'
comment about clients speaking for themselves, that they lie
once too often, how that same lie was the tip-off that ther

were more. But the one "lie" on Kevin's videotape—that the police had betrayed him—turned out *not* to be. At the time, Glitsky simply hadn't known about it. He told her: "Everything Shea said on the tape is true."

Elaine was shaking her head. "I don't understand what she could possibly get out of all this, assuming what you say is true. Why would she . . ."

"She's got her man in the DA's office, she got Philip Mohandas and his people thinking she's on their side, even got the president of the United States—"

"Get real, Abe, that's just—"

He held up a hand, stopping her, and told her about Hunter's Point. It had an effect. Elaine became silent, taking it in.

"We're talking a hundred thousand votes, Elaine, minimum. We're talking another term, more influence, more power, maybe even the vice presidency. And guess what? It all goes away if Kevin Shea is innocent, if there's even a serious perception that he's innocent."

"It wouldn't all go away. Not just over that."

"Yes it would. You think about it."

Elaine could do the figuring. If Shea was guilty, then Loretta Wager was the crusading personification of justice who had the guts and vision to put her outrage to use in the service of her people. But if he was not, if he were innocent and she'd led the rush to judgment, she became a strident harpy, a bigot herself, seeking only a white scapegoat. To satisfy the gaping maw of her own ambition.

"She can't let him be innocent, Elaine—she's invested too much in his guilt. She doesn't have a choice . . ."

Elaine sat there. "But what if it came out after . . ."

Glitsky was shaking his head. "How would it do that?"

"Well, *you,* for example. You could—"

"No, I'm a discredited police inspector who didn't follow orders. My credibility is shot as it is. I pull anything like this and it only gets worse."

"Okay, then, Wes Farrell . . ."

"Shea's own attorney? I don't think so. And I don't think *you're* it either—not after the fact, if something *does* happen with Shea, not if you don't have any hard proof that Shea didn't do it."

"I could find—"

But Glitsky was shaking his head. "No you couldn't. You can't prove a negative, which is the bitch about getting accused in the first place. I think it's why we're supposed to prove people *did* do something, not *didn't*, although normally I don't go around preaching for the presumption of innocence. But it does have its place."

Glitsky stood and walked back to the windows, to the blessed clarity. "And that leaves nobody to argue for Kevin Shea, not after he's dead. Can you think of anybody else? I can't. This has been well thought out. Reston, the FBI, getting rid of me—and after Shea is gone and it's over, the whole thing gets—pardon the phrase—whitewashed. And it's going to work unless we do something now."

Elaine sat back in her chair. "And what do you propose, without destroying my mother?"

"I want to bring Kevin Shea in to you. You're still the DA of record on the case, right?"

"I think so." Then, at his sharp glance. "Sure. Yes."

He crossed back to her. "All right. I think you're a lot safer right now than the jail. I also don't believe your mother would ever let anything threaten you. If he's with you, he's safe. So I've got to contact Farrell, get in touch with Shea, bring the boy in."

"And then what?"

"Then I don't know, tell the truth. We're guaranteeing Shea's safety, and essentially, that's all he wants."

"All right, that can be arranged. We can go to one of the towns down the Peninsula . . ."

"Try someplace small and upscale. Say, Hillsborough or Atherton. I've got to have something I can give Farrell."

"Abe." She reached a hand out and touched his knee. "Do you *really* think this is what's happening?"

He fixed her with his eyes. "Yep."

"And you think you can really do this, get Shea in custody this morning?"

"I'd better." Then: "You want to call your Sergeant Stoner for me, see if you can find out if he remembers where Farrell lives?"

"Can't we just call Farrell and ask?"

Glitsky shook his head. "I don't know if I mentioned. I'm pretty sure Farrell's phone is tapped," he said. "It gives me pause."

66

Philip Mohandas normally would have been gratified by the turnout so far, but he'd been wrestling with demons for the better part of the night and they had beaten him down.

It was just seven-thirty and already there were hundreds of people milling about Kezar Pavilion on the southeastern border of Golden Gate Park (about three hundred yards from the apartment at Stanyan and Page where Kevin Shea and Melanie Sinclair were just waking up). He could see the stream of people flowing down the side streets across the lawns of the park. It was a beautiful morning, a little windy with a heavy smoky smell to the air.

Mohandas knew that the combination of wind and fire was making problems in Bayview, for the first time in North Beach, and he noticed a small pillar of smoke rising due east and a little south, perhaps over by Divisadero. The march might have to jog north a few blocks if it got much worse, but the wind wasn't really his problem.

His problem, if he was going to have one, would be crowd control. This was the case often enough that he was used to it, but it always caused him concern, especially here today when his credibility was so clearly on the line. This was his show. He'd called it into being, and the response—from the look of things so far—was going to be overwhelming. He couldn't allow things to get out of hand.

And unfortunately, in spite of the early arrivals—a good thing—there were signs of other, potentially disruptive elements.

First was the presence of so much armed authority—he'd passed truckloads of National Guard troops on his drive out here earlier, mobilized and ready to roll, parked all along Fell Street. In addition, at least a hundred city police were on patrol, many on horseback but a large number on foot, too, in the open pavilion and its surrounding streets, even by the tent that he was using as his staging area.

The uniforms weren't the worst of it. Since the release of Kevin Shea's tape the previous afternoon, he had become increasingly aware of the backlash problem, which—to be honest—he'd expected a little sooner. But now, even though the official response to the tape had initially been skeptical across the color spectrum, he had been hearing reports of spontaneous outbreaks of angry white people taking to the streets.

Already this morning he had seen the police subdue and carry away one belligerent white man with a placard. True, it was an isolated case, but it was worrisome. That the man had come out at all, knowing how badly he'd been outnumbered . . . he must have thought there would have been others, perhaps many others.

Mohandas held no illusions—he knew any meeting between a white and black group, in this context, today, could get ugly fast. He had to get the show on the road as quickly as he could, keep his crowd moving and focused. That was the key.

Suddenly Allicey was standing next to him. "Lot of the people with us, Philip, hearing us, what we're saying."

He nodded. She motioned out to the growing crowd. "This is it," she said. "This is the difference between you and Loretta Wager. You are with the people."

"You think so?" He often thought that the most important function Allicey served for him—out of hundreds—was her *belief*. She never wavered. The mission was the freedom of her people, of their people. They had been oppressed for so long, still were. And that's because they had struggled to be *included*. That had been wrong, he'd decided. The path lay in separation and connection with your own. It was a spiritual thing, a constant battle, and you could not afford to lose your faith, to mingle with those who would dilute it. Or, like Loretta Wager had done, sell it out for power and influence.

"You are, Philip. *With* the people."

He shook his head. "I must be getting old. My vision is a little blurred."

She rested a hand on his arm. "You have been tempted."

He nodded. "So much of it now seems to be logistics, money, getting concrete things done."

"But, Philip, the world isn't made of concrete."

"More than you'd think, Allicey." He sighed, smiled weakly, then turned toward the tent behind them. But he did not walk on. Instead he stopped and faced her. "I can't put a name to what it is."

"What *what* is?"

"The temptation."

"To what?"

There was sadness in his face—his eyes were shot with red. The week had been grueling. "To not believe. To not believe it's going to change. And if not, should I take the devil's offer? That way, something I do might have an ending." He folded his hands together in front of him. "Something might close up, Allicey, feel finished. You hear what I'm saying?"

"The river just flows on, Philip. It doesn't close up. It doesn't end."

"But where's it goin', girl, where's it all goin'?"

"The point is, it's going, Philip. It's moving ahead."

"Is it?" he asked.

Carl Griffin pulled into the city lot under the freeway overpass behind the Hall of Justice. Exhausted from the long, late fruitless nights and only marginally aware that it was a Saturday, he wasn't even hungry.

Griffin was a working dog who basically liked his weekends and his Monday Night Football, but when he had a report to finish he liked to get it done so it didn't hang over his head, and he and Marcel Lanier had interviewed, together, over twenty people last night. All of whom had agreed that there had been a riot, that the DA had gotten killed, yeah, all of that, but so what? What else was new?

People seemed sick of it—talking about it, dealing with it. Others, not knowing what they should admit they saw or didn't see, did or didn't do, were scared of the cops. Griffin could see it in faces, in their body language. Nobody was talking very much. But the reports had to get done— lack of paperwork would bite you every time you didn't get to it, or did it sloppily. Griffin thought they didn't call it the homicide *detail* for nothing. Griffin himself was not what he would call an idea man, but he remembered every step of things he did and could assemble the basic package in twenty-five minutes or less.

So he and Marcel had flipped a coin at the Doggie Diner on Army at a quarter to twelve last night to determine who would come in this morning—or before Monday at least—and write the report on what they hadn't found, and Griffin had lost.

The roasting-coffee smell—was it coffee?—was strong here in the lot, riding on a morning breeze coming off the bay. Griffin schlumped across the pavement, down the corridor by the morgue and the new jail, into the back door, around the metal detector.

Glancing into the lobby, he saw that the lines of cited rioters had vanished, perhaps in response to the outbreak here a couple of nights ago. He didn't know what the sheriff was doing with those people anymore and he didn't much care just so long as they were kept out of his way.

Only Ridley Banks was in the office, arms crossed, slumped in his chair, feet on his desk. He appeared to be sleeping, maybe had spent the night here. Griffin put on a pot of coffee, emptied his pockets and plopped his papers down on his desk, pulling his chair up to it with a sigh.

The phone rang in Glitsky's office and he sighed again, let it ring once more—Ridley wasn't going to get it—then pushed back and stood. There was a police department notice on the wall next to the open doorway that he ignored as he went inside and picked up the phone.

"Homicide, Griffin."

"Hey, Carl. Abe. How you doin'?"

"The band's just settin' up and the chicks aren't here yet so it's kind of slow. What's up?"

"I got a favor to ask. What's your day look like?"

"Nothin'. I'm in for the report on last night. After that, before that, whenever, you name it."

"How'd last night go? You find anything?"

Griffin eased a leg over the corner of Glitsky's desk, put his weight on it. "The short answer's no. Nobody really even heard the two shots, would take an oath on it."

Glitsky hung back a second. "I thought you already had those. Yesterday, those old ladies . . ."

"Yeah, I know. But they didn't hear two shots. The two of 'em heard one shot each. Lot of folks heard one shot."

"So what does that mean?"

"Hell if I know. I just write down the answers and let the lawyers figure it out. Probably means nothing—somebody heard the first one, thought it was a backfire, it got their attention, then *bang*—oh yeah, maybe a shot. People weren't their usual talkative selves, some reason."

Okay, Griffin was thinking, so we got nothing. He didn't want to spend more time doing the third degree on what they didn't have. "So what's the favor?"

"Elaine Wager may be coming in with Kevin Shea, could be an hour, maybe a little more."

"You're shittin' me. Kevin Shea himself?"

"What I want is for one of our guys—I don't want any other DA or the sheriff involved—one of *you* to escort her and Shea down the Peninsula, to wherever Elaine tells you."

"You really got Kevin Shea?"

"Almost, I think. I just want to be prepared. And, Carl, this is a favor, not an order."

Same difference, Griffin was thinking.

Just at that moment Banks appeared in the doorway holding the PD notice. "Is that Abe?" he asked. "Let me talk to him." He handed the paper to Griffin, took the phone.

"Lieutenant, this is Ridley . . ."

Griffin heard it in the background as he scanned the paper. What was this bullshit? Glitsky placed on administrative leave, questions on current homicides should go upstairs to Frank Batiste, the assistant chief.

Banks was telling Abe that the lab hadn't been able to find any fingerprints on the yellow rope that had hung Arthur Wade but that he'd been frustrated with an evening gone into the pisser and he'd gone over to Jamie O'Toole's place last night and told him they were pursuing the knife wounds on Mullen and McKay with doctors in the area and were sure they would be bringing them downtown, perhaps under arrest, by the afternoon.

"No, I know it's unlikely," he was saying, "but I think Mr. O'Toole's about ready to cave, cut a deal, do a little talking about the principals who might be involved here, save his own sweet white ass." Banks cast a look at Griffin, smiled blandly. "Figure of speech, Carl," he said. Then, listening another moment: "Anything else you want out of the lieutenant?"

Griffin looked down at the paper in his hands. This was why it was a favor, not an order, so it wasn't, in fact, the same difference. Still, Abe was a good cop, a fair guy. Whatever it was probably had to do with the brass and Griffin didn't get involved with that. "No. Tell him I'll be there."

Banks did, then hung up, pointed to the paper. "Can you believe this idiocy? What's this about?"

"Yeah, I know," Griffin said, putting it on Abe's desk. "When they first started talking about making him lieutenant, I warned him."

"You warned him?"

Griffin nodded. "You get to lieutenant, you stop being a street cop, which is what Glitsky is. Like me. You can't change what you are."

Banks, in the longest discussion he had ever had with Carl Griffin, flashed on his girlfriend—maybe now ex-girlfriend—Jacqueline coming to the same conclusions as this overweight flatfoot. It amazed him. "Beware of any job that requires a change of clothes."

"Yeah, that's what I mean. That's exactly it."

"Thoreau wrote that."

"Who?"

"Thoreau."

"The guy who wrote *Presumed Innocent*?"

Banks couldn't help himself. "Yeah, him."

Griffin, oblivious, was moving on. "I liked the movie but I still think the guy—the attorney—he did it, not his wife." Then, without missing a beat: "Did I hear you talking about knife wounds with the lieutenant? I ever tell you about Colin Devlin?"

Chief Dan Rigby, trying to keep a low profile, was on a field telephone with an irate and frustrated Mayor Conrad Aiken.

"Mohandas is there? He's going ahead with it?"

"Unless I stop him, sir, but I thought I'd call you first."

"What's he trying to accomplish by *this*? Goddamn it!"

"Yes, sir." Rigby waited.

Yesterday, after a series of referrals from cowardly lesser city bureaucrats had moved the request along to his office, the mayor had had a long and heated discussion with Philip Mohandas about the wisdom of his projected march on City Hall. The mayor pointed out the concessions he had already made—the increased reward on Kevin Shea, the appointment of Alan Reston. The city was genuinely trying to respond. The mayor, through his man Donald, had even gotten wind of the Hunter's Point deal and knew that Mohandas was still in the pipeline for administration of that pork barrel. What did the man want? Wasn't it ever enough? And Mohandas had replied that all he wanted was a permit to allow his people peaceably to assemble, as guaranteed by the United States Constitution.

Deaf to arguments about the potential for violence, the inflammatory nature of the demand for Kevin Shea's head, as well as the difficulty in meeting that demand even with the best of intentions, Mohandas had informed the mayor he was going ahead with the march. His people deserved it. With or without the permit, the application for which had led to this meeting in the first place.

"Without a permit, the gathering will be illegal," Aiken had warned. "I could order and enforce dispersal, even your own arrest. Extend the curfew, declare martial law, and if you think things are bad now . . ."

"I understand all that," Mohandas had said.

In the end Conrad Aiken—feeling a little like Pontius Pilate—had decided he could not issue the permit. The rally, gathering, whatever it was, might go ahead, but it would be without his imprimatur. His threats, he knew, were bluffs. He wasn't going to make a bad situation worse by calling up more reinforcements.

But until Rigby's call, Aiken was hoping against hope that Mohandas would—for once—not push things beyond their limits, that he would see the light and act responsibly. Now, clearly, that was not going to happen. The crowd, according to Rigby, was already at about two thousand and the streets surrounding Kezar were packed.

Well, Aiken was thinking, it could be Mohandas had heard at least a little of what he had been saying. The man wasn't budging on pushing his agenda, but there was one sign of conciliation, even in his intractability. At least Mohandas had not gone public with the mayor's decision not to issue the permit—not yet.

"My advice, sir," the chief was saying, "is we watch it closely, but I think to try and stop things at this point would be to invite a disaster. Permit or no permit."

The mayor swore and the chief agreed with him.

And then the horrible, ugly, unbelievable reality struck Aiken like a club. Suddenly he *knew* the strategy Mohandas was contemplating . . . he was saving the news that the mayor had refused to grant permission for this march for greater effect as the rally progressed. And that would let loose the furies.

Aiken could not allow that to happen—not only would it ignite the volatile crowd, it would be a political disaster. How had he overlooked this possibility while he was talking to Mohandas yesterday? He'd simply wanted to have the march not happen—he'd had enough of riots and this was certain to become another one. He'd been trying to do what was right and keep the city from another explosion of violence and rage. He'd really thought there had been a chance that Mohandas might call it off. Yesterday, Aiken had needed his no-permit stance as a fallback for those who would accuse him of irresponsibility for condoning the march at this critical time.

But it was going to backfire on him. He saw it clearly now. Mohandas was going to exploit his refusal to issue the permit in the worst possible light and make the mayor into a racist, the worst epithet there was for a San Francisco politician.

He could not let it happen.

Dan Rigby was still on the line, waiting for instructions. "Chief," Aiken said, "I think you're right about not interfering unless there's trouble, but I'm going to go you one better. I'm going to issue the permit."

"Look at this!"

Melanie was peeping through the apartment's front window at the mass of movement below. Kevin came up behind her and rested his hand gently on her rear end, leaning over to look.

"It's Mohandas's rally," he said. They had both heard about it on television. "Wes better come through here. If I'm not mistaken, this whole thing is about finding us."

Melanie turned around, pulling the shade down all the way. "You want to call him now?"

Kevin thought about it. "He said nine. But yeah, I do."

"So do it."

Kevin would be calling precisely at nine o'clock, so Wes thought he'd take care of Bart, get that out of the way early. He made it all the way down the stairs into the apartment's lobby, didn't even hear the phone ring this time.

Special Agent Simms was back in the van with two techs and one marksman. She had decided to keep one of the shooters on hand at all times—there might not be time to round up both.

After the close call at Pizzaiola, she had not been able to sleep until nearly three in the morning. She had given instructions that *any* call to Wes Farrell, no matter how mundane, and from whatever source, was sufficient grounds to awaken her.

There had been none.

The last call had been long before sleep came, the warning that his phone was being tapped, from some leak somewhere. It infuriated her. Too often somebody discovered these things—she thought the penalty for exposing a secret tap to its mark should be death, but Special Agent Simms thought that, under certain conditions, the penalty for jaywalking should be death, too.

The good news was that Farrell had not unplugged his phone. He hadn't even taken it off the hook. It was possible, she supposed, that he didn't believe it was tapped. Some people were that way—you could tell them you were sleeping with their spouse and they'd smile and say they didn't believe their spouse would ever be unfaithful. He/she just wasn't that kind of person.

More realistically, though, and her real hope, was that Farrell had no way to get in touch with Shea except by phone. It was their only link, and he'd have to use it at least once. She was also counting on the public's perception—no longer true—that you had to stay on the lines for a reasonably long period of time before they could pinpoint a location for either party. Maybe Farrell was thinking he'd keep it quick if Shea called him, get him off in ten seconds or so. But that would be enough.

And, in that ten seconds, they'd have to make arrangements about how to connect again, wouldn't they? And it would all be on the tape here in the van.

They'd get him. It wouldn't be long now.

67

With three separate telephone numbers, each with its own answering machine, Loretta Wager could be here and gone at the same time at any moment of the day or night.

Last night, for example, she had been here for Alan Reston, gone for Glitsky. She didn't feel good about what had to happen with Abe, but she would make it up to him when this was all over. In a way, she loved his tenacity—but she couldn't have even Abe compromising her position right now. If he could just be made to leave things alone until this was over they could pick up where they were. And she thought that might even be by tonight. Reston had brought her up to date on the Wes Farrell phone tap, and the assumption was that the FBI would be able to move by sometime this morning at the latest.

After Abe had left her at City Hall, when she had called Reston's *real* number (not the one she had randomly punched in while Glitsky was standing there) and talked to Alan about Glitsky's request that she step in and straighten out the new DA's head—there really wasn't much discussion about whether or not to complain to Chief Rigby and put the lieutenant out of commission, temporarily. It had to happen.

Once that was done, she fully expected to get a call or two from Abe. And she simply wouldn't be available. She had pulled her curtains, turned out the front lights. If he drove by to see her she wouldn't be home. She didn't think that if he came by he would wait all night, but if he did she had a story for that too—exhaustion, earplugs, a Dalmane.

But he had not come over, had simply phoned twice and left messages and that had been that. He was a man's man, she was thinking. He wouldn't come whining to her about his problems. She liked that about him, too.

He'd simply wait until they were together again. He'd bring up his questions about where she'd been—not in any accusatory way—what reason to accuse her of anything?—and she would come up with something plausible that had unexpectedly prevented her getting back to him. There were any number of excuses that she knew she could make him believe. He was upset and she couldn't blame him, but she just couldn't talk to him until after . . .

Drinking her morning coffee, now having decided it was safe to open the curtains, she allowed herself a moment of repose. She had decisions to make about who she was going to call back—her daughter and the mayor had both left urgent messages, but five minutes wasn't going to make any difference.

There was, she thought, something truly thrilling about physical infatuation. She wasn't immune to it herself, now with Abe. She was thinking back to when he'd been her young stud at San Jose State, how—remarkably—his body hadn't changed much at all. The chest had filled, broadened somewhat, but the belly was still a flatiron.

There would be such sweet—bittersweet—irony if they could somehow, against all these odds, stay reconnected. She smiled unconsciously. On the desk at City Hall, my, my . . . the man was a piston.

But more than that, she loved how he seemed truly to envision himself as such a pragmatist, a working cop, down-playing the brain of the Talmudic scholar that she knew his father was. And really such an idealist. If he only knew the truth of some of the hard—impossible at the time—choices she had had to make . . .

Maybe sometime in the future she could let him know. When it would either matter more or not at all. Later, if their infatuation developed into the real thing. She was so incredibly moved by his sweet trust of her.

Would he ever forgive her?

Well, after this she would make it up to him. She'd try. She owed him that much for the part of him she had carried with her, lived with over the years. And the other part now—the one that she had found again.

*   *   *

"What is it, honey? You sounded so upset."

Elaine had been fighting herself over it, and in the end blood had won out. She had to talk to her mother—she couldn't just take Glitsky's word for something so important—and get a straight denial or a confirmation. Either way, then, she would know, and would better be able to act. Her mother would never lie to her.

Loretta answered her that she didn't know why Abe would have said such things to her. "I just saw him last night, honey. He told me about this and I passed it along to Alan Reston. Didn't he tell you that?"

"He said you didn't call him back."

"That's true, but how could I? I didn't get home until nearly one—I was out with a couple of the supervisors' aides, trying to work out the administration of this Hunter's Point thing. I've got a few other things besides Lieutenant Glitsky on my mind just now, hon. I think Abe must be just feeling the pressure. I've got to talk to him. Is he there now?"

"No, he's gone over to Farrell's. I just wanted to know what you'd do . . ."

"It sounds to me you're doing just right, Elaine. I'd do the same thing. If Abe can bring you Kevin Shea and you can guarantee his safety, then of course you've got do it. That's all I've called for time and time again, is the man's arrest."

"That's all you want?"

"What else could I want, child?"

"Even if he's innocent?"

"Of course. *Especially* if he's innocent, which I don't think he is, mind you. I think Abe might be losing his perspective a little bit. If you hear from him, you have him call me, hear? Get this boy back on the right track."

"All right, Mom . . . I will."

"And as for you, I'd be a little careful." Loretta went on about the pitfalls of abandoning procedures, then ended: "All right, now you take care, I've got to talk to the mayor. You need anything else, just jingle me back, okay?"

*   *   *

Damn damn *damn* you, Abe Glitsky! You don't know what you're messing with.

"So I thought, Senator, that you might be able to put the best perspective on this oversight by personally delivering the permit to Mr. Mohandas. I mean, the whole point of the rally is to protest the city's foot-dragging. I thought you could offset that . . ."

"I think you're right, Conrad. If you want the truth, I don't think I would have approved the permit on this thing yesterday either if I were in your shoes. That's off the record now, but I believe you did the right thing. Now, though, since the rally seems to be going forward . . ."

"I could send a limo. Be there in fifteen minutes with the signed permit."

"If you could make it a half hour I'd look a little better on television." She laughed conspiratorially.

"Thank you, Senator. I don't know how to thank you but I'll remember this."

"Oh, nonsense, Conrad. It just gives me an excuse to say a few words in public, and you know I just live for those moments." She laughed her deep, throaty, self-deprecating laugh.

"Still . . ."

"You hush now. Send your limo over. Bye bye."

68

Glitsky had stayed with Elaine, discussing how they'd do it, for most of a half hour, then had called the office and lucked out by getting Carl Griffin, who'd drag a log a mile through deep sand and never ask why. After that he'd planned to drive directly down to Farrell's, but when he had gotten into his city-issued car, by habit he checked and adjusted his rearview mirror, fiddled with the seat, moved it back a notch—and stopped dead.

It was a full ten minutes before he turned the ignition key.

Farrell, wary as a terrier but not quite half as cute, greeted Glitsky in a blue-tinted suit that fit him perfectly. With his hair slicked back and ponytail tied up he almost looked like a practicing attorney except for what looked like an ink stain or something that colored his lower lip and part of his chin.

In the living room papers were lying around, old food containers, beer bottles, soda pop cans, pizza cartons. Farrell introduced his visitor to Bart the dog and then, catching Glitsky's look, told him the cleaning lady had unexpectedly taken some time off.

Thinking "What? A century?" Glitsky picked his way across the room and plunked himself down on an overturned milk carton. "Business a little slow lately?" he asked. Bart came up and sniffed at his shoes, his cuffs, his pants. Glitsky petted him.

Farrell came back from doing something in another room and was looking at his watch. "I got about eight forty-one."

Glitsky checked his own. "About."

"I can't figure how I can avoid the call with Kevin. There's no way I can reach him to warn him off. I've got to be here for him when he calls," Farrell said, lowering himself onto the futon. "That was *you* last night, wasn't it?"

"That was me."

"So how do you think we ought to handle it?"

Glitsky reached down and scratched at Bart's head again and the dog nuzzled up against his shoes.

"You really don't know where he is?"

Farrell acted offended. "Look, Lieutenant, I'm here. I'm here for no money because I believe Kevin Shea is as innocent as you or me. If I knew where he was I'd be with *him*. That's my story and you can take it or leave it. I'm not playing any lawyer games. I'm out of the trade."

A nod. No apology, though. "So the only way we find out where he is, we got to take the call?"

"That's how I see it."

"Then it's going to be a race. You got a backup place, someplace you decided you'd meet if everything fell apart?"

"No," Farrell said wearily. "You know, Lieutenant, we hadn't exactly planned all this. What do you mean, a *race*?"

"I mean as soon as the FBI places your boy, they're going to be rolling, and you'd better plan to be doing the same thing. I've met Special Agent Simms, and she's here to put out fires, no questions asked."

"Kevin Shea is a fire?"

"I know she's considering him armed and dangerous."

"But he's not. He's nothing like that."

Glitsky shrugged—people got things wrong all the time.

"So I just ask him where he is and head out there?"

"Yeah, I think so."

Farrell shook his head, blew out a long breath. "And then what?"

It didn't take long. They were still in San Francisco's jurisdiction, regardless of the FBI's presence. Glitsky—he omitted the fact of his administrative leave—could make a formal arrest, with the bonus of it being in the presence of Shea's attorney and another witness. The assistant district attorney, Elaine Wager, was on board and she'd agreed to help, get Kevin Shea down to a safe zone, maybe even assist Farrell in trying to get the indictment quashed.

The telephone rang. Both men looked at their watches—
it was well over fifteen minutes before the call was due.

To Farrell, there were still logistics, a lot of them, to
discuss. He didn't feel ready, but he grabbed it before the
second ring was over. Listening, he began to frown. "Yeah,
he's here, just a minute." Then, to Glitsky: "Elaine
Wager."

Elaine told Glitsky she had talked to her mother, who had
denied all of his allegations. All she wanted was Kevin
Shea's arrest—that's all she had wanted all along. Loretta
didn't really think—and Elaine had come to agree with
her—that it would be a good idea to transport Shea out of
the city and county. That was really a police matter, and
Elaine was with the DA's office, not the PD. It was beyond
the scope of her professional responsibilities. She had to be
careful not to go outside the accepted procedures—look at
all the problems that kind of thing had caused for O.J.
Simpson's prosecutors. Did she want that kind of circus?

No, the smart thing was to play it by the book. She could
still have Abe deliver Shea to her, and then they could all
go downtown and book him and somehow guarantee his
safety. To think anything would happen in jail was really
just paranoia. People rarely got killed in jail, especially if
there was the kind of notoriety that there was in this case.
Whatever, Kevin Shea would be especially protected. He
should not be concerned about it.

Glitsky was thinking maybe she should ask Jeffrey
Dahmer about that, but held his tongue. Then he told her
that her whole new idea wasn't going to fly.

"Why not?"

"Because Mr. Farrell isn't delivering Kevin Shea to the
San Francisco jail, not without more assurance of security
than that."

Which was where it ended, except for the final note that
Elaine thought that Abe might be working too hard, seeing
things that weren't really there.

He replaced the phone gently into its cradle. It was five
minutes of nine. He relayed the message to Farrell, who
had been hovering, getting the gist as it developed.

"So now what?"

Glitsky stared across the room. "I don't suppose you'd be amenable to taking your client downtown?" He didn't even wait for an answer. It was going to come down to him and Loretta, as something in him had known it would have to. Farrell started to reply but Abe stopped him with a gesture to show the question hadn't been serious. But this next one was: "How about if I can get the senator herself?"

Farrell, embittered by Elaine's turnaround, was shaking his head. "I don't know if she—"

"She can. Reston's her man. She could get him to promise protection, and meanwhile call off the FBI, take the message to the community, get Mohandas to call off his Dead or Alive rhetoric." He paused. "She's the only one who can do it."

"But why would she? Didn't she just tell . . . wasn't that her daughter . . . ?"

"She's protecting her daughter's job, her career. This is different."

"She won't do it, Lieutenant."

Glitsky was grim. "She might." He was on his feet. "You got a beeper?"

"No. I used to."

Glitsky pulled at his belt. "Here, take mine. If she'll do it, if we can deliver Shea to her, if she stands up for him in public, you won't get a better guarantee than that."

"But even if she does, how will you . . . ?"

Glitsky pointed at his beeper. "I'll call that number. If you get a chance, call me back and tell me where you are, where Shea is. If you get there before the FBI, get the hell out of wherever you are, go someplace else and wait for me to call you again. If not—if the feds are right behind you, call nine one one. Point is, get some other people there. Get some witnesses."

"And what if Loretta Wager just won't do it?"

At the door, Glitsky turned. "Same basic plan, counsellor, except if you don't get beeped and do manage to get out in front of the feds . . . ?"

"Yeah?"

"You didn't hear it from me, but ride like the wind."

69

There was the doorbell—the limo, she supposed. She had told the mayor a half hour and apparently he was in such an all-fired hurry that he'd sent it in half that time.

She was just finishing her hair. Well, she wasn't about to do the rest of her makeup in the car. She'd tell the man he'd have to wait.

Her steps echoed on the hardwood as she walked up through the back rooms to the foyer.

"Abe!"

"I tried to call," he said. "Nobody answered."

"No," she said. "I know. I got your message but I got in so late . . ."

"Elaine said she'd talked to you." He squinted out at the sun, into the wind. "You mind if I come in a second?"

"Well, I'm expecting a . . . sure." She smiled brightly at him. "It can only be a minute, though. I've got to get to the rally."

He stopped midway through the door. "You're going to the Mohandas rally?"

She reached out and touched his sleeve. "Not what you think. The mayor asked me to deliver the permit for it, that's all." She shrugged. "Political favor. The limo ought to be here any—"

He brought the door to, closing it with the flat of his hand. She tried a smile—confused, actually concerned about him, the pressure he was under. She moved toward him—

"No," he said.

She drew back. "No what, Abe?"

His gaze was flat, without expression. Cop mode. She tried again, reaching out. He moved to the side and away from her. "I was a half hour away from picking up Kevin Shea, getting this whole thing over with the only way I could," he began, "and you sandbagged me." He was moving slowly away from her, keeping a steady distance, back through the cavernous living room toward the library.

"Abe, *please,* I did nothing of the kind. If anything I was trying to help you both. Elaine from making a mistake that could cost her her job, her career, *you* from being drummed out of the police department altogether."

He nodded, something had been confirmed. But he was holding it close, giving nothing away. "As opposed to what?" he asked.

"As opposed to this administrative leave, that's what. You're hurting yourself, Abe, with such a—"

"How do you know about the administrative leave, Loretta?"

A blip of lost control. A vein showed in her temple. "Well, I . . ."

"*I* got the word around midnight last night. When did you get it?"

He had maneuvered them both back into the library, where they had come the first night. It was the closest thing in the house to his turf.

Loretta was framed by the door.

"I don't know," she said. "Really, I just don't know." Her eyes looked wounded. She took a step toward him. "Why are you being so cold, Abe? Why are you talking to me this way. *All* I did was tell Elaine to make sure she followed the rules." She ventured a couple more steps, stopped. "*That's* who told me about you. It was Elaine."

"About the leave?"

"Yes."

He nodded again. "How did she know? I never mentioned it to her."

A narrowing of vision? "Well, then she didn't get it from you. Maybe she talked to Alan Reston. Maybe she heard it on the news. All *I* know is that she told me." She closed the last few feet between them. "Abe, please. Why are you doing this?"

Now, her eyes glistening from the pain he was putting her through, she lay her palm on his arm. "Please."

He stepped back. Her hand fell. "I want you to call her," he said.

"And say what?"

"Tell her I've explained things to you. How they stand. Tell her it's the right thing."

"But it isn't. It could ruin the case, ruin her."

"There is no case, Loretta. Kevin Shea is innocent and you know it."

The response had the quality of a reflex, but she took a little extra time to phrase it. "No white men are innocent, Abe. *You* know that."

He'd heard this a thousand times in one form or other, and it had no effect on him now. "Some are," he said simply. "Kevin Shea's one of the good guys, Loretta."

"Oh, so why don't we put up a statue to him?"

"He didn't do it and you've railroaded the whole country thinking he did."

She narrowed her eyes. *"So what?"*

"So what? You can undo it."

"Get a life, Abe. Even if this boy *himself* didn't do it— don't you see?—he represents what happened. It doesn't matter if it was actually him, Kevin Shea the person. It doesn't matter at all."

"That's exactly what does matter."

She stood firm. "What would be worse, Abe, is if *no one* got arrested or punished for what happened to Arthur Wade . . . if it just went unavenged."

Suddenly he'd had enough. He wasn't here for politics or philosophy. "You have to call Elaine."

Her back stiffened. "I'm not going to do that. It could ruin her, it could end her career, everything she's worked for—"

"No," he said, "it could ruin *yours.*"

She let a brittle laugh escape. "You think this is about *me.* Abe, please, come on . . ." She kept following him, slowly moving in closer, one step. Another. Hesitant on the face of it, a confidence underneath. It had always worked before. "This *is* about Elaine. *Only* Elaine, not me."

She was cornering him, giving him no other way—he

didn't want to take it as far as it could go, not unless—until—she forced him. And that's what she was doing.

He knew what he knew, but if he could just get her to back off on Kevin Shea, that would be enough. Enough for him. There would be a certain justice in that, and sometimes that was all you got.

But she wasn't going to leave Elaine. She *couldn't* leave her—Elaine was something she hadn't ever wanted to use in this way, but now it was developing that she must. It could end this impasse with Abe. It could save her . . .

Loretta Wager had molded a life using the clay she was given—every daub of it. If you had a secret, knowledge, you hoarded it until it could provide its maximum effect.

This was the time.

She sat on the arm of the chair, weary with the weight of it. "Abe, don't you know? You really don't know?" A tear finally broke loose and she let it roll down her cheek. "We cannot hurt Elaine, Abe. We cannot let her be hurt. Not *either* of us . . ."

"It's not Elaine," he began again impatiently, "it's—"

She slapped the leather on the back of the chair. "Goddamn it, Abe, listen to me. It *is* Elaine. *It is Elaine.*"

She let the moment simmer. Watching him as it registered. A beat. Two.

"What are you saying?"

She paused again. Then: "Do you think I wanted Dana Wager instead of you? Do you think I wanted him for *me*?" She shook her head. "I wasn't going to force anyone—force *you*—to marry me because I was carrying your baby. Okay, you weren't ready to marry me for myself. Don't you understand? I had to have someone who would. And Dana was there. He never had to know. He never knew." She stared at him. "And neither did you."

No reaction. A still frame of the moment of impact. Next, slowly—so slowly—Glitsky's arms coming uncrossed, his face going slack.

Loretta, nodding now, the tears beginning to fall freely. On her feet, another tentative step toward him. "She's *your* daughter, Abe. *Elaine is your daughter.*"

*   *   *

"Get the hell away from me!"

"Abe!"

"Get away!" Somehow, he had crossed the room. His face—flashes of heat. A tingling, terrifying. A jab in his left arm—his heart was stopping.

"Abe, please . . ."

"Goddamn it goddamn it . . ." A snifter. On the bar. Grabbing it up, squeezing. Impossible. No more control.

The explosion on the hardwood. Shards of broken crystal.

"YOU TELL ME THIS NOW?"

"Don't yell at me, Abe. Please . . ."

"DON'T YELL AT YOU? Don't yell at you? Jesus . . ." Walking in small circles, turning. Nowhere to go. "Goddamnit."

Another try. "Abe . . . ?"

He pointed at her. "Don't come near me! Don't you dare take another step."

She waited, hands at her sides.

Slumped in the chair, he heard her moving around in the house.

Minutes had passed.

He still had to do it—do his job—but he found he couldn't move. It had come to where he had known it must. But she had rocked him. He knew it was true. The old nagging sense of familiarity, of vague but real recognition. *Elaine was his daughter.*

He could not make himself stand up, go in and accuse Loretta, face her. He was afraid of what he might do.

The doorbell rang. Her limo.

He had to move.

Get up, Abe, get up!

If he moved, if he saw her face . . .

Steps echoing on the floor, the door opening. "Hello. Yes, I'll be ready in five minutes. You can wait in the car."

He couldn't let her.

He couldn't stop her.

She'd beaten him. She'd won.

70

"All right, Kevin, call." Wes Farrell stood in his coat and tie by his kitchen wall phone, talking to it like an idiot. "It's eight after nine and you said you'd call at nine on the dot and this isn't the time to go flaky on me."

He had the television on in the war zone of his living salon, and CNN was broadcasting, live near Kezar Pavilion. The whole country was following San Francisco this Saturday morning. Mohandas had appeared a couple of times, the same sound bite about the plans for this to be a peaceful march, a demonstration to the city's leaders, the *country's* leaders, that . . . blah, blah, blah.

The phone jangled. Wes snapped for it, knocked it from its cradle, grabbed again but the receiver fell to the floor. He snagged it up. "Kevin? Give me your address."

"Drop the phone, Wes?"

"Kevin, listen to me. We got some big problems. Just give me your address and I'll be right over there."

"Are you watching this thing on TV?"

"Kevin, give me your fucking address right now."

"What kind of problems, Wes?"

"I'll explain when I get there. Give me your address."

Kevin's tone shifted. "We're still on 'go,' though? I mean, the basic plan . . ."

Wes was silent. Then: *"Where?"*

Kevin gave him the address, the apartment number. "Fourth floor, in the front," he said. "Looks right over the park. There's a million people down there."

Wes was swearing at himself all the way down to his garage. He *couldn't believe* that his own brain was failing him so badly. What he should have done was just give Kevin the phone number on Glitsky's beeper, tell him to get out *now* and go someplace else, then beep him and tell him where he was, which would be where they'd meet.

But, of course, he was too incredibly stupid to have thought of that. Not when it could have done any good.

Special Agent Simms was in her car with her three fellow agents and moving before Farrell had pulled out of his garage, so she had at least some blocks on him.

It had been unwise of Farrell, she thought, but good for her side, to ask Shea for the address. Still, what else could he have done? Anyway, she had all of the advantage now. The address, the apartment number, the jump on the chase. Maybe they wouldn't need to use any firepower, unless . . .

Well, she would see. Certainly she wasn't going to get scared out of using the tools they had brought. She wasn't about to show any weakness on *that* score. The public might have screamed about that woman and her kid the FBI had had to kill up in Idaho, but within the ranks of the Bureau it was generally conceded that the whole thing had been unavoidable. It had been—what was his name?—the guy Weaver's fault for getting them all in that position, certainly not the Bureau's. Start worrying about criticism, the *media* response, you might as well hang up your badge. You wouldn't get anything done.

She would do what she had to do.

The first action would be the simplest and most direct. She would go up and knock on the door, say she had a federal warrant and he was under arrest. In a perfect world he would open the door and come out with his hands over his head.

Somehow she didn't have the feeling it was going to go down exactly like that.

In spite of Mohandas's best efforts to get things going, the rally wasn't about to start on time. They never did. His mouth was dry in spite of the constant popping of Tic-Tacs. He couldn't stop pacing inside the tent. Allicey, taller than he was, kneaded his shoulders whenever he passed by her.

It was nearly nine-fifteen and there were still people pouring into the Pavilion. The police were patrolling but all seemed calm. There had been two more skirmishes that he had seen from up here, but both had been quickly suppressed.

The smoke from the Divisadero fire was getting a little worse—the wind and all. He'd definitely have to skirt north when the march began. He wasn't going to give much of a speech. There wasn't that need today—he'd already said it publicly so many times—and the turnout was so great that he thought it would be more effective just to get them moving, let it speak for itself.

What he'd do was welcome everybody, talk a minute about the *reality* of how things worked, not the lip-service they always got but the way results just didn't seem to come all the way to them. The mayor had played into his hands so beautifully he couldn't believe it, but he'd have been a fool not to use what he'd been handed on a platter. He could almost hear himself: ". . . but in spite of the *words* we have all heard time and time again about this city's cooperation, the plain fact is, my brothers and sisters, that even this rally, even this peaceful gathering to show our concern, our *despair,* over the denial of justice for the tragic murder of our brother Arthur Wade . . ." He would pause here for the outburst to die down. "The plain fact is that they have even made *this* gathering illegal. They said we couldn't have this march. They wouldn't give us the permit. But I say our strength is our permit. Our unity is our strength. And let God himself be our judge!"

It was going to sing all right.

And then he'd lead them out, down the seething streets all the way to City Hall. In righteousness, in rage, and in glory.

71

She came briskly out of the back room. She was wearing her dark blue—hat, suit coat, clutch purse. Things were moving along. She had defused Abe, and now she had to hurry.

As she got to the foyer she stopped, her body sagging. She, herself, was wearing down. "I've got to go out. Please get out of my way."

Glitsky stood blocking the front door. "I'm going to call Wes Farrell from here and tell him that you're coming with me to personally guarantee Kevin Shea's safety."

"I'm going to the rally, Abe. The mayor has asked me to deliver a permit—"

"I'm not asking, Loretta. I'm telling you. Forget the permit. I'm giving you a last chance, although God knows why . . ."

"A chance for what?"

"You've been saying all along that all you wanted was Kevin Shea arrested. *Of course* he deserved some consideration, some safety. Well, I'm giving you a chance to prove you're not lying."

"I'm not lying. Why would I lie?"

"Why? Because your career is over if Kevin Shea is innocent and you know it. You *can't* have him be innocent. You can't let him be arrested and get a chance to be heard. That's why you've been blocking me."

"This is stupid . . . I haven't been blocking anybody, Abe. Not you, not anybody. You've just gotten—"

He raised a hand. "I know, I know. Paranoid, overworked, irrational, any and all of the above. Yeah, that's me. You got me."

She moved forward. "I've heard enough of this. Let me by!"

Pushing at him, he might have been a wall. Until he exploded, grabbing her by the shoulders and shoving her backward. She stumbled, nearly went down, recovered. Her eyes blazing, she straightened up. "You want to talk about careers being over, Abe. You just ended yours."

Glitsky didn't care. He spoke with a forced calm. "You're not getting by. Understand that. You've got about ten seconds to agree to go out of here with me. And then you're not going to have a choice about it anymore."

She stared for a beat, then told him he was crazy.

"Six seconds," he said.

"Why would I agree to something like that? I've got a driver waiting right outside the door here. I've got to—"

"All right. Time's up." Glitsky's face was set, ashen. "Don't say I didn't give you an out, Loretta. You wouldn't take it." He took a labored breath. "I'm arresting you for the murder of Christopher Locke."

The reaction took a moment—a squinting, a half-turn, lack of belief. "You can't . . . this is *absurd.*"

"No, Loretta, this is the truth."

"Did you dream this up last night or something? Abe, you're out of your mind. I wouldn't . . ."

He was shaking his head. "He wasn't turned around in the car, looking out the back window. He was sitting next to you, without a clue."

"You're insane."

He ignored it. "You were *near* the riot all right, even driving toward it, inside the car. But you never made it, did you?"

"Of course, we did. How can you even say—?"

"Because there's this thing I work with called evidence. There were no signs that a crowd had been anywhere near your car, much less throwing rocks at it, kicking it from behind. I walked all around it. I looked."

"Then you missed it."

"No, I didn't. I wondered about it the first time I inspected the car. What I missed was what it meant."

"And what did it mean?"

"It meant that what you *did* do was you pulled up a

couple of blocks short of the action and shot Locke behind the ear. That was the shot no one heard."

"I did *not*. That did not happen—"

Glitsky's voice didn't waver. "But it was also the shot that left no glass shards at all in the wound and too many powder burns around it—but you wouldn't have known about any of that. That isn't politics. It's just stupid, grinding police forensic stuff—not very interesting."

She folded her arms in front of her, shaking her head. "And what did I do then?"

"You drove down a dark dead-end street—all the street-lights were out—and walked around the car and fired a shot through the passenger window that would appear to have been fired at you, and then you probably used the butt of the gun to knock a bigger hole in the safety glass."

"Probably. Only probably? You're not sure?"

"I don't know for sure what you used, but probably we'll find out eventually. But what it was—it was another mistake."

He waited. She didn't ask, eyes fixed, unyielding. So he continued. "There was just the one bullet hole in the safety glass, which was the problem. You thought the window would break with the shot, but it just made a nice neat little hole, didn't it, some spiderwebs around it? So you had to hammer a bigger one, something two bullets might have passed through. Except for the reality that even *two* .25 caliber bullets won't put a fist-sized hole in safety glass. You probably couldn't get one with four."

Her expression remained impassive, but she eased herself down onto the bench against the hallway wall. "This is fascinating," she said.

"Right. The other thing, the clincher if you want to hear it . . ."

"Oh, please . . ."

The venom in her voice paralyzed him for a second. In a way it was salutary, helping wipe out the last traces of any sympathetic feeling. He felt the scar stretch through his lips, knew he was giving her his piano-wire smile, the one Flo had told him could give nightmares to mass murderers.

"This was the moment, just this morning, when it all

came together. Before that, almost everything was there—I didn't know that nobody had heard two shots, but the rest of it. Except I didn't *want* to see it. I went to adjust the seat in the Plymouth. You know the car. It's the same one you and Locke rode in."

Still nothing. No reaction.

"Remember the other night, you and me counting 'one two three,' pushing the seat up so you could drive? You remember that? So this morning, there I was sitting in the driver's seat, and it struck me what was so wrong about the bullet hole in the door of *your* car, the driver's door. You want to know what that was?"

Silence.

"It would have had to go through *you* first."

Finally, against her will. "*What* are you talking about?"

"I'm talking about you being unable to drive, to reach the foot pedals without the seat pushed all the way forward. And if the seat was forward, which it had to be, the trajectory of the shot from the hole in the window to the hole in the upholstery would have had to hit you. It would have had to go through you, Loretta." He waited. "So you weren't in the seat. You were outside, in the street, firing the one shot—the *one shot* everybody heard—through the safety glass. The one you said almost hit you."

"You're wrong. I was trying to get away from there. Chris had just been shot, the seat must have slid back with the acceleration."

Glitsky had broken witnesses before, and when you started getting denials of the details, you knew you were there. He crossed the foyer, sat at the opposite end of the bench. He didn't intend to break her. Not before he made her undo some of the damage she'd done—to herself, to Elaine, to Kevin Shea—and she was the only one who could do it. He needed her for that first; then he'd deal with the rest.

He almost whispered it. "You killed him, Loretta. You had to."

She wasn't giving it up. "*Why* should I have killed Chris Locke?"

She was leading him there.

"The simple answer is because you couldn't control him anymore. But it really wasn't that simple. He was blackmailing you, you were blackmailing him. You knew each other's secrets."

"About *what*?"

"About the money you laundered through the Pacific Moon."

That he had come to this knowledge, finally, rocked her, although she covered it—her tightened lips were all that betrayed it. "I explained that to you, Abe. That was completely legitimate."

"No," he said. "Chris Locke was prosecuting the case, and then he met you and the two of you became involved, wasn't that it?"

"No. None of this is it."

"He represented the DA's office and dropped the charges, said there wasn't a case and you got to keep the money . . ."

"That's not true. This is . . ." She was standing up, but he took hold of her by the wrist, held her. She sat back down.

"But the money wasn't why you killed him. What he knew made you nervous maybe, but the records had been destroyed, cleaned up, sanitized. You had the same thing on each other. You could live with that."

She looked at him, waiting. She'd give him nothing.

"Because he rejected you and he took up with Elaine. Because now he was really out of your control. He was going to play fast and loose with your daughter, your baby. You could handle that for yourself—but your *daughter* wasn't going to have it like you did. She was going to have it better. You were going to protect her because you knew what Chris Locke would do. It would be what he'd done to you."

"And exactly what was that?"

"He'd use her, then throw her on the slag heap when she became . . . inconvenient."

"I haven't been with him in years. I wouldn't . . ."

Glitsky nodded, the first admission.

"Besides, you can't prove any of this. I did not kill Chris, I did not launder any money. For God's sake, Abe, it's just . . ."

He stood, walked to the window next to the door and looked out, his back to her.

The limo was parked right there.

He counted to fifteen, then without turning, said, "The

proof is in your hand, Loretta. You going to shoot me in the back? What are you going to say? That you thought I was a burglar? A rapist?"

He turned around.

Loretta was standing by the hallway bench, clutch purse in one hand, the small gun levelled at him in the other.

Glitsky's eyes went to it. "I've got a good friend who's an attorney and I've left a letter with him," he lied. "It says that in the event of my death, they should compare the ballistics on the bullet that killed me with the one that killed Chris Locke." He nodded at the gun. "They're going to match, Loretta. And the letter goes on about a few of the other things we've talked about this morning. It also mentions your name."

He took a step toward her. "It's over, Loretta. It's over."

Slowly she lowered the gun.

"I had to kill Chris. He was going to ruin my daughter . . . was already doing it . . ."

Glitsky nodded. He already knew this. "I'm going to need to take that gun for evidence," he said.

"You can't think I'm going to give you this gun."

"I'd prefer it," he said, "but it doesn't really matter. I don't need it."

"Without it you don't have any physical evidence. You don't have a case." She took a step toward him, her expression set, tone low. "We don't have to have this happen, Abe. I can throw it away, get rid of it . . ."

He reached into his pocket and pulled out the pocket recorder he always carried, turned it off, played back the last few moments, her admission that she had killed Locke. When he flicked it off, he held out his hand. "The gun," he said.

She gave it one last try. "Abe. This won't work. Alan Reston won't prosecute me. You won't even get him to go to a judge for an arrest warrant."

"That may be so. But I can arrest you for murder without a warrant. When I book you into county jail, the press will be there, and they'll ask me why and I'll tell them. And then Alan Reston will either have to prosecute or explain why he doesn't, which he can't do. And even if he doesn't, okay, then, you get away with murder, but I've done my job." Glitsky took a step toward her, his hand outstretched. "Now either use that gun or give it to me."

It took her a long moment, but finally she turned it barrel in and handed it to him. As he put it into his pocket, she asked him, "What do you really want, Abe?"

"The same as I've always wanted, Loretta. I want to arrest my suspect. I want some protection for Kevin Shea."

"And what do I get?"

Her singularity of purpose continued to impress him. It never ended. "There's always a deal, Loretta, isn't there?"

She waited.

"You think I'm about to let you walk on a premeditated murder?"

"I don't know what you're going to do, Abe." She stood in front of him. "I'm telling you what I *need*, that's all. It's your decision."

"Either way," Glitsky said, "you're dead politically."

"Maybe." Her eyes rested on him. "You're such a fool," she said, "we could have had it all."

The doorbell rang, followed by a knock at the door. Another. "Senator?" The limo driver.

"Do we have a deal, Abe?"

Another knock. "Senator, we're running a little late here."

"I need your word, Abe."

Glitsky, in spite of his official administrative leave, was still the nominal head of homicide, *and* a cop inside out. He had known she would probably try something like this devil's trade, but there was still the moment before it was irrevocably done. The temptation to let it go—he didn't have to take it out all the way . . .

He suddenly felt clammy, sick with the portent of it.

"We'll talk about the *possibility* of a deal later, *but no guarantees.* I want you clear on that. You either go with me to Kevin Shea right now or I take you downtown. And if I do that, it's beyond the control of either of us. You're charged with murder and it can't be undone. Or"—he pointed a finger—"or I take you out to Kezar Pavilion, where you might do a little good. It's *your* decision, Loretta. You decide."

Her bluff called, she hesitated, took in a breath, then crossed the foyer to the door. "I'll tell him I'm driving over with you."

Glitsky went to make his phone call to Wes Farrell.

72

In response to the four outbreaks of interracial scufflings and five serious injuries in the last half hour, the National Guard had moved into positions of closer conformity with the proposed march route, and the trucks with their troops had closed off all traffic and were lining the streets on either side of Golden Gate Park. New arrivals wanting to join the march were going to have to leave their cars blocks away and breach this wall and its security measures as they walked in, and hundreds were doing just that. In the park's panhandle the tent city took up the center and the tide of people would in theory flow around the roped-off living areas.

Special Agent Margot Simms—who had elected not to act in concert either with the San Francisco police or the National Guard—had her driver pull to the side of the road only four blocks from Kevin Shea's apartment. She looked down the hill at the flood of people moving toward Kezar, the troops, the stalled traffic.

How to get through that? Well, she was with the FBI, that was how. She wasn't going to put her own men at risk, and she was going to do her job, which was apprehend Kevin Shea, by force if necessary. She gave the order to circumvent the sawhorses that closed off the streets and head down, past the Pavilion, to her destination. She did not give a good goddamn what, or who, might be in the way. She knew that Wes Farrell, the lawyer, was going to be facing the same problem she was, and he would have no identification to flash to get him by this hurdle.

They were still ahead.

The car crept through the pedestrians, several of them whacking the roof, the hood. Two blocks in three-and-a-half minutes—then they were stopped by a couple of teen-aged National Guardsmen, rifles out and jittery.

Simms got out of the front seat, held up her badge, identifying herself. The two boys—one with a black nametag reading "Morgan," the other a thin, hawk-faced boy whose tag read "Escher," looked at one another, and Morgan said, "Yes, ma'am?"

"My colleagues and I need to breach your line here."

Again, the silent consultation. Morgan said, "I'll have to get permission, ma'am."

Simms stiffened. "*I'm* giving you permission, son. This is the Federal Bureau of Investigation and we are in a hurry."

"Yes, ma'am." But neither man moved.

"Well?"

"Well, our orders are to keep vehicular traffic out of the parade route . . ."

"I'll go check." Escher ran off. Morgan made a gesture. "It won't be long," he said. "Five minutes."

Farrell, more familiar with the city than Simms, figured the rally would be a mob scene, so he went the back way over Portola and Twin Peaks, thinking he would wind up on Ashbury and then park. He could walk the rest of the way, which he supposed he'd have to do in any event.

The beeper went off as he was passing by a gas station on 17th. He pulled in, ran to the pay phone and punched numbers.

"You've got the senator with you? Herself?" Farrell couldn't believe it.

Glitsky was curt. "Give me the address. I don't have any time."

Farrell did, and Glitsky said, "That's right in the middle . . . that's where the march is starting."

"You got it, and I hear on the radio they've closed off the park. Where are you coming from?"

"Pacific Heights."

"You're going to have to come around the back way, maybe up Judah."

Glitsky thanked him. "Take me ten minutes," he said.

"Don't bet on it, and by the way, your idea of getting out if I'm there before the feds . . ."

"Yeah?"

"I don't think so. Not today."

Simms was talking to another man with another nametag—Florio. The stripes on Florio's sleeve indicated he had some rank. She explained her position—the Guard would have to let her through the park, they had an arrest to make. Federal warrant. Most Wanted List. Florio raised his eyebrows. "Kevin Shea?" he asked. At the mention of Shea's name, both Morgan and Escher snapped up.

She looked right, left, then back to Florio. "No comment on that," she said. "Can we get through here?"

She was back in the car and it started moving again through the pedestrians, Morgan walking on one side, Escher on the other, escorting them.

"He should be here," Kevin said.

"He got caught in the traffic."

He couldn't stop looking out the window, pulling up the shade, glancing down. Melanie came over to him, moved the shade back. "Sit down. Come on, Kevin. Looking out isn't helping anything."

"*Sitting* here isn't helping anything."

"Sitting here is waiting for Wes. He'll be here."

Kevin started snapping his fingers, his nerves eating him. "We should have—"

"Hey." She touched a finger to his lips. "We're doing it." She leaned over and kissed him. "I love you. Just wait, Wes will be here. It'll be all right."

He was reaching for the shade again, going to look down on the park. The downstairs doorbell sounded. "There he is," Melanie said, crossing to the buzzer that unlocked the lobby door. She was about to push it when Kevin jumped up from his chair. "Wait!" and went to one of the side windows. Opening the shade a crack, he looked out and down. "Okay," he said. "It's him. I think . . . I've never seen him in a suit."

"Kevin, who else would it be? Nobody knows we're here."

He gave her a look. "Famous last words," he said.

*   *   *

As directed by their supervisor, Morgan and Escher remained at their new positions as escorts of the FBI vehicle, which had pulled to the western curb at Page and Stanyan, across the street from the apartment. Simms sent one man with a field telephone and a suitcase into the park to find a reasonably elevated spot from which he would have a clear shot at the fourth-floor front window of the apartment building across the street from them—a tree or a telephone pole—should it be necessary, should the order be given. (Their backup unit was on the way, but with the traffic problems, she didn't want to have to wait for them. They might not encounter a Florio who would cooperate.)

Simms took her two other men and they made their way through the pulsing crowd onto the street, eventually into the open courtyard that faced the park, and to the front door of the apartment. She rang the entire bank of doorbells for the first floor, and someone buzzed open the outer door.

"Cake," she said, holding the door for her men.

Out in the street Morgan and Escher were guarding the car, the only one parked on Stanyan. People kept washing by, around it. Someone's amplified voice came ringing over the distance—the rally was getting under way.

"Who's the car, man? I been walkin' ten blocks, my dogs be achin'. Thought no cars allowed in here. They was, I woulda brung mine."

Morgan wasn't supposed to talk to the crowd except to answer informational questions and give directions, but this big guy had one of those immediately friendly faces, a big smile, a wife and kids in tow, here to support the cause. But he wasn't trouble. Everybody wasn't on the warpath.

"FBI," Morgan said, then added: "They got Kevin Shea tree'd in that building. Bringing him in."

"Hallelujah," said the man, his smile brightening. "Don't got to walk so far now, all the way City Hall. Ought to just park my dogs here." Then, turning to the crowd behind him, spreading the good word. "Hey, you all hear this? They got Kevin Shea." Pointing. "Yeah, right over yonder."

*   *   *

Upstairs, the deadbolt thrown again, Kevin, Melanie and
Wes decided that even with the crowd outside, their odds
were far better facing it than an armed, trigger-happy and
belligerent FBI.

No one except possibly the FBI knew they were anywhere within miles of here. They'd be an all-but-
anonymous few white faces in the crowd, and Wes assured
them that there were a lot of others, more than he would
have thought. Everybody with a placard, a message, or a
cause had come to the party.

Kevin could wear his ski cap. They could get away from
the heat here and then wait for Glitsky's call on the beeper
when they got to a safer spot.

In the apartment's lobby Simms spoke by walkie-talkie to
her sharpshooter and decided she would give him the extra
few minutes he needed to get into position before she took
her two other men upstairs with her to make the arrest.
With the crowd, he had found it difficult to blend in, find
a spot, get set up. She told him she would give him ten
minutes max—call her if it was going to be sooner.

In the interim the three of them would split apart to
check the layout of the building, identify any potential hidden exits, back doors, fire escapes. Make it airtight.

They would meet back here in the lobby, then go up and
take him.

". . . and we have just received an unconfirmed report that
Kevin Shea has been located at a building not five blocks
from where we are standing right now at the Kezar Pavilion. Philip Mohandas has left the podium, almost at a dead
run, and is leading the marchers—it's a tremendous and
very angry crowd and I'm sure you can hear them chanting
Shea's name over my voice—he's leading the way out
toward the edge of the park.

"We'll be trying to follow Mohandas as he . . ."

*   *   *

Glitsky had pulled his siren and flasher and put it on the roof. Loretta was sitting next to him, silent and withdrawn as they careered through the narrow streets, now south of the park, almost there.

Glitsky felt he'd been awake for days. He had the AM radio on, had heard the latest reports. Somehow—how did these things happen?—somehow it had gotten out.

Now Philip Mohandas and a crowd estimated at between five hundred and several thousand had converged on the Stanyan Street apartment building. The FBI was, reportedly, inside the building, but so far—according to the news reports—had not moved to make an arrest. In actual fact, no one seemed to know for certain what was transpiring inside, or whether Shea was there at all, or if anyone was with him.

Except Glitsky. Glitsky knew.

He had to keep turning away to get closer—Lincoln Boulevard was closed so he came east a few blocks on Irving, then had to jag up Judah, which turned into Parnassus. Finally, he stopped a few blocks short of Stanyan—even with his siren there was no moving through the masses. He turned to Loretta, jerked open his door. "Let's go."

Loretta was recognized immediately, hailed and surrounded by the mostly adoring throng. They loved her, arriving at the moment when it was all coming down. Of course she was here—she'd led the charge all along . . .

The charisma had switched back on—her face was alive, her eyes bright. Glitsky had his badge out and did not let go of her arm as they were swept along into the heart of the crowd. "It's Senator Wager! Out of the way! Give the woman some space! Let her by, let her by . . ."

As the locus of the greatest intensity became recognized, as the flow began to move in the direction of the apartment, Florio got an urgent call from Morgan on his field telephone that ordered him, Escher and three hundred other National Guard troops to mobilize in front of the building, to try and keep the courtyard clear if they could.

They had moved out double-time, beating Mohandas and the bulk of the crowd by no more than five minutes, getting deployed, breaking out their heavier gear.

Now the soldiers—helmets on, batons and riot shields up—had the place tightly surrounded, keeping the crowd back, but it was an insecure toehold. The multitude was everywhere, the air thick with shouts, screams. The blaze that had started on Divisadero had grown. Smoke from it was drifting low, blinding and acrid.

Sirens moaned in the distance.

The chant rose and fell, moving through the masses, never stopping, never losing its tenor of rage and urgency. "We want Shea! We want Shea!"

They had been ready to get out when they started hearing the chant. Wes Farrell moved to the front window, cracked the shade, looked out, let it fall back, and then turned. "This doesn't look too good."

Melanie was holding Kevin's hand by the door. "I love it when you talk like that," she snapped at Farrell.

"The place is surrounded, Melanie. Look for yourself."

"So now what?" from Kevin.

"Now we hope Glitsky shows up in time with the senator."

"He *is* coming?" from Melanie.

"He said so."

"And then what?" Kevin said.

They could hear the chant clearly up here. It wasn't going away.

"What about the FBI?" Melanie asked. "I thought they were—"

"Except," Farrell said, "they're going on the assumption that you're armed and dangerous, so if we do hear from them, probably the first we'll know of it is they'll come shooting through this door . . ."

"God, Wes, you *are* a fount of good news."

"I didn't make it," he said, "I'm just reporting it."

"So what do we do?" Kevin asked for the third time.

"You want to go out there?" Wes said. "Face that? No? Then we wait."

*   *   *

Florio was looking at a sweating, breathless man in full
uniform who was identifying himself as San Francisco's
chief of police, Dan Rigby. He was outside the line of
troops with a few of his uniformed men. Florio waved them
through and inside to the courtyard.

"Is Kevin Shea in this building?" Rigby was already
moving, jogging to the building's entrance. "Do we know
this? Who else is here? Is the place secured?"

Inside, the lobby doors hanging open, Rigby went up to
Special Agent Simms, who had just returned to the lobby
and was planning to begin her assault upstairs.

But she couldn't do that, he told her. Not now. Not without more reinforcements. It was turning into anarchy out
there in a hurry. If she came out with Kevin Shea, tried to
get through this mob, what did she think was going to
happen?

Simms was beside herself. How had this developed so
fast, gotten away from her? She had her men with her, she
had her warrant—she should just tell this local yoohoo
Rigby that she was going up to make the arrest and let the
chips fall. But now—after first exploding at her for not
informing the SFPD of her intentions and movements—he
was trying to claim some jurisdiction of his own.

"What I'm saying," he was saying, "is that I think we've
got a bigger problem than you're acknowledging. How the
hell are you going to get him out of here if you do pick
him up? You have any idea what's going on out here?
Where is he anyway? We need more people here. Jesus
Christ."

The other FBI agents and the city policemen were warily
circling each other in the lobby, which was also now back-
filling with residents of the building. Saturday morning, everybody home and wide awake.

Simms and Rigby—the knot of authority—had to move
just outside the lobby doors, into the well of the courtyard.

"He's my prisoner," Simms said. "Let that be my
problem."

Rigby wasn't having that. "It's in *my* city. Like it or not,
it's my problem. What's happening right here" . . . he mo-

tioned out in front of them . . . "is my problem. I'm not having another lynching in one week. We try to take Kevin Shea out through this, that's what we're going to have."

Simms caught sight of something over the crowd. "Who the hell's that? Somebody's on top of my car!"

Rigby turned. Philip Mohandas had a bullhorn in his hands, trying to get the crowd's attention. "Get that lunatic in here!" Rigby barked at one of his men. Then, to Florio: "Be nice, invite him in here if you have to."

Then something else. Another noise, a further disturbance off to the left, one of the troops running up. "Sir," he said to Florio, "there's a policeman here—no uniform— who says he's got a U.S. senator—"

But before he could finish, the crowd had been pushed aside and the line had given enough to let Glitsky and Loretta Wager through.

Simms took the field telephone from her hip. She nodded, looked up at the fourth floor, said, "Hold on" into the phone, spoke to Rigby. "They're lifting the shades. My man could take them out."

They were all assembled at the fountain in the center of the courtyard—Rigby, Simms, Mohandas and his assistants, Florio, Glitsky and Loretta Wager.

Rigby gaped in disbelief at the senator, at his lieutenant holding her arm. "What the hell are *you* doing here?"

"I'm here to arrest Kevin Shea," Glitsky said.

"Like hell you are," Simms broke in. "He's mine."

"You're on leave, Glitsky. Maybe you didn't get my message . . ."

"What's happening?"

Farrell tried the shade again. "I don't know. They're all down there at the fountain. Glitsky's made it—he's got Loretta Wager with him."

"Then why doesn't he come up here? Why don't we go down?"

"I don't know. I don't know."

"Going down is not a very good idea, Kevin. I think we better let them come up."

*   *   *

The chant had ceased, at least in the forefront of the crowd. There was a restless milling, an awareness that something was happening—being decided in the center of the courtyard—and it was spreading backward into the mass.

Pulsing, waiting.

One of the uniformed cops came up to the group, then left on a run, crossing outside the line of troops, disappearing. In fitful starts, the chant would begin again, pick up, fade.

Glitsky, alone, peeled off from the group gathered at the fountain, walking slowly, hands in his pockets, shoulders hunched. He entered the building and made his way past the federal agents and policemen and disgruntled and curious citizens that now crowded the lobby.

There were four flights and except for the first—where some of the apartment dwellers had clustered—all of them were deserted. He walked at a steady pace, turning the corners, his hands on the bannister, twelve steps a flight, then walked the dingy rug to the end of the hallway and rang the bell.

The door opened. He had his badge on but his weapon was not drawn. "Mr. Farrell, how are you? You got a client you'd like to surrender to me?"

"Is this really going to work?" Farrell said, stepping back.

Nodding more confidently than he felt, Glitsky walked to the window and raised the shade, the signal they were waiting for down below.

Melanie and Kevin were standing together, arms around each other. "Are you ready for this?"

He nodded.

"I'm with you," she said, a whisper now.

"I'm with *you*. Whatever happens, however this comes out. You got that?"

"I got it."

Farrell was leading Glitsky over to them, talking logistics, the law, the deal. Then it was time.

"Kevin Shea," Glitsky said, "I am placing you under arrest for the murder . . ."

73

Loretta Wager stood on the steps of the fountain, bullhorn in hand, facing the crowd.

Mohandas had not liked it (Allicey Tobain had hated it), but the senator had prevailed with the argument that the march was all about apprehending Kevin Shea anyway, wasn't it? So Mohandas had succeeded—the march had succeeded. They all had what they wanted. And if he didn't introduce Loretta, if they didn't somehow get this thing defused, what then? Another riot, more violence? Who would that benefit?

She had cut Mohandas out of the group—three steps away—for long enough to get it said—did he want to be on the short list for administering the Hunter's Point Shelter, or did he not? If he did not come across *right now,* he could forget she had ever mentioned it.

One last thing Loretta wanted—and this was a good time to bring it up because the chief of police was right here . . . Mohandas must clarify that the original one hundred thousand dollars reward was *not* for the death of Kevin Shea—they'd all heard that rumor on the streets and it was false. It was for information leading to his arrest—that was all.

That was all.

"My brothers and sisters," she began, looking up as the shade was lifted. *"Kevin Shea has been arrested."*

A roar, an outpouring of relief and anger and frustration bouncing off the U-shaped structure behind her, echoing through the courtyard back on itself, multiplying in a crescendo of noise that rolled on, picked up, rolled on again.

"My brothers and sisters," she said again, and at last the

wave of sound broke, flattened, became still. She raised her voice. "No one has fought harder than myself to see this moment. No one has kept this issue on the table more faithfully than Philip Mohandas." Another round of applause. "And it has come to pass."

She paused, then pushed on. "But this is not the end of the story for us. Nor is it for Kevin Shea."

"Kill him!" Someone yelled out. "Lynch *him*!" And a chant—"Kill Kevin Shea, kill Kevin Shea . . ."

"No!" The bullhorn amplified it again. "No!"

Gradually the crowd went silent.

"We've *got* Kevin Shea. Hear me. We've got him." They were listening. "Philip Mohandas is here. I am here, and we are with you. Your interests are *our* interests. It is not the San Francisco police that have apprehended Kevin Shea. It is not the FBI. It is us. All of us . . ."

A roar went up. More "Kill him, kill him," but something else, and Loretta rode it. "And now I'm asking you, I plead with you, you've got to believe *us*. We're going to see justice done." She raised her voice, pointing over the crowd. "But justice is not going to be served by another lynching today."

A hesitant chorus, a murmur of "Amen amen amen." Then silence in front of her, until abruptly someone yelled, "Not Kevin Shea, he's got to die!" A reverberation, the sentiment spreading, and then wearing itself low.

Loretta looked down at Rigby, Mohandas, Simms. They couldn't help her. This had been her suggestion (they thought)—the only way to pull it off, and she had to do it. *"No one"*—she raised her voice—*"no one* hates more than I do the bigotry and the hatred that Kevin Shea stands for." Now, more quietly: "But I'm telling you that it is over here. We have him. Philip Mohandas and I are walking out of here with Kevin Shea and taking him downtown. He is our prisoner. I promise you that neither of us will rest until justice has been done. You all have my most solemn word . . ."

". . . I don't believe this, ladies and gentlemen, Senator Wager has gone back into the building with Philip Mohandas, and now they are coming out surrounding, yes, I think

I can see clearly—it is! It is *Kevin Shea*! A handcuffed Kevin Shea—an unidentified black man—perhaps a police officer—is on one side, Philip Mohandas on the other. Senator Loretta Wager is leading them out. Behind Shea is Chief Rigby. With them is a young woman—that must be Melanie Sinclair—and another unidentified man—a white man—in a business suit. The crowd, ladies and gentlemen, is silent as the grave.

"They're moving now through the courtyard, across the fountain area where the senator just gave her powerful speech. They appear to be—yes, there's a black-and-white police car at the curb, the crowd is all over it, nearly swarming over it. The situation is highly volatile, as this reporter sees it. They're approaching the line of National Guard troops. You hear the anger, the outbursts of rage at Kevin Shea, but so far the crowd is . . . The troops are letting them through now. They're *in* the crowd. There is nothing between them and the fury we've been witnessing here all morning, especially the last half hour.

"Now they're actually making way for Kevin Shea and the rest of them. They've gotten to the police car, the back door is open, the senator—Senator Wager—is inside the car now. Now Shea. Mohandas. The car is starting to move now, slowly, its flashers on. The crowd is making way, slowly giving way. Amazing. I believe they're actually going to get through . . ."

.

74

There were two cars. The police car with Wager, Shea, Mohandas and Glitsky, and Simms's FBI vehicle with herself, Rigby, Melanie, Farrell. The lobby and front steps of the Hall of Justice were jammed by the time they arrived—to Loretta it looked as though they had gathered every television camera in the western hemisphere, all the newspapers and magazines, radio stringers, off-duty cops, staff members, transients and regular citizens. But it was not a mob anymore. It was a crowd.

Behind them, back at the park, they were getting the word that the people who had attended the rally were dispersing. Loretta felt vindicated. She had been right. They had needed the symbol of Kevin Shea. The embers might still be smoldering to flame again later, but at least there was a sense that, for now, the crisis had passed.

Loretta thought it was the strangest ride she'd ever taken. Sitting there right next to Kevin Shea, she was startled when he had turned to her and thanked her for her involvement, her courage. He was innocent, he told her. He had tried to hold Arthur Wade up, not pull him down . . .

Even Mohandas, by the time they reached the Hall, seemed responsive at least to Shea's open nature. For all Shea had been through, he was remarkably gracious, with a kind of nervous humor, no trace of surliness. It certainly didn't seem to bother him to be tightly wedged between two black people. He seemed, in fact, glad to be there.

They didn't book him on the sixth floor but brought him immediately to Alan Reston's office, which no longer bore any sign of his predecessor. Reston, of course, had followed the drama at the park on television and was waiting for them when they arrived. So was Elaine Wager.

A discussion led by Wes Farrell and largely corroborated by Lieutenant Glitsky finally brought the flawed evidentiary package out into the open. Rigby wanted to know more about the investigation into the other suspects—O'Toole, Mullen, McKay, Devlin. They waited while Carl Griffin and Ridley Banks came down and did their little song and dance.

After all of that, however, Reston still wasn't inclined to an outright dismissal of the charges on Shea, not this soon and not on his lawyer's arguments. He dismissed Mohandas and the homicide inspectors, thanking them all for their cooperation, and then, behind his closed doors, announced to Loretta, Elaine, Glitsky and Rigby his decision to move Shea when night came to an undisclosed location and keep him under guard until they could get the evidence in front of a judge.

It was one-twenty when the bailiffs came down and led Shea upstairs to his solitary cell.

Glitsky had not left Loretta's side. She had watched him for any sign, any reaction when Elaine had come into Reston's office, but he had only nodded—a professional conducting business. Seeing them together, now, father and daughter—she realized it was the first time that all three of them had ever been together in the same room. A reunion. No, a union. A closure of some kind.

She requested a short conference alone with Glitsky in Reston's office. When the door had closed behind all the others, she turned to him. "All right, Abe," she said. "I got Kevin Shea for you. That was the deal."

Glitsky stood leaning against Reston's desk, five feet from her. Maybe Loretta had been in Washington too long and just didn't understand that in Glitsky's world everything didn't come down to a deal. He had been careful about what he'd told her—that once Kevin Shea had been arrested they could talk about the possibility of a deal, which they were doing now.

His hands were in his pockets, his face a stone. He couldn't let himself remember what had happened between them—or forget what she had done. He walked by her, across the room to Reston's door. Opening it, he looked back at Loretta and shook his head. "Loretta, we never had a deal," he said.

In the hallway just outside the DA's office Elaine was waiting, wanting to talk about what they had done, where it would go from here, oblivious of what had gone on inside.

Glitsky, trapped by convention and gutted by tension, couldn't get himself away. He was still there with Elaine when Loretta opened the DA's door. Seeing them, she put on a public face, then—for her daughter—a smile. She came up to them, her eyes glistening. "I just needed another minute," she said. "All this happening . . ."

Elaine asked Glitsky if he wanted to join them for lunch, try to start the healing.

Glitsky said no. He had to go upstairs to finish up some work. Rigby had told him he could pick up papers on his desk but still wasn't to consider himself back on active duty. They would review the administrative leave and the reasons for it on Tuesday. Rigby didn't much care what the reasons were—whether they were good or bad. Glitsky had disobeyed his orders. That was enough. Glitsky even tended to agree with him.

"I'm seeing your mother tonight," he told Elaine. Turning, he said to Loretta, "Eight o'clock?"

Suddenly he leaned down, held her for the shortest instant against him, his hand behind her neck. *"It's your decision,"* he whispered into her ear. Then, straightening up, smiling his non-smile, pointing a casual finger. "Eight o'clock, then. Sharp."

Sharp.

Elaine was going to be all right, her mother decided. Her zeal to prosecute Kevin Shea was not going to be the end of her career, not with Alan Reston there to run the screen for her. She might not even need Reston. She was stronger than her mother gave her credit for. She was looking ahead, moving on. She realized Chris Locke and herself would have gone nowhere. Maybe it had been for the best—

although now, of course, it hurt. It would hurt for a while. She knew that.

But that, Loretta thought, was the point—Elaine had some perspective on it already. She'd survive. Her daughter would not break. She must never break, she was her mother's daughter.

They had finally gotten away from the cameras and madness and driven together out of the city, north to the Marin coast. It was so peaceful up there. They'd had the whole afternoon together, mother and daughter, something neither of them had had the time for in years. A quiet lunch at some little out-of-the-way place. No one bothered them, knew who they were or cared.

On a rise of the winding road back to San Francisco, they had pulled over and looked at the famous view, south over the bridge and the city. For the first time in days, there was no smoke.

Elaine had dropped her off at home at five-fifteen.

Sharp.

It's your decision.

The wind had died down. She walked out onto the balcony—outside the library—that looked back over the Golden Gate Bridge. The sun was low but the evening had remained warm.

She was wearing a shimmering purplish sheath over black pants. Pearl earrings. She had made reservations at Stars, and of course even at this last minute there would be a seat for the senator. Would she like a screen set up, some additional privacy? Jeremiah himself would be in—might he stop by and offer her a little *cadeau*? He was a big fan of hers.

There were the formalities to attend to. She had finished the letter to the president, thanking him profusely for his humanitarian gesture regarding Hunter's Point and forwarding her strong recommendation that he consider Philip Mohandas as the administrator for the area's program. A deal was a deal.

She dictated five short letters on administrative and committee issues onto her microcassette and sealed and franked the envelope addressed to her office in Washington. It was on the small table next to the bench in the foyer where she would remember to put it in the mail.

It's your decision.

Her mind turned to the election, to her Senate seat. Actually, there was a lot of irony there, she thought. The way Glitsky had arranged it, she had come out a hero in spite of her earlier stridency, her earlier calls for near-vigilantism. No one except Abe really had a take on what she'd done behind the scenes. She had miscalculated, but luck had been with her. Her reputation was going to survive pretty much intact.

Of course, there would be some, perhaps quite a lot of political flak she'd have to endure. She'd come out too strongly and too soon on Kevin Shea, before she had all the facts. People—the public, allies and enemies as well—would question her judgment, but she didn't think on balance it would hurt her chances. The Hunter's Point coup was going to get her a half-million black votes, which she thought would more than compensate for the loss of her moderate whites.

Shivering, though it wasn't cold, she let herself back through the French doors. The sun was casting prisms of light onto the hardwood. It was a beautiful house. She should spend more time here. Someone should appreciate all of this, all she had . . .

Crossing over to the bar, she lifted one of the crystal glasses and poured herself a good inch of the cognac she had shared with Abe.

There was a gold clock—it had been an early anniversary present from Dana—under a glass dome on the opposite bookshelf. The hours were marked in Roman numerals and the gold mechanism spun leisurely back and forth, around and around, underneath the clock's face. The hands pointed at the seven and the four. She found she could not take her eyes from them. There was no distracting second hand busily ticking the flying time away.

It was seven twenty-two.

The cleaning supplies—the brushes, picks, cloth, oil—they were all laid out on the velveteen that she had spread over the glass on the makeup table in the dressing room on the second floor just off her bedroom. It was a small room with one small circular window high up in the wall.

She put the snifter of cognac, half gone, beside the velveteen.

There was her note to Abe.

One of the clocks downstairs chimed the half hour. Seven-thirty. Suddenly she couldn't remember if she had left the front door unlocked for Abe when he got here. That would be important. She did not want to forget that.

So she walked downstairs again, through the foyer, took another few sips of her drink. The door was unlocked.

A glance back through the library. The sun had moved lower—the prisms had vanished.

He would be on time when he came to arrest her. She was certain about that. He had said eight sharp.

It was her decision.

She walked back up the stairs into her dressing room, put down the snifter where it had been before.

She picked up Dana's old Colt revolver which she had always kept up here.

The note, in light pencil strokes, read: "Abe. Remind people that Dana and I used to go target shooting together. There must have been an accident when I was cleaning his old gun . . ."

Glitsky carefully lifted the piece of paper. Going into the bathroom, he folded it over and tore it into little pieces, then dropped the pieces into the toilet and flushed three times.

He walked into the bedroom and lifted the phone next to Loretta's bed, punched the numbers nine . . . one . . . one.

Monday
The Fourth of July

75

Elaine Wager held herself erect. She had been through it all the past week. Was there almost a sense of relief in her bearing, Glitsky wondered, that nothing more could happen to her, that she had survived?

He leaned over and pushed the passenger door open after he had stopped at the curb. Elaine was wearing jeans, lace-up brown shoes, a baggy sweater. Her hair was held back severely.

"Thank you for picking me up," she said. "You didn't have to."

"Yes I did," he said. At her expression, he clarified it. "Not pick you up. Go see her."

"I heard you found her . . ."

He was driving now, didn't have to look over. "We had an appointment," he said.

"Abe?" Her voice was suddenly tentative. "What was she like, as a woman. I mean, if I can ask that?"

He was pulled up at a light. "Beautiful," he said, "she was beautiful."

Elaine closed her eyes, nodded. "That was how she was as a mother."

Glitsky was hunched forward on the first two inches of the plaster chair, his elbows on his knees, waiting, his hatchet face chiselled in a scowl of impatience. Across from him, Elaine stared at the tiny holes in the acoustic tile of the ceiling.

The coroner, John Strout, opened the connecting door with a little *whoosh* and everybody was suddenly standing.

When he nodded, Elaine steeled herself and walked into the morgue. Glitsky stayed behind.

"I'm due for a few days off," Strout said. "I can't keep this up. People I know winding up in here . . ."

"Do you know what happened?"

"Looks like about what it did before."

"I want to know your ruling," Glitsky said. His voice had a hoarse quality—it raised a flag for Strout. "I knew her personally, John." He paused, wondering how much he had to say. He decided not much.

"Well, you know as well as me, you cain't ever say with pure certainty in a case like this, but I'm going to rule accidental death. I don't think she killed herself."

"Why not?"

"Well, mostly because of everything else I know about her last hours. Spent the day with Elaine in there, who said everything seemed hunky-dory, better than it had ever been. Then, *you* know, she'd just had a couple of major successes. Shit, Abe, the woman was on fire. She was flying. That, plus you don't make dinner reservations and then kill yourself. You don't dictate five memos on next month's business and then kill yourself."

Unless you plan it so carefully that your daughter, above all, will never know, Glitsky thought. But he asked, "Anything forensic?"

"Actually, strangely enough, yeah. The angle, the distance. Gun went off far enough it didn't give her any powder burns—she wasn't holding it against her temple, in her mouth, anything like that. Most folks do. Come to think of it, I never once had a suicide shot through the heart. Not from an arm's length away, Abe. I believe the gun just went off." Strout pulled at the sides of his long face. Studied the lieutenant a minute. Carefully placed a hand on Glitsky's shoulder. "It was an accident, Abe. There's nobody to look for."

Glitsky felt his legs go loose. Maybe his little talk to Loretta about the importance of forensic details had borne this fruit.

He sat down a minute, then looked up at the coroner. "It's what I wanted to hear, John. Thanks."

*   *   *

Superior Court Judge Marian Braun was extremely displeased to be contacted by the new District Attorney on her holiday weekend, but thought that it probably served her right for not getting the hell away to Hawaii or Puerto Vallarta or Palm Springs as most of her colleagues on the bench did. Next year, next year she'd remember.

But, of course, this was an important case and the city had already played it so poorly . . . If she thought she was having a bad Fourth of July, she thought it didn't really compare to what they'd put this fellow Shea through, and he was still in custody.

She'd read the moving papers of the attorney, Wesley Farrell—a vague memory of competence from somewhere, but she couldn't put a face to it—and then carefully gone over the three independent confirming stories from the police interrogations of the other witnesses. Three of these people—James A. O'Toole, Brandon W. Mullen and Colin Devlin—seemed to be attempting to trade immunity or lesser pleas in exchange for avoiding a murder charge, while the fourth, Rachel Koshelnyk, seemed credible, never mind her poor English.

She'd also read over the testimony of, so far, the only suspect to be charged in the murder, Peter M. McKay. Also the testimony of homicide lieutenant Abraham Glitsky. The file was nearly an inch thick and she'd read it all. Everybody seemed to agree that Kevin Shea had done nothing wrong.

Judge Braun couldn't do a thing about possible federal charges against Kevin Shea. She couldn't quash the Grand Jury indictment without hearing all the evidence in the case. But she had heard enough, and what she could do was her good deed for the month and order Kevin Shea released on his own recognizance. She didn't think he was going to go anywhere.

Farrell took Kevin Shea back to his place. Emotionally drawn and quartered, the young man did not want to go out to lunch, did not want to celebrate, did not want to hear instructions about his future behavior or strategy about his defense in the event that he would need one. What he really wanted to do was go home.

Farrell understood and didn't press him. Kevin had been through the wringer and needed to decompress. Farrell, on the other hand, betook himself to lunch at John's Grill, where he thought he fit right in with the consolation party they were having in honor both of the Fourth of July holiday and of the owner's unsuccessful trip to New York City, where he had gone over the weekend to bid on one of the two original Maltese Falcons that had been used in the movie. His top bid of thirty thousand dollars fell a little short of the six hundred thousand dollars the trophy had eventually gone for, but the publicity and goodwill he had generated by the effort wasn't hurting his restaurant business.

Farrell ordered sand dabs—butter, capers, lemon. He'd had enough frozen food, delivered food, plastic food to last a lifetime. Things were going to change. He had his day planned out, maybe the rest of his life. At least now it was going to start—he'd also go home and take Bart out for a long walk (the dog deserved a little attention), clean up his living room and wash the dishes in the sink, do a couple of sit-ups (not too many the first day), then pour himself one and only one extra bone-dry Bombay Sapphire martini and watch the fireworks from the roof of his apartment.

Tomorrow morning, first thing, he was going to cut his damn hair, then place calls to some of his old colleagues, polish up his résumé, put the word out. He was back in the business.

Glitsky made it down to Monterey by one twenty-five. Nat had persuaded the skipper to hold the afternoon boat until he got there. After all, this was five paying customers they were talking about at twenty bucks a pop. It was all Abe's money—Nat loved to watch it go. That's what money was for, though he hadn't thought so when he was younger. Well, that's what life was—you learned.

The other three potential whale watchers didn't mind so long as the wait wasn't too long, and it hadn't been.

By two o'clock they were four miles outside the breakwater in bright sunlight on calm seas. Isaac was sitting cross-legged on the coil of anchor rope, scanning the horizon with binoculars. Jacob was reading his horror novel and

Orel—little Orel—was practicing some of his hip-hop dance moves to the delight of the other customers, his small portable radio propped on the wooden table in the center of the deck. Nat had stretched himself out on one of the benches and fallen asleep.

Glitsky chewed saltwater taffy and walked to the bow, back to the stern. Disoriented, out of place. Out of a job, too, probably.

He hadn't mentioned that to anyone. Not yet. God knew, there'd be time. Plenty of time.

He wasn't fooling himself. He didn't want to be there, with his boys, with his father, with the only people left in his world. What did that tell him? Why had he driven down here anyway—maybe see a fat seagoing mammal for eight or nine seconds? Whoopee. He couldn't wait.

Nobody needed him anyway. He ought to leave the boys with his father and—

"Hey, Dad!"

"Yo." He jumped. Force of habit. It was Isaac. He checked the other two. Still reading. Still dancing. Everybody okay. He walked back next to his son, who patted the rail in front of him. "I was just watching you walking back and forth. What are you thinking about?"

The question caught Glitsky like an uppercut to the ribs. "I don't know, Isaac. I guess I was thinking I ought to see more of you guys," he lied. "We ought to do more together."

Isaac gave him one of those teen-age expressions. "No," Isaac said, "that's a dad answer. I mean really."

Glitsky leaned back against the railing. "Really?"

"Right. Like what are you really thinking about? Like what is the world really like to you?"

"Where does *that* question come from?"

"It's the kind of stuff we talk with Nat about, I guess."

It struck him as funny. "That's the kind of stuff *I* talk to Nat about."

"Your father . . ."

"Yeah, Nat's my father . . ."

"So why don't you talk to *us* about any of that stuff? About any real stuff? I mean, ever since Mom, it seems like you've just been doing what you had to do. I mean with us, your job, everything. Like nothing got to you."

Here, stab me someplace else, Abe was thinking. "Things do get to me," he said. "A lot of things. You, for instance."

"What about me?"

Glitsky let out a breath. "*Like* why you don't ever talk to me. Why everything's territory, everything's a fight, everything's something you don't want to do . . ."

His sixteen-year-old son was nodding, listening. "That's because the only time you talk to me is when you're telling me to do something. Like you're a cop at home, too."

"I am a cop, Isaac. What do you want to talk about?"

The boy swallowed. "I don't know. How about sometime you talk to me just to say hi there, how's it goin'? Like that."

Glitsky looked up. The blue horizon was out there, limitless and empty, and he was here, floating in the vastness of the sea with his oldest son reaching out to pull him aboard. What the hell was he waiting for?

He could feel his face, the start of a real smile. "Okay, hi," he said. "How's it really going?"

Even to a city numbed by tragedy and violence, the accidental death of Senator Loretta Wager at the moment of her greatest triumph was a great calamity. The president of the United States himself was flying out in the middle of the week to attend the state funeral. Mayor Conrad Aiken declared a month of mourning in the city of Saint Francis.

Philip Mohandas was already proposing a new name—the Loretta Wager Memorial Playpark—for the Hunter's Point project for underprivileged youth that he, in all likelihood, would be administering.

The chairman of the Democratic National Committee said that Senator Wager's untimely death would send the search for a vice-presidential candidate in the next general election back to the drawing board. After her heroic personal intervention in the events surrounding the arrest of Kevin Shea, she had been a shoo-in for the nomination.

"She was," he said, "a very special woman with enormous personal stature, absolute integrity and a feeling for the common man that set her apart from all of her contemporaries. She was not first or even most importantly a politician, but a person with traditional values and real emotions who somehow managed, at the same time, to be larger than life. I believe that, had she decided to pursue the office, she could have been our first female president of the United States."

And a Harris Poll conducted late Sunday afternoon—the day after the accident—concluded that, had the coming November's Senate election been held on that day, Loretta Wager would have beaten her nearest opponent by twenty-four points.

Kevin walked slowly, exhausted, flight by flight, all the way up the stairs and turned the key to his door.

The bed had been made, the covers turned down. The windows were open, the blinds up. He didn't remember the place being so *light*. Outside, the view sparkled in the clear air. A light, warm, flower-scented breeze ruffled the curtains.

The dishes—mostly coffee cups and beer mugs—had been washed and a large bouquet of flowers had been placed on the occasional table next to his chair. He surveyed the room once, walking in a big circle, then came back around to his bed and sat on the edge of it, facing one of the windows.

Where was she?

He took a shower—got the jail smell off. Put on a pair of clean blue jeans, went back to the bed, bare to the waist, letting the breeze dry him.

Fifteen minutes, twenty. He didn't stir, wasn't moved to think. He was just there, sitting, waiting, letting some of the nightmare recede.

He knew she was going to come. He knew.

From behind him on the landing, steps on the hardwood. He stood and turned and was going for the door when it opened.

She was carrying a brown paper shopping bag with a loaf of bread sticking out of the top.

The impression—the sense of her—all at once in a rush—her hair down and shining. An unadorned light yellow dress, simple lines, the thin material of it shimmering with the beating of her heart. He could see it.

She put the shopping bag on the bed, straightened up,

meeting his eyes. Her smile broke—relief, joy, with him again.

"Remember that key I was going to send back to you when we broke up? I didn't." Then: "I thought you'd be a little later getting home. I wanted to be here."

"Wes dropped me right off."

She stopped, afraid to move forward, the last tentative doubt. A tenuous smile, and in it the question. Did he still want her?

It was all there—he could read it.

Silence. Both of them skittish. Afraid they might blow it right now, the first minutes here in real life. Aware of how much it all meant.

She stood across from him, two arms' lengths, hands straight by her sides, her eyes . . .

Something he had never seen before, anywhere, had really never believed he would. She *saw* him and still loved him. It was everything he wanted in the world.

She asked him, "Do you need to be alone right now? Do you want me to go?"

He moved forward and put his hands on her arms. He felt a tremor there. "Not ever," he said quietly, "not ever."

Her arms came up around him, moving into him. He could feel her heart against him. He could feel his own.

They were beating in the same time. Together. Real time, real life.

In the old days, not the *old* old days (since the Little Shamrock had been in existence since 1893) but back in the fifties, the bar had been as popular for its lunches as for its drinks.

Moses McGuire and his silent partner, Dismas Hardy, thought it would be a good promotional move and a pretty good time to roll back the clock for the Fourth of July, and they had obtained a city permit to cook hot dogs and serve clam chowder (ten cents and fifteen cents, respectively) out on the sidewalk in front of the bar, on Lincoln, across the street from Golden Gate Park. They had draped a huge American flag from the roof of the Shamrock and it covered the front of the building down to the top of the windows. The whole area out front was cordoned off with sawhorses, and the weather had cooperated as it so rarely did in San Francisco.

Now at seven in the evening it was warm and still. The holiday traffic was light on Lincoln, and Hardy and McGuire were standing behind a table under which kegs of Guinness Stout, Bass Ale and Anchor Steam sat in metal containers filled with ice. All around them, inside and outside the sawhorses in front, spilling out and over into the street, in the bar behind them, a mixed crowd of at least two hundred people ate and drank to a background of some John Philip Sousa marching band music, which Moses had thought would be appropriate and which Hardy had agreed to, although it wasn't his favorite. McGuire was the three-quarter majority owner.

They had been pouring beer as fast as it would flow for the past hour and suddenly there was a lull.

"Where's your friend Glitsky?" Moses asked. "I thought he was going to be here."

"He might show yet—he said something about going down to Monterey. Priorities." Hardy gestured at the throng. "Glitsky or not, though, this looks like it's working."

"It may be our best idea ever," Moses answered. He tended to hyperbole even when he wasn't drinking, and he'd had about four beers already.

"It might be *your* best idea, but I personally have had better ones."

"Yeah, such as what?"

"Such as marrying your sister."

Which, of course, Moses couldn't dispute.

"Still"—Hardy was conciliatory—"I have to admit I was worried."

McGuire had poured himself another paper cupful of stout. He drank off a third of it. "About what?"

"About what? he asks. Oh, nothing, Mose, it's been so mellow in the city lately, what ever could one find to worry about?"

Moses drank again, shook his head. "Not here. It would never happen here. Not in my bar."

"I've heard that song before . . . never in San Francisco either, but guess what . . . ?"

Moses gestured. "Hey, look out there now, Diz. Just look."

Hardy's eyes raked the crowd. There was a sea of faces, all kinds. "Okay . . . so? This proves something?"

"I think so, Diz. I really do. Hey, two days ago, all last week, you remember . . . now look at this. We're moving on."

Hardy hit his Guinness tap and let an inch or two of the black nectar fall into his cup. He drank it off in a gulp, scanned the crowd one more time, turned to his brother-in-law. "Maybe," he said. "Let's hope so."

Read on for a preview of John Lescroart's
riveting novel

The Motive

Available from Signet

By location alone, a block from Fillmore Street as it passes through the upwardly challenged Hayes Valley, Alamo Square would not be among the sexier neighborhoods in San Francisco. But one of the most popular and recognizable posters of the City by the Bay captures a row of beautifully restored and vibrantly painted three- and four-story Victorians that face the park on Steiner Street—the so-called Painted Ladies. The poster created a certain cachet for the area such that the cheapest of these houses now go for three-plus. Million.

The blaze at Paul Hanover's, in the middle of this block, began around eight p.m. on May 12, although the first alarm wasn't called in until nearly 8:30. Fires love old Victorians. Even though Hanover's house had been stripped to the bare bones twenty years earlier—retrofitted for earthquakes and freshly insulated with fire-resistant materials—it is the nature of Victorian design to have funky interior spaces, oddly shaped rooms, crannies and closets and unusual passages. Within the walls, since heat wants to travel up, fires employ the vertical stud lines as flues, almost as chimneys, to transport themselves effortlessly and quickly up and up into the roof spaces, where billowing smoke is most often noticed first.

Even in a neighborhood of great sensitivity to the threat of fire—of old, very valuable wooden houses in wall-to-wall proximity—no one noticed anything amiss at Hanover's until the fire had progressed to the unfinished attic. The late-arriving fog camouflaged the first appearance of the smoke, and the wind blew it away. By the time one of the local residents realized that what he was actually seeing was not fog but thick clouds of smoke pouring out from under the eaves of his neighbor's roof, the fire was well advanced.

As soon as the first alarm's fire trucks arrived—three engines, two trucks, two battalion chiefs, an assistant chief, and a rescue squad—the two-man aerial ladder team from the first engine began climbing to Hanover's roof, intending to ventilate it by cutting a hole into it with axes and chainsaws. Meanwhile, four men in Nomex turnout pants and coats and wearing Scott Air-Paks—the initial attack squad—got to the front door, found it unlocked, and opened it right up. Although they were armed with Akron fog nozzles that could spray water over a wide angle and get them closer to the flames, in this case they were greeted by a roiling cloud of hot thick black smoke impossible to see through. They could make no progress.

Al Daly, officer of the initial attack squad, spoke matter-of-factly into the headpiece of his walkie-talkie. "Front door is breached, Norm. We got a *working fire* here." Daly was speaking to his battalion chief, Norm Shaklee, out front in the street. The words conveyed great urgency. A working fire meant they would need least one more alarm—four more engines, another truck, two more chiefs. In a house this size with so much exposure to the homes on either side, this working fire could go to five alarms, San Francisco's maximum.

All four stories of Hanover's home might already be—probably were—involved. Shaklee, in his white helmet, placed the next alarm call and looked up as the sound of chainsaws stopped. Over the roof, a churning pillar of black smoke erupted into the sky, and he spoke into his walkie-talkie. "They're through on the roof, Al. Back out a minute."

He was telling Daly that ventilation was about to start working, potentially a very dangerous moment. If the smoke inside the house was hot enough—and no one knew if it was—the addition of oxygen to it might at this time cause a tremendous and often lethal backdraft explosion. So the initial attack squad waited in a kind of suspension down the front steps out in the street until, a minute and forty seconds later, the smoke column spewing from the roof suddenly exploded into a fireball that lit the night around for blocks and rose to a height of a hundred feet and more.

By now, the first hoses had been attached to the hydrant at the corner, and eight firefighters on each of them were blasting six hundred gallons of water per minute into the open space. For all the apparent good the firefighters were doing, they might as well have been standing around spitting on the flames, but appearances in this case were deceiving. The hydrant water was lowering the temperature sufficiently so that Daly and his squad could advance again into the building.

Because of the ventilation, the smoke that filled the foyer had now begun to dissipate upward, as did the thick cloud of steam generated by the water from the hoses. Within a few seconds after the hose teams stopped soaking the entryway, Daly and his squad were back at the front door. With his night helmet's beam on and glowing, he had relatively clear sightlines through the foyer and into the house beyond, to the flames still licking at the walls on all sides. Wielding his Akron, spraying in a wide arc, he advanced into the darkness, following the beam from his helmet. All around was noise and chaos—the rush of air behind him as the conflagration sucked it in, the roar of the actual fire, the creaking and splintering of wood, the hail of ax blows, disembodied voices yelling both within and outside the building.

Daly sprayed and advanced, sprayed and advanced. One foot or so at a time. The foyer was circular, high-ceilinged, and quite large, perhaps fourteen feet in diameter. He could make out the shapes of burning furniture along the walls—what appeared to have been a coatrack, a sideboard, maybe an umbrella stand or waste basket. Drapes over a pair of windows, curved to the shape of the house, were all but incinerated. One opening to Daly's right led into another open room, and directly ahead of him another doorway fed into a hallway. Everywhere he looked there was flame—total involvement of the ground floor.

Despite the hoses' soaking, the fire was growing again, heating up. It was excruciatingly hot, dangerously hot. Daly felt a sloshing like water in his ear, but knew that it wasn't water. It was his ear wax, melting. He had to get out of here, right now. He wasn't going to be able to check for potential rescue victims until the fire died somewhat, and by then—by now, he knew—anything living in the structure would have died as well.

Still he pushed forward, forcing himself to take another step or two, spraying as he went. It was full night, his only light his helmet beam. Looking down at the entrance to the hallway, he suddenly became aware of two shapes that stopped him where he stood. Leaning in for a closer look, not that he needed it, he forced himself to speak in his most neutral tone. "There's two bodies in here, Norm. In the foyer."

Out in the street, the second-alarm units had begun to arrive and Shaklee was issuing orders to nine people at once back by the rehab unit, which itself was already nearly overwhelmed supplying drinks, fresh air bottles, and first aid. He asked Daly to repeat what he'd just said, and Daly did, adding, "No ambulance needed." Which meant they were obviously dead.

Shaklee took only another second to process the information, then turned and spoke to his operator-aide, who functioned as gopher in the field. "Find Becker," he said, "and put in a call to homicide."

Arnie Becker, the forty-three-year-old lead arson investigator attached to the Bureau of Fire Investigation, arrived with the second-alarm unit. In situations like this, Becker's task was to determine the origin of the blaze. To do that, he'd have to enter the building and investigate all the indicators—"V" patterns on walls, decalcification of Sheetrock, "alligatoring" of studs, condition of electrical components, and so on—and by doing so hope to locate the spot where the fire began and, if possible, discover what might have caused it.

Becker was a twenty-year veteran of the fire department. In San Francisco his whole working life, he was particularly familiar with Victorians, and he knew that this house, with all the places in which a fire could hide, would in all likelihood burn through the night and perhaps well into the next morning. He wasn't going to have an answer anytime soon.

But that didn't mean he didn't have a lot to do. A huge

crowd of onlookers had coalesced on the block, and more were streaming out of houses both up and down the street and across the open space of Alamo Square behind them. This was his potential witness pool—people he and his team would need to talk to. Some percentage of them might live on the block, might have seen something suspicious.

He needed all the information he could find from a near infinite universe of possibilities, the most tantalizing one being that if this fire was arson, if someone had started it, then that person was probably among the crowd, enjoying his handiwork, possibly even sitting in one of the cypress trees in Alamo Square getting sexual satisfaction from it. Becker had seen it before.

In San Francisco, police officers from the Hit & Run Detail are assigned to fire investigation, so Becker had a staff of helpers and he sent them out to talk to everybody they could. They would not conduct formal interviews—not now, anyway—but he wanted names and phone numbers of everybody. If people didn't want to provide that, that could be instructive. If still others wouldn't shut up, that might tell him something as well. Becker didn't know anything, including what he didn't know. So this was his chance to start gathering information from whatever source presented itself, and he took it very seriously indeed. His men fanned out to either end of the crowd and were working it to the inside and from behind.

Becker himself was on his way to talk to the neighbor who'd called in the fire and who had waited around to help guide the trucks when they'd arrived, not that they had needed it by then. But suddenly Becker's partner in the Arson Unit, J. P. Dodd—twenty-eight years old, Army trained, competent yet relaxed—appeared at his elbow. The night around them was a kaleidoscope of lights in the darkness—the yellow flickering fire, the red bubbles on the trucks, the white glare from the firemen's helmets, now the kleigs of the TV camera crews. Dodd's earnest face looked particularly grave. "They've found two bodies, Arn. Shaklee needs you to come on up."

The fire still raged in the back of the house and on the upper stories. The two manned firehoses at the front door snaked across the floor of the foyer and disappeared out the right-hand doorway, leading somewhere back into the inferno. Becker, now suited up in his turnout coat and night helmet, his Scotts down over his face, also held a wide-beam flashlight that he trained on the bodies. He squatted like a baseball catcher, having learned that to put a knee on the floor was an invitation to pain and suffering.

The clothing had been burned off where they had been exposed, but even though both figures were lying on their backs, he couldn't tell what sex either had been. One was larger, and one smaller, so they were possibly a man and a woman, but he wouldn't be sure until the coroner was finished with them. The hair and any distinguishing characteristics on the faces, likewise, were burned away.

Something in the resting attitudes struck him, though. He had seen many dead people before, the victims of fire, as well as victims of murder and/or suicide, who were at fire scenes but dead before they burned. In his experience, the bodies of people who died from smoke inhalation as the blaze grew around them tended to curl protectively into a fetal position. Victims of murder or suicide most often lay as they fell, and these two bodies fit that profile.

The *New York Times* bestseller from
John Lescroart
THE MOTIVE

With their park view and old-fashioned detail, the Victorian
houses on San Francisco's Steiner Street were highly valuable. But with their wooden construction, they were also
highly vulnerable. So when Paul Hanover's multimillion-
dollar home went up in flames, it was all over very quickly.
And when the bodies of Hanover and his girlfriend were
found in the charred debris, it appeared that the end came
even more quickly for them—judging from the bullet holes in
their heads. But this isn't just any double homicide. Hanover
was a friend—and donor—to the mayor, who wants answers.
And in trying to provide them, Abe Glitsky and
Dismas Hardy will face an old lover and an old enemy—and
follow a trail of evidence that stretches far beyond
their usual jurisdiction.

**"Surpasses anything Grisham ever wrote and
bears comparison with Turow."**
—*The Washington Post*

**"A powerful rollercoaster ride through the
twisting streets of San Francisco."**
—*The Hartford Courant*